To Antigone Elizabeth and Cyrus Lawrence,

I leave you this, my Empire of Bones. Keep it tight to yourselves. Secret. If Ashtown grows unsafe, run and don't ever look back. Every little thing that I collected and hid in my outlaw years is charted in this map. All of it is yours—allies and artifacts, weapons and wealth, enough hidden paths and hidden doors to last you through lifetimes of running. The keys I gave you will open every door.

Be good. Be brave. I wasn't.

Billy B

# EMPIRE OF BONES

## BOOK 3 ASHTOWN BURIALS

## OF

# N. D. WILSON

A YEARLING BOOK

Text copyright © 2013 by N. D. Wilson
Cover art copyright © 2013 by Jeff Nentrup
Map art copyright © 2013 by Aaron Becker

All rights reserved. Published in the United States by Yearling, an imprint of
Random House Children's Books, a division of Random House LLC,
a Penguin Random House Company, New York.
Originally published in hardcover in the United States by Random House
Children's Books, New York, in 2013.

Yearling and the jumping horse design are registered trademarks of Random House LLC.

Visit us on the Web! randomhouse.com/kids
Find out more at AshtownBurials.com!

Educators and librarians, for a variety of teaching tools,
visit us at RHTeachersLibrarians.com

The Library of Congress has cataloged the hardcover edition of this work as follows:
Wilson, Nathan D.
Empire of bones / N.D. Wilson. — First edition.
pages cm. — (Ashtown burials ; book 3)
Summary: "Hunted and on the run, Cyrus and Antigone Smith race to find the inheritance left to
them by their benefactor, Billy Bones, before rampaging transmortals can descend on Ashtown and
free their buried brothers." — Provided by publisher.
ISBN 978-0-375-86441-4 (trade) — ISBN 978-0-375-96441-1 (lib. bdg.) —
ISBN 978-0-375-89574-6 (ebook)
[1. Secret societies—Fiction. 2. Supernatural—Fiction. 3. Brothers and sisters—Fiction.
4. Apprentices—Fiction. 5. Magic—Fiction.] I. Title.
PZ7.W69744Emp 2013 [Fic]—dc23 2013015916

ISBN 978-0-375-86398-1 (pbk.)

Printed in the United States of America

First Yearling Edition 2014

*For JKT the IVth*
*(because you changed everything . . .)*

# PROLOGUE

# GRAVEGARDEN

ON A WIND-BATTERED HILLSIDE, above a lifeless house, beyond the jagged battle line where sandstone cliffs held back the gray churning sea, in soft mossy earth beneath a towering redwood tree, there was a hole in the ground six feet deep. Two brothers, breathing hard, scrambled out over the wet sandy mound beside it and dropped their shovels. A sister watched them pick up ropes beneath a long pine box. A tall man with dark skin and another with a thick, square beard stepped in to help.

With arms crossed against the cold, Antigone Smith watched her father's pine box being lowered into shadow. Her cheeks were wet, washed with rain, wiped with wind.

Wood sighed as the box settled in its hole. The brothers dropped their rope ends into the grave and backed toward their sister.

Rupert Greeves raised his face to the wet sky and spoke the words of blessing for an Explorer gone ahead.

Antigone stood between her brothers and knew that

this was where she would always be standing. For the rest of her life, her soul would keep roots in this place, at the foot of her father's grave in the California hills, above the cliffs, above the sea.

Cyrus and Daniel Smith picked up their shovels. Gravel and sand and earth slapped down onto the box of pine and trickled through the cracks. And while the brothers worked, planting a man, the Captain sang a dirge of departing, his voice swaying like a sailing ship, his words lost in ancient English but his sorrow as real as the rain. Finally, when the box was swallowed like a seed, Antigone lifted her eyes to where the bark had been cut from the redwood tree, to the carved words that marked their father.

## LAWRENCE JOHN SMITH
through deepest shadow
across darkest sea
he sails for the sun

# one

# POOL PARTY

People wear places like they wear shoes. A place shifts around you, and you shift inside it, growing blisters and then calluses, becoming used to each other. But shoelaces tatter. Soles grow thin. Every day spent in a place frays the carpets, compresses the dirt, scuffs the sidewalks, or kills the grass just a little bit more. Floors creak, stairs bounce, trees, moss, weeds, and mildew grow, walls sag, pipes chatter and finally leak. Every breath changes the paint in a room, or the growth of green things beside you; every switch of the lights sends lightning rivers racing through secret grooves in hidden copper wires.

No place is ever the same tomorrow.

Take off your shoes and leave them in the tall grass for a year. Return and slip them on if you can. Disturb the ants and centipedes and beetles that now live inside. Wiggle your toes. You have changed.

No place is yours forever.

The evening sun dragged its light sideways across a lake, across miles of hills and barns and highways until it found Cyrus Smith, tipping back in a wooden patio chair in a place that had once been his own. Cyrus inhaled a rich slice of autumn air, scented with distant cattle and ripe fields and dusty asphalt and whole forests of yellowing trees. The smell was familiar, and it plucked memory strings inside him. But everything else had changed. The Archer Motel was nothing like the decaying roadside carcass that he and Antigone and Daniel had once made their home. As Cyrus looked around, he felt like he was being lied to. The motel was a little bit taller now, and the new metal roof gleamed. The walls were bright Jamaica blue, new windows set inside angel-white trim threw perfect reflections back at him, and working air conditioners hummed to themselves in diligent boredom. At the far end of the building, the motel had even grown a sparkling diner with huge windows and bright-red bar stools. Out front, smooth asphalt wore fresh yellow reflective parking stripes with casual pride. And at night, the Golden Lady, with her arrow drawn, bathed the motel with warm, uninterrupted neon.

Strangest of all, immediately in front of where Cyrus sat, tipping in his chair with one knee bouncing, chlorine-blue water slurped gently at the edges of a swimming pool that had once held only a collection of cast-off tires.

To be completely fair, Cyrus Smith wasn't much like the boy the motel remembered, either.

It had been well over a year since he had called Room

111 his own, since he and his sister had been swallowed up by the Order of Brendan. A year of training, a year of struggle, a year of blood.

Cyrus's shoulders were broader than when the motel had seen him last, and his arms were longer and knotted. Veins striped his dark forearms and the backs of his hands. His black hair was short enough to be uncombable, but long enough to jut out from his scalp in whichever direction it liked. A seamless white silk bandage was wound tight around his left wrist, stained on the inside with the ooze of an unhealed wound where Oliver Laughlin, nephew of Phoenix, had slashed him with the Dragon's Tooth.

He rubbed the bandage with his thumb while his knee bounced.

The biggest change was in his dark eyes.

Cyrus Smith knew who he was. He had seen nightmares become real. He knew what it was to be hunted, and he knew what it was to hunt, to run and to attack, to stand his ground, willing to kill and willing to die. He knew the smell of Death's breath and how cold it felt on his skin.

And he knew how sluggish and tired he felt every time he even thought about trying to learn something. It was like being a bug stuck in tree sap.

Cyrus looked at an old leather-bound book open on a little table beside him, and the pad of paper where he had been using a heavy two-legged compass to spin circles and transcribe triangles. He had done more of the proofs than he'd expected, but less than he'd promised himself he would. There were too many distractions, inside his mind and out. He hated it when Rupert Greeves left him behind. And Cyrus was sure that this time Rupert was sneaking back into Ashtown—where Cyrus's mother was being kept in the shiny, lemon-smelling hospital wing.

She'd been awake for weeks now. *Weeks.* And if Bellamy stinking Cook hadn't been named Brendan, and if he hadn't sold out and gotten the treaties with the crazy transmortals voided, then Radu Bey and his stupid *Ordo Draconis* wouldn't have put their little death order out on Cyrus and Antigone, and the O of B wouldn't have ducked and groveled, and Rupert wouldn't have yelled at the Brendan, and maybe he wouldn't have to be running from his trial or whatever the O of B used to depose an Avengel, and Cyrus could have been there when his mom woke up. He could have just been sitting in the room with his sister and his brother, and he could have seen her eyes open.

He could hardly imagine her awake. Sitting up. Smiling. It made him ache. Of course, they had sent her letters. Antigone had sent one every single day for two months, ever since they'd heard. Rupert had someone inside deliver them. But they'd never heard anything back. How could they? They hadn't slept in the same place more than two nights in a row since Diana Boone's house right after the brawl in the old cigar factory. They hadn't even stayed *one* night in California when they'd buried their father.

For two months, Rupert Greeves hadn't stopped moving, and Cyrus and Antigone had been dragging around behind him like a forked tail. Strange people, strange houses and estates and airplane hangars. Strange meetings and messages and men with trucks full of fuel waiting beside tiny airstrips with only one tattered old wind sock flapping above an outhouse.

Strange looks. Lots of those. And always directed at the two strange kids who stood behind the tall black Avengel, running from the Order he had sworn to defend, and still struggling to defend it. Cyrus knew that for many members of the O of B, the long list of what-ifs and if-onlys didn't start with Bellamy Cook becoming Brendan. They started with him. Cyrus. *That* Smith kid. From *that* Smith family. The kid who'd had the Dragon's Tooth and hadn't told. The kid who'd lost it . . .

Every night, as he slipped toward sleep, in this house or that one, in this barn or that warehouse, or in the back of a thrumming plane, he could feel the tooth being torn away from him all over again. And then he saw the tooth on the end of a broken cane in poor Oliver's hand, just within reach. He saw the tooth slashing at him, and he felt its cold edge parting the skin on his arm.

Every night, he jerked out of half-sleep, clawing at the wound beneath his snug spider-silk bandage and blinking away sweat.

Cyrus wasn't going to think about it. There was no point. He let go of his arm and flipped the book shut on the table beside him. His knee was still bouncing.

At least tonight he'd be in his old room. And if Rupert had to ditch him, being left at the renovated Archer had been interesting. At first. But he and Antigone and Dan had been here since breakfast. He'd seen every new little thing.

And the swimming pool bothered him. Two brutal years he had lived in this motel with this stupid pool refusing to hold water. And now? The pool was making it look easy.

Cyrus's knee stopped bouncing. The clear water rippled gently, licking the line of fresh blue tile around its rim like a liquid puppy waiting to be played with.

Cyrus stood up, kicked off his flip-flops, and began unbuttoning his faded green safari shirt.

Across the pool, Antigone Smith looked up at her brother. She was in a tank top and shorts, her dark hair in a blue bandana, and she was seated at a table with two large and delicate rice-paper globes covered in ink gibberish perched in front of her. Both had belonged to the outlaw William Skelton. One had been left to them in his will; the other they had found hidden in his rooms.

Cyrus dropped his shirt on his chair. The pool water licked the walls, waiting.

"Do you have a change of clothes?" Antigone asked.

Cyrus grinned. "Do I care?" He stepped forward, his toes tracing a fresh black proclamation painted onto the concrete:

# NO DIVING

Cyrus dove. The cool water swallowed him, tugging at his heavy pocketed shorts. Patricia, his hidden little silver snake, tightened around his neck at the sudden cold. Cyrus bent his back and flared his arms, keeping his dive shallow, but his bare chest still grazed the rough bottom. He relaxed, twisted onto his back, and let himself drift beneath rippling light.

Rupert Greeves should have called already. He should have given them a time when he would be back, or at least explained what he was doing.

Since when had Rupert ever cared about explaining things to Cyrus? No. That wasn't fair. Rupe had done hours of explaining and planning and discussing in the past two months. Just never as much as Cyrus wanted. And not at all this time. This time he had gone back to being his old mysterious self.

Cyrus stood up and surfaced, flinging water off his head.

"Tigs," he said, wiping his face. "What time is it?"

Antigone didn't answer. Cyrus blinked, looking around. Antigone was on her feet, both hands over her mouth.

Rupert Greeves stood on the patio, just outside the sliding glass door to the motel office. His hair was shaved on the sides and short on the top, but his pointed beard hadn't been trimmed in a while. The big man rubbed his jaw with a dark scarred hand. He looked from Antigone to Cyrus. Then he grinned.

"She's not strong yet," he said. "Not physically, least-ways. But she's here."

Rupert Greeves stepped aside.

John Horace Lawney VII, the round, tweed-suited lawyer who had been with the Smiths from the beginning of their adventures, pushed a wheelchair out onto the patio.

Seated in the wheelchair, thin but bright-eyed with happiness, Katie Smith looked at her children. Her deep-olive skin glistened with life, and her smile was pearl and sunlight. Three years of pure white hair had been shorn from her head and lay in a braid across her lap. Raven-black hair still shorter than her sons' grew in its place. She reached out a slender arm to Rupert and he took her hand. Slowly, wavering only slightly, the woman who had slept for three years rose to her feet.

Cyrus Smith had never seen anything so beautiful in his life.

Cyrus didn't know how he got out of the pool. One second he was in water up to his ribs, and the next he was dripping on the patio. Antigone was already racing forward, yelling for Dan to come quick. Cyrus watched his sister slide her arms gently around their mother. He saw his mother's tears and his sister's ribs shaking. He moved forward, and then he froze, dazed, unsure what he should do next.

His mother was so small. And she looked so much like Antigone, with her high cheekbones and wide smile, but shorter, and far more fragile. Cyrus suddenly felt how much he had changed. He'd grown at least ten inches in the three years since his mother had gone to sleep in the ice-cold sea, since Dan had dragged her out of the surf, unconscious. Cyrus saw the wonder in his mother's eyes as they took him in, and he felt like an ape next to a doll. And then his mother reached for him. Her hand found his face and her eyes settled on his.

"My Cyrus," she said. "You are your father and your uncles bound into one." She pulled him in with one arm. Wet and dripping, Cyrus wrapped his mother and sister together, and he began to laugh.

Dan exploded out of the motel and his arms joined Cyrus's. Rupert Greeves stepped back and laughed, and Horace said things that were probably funny, and Antigone was trying to tell her mother something, and all Cyrus tried to do was *feel*.

The wind was blowing through the fields and over and around and under distant cows. The sun was still dropping, and the pool still licked its new blue tiles, and beyond a chain-link fence there were dense scrub plums with paths that had once known the sound of Cyrus's feet and ditches where Cyrus had fished for tires and drowned his homework. In the trees and on the telephone poles, old-man cicadas whirred anger at the world for changing. In their youth, the world had been in a spring of green and flowers. Now, they buzzed, everything was coming to an end. Nothing would ever be the same again. And they were right.

Another three years could have passed for Cyrus, standing there, dripping and laughing beside the pool that now held water. Another three years, so long as nothing changed again. But everything changes. Even moments die.

Cyrus's mother was pulling away. Still holding his hand, she sat back in her wheelchair and said that she was hungry. Looking into his eyes, she spoke strange words in a rolling language he had not heard since he'd been a much smaller boy, rooting through kitchen cupboards in the old California house.

"*My hungry son could swallow mountains*," Katie translated.

Cyrus smiled. "I remember," he said. "And yeah, I think I could."

Dan took control of his mother's wheelchair, turning her back inside the motel.

Antigone leaned her head against Cyrus's bare shoulder.

"Wow," she said quietly. "Cy, can you even believe it?"

Cyrus inhaled slowly, watching his mother go. No. He couldn't believe it. Not any of it. He couldn't even believe his mother had ever been gone. He couldn't believe she was back. His mouth opened and shut, but he had no words.

"Insightful," Antigone said. "Good chat." She straightened up and poked his arm with a sharp finger. "Clothe yourself, Rus-Rus. Make like a gentleman. I don't want Mom to find out that I've let you go totally wild."

Cyrus reached out to mess up his sister's hair, but she ducked away laughing and shot into the motel.

Rupert Greeves still stood on the patio. He walked around the little pool and picked up Cyrus's shirt and flip-flops. Then he came back to Cyrus and held them out.

"Sorry I didn't say much," Rupert said. "Didn't want

you two frantic with waiting when it mightn't work. Almost didn't, point of fact. Touch and go in the hospital, and again getting her off the grounds. Bellamy Cook has an entire bleeding army at Ashtown now. Dennis Gilly and Nolan were pure gold. Wouldn't have come off without them."

Cyrus took his shirt and held out his right hand. His big Brit Keeper swallowed it with his own rough hand.

"Thanks, Rupe," Cyrus said. "Don't know what else to say."

Rupert turned Cyrus around and led him toward the door. "You could say you spent the whole afternoon working on cartography, that's what you could say."

"I *could* say that. . . ."

"And I'd be daft to believe you, yeah?"

"Would you believe Euclidean geometry?" Cyrus asked.

Rupert's laugh exploded up from his chest.

"I did!" Cyrus said. "I did! And it was even kind of cool. I like math with no numbers. In small doses, at least. Tigs said it might help with the map stuff."

They disappeared inside.

Behind them, the pool slurped. Shadows lengthened, and prophet cicadas sounded their autumn alarm.

*The nights grow cold! The world is dying! Look on the yellowing trees, ye mortals, and despair!*

No one listened.

Pats' Diner was as bright as Pat and Pat, the Archer's new owners, had been able to make it. A dense flock of white-wired lights, each with a red enamel hood, dangled from the polished beam ceiling. The long white countertop bar was set inside sparkling chrome edges. The black-and-white linoleum floor had been waxed until it gave off starlight, and the red vinyl bar stools sparkled with built-in glitter. The bar window that opened into the sizzling kitchen where big Pat and his beard worked the grill was set beneath a large mirror painted with the Golden Lady and her bow.

And the whole place smelled like bacon.

Pat the waitress moved between tables with plates loaded with breakfast dinners and burgers and chicken-fried steaks and sides of fries and two heavy loads of biscuits embalmed in sausage gravy. And if she was the size of three women, she had the grace of three as well, because not one drop slopped, not one fry slipped, and every diner was remembered, and every diner was *doll* or *honey* or *darling*, and big Rupert Greeves was *sugar*.

Cyrus ate, but he couldn't taste. And he couldn't stop blinking. Every time he shut his eyes, he expected the world to pull back a curtain, to laugh at its terrible joke, to shatter the scene in front of him with some horrible punch line—the old Phoenix and his new crop of gilled warriors would spring through the glass with fat-barreled fire-breathing guns raised. Radu Bey would burst out of the kitchen and snatch back Antigone. Or maybe Dan's heart would stop. Or sad Oliver Laughlin possessed by the soul of Phoenix would be waiting for Cyrus in his room, with Dragon's Tooth raised.

The unhealing slash on Cyrus's forearm stung beneath its bandage, as fresh as today's paper cut. Cyrus pressed on it with his thumb and shut his eyes again.

He couldn't trust happiness. Not even a little bit. Maybe this was all a complicated daydream, conjured up by a Cyrus crouching in the fields or beneath a plum tree or in musty Room 111. His room had never burned. His mother was still asleep. His father had been lost at sea, not shot and frozen for three years by Phoenix's bone-tattooed crazies. He and Antigone and Dan would be forever living on waffles in their slowly rotting motel. They would be forever stuck where tragedy had first dropped them.

Cyrus pushed the mistrust as far away as he could and opened his eyes, looking down the train of small tables that had been shoved together to handle their party. He was on the end. His mother was on his left, with Antigone beside her. Katie Smith was leaning against Antigone, smiling, listening. Antigone seemed incapable of turning her words off, incapable of letting one second of the last three years go unreported, though she'd already written it all in letters that her mother had been poring over in the two months since her waking. Across from them, Dan leaned over the table, smiling, absorbing everything, as alive in the moment as Antigone was.

Horace was buttering toast beside Dan, and pale, deathless Nolan was leaning back in his chair with his paper-colored arms firmly crossed and a wry smile tugging at his mouth. Arachne sat across from him with her eyebrows up, feigning irritation at some comment, a heavy bag in her lap. Cyrus knew that it held her eight-legged army. The bandage on his left arm had been woven in place by those spiders. Not long ago, standing above his father's body, he had watched thousands of them unweaving the white coat that had long been Phoenix's strength and curse. Antigone had a shirt of Angel Skin that had been woven by that living womb and infused with all the magic of Arachne's fingers. Cyrus couldn't imagine holding still for that ticklish spider-marching process. Just the thought made his throat tighten.

His mother's hand suddenly rested on his forearm, sliding gently up and down over his silk bandage. Cyrus looked into her eyes, dark as cool shade, flecked with rare pricks of green like hidden emeralds.

*No joke*, the world said. *This is real.*

Cyrus exhaled and smiled and then looked away. He didn't want tears. He'd slow-blink and dream-wonder as much as he had to, whatever it took to keep him from crying, from scooting his chair up tight against his mother's and worming his way under her arm like the Cyrus of three years ago. But even then, he wouldn't have cried.

At the other end of the table, Rupert Greeves sat, leaning back in his chair, rolling a toothpick on his lip, watching Cyrus. Cyrus steadied his breathing and met his Keeper's eyes. Rupert seemed tense, uneasy. The big man nodded toward the big front window of the diner, and then pushed back his chair to stand.

Cyrus started to stand, but his mother's hand tightened on his arm. He looked down at her.

"Are you all right?" she asked. "Cyrus?"

Cyrus nodded and smiled. He stood and leaned down, gently wrapping his mother with a one-armed hug, stealing her from his sister. He was only crossing the room, and yet he felt like he had to say goodbye, like this hug should provide enough affection for another three-year separation if need be—as if any hug could.

Still smiling, Cyrus backed away and turned toward Rupert Greeves at the window.

"You good?" Rupert asked.

Cyrus looked out at the mostly empty parking lot, at the leaning Archer and her bow—her neon dull and muted beside the setting sun.

"Yeah," Cyrus said. "It's all unreal." He looked at Rupert and then back out toward the road, trying to see through the fog in his mind, to find the right words for what he'd been feeling. "I want the world to stop," he said. "I want Phoenix and the transmortals and their dumb *Ordo Draconis* to just hold off for a little while. I want a time-out so I can be with my mom without thinking about everything else that's going on."

Rupert nodded. "Feel the moment without fear of future moments. But it's not the world you want to stop. You want your mind to stop. Focus on right now." He looked down at Cyrus. "Can you?"

Cyrus shook his head. "I try. But I want to know where Phoenix is. I want to know if he's still in Oliver's body. I want to know what he's planning and what the transmortals are planning and if they're still looking for me. I want to know where you sent the Captain and Gilgamesh, and what's happening at Ashtown, and where Jeb and Diana Boone are—you said they would meet us here—and what Skelton's old paper globes are supposed to mean, and I want to *stop* wanting to know all of those things and just be with my mom and my sister and my brother." Cyrus put his knuckles against the air-conditioned glass of the window and studied the parking lot. A semi chattered past, hauling a loaded cattle trailer. "And where are Gunner and Dennis? Weren't they with you?"

Rupert smiled slightly. "You have the makings of an Avengel. My mind chews much the same. Our war is far from over, and worry never rests." He sighed. "Jeb and

Diana should be here. They were stationed along our route to see if we were followed. I sent Gunner and Dennis back to find them. Even assuming that everything is fine and that they roll in late for some mundane reason, we're no longer staying here tonight. As outnumbered as we are, this close to Ashtown, I would relocate for a hiccup."

Cyrus scanned his Keeper's face. He didn't look worried. He looked . . . hard. And still. But Cyrus could feel his own pulse quickening. Rupert thought something had gone wrong. No. Something *had* gone wrong. Now it was a question of what and for whom. Diana? Jeb?

Cyrus looked back out at the road. "What do you mean, *mundane*? Like what?"

A small orange motorcycle with a milk crate on the front wobbled into view, trailing smoke. It slowed beneath the Archer and then turned into the parking lot. A round man in a brown fluttering monk's robe dwarfed the bike. His thick calves barely tapered into his ankles, and fat feet splayed out of his leather sandals. His head was shaved except for a short curly Mohawk. Strangest of all, Dennis Gilly, onetime porter of the Ashtown Estate, slumped limply on the back of the teetering bike, his hands tied together around the Mohawked monk's thick middle.

The monk parked the little bike thirty feet from the diner windows, uncinched Dennis's hands, and lowered the former porter onto the asphalt. Dennis was unconscious. This close, Cyrus could see that the monk was actually young, baby-faced despite his punk hair, and soft all over. This close, the monk could see him, too. But he wasn't looking at Cyrus. He positioned himself beside Dennis, adjusted a long rope belt that had been wrapped three times around his large middle, spread his feet, and grinned straight at Rupert Greeves.

Rupert did not grin back. He plucked out his toothpick and flicked it away.

"*Mundane*," Rupert said quietly, "looks nothing at all like this."

# two

# BROTHER NIFFY

THE BULKY MONK RAISED BOTH OF HIS ARMS and splayed his fingers to show that his huge hands were empty. They were empty, but they were also covered with dried blood.

"Rupe?" Cyrus glanced at his Keeper.

Rupert didn't answer; he was already striding toward the door. Cyrus hurried after him, looking back at the table as he did. Antigone and Nolan were on their feet. Dan had twisted around in his seat. Horace was still eating.

"Cy?" Antigone asked. "Who is that? Is that a body on the ground?"

Rupert pushed open the glass door, and Cyrus followed him out of the air conditioning, into the asphalt-baked air of the parking lot.

"Name!" Rupert bellowed before the door had even shut behind Cyrus.

The monk's grin widened, his cheeks rising until they pinched his eyes almost closed.

"Why the wrath, there, Rupee?" he asked. "I've done

no harm. In fact, as I'm seeing things, I've undone a great deal o' harm alreadies, and more to come."

Rupert stopped ten feet from the monk, and Cyrus stopped beside him.

The monk looked at Cyrus. His smile quieted, but his eyes sparkled.

"You'll be the Smith lad, then," the monk said. "And with the devil's own nose for trouble, too, or so I've heard."

Dennis groaned and twisted slowly on the ground, until his face was pressed into the asphalt. Cyrus could see a nasty gash behind his right ear. His shirt was stiff with blood.

"You know who I am," Rupert said, moving forward. "You must know what I can do. Give me your name, monk, and your purpose, and tell me why one of mine is groaning at your feet before I put you on the pavement beside him." Rupert drew a long-barreled revolver from the small of his back and let the gun dangle at his side.

The monk snorted and then saluted. "Brother Boniface Brosnan, reporting for duty, sir! Aye, aye, capitanny! Hup, hup, hup, yessir!" Then the monk lowered both his arms and slid his thumbs into his triple-looped rope belt. The laughter and smiles vanished. "I am the seventh Cryptkeeper, eighty-sixth to hold the seat of Monasterboice, established by the Navigator's own self. I was birthed on the Brendan Stone in the ruins of Fenit Isle; at twelve I tamed the king-wisps of Iona; at fourteen I faced the gin-thralls of Axum; and at sixteen I loosed the curse-knots that bound the eight thousand warrior souls in the statue army of Shaanxi. Now, at nineteen, I stand on a wee patch of tarmac listening to the threatenings of one Rupert Greeves. Do you think I fear your little gun and the metal it spits? I have held the breath of Brendan, and the power that bound him binds me. As for my purpose? I am here because of your own failings, so-called Avengel, because the Brothers of the Voyager will not have the long war lost on account of the follies of Ashtown and the rot of your unbelieving Order. One of your own groans at my feet because he is a weakling, and because he resisted me as I saved him. My favorite band is U-bloody-2, my sport is rugger, and I admire the films of John Wayne. Is that enough for you, then, Master Rupert?"

"Yeah, but who does your hair?" Cyrus blurted the question before he even knew it was coming. His whole body had tensed through the monk's speech, and his jaw snapped shut behind his words.

He hated it when people tried to intimidate him. He hated it even more when the intimidation worked.

Rupert glanced at Cyrus, surprised. The monk named Boniface smiled slightly.

"I do me own shearing," Boniface said. "Are you in need?"

"Cy," Rupert said. "Get Dennis inside and have

Arachne look him over." He stepped forward and reached for the monk's arm. "This Irish gob and I will have words in private."

The thick young monk was rabbit-quick. He snatched Rupert's wrist and jerked him forward. In one burst of motion, a bare leg flashed up, smacked into Rupert's face, and bent, hooking around Rupert's head. The monk dropped onto his back, slamming Rupert to the ground with two white legs scissored tight around his throat. The monk's robe was bunched up around his waist, and his boxers were striped with the green, white, and orange of the Irish flag. He was laughing,

Cyrus stepped forward, planted his left foot, and kicked Boniface in the jaw.

Pain shot through Cyrus's leg. It was like kicking a fire hydrant. He saw blood spray up around his foot in a little cloud, and then two large hands closed around his ankle and he was falling. Asphalt jammed loose gravel through Cyrus's shirt and into his back. An anaconda arm twisted him sideways and wound beneath his arm and behind his head. He was looking into the blood-spitting, grinning face of Brother Boniface, he couldn't move, and deep grinding pain shot through his shoulder.

"Do you prefer your arm in or out of its socket?" the monk asked.

Cyrus kicked, but the pain and the pressure only sharpened. He heard Rupert scuffle, and then a hammer cocked and Rupert's revolver slid up the monk's chest, pointed right at his face.

Behind Cyrus somewhere, a shotgun pumped. And then pale Nolan dropped into view, grabbing a fistful of the monk's Mohawk and levering his head back. With the other hand, he pressed a long knife against the monk's soft throat.

"Release them both," Nolan said. "Slowly."

Boniface licked his bloody lips, then spat out a molar. Cyrus heard it click away across the asphalt, and he heard Rupert gasp, breathing suddenly. The pain in his own shoulder suddenly vanished. He rolled away quickly and rose to his knees.

Pat the cook held a short shotgun, and Dan and Antigone stood beside him. Rupert rose slowly, coughing, chest heaving, and then he pointed his gun down at the monk.

Brother Boniface Brosnan looked up at them all with his thick white limbs splayed and Nolan's knife at his throat. He snorted and spat a glop of blood after his tooth. Then he grinned.

"Well," he said, "shall we try, try again? My best mates call me Niffy. It's truly a pleasure to meet your little outlaw band."

Nolan turned his deep, timeworn eyes onto Rupert, waiting for instruction.

Rupert shook his head and wiped a trickle of blood

from his nose onto the back of his forearm. Nolan with-drew his knife as Rupert looked at the road and another passing semi with a chattering trailer.

"Get our dear Brother Niffy inside," Rupert said. "Guns and blood and brawling, we'd best get out of sight and quick." He turned to Cyrus. "Your shoulder okay?"

Cyrus nodded. "But my foot hurts from kicking him."

Niffy stood and straightened his robe. "And my jaw's just brilliant, thanks. A lovely boot you have."

"Don't start, Irish," Rupert said. "Get inside and have your story ready. I'm missing people."

Dan and Antigone were lifting a whimpering Dennis between them. Dan paused, cocking his head. "Are those for us?" he asked. "The sirens?"

Everyone froze. Cyrus looked at Antigone, at Rupert, at Dan and Nolan. He heard nothing but cicadas. Then a van passed and faded. But Daniel wasn't working with normal human ears. He'd gone through horrors on Phoenix's table, and his heart could still beat thanks only to the flesh-weaving magic of Arachne. But there were some upsides to the modifications. Dan turned to Rupert and nodded.

"They're coming closer. And a car. Fast. Someone is seriously hauling."

Slow seconds passed. And then Cyrus heard it, too. At first, only the distant whine of sirens. Definitely more than one. And then tires screaming on asphalt, sliding on unseen corners.

A classic limo-long black car fishtailed around a corner and into view. Smoke rose behind its tires as it again accelerated. Cyrus had ridden in that car before, and he knew it couldn't have been any faster if it had been part rocket. But speed didn't help on corners.

The car whipped around, nearly kissing the Archer's pole with a chrome fender, and then entered the parking lot sideways, dragging smoking stripes of black rubber behind it.

As it rocked to a stop, Diana Boone leapt from a rear door. Her strawberry hair was cinched back in a tight braid. She was wearing a long safari shirt belted with a caramel leather double holster. One gun was missing. One shirtsleeve was black and smoking.

"Jeb's hurt!" she shouted. "Rupe, it's bad. And we lost Dennis. Some monk . . ." Her green eyes landed on Niffy, and then darted to Dennis.

Rupert was already running toward the car. Gunner, Horace's tall Texan nephew, rose out of the driver's side. He was in a black suit minus the jacket, and twin revolver butts peeked out from under his arms.

"Mr. Greeves," Gunner drawled. "There ain't no time, sir. Two minutes tops. We need to move on out and now. They're hot after us. Two dozen, at least, loaded for bear."

Rupert stopped at Diana's door and looked inside

the car. Cyrus watched the big man's face fall and his chin drop to his chest. But the sadness was only there for a moment. Rupert tugged a small card and a pen from his pocket. He began scrawling on it while he spoke, his voice as calm as it was quick.

"Daniel Smith, get Dennis into this car now." He looked up and bellowed, "Arachne!" Cyrus turned back to the diner and saw his mother and Horace standing at the window, watching. Arachne hurried out the front door, cradling her heavy spider bag like an infant, but it sagged like a sack of mud.

Rupert handed Diana the card. "That's where you're going. Do not relocate again before we arrive unless there's an emergency—your secondary location is on there as well. Cyrus flies tonight. You're too shook, but keep him sharp. Nolan"—Rupert turned and pointed at Niffy—"if he gives you any heartache, deal with him. You listening, Irish? I want you as proper as the pope."

Daniel had gotten Dennis into the front seat. He shut the door and stepped away from the car. Arachne slid into the back, and Cyrus saw her ice-blue eyes widen as she looked at the floor.

Diana shook her head. "Rupe, I have to stay with him." She grabbed at Rupert's shirt as he climbed into the car. "Please."

Rupert put a big hand on her shoulder. "I'm sorry.

No discussion. We'll get him help." He looked around at the little crowd. "Go!"

With that, Rupert ducked into the back of Horace Lawney's modified limousine. The engine throbbed, Gunner spun the car around, and it bounced out onto the little road.

Diana Boone's shoulders shook.

Cyrus looked at Antigone, at Dan, and then at Nolan. Pat the cook rested the shotgun on his shoulder and turned back toward his diner.

"I know I'm new to the club," Niffy said. "But it seems we'd best be off."

Cyrus nodded. The sirens were growing louder, and the people they really needed to worry about would be even closer than the cops.

"Dan," Cyrus said. "Get Mom. Leave the wheelchair. Do you think you can carry her?"

Dan was already jogging away.

"Di?" Cyrus said.

Diana Boone spun on her heel. She dragged her hands quickly down her cheeks, streaking soot over her freckles. She looked from Antigone to Cyrus with wet wide eyes.

"We need to go," she said. "Right now."

Cyrus led the way, ducking through the old tunnels beneath the overgrown plum trees and holding back branches for Dan, with their mother in his arms. Antigone and Diana followed. Horace, Niffy, and Nolan brought up the rear.

Cyrus was still wearing flip-flops, and he'd almost forgotten to snatch his canvas pack out of Room 111, where he'd hoped to spend the night. He had completely forgotten to thank Pat and Pat, but he figured they would understand.

"Daniel, I can do it." Katie Smith patted her son on the chest. "Set me down and I'll walk."

Daniel didn't answer. Cyrus slid out of the plums into a dry pasture and pulled a bundle of branches aside until they popped with concern.

"Daniel . . . ," Katie said.

"Mom," said Cyrus. "We have to be quick. And quiet. Just let him carry you. And hang on."

As the train emerged, Cyrus turned and began to jog through the tall grass, glancing back to make sure Dan could keep up without jostling their mother too much. He shouldn't have worried. Daniel's head was high and relaxed, and he wasn't even breathing hard. Cyrus hated admiring his brother's strength. It meant that Phoenix was good at what he did. And it always reminded Cyrus that he would never again see his tall, straw-haired, blue-eyed California brother. Dan was a quick brown-haired ox, with a patched-up heart and dark-brown eyes that saw things he didn't like to talk about.

Cyrus wondered what his mother thought of Daniel's change. She'd known about it; she'd been brought up to speed on almost everything during her two months of therapy in Ashtown. But she hadn't commented on Dan. She'd said more about the changes in Cyrus.

The group shuffled across an old beam over a muddy pasture stream, and then Cyrus led them up a low hill, through a cattle gate, and down into a green bowl. Milk cows looked up, still chewing, and watched them descend. The motel disappeared from view behind them.

At the bottom of the bowl, beside the ruins of an old barn with a broken back, an odd-looking tilt-rotor plane basked in the long grass. Two large propellers had been rotated up above the wings, making it look and act part helicopter. Once in the air, the props could rotate forward. The strange plane had once belonged to Rupert's old Keeper. It had been borrowed from his widow, and the loan had become mostly permanent.

Cyrus had never flown it.

Diana got the cabin door open and climbed up and forward into the copilot's seat. Dan set Katie down and helped her climb inside. Horace hopped in, but Niffy paused to admire the plane before Nolan nudged him from behind. Antigone stopped at the door.

"Cy . . ." Antigone's voice was one shade short of panic. She turned back toward the motel. "Oh, gosh. Cy . . . the globes."

Cyrus stared at his sister, not understanding.

"Skelton's paper globes," Antigone said. "I left them by the pool when Mom came and then I forgot them. We have to go back."

Cyrus sighed. "Why? We never even figured out what they meant."

"Yeah, but *they* might," Antigone said.

Cyrus turned and hopped up into the plane's open door. His mother was in a rear-facing seat, and Dan sat with his legs crossed on the floor at her feet. Niffy was facing forward, perched in a middle seat between Horace and Nolan. The little lawyer was pinned against the rounded cabin wall.

"Horace," Cyrus said. "What would you say if I told you we lost Skelton's paper globes?"

Horace snorted. "That I warned him against taking you as his heirs, and that I hope he haunts you into an early grave. I've told you that the money and the accounts he had me hiding were only a fraction of his real worth. His real shadow empire, the one he spent his final years sheltering from the O of B *and* from Phoenix—"

"Yeah, yeah," Cyrus said. "I get it."

Cyrus leaned in until he could see up into the cockpit. Diana looked back at him from the copilot's seat. She already had her headphones on, but she lifted one ear-piece.

"Give me two minutes, Di," Cyrus said. "Fire up in one and be ready for me."

Diana nodded and turned back to her controls. Cyrus dropped his pack on the floor and then backed out of the cabin.

"Cyrus . . ." His mother's voice stopped him. Her eyes were wide with worry.

"Love you, Mom," Cyrus said. "Be right back." He turned away, sidestepping Antigone as he did.

"Cy . . . ," Antigone said.

"You're not coming, Tigs, so don't even say it." He kicked off his flip-flops and handed them to his sister. "Stay with Mom."

And with that, Cyrus Smith began to run.

Antigone watched her brother race through the pasture, weaving a slalom course around grazing dairy cows. As he reached the lip, he ducked low, and then disappeared.

Antigone sighed and climbed up into the plane, dropping into the one empty rear-facing seat, across the cockpit door from her mother. Her eyes stayed focused on the pasture, and her thumbnail rose to her teeth.

Katie Smith took her daughter's free hand.

"He's changed a lot," Antigone said.

"Cyrus?" Katie laughed. "Have you forgotten the boy who ran the cliffs, who always left a worried sister behind?"

"More like an angry sister," Antigone said. "It was stupid. And he fell, too. He was lucky."

"Cyrus has grown larger," Katie said. "But he is the same boy." She squeezed her daughter's hand. "I am sorry I left you. It must have been hard to be the one who had to worry for Cyrus."

"Oh, she wasn't the only one," Dan said. "And I wasn't any good at it."

"I'm here now," Katie said. "And I think I will worry enough for all of us."

Niffy massaged the side of his swollen jaw with two fat fingers. "Touching," he said. "Truly."

Cyrus slipped out of the plums and over to the chain-link fence at the end of the pool and patio. He couldn't see the globes anywhere, but the sun was just down and shadows were deepening. An evening breeze wrapped around the motel and made the short hairs on his neck tingle.

Cyrus could hear voices. They were coming from the front of the motel. Not much time.

And then the door to the pool patio slid open. Cyrus retreated beneath the brush and waited. Two men stepped out.

These were not Phoenix's men, at least not visibly. No gills fluttered on their necks. No bone tattoos traced their limbs. These were men of the Order of Brendan, men dressed like Rupert Greeves and hundreds of other Explorers and Keepers of Ashtown.

They wore canvas shirts, safari shorts, and boots. Wide leather belts held holsters and short sheaths.

One of the men was shorter than Cyrus, with immense shoulders. He had brown hair and a short reddish beard. Cyrus had seen him dozens of times in the dining hall, but even more often training Acolytes in the great yard of Ashtown. His name was Eric Romegas, but the Acolytes all called him Eric the Red.

The other man was taller, leaner, blonder, and looked more like someone who wanted to be photographed for a living. A short, heavy gun was slung over one shoulder, and he cradled it against his stomach. Cyrus had never seen him before.

Eric the Red squared up and faced the taller man. "You hear me, Flint. I trained Jeb Boone. He was a member in good standing."

The man called Flint smiled with half of his pretty face. "They took the bait. But we didn't take them, did we? Funny how Jeb and that brat Diana just happened to lead us off the trail. If they hadn't, the Smiths and that mutineer Rupert Greeves would be facing their Brendan tonight." He shrugged. "Or lying in their own blood at the feet of their Brendan."

"What you did was evil," Eric said. "I'll have no part of it."

Flint walked toward the fence and Cyrus held his breath, fighting to slow the thunder of his heart.

"'I'll have no part of it,'" Flint mocked. "No part! Not for Saint Eric! Well, too late, lad. You knew the game. You came to play."

Eric shook his head. "The Brendan has a right to question any members of the Order, and the Avengel must stand before him prior to being removed. Any rule-respecting member would help bring them in. It's all in good order. Pumping Jeb Boone full of lead is not!"

"Oh, don't play dumb," Flint said. "You're dumb enough already." He turned and walked back toward the motel, and Cyrus exhaled. He preferred having the man's back toward him. "You know the Smiths will be sent off to the transmortals as a peace offering, and Rupe is as good as dead. *And* you know the Brendan is cleaning house until Ashtown sparkles. The Boones are all gone either way."

Flint flipped a switch on the motel wall. The pool suddenly glowed with pale light. Cyrus could see the paper globes.

They were in the pool, flattened like trash and floating in a cloud of dark dissolving ink.

"Hello," Flint said. "What's this?"

From beyond the fence and one green fold of pasture, two huge engines shook the evening air.

Old-man cicadas grew silent. Surely, the end had come.

## ⚜ three ⚜

# SOGGY

CYRUS BIT HIS LIP. Flint and Eric both stared across the pool and over the fence.

"Helicopter?" Flint asked.

"Plane," said Eric. "But I'm done. And if this is how Brendan Bellamy Cook wants Keepers to behave, the whole Order can go to hell. It already has. . . ."

He turned toward the sliding motel door, but Flint raised his gun, pointing it squarely at Eric's back. He tucked two fingers into his mouth and whistled long and hard.

"Just so we end this honestly," Flint said. "I'm glad I get to be the one to put you down. Turn around."

Cyrus vaulted the chain-link fence, and then leapt the corner of the pool. Eric the Red turned to face Flint, angry and defeated. His eyes widened as Cyrus picked up a wooden patio chair and smashed it over Flint's head. The tall man crumpled.

Cyrus didn't have time to talk. He dropped into the

pool, scooped up the two paper blobs, slapped them over his shoulders, and exploded back out of the water.

Two more men stepped out of the motel door. They raised shotguns.

Eric the Red roared, lowered his shoulder, and drove them back into the doorway. A shotgun fired. Glass exploded. Cyrus turned toward the end of the pool, the fence, the scrub plum trees.

Six men rounded the corner of the motel and stopped beyond the fence. Heart racing, Cyrus slipped to a stop on wet feet. They had cut off his path through the plums. He could jump the fence straight at the pasture, but the brush was too thick and too tall. He'd be stuck until they plucked him out.

Another gun fired, and Eric the Red staggered and fell. Tall Flint rose slowly to his feet, bleeding from his scalp, gun smoking.

Cyrus stepped onto a patio chair and hopped onto the top of the chain-link fence. Metal dug into his feet, and the plums walled him in. He turned, wobbling, racing along the fence, grabbing at branches. Then he jumped for the Archer Motel's new gutters.

Fingers caught, metal bent, but both held. Cyrus chinned himself up, hooked his right leg onto the hot metal roof, and rolled himself up.

He scrambled toward the peak, keeping low and

breathing hard. From here he could clear the plums. But it was a big drop. A bone-breaker.

"Tuck and roll," he said. "Tuck and roll." He exhaled and crouched on hot feet, ready to dash and leap and crash.

He paused. There were already men in the pasture. They were running away from Cyrus, toward the sound of the plane.

Something thumped onto the gutter at the edge of the roof. Two hands.

Cyrus dropped into a baseball slide straight toward them. His wet shorts shot him down the hot metal roof, but he dragged his palms and they squealed like bad brakes. He leaned back and cocked his right foot.

The hands quivered and Flint's head rose between them. Cyrus stomped his bare heel into the bridge of the man's nose. Bone crunched and blood spattered up between Cyrus's toes. Flint dropped to the concrete, half-unconscious.

Cyrus twisted onto his belly and tried to scramble back up to the peak, slipping on his bloody right foot. Behind him, guns fired and sparks kicked off the metal roof all around him. Ricochets went whining up into the sky.

He dove over the peak for shelter, and as he did, a swarm of bees stung him in the calf. Not bees. Pellets. Hot, fiery, shotgun-belched pellets. With one hand gripping the roof, he grabbed at his leg and bit his lip against the pain. Little craters, erupting blood.

He could hear shouting, but it didn't matter what was being said. He knew it was about him. They would surround the building. They would shoot him again. He had to get to the plane. But that meant standing. And then running. And then jumping into the pasture and slamming into the ground. Then standing back up and dodging and outrunning grown men with guns in a four-hundred-meter cross-country sprint. Not likely.

But the other option was dying.

Cyrus rose to his knees. He could hear gunfire that was not meant for him. Distant gunfire. And then he heard the airplane change its roar. Diana was taking off.

Cyrus could hear men below him on both sides. He heard a metal gutter pop and squeal. They were coming up for him.

The turbo-prop, tilt-rotor plane rose above the pasture and glided forward like a helicopter. It drew every pair of eyes. Nolan was leaning out of the open door with a revolver, taking aim and firing whenever a gun was raised below him. Dairy cows bellowed and thumped around in panic, trying to organize a stampede.

Cyrus clambered to his feet and began to wave his arms.

He couldn't see Diana, but he knew when she saw him. The plane swiveled, and swooped in above the motel, beating the air down around him, sending Cyrus slipping back to his knees.

The men below finally had a target that was easy to hit. Sparks rattled off the wings, but every time Nolan fired, another gun on the ground went silent. Two men were scrambling onto the roof, and then Niffy dropped out of the door of the plane, robes fluttering as he fell. He landed on the metal roof like a ninja elephant and immediately somersaulted down toward the climbing men. As they raised guns, Niffy tore his rope belt loose, and in his hand, it lashed out like hemp lightning. The end cracked the first man in the face and sent him toppling backward over the edge. The rope wound around the second man's legs, and Niffy jerked his feet out from under him. The man fired into the air as he fell.

Cyrus crawled beneath the plane, looking up at Nolan leaning out of the open door at least ten feet above him. He had to stand, to jump. And then a huge hand slid beneath Cyrus's left arm, and another hand grabbed him by the seat of his shorts.

Cyrus rose until he was perched just above Niffy's right shoulder. The thick monk suddenly dropped into a crouch, sucking in a long whistling breath, his grip tightening on Cyrus's rear.

Cyrus flailed. Niffy heaved.

Cyrus floated up through the wind like he'd been spat by a trampoline. Nolan's eyes widened; then Cyrus smacked into him, and the two tumbled back into the cabin in a tangle of arms.

The end of Niffy's rope flopped up onto Cyrus's back, and Dan grabbed on to it, threading it quickly through the metal bones beneath Antigone's seat and then gripping the end tight with both hands.

"Go, Di! Go!" he shouted, and the plane slid to the side, away from the motel.

Cyrus sat up on Nolan's legs, grabbed the edge of the open door, and hopped up onto his good leg. Nolan slid back into his seat.

Cyrus leaned out of the door and looked down as the plane moved over the parking lot and the road and the trees. Niffy dangled from the end of his rope belt with only one hand. His thick bare legs were cinched tight around the arms and chest of a bloody-faced and panicking Flint. While Cyrus watched, Niffy swabbed his free little finger around the inside of his own fat cheek, and then wiggled it in Flint's ear.

"Cy!" Antigone shouted. "Cy! Your leg!"

Cyrus looked back at his sister and his worried mother. Then he twisted, glancing down at his calf. He grimaced at the sight but was actually surprised that it didn't look worse. He had expected something gorier, more chewed. It felt like it should belong to the shark bite school of wounds. But this shark had bitten with only a dozen or so very small and scattered teeth that had left behind oozing golf ball puckers in his leg. Still . . . *ow*.

"Ricochets!" Horace yelled, the hair above his ears lashing his bald scalp in the wind. "You're lucky. Not much worse than a BB gun! You'll be fine! Where are Skelton's globes? Or was all of this without purpose?"

Nolan laughed. Cyrus snorted, and then shouted back, "How 'bout I shoot you twenty times in the leg with a BB gun!" He peeled the soggy paper off his shoulders. Horror flooded Horace's eyes. "They were in the pool!" Cyrus yelled. "I don't think they ripped, but the ink is pretty bad."

Antigone looked like she was going to be sick. Cyrus draped the two paper mats over her knees. Then he smiled at his mom and limped into the cockpit. He wormed down into the pilot's seat and slipped on his headset.

Diana looked at him. Her voice crackled in his ears. "Is that fat monk dangling from the plane?"

Cyrus nodded.

"I knew we were dragging something heavy. Can we drop him? Or should we tilt these rotors down and flap him off at three hundred miles per hour?"

Cyrus shook his head. "Find somewhere close and set it down. He's one of the good guys."

Diana nodded. She banked the plane back over the

road toward a low, flat-roofed building with a cracked and weedy parking lot. Cyrus knew it had once been a grocery store, but the windows had been boarded up longer than he knew.

"How's the leg?" Diana asked. "Didn't look great."

Suddenly, Cyrus's leg didn't feel quite as bad.

"Still attached," Cyrus said. "Hurts. But I'll be fine."

"Good," Diana said. She began to lower the plane toward the parking lot. "They got Jeb with a shotgun, too." Cyrus watched her profile—soot-streaked freckles, flexing jaw, angry, *angry* eyes. "In the chest and face. I . . . we—" Her voice broke off in Cyrus's headset. He felt sick. His leg was nothing. He watched Diana sniff. Swallow. "We even knew some of those bastards, Cy. Eric the Red trained us both."

"I don't think Eric made it," Cyrus said. "He was mad about Jeb. Then he helped me, and they shot him."

Diana said nothing. But she nodded, turning the plane as she did. Cyrus felt Niffy's weight release. The plane surged up slightly, and then Diana set it all the way down.

"Are you going to be okay?" Cyrus asked.

Diana nodded. Then she wiped her cheeks again. "Get the chunky monk in if you're gonna. We've got a long flight."

Not too far above an altitude of ten thousand feet, Cyrus blinked, squinted, and shielded his eyes. Flying due west, the little plane had caught up to the setting sun.

"Bright," Diana said simply. She reached beneath her seat and handed Cyrus an old pair of aviator glasses. "Push her a little faster and climb. This is the only way you'll ever see the sun rise in the west."

Cyrus put on the shades and did what she said. He pushed the plane harder and climbed higher, until the sun rose above the horizon. Diana actually laughed, and even though the sound was quiet and crackly and filtered through a headset, it made Cyrus feel better.

The plane shook a little more at this speed, battering its way through rough air.

"Did Rupe ever tell you about the Sun Chaser?" Diana asked.

"No," Cyrus said. "He doesn't do a lot of telling."

"It was the first time Jeb helped him," Diana said. "There was this Greek family, in the O of B but never that active. Close with some of the goofier, more harmless transmortals. Big money. Not just private-island people. Private-islands-all-around-the-world people. But they went nuts. Decided they were descended from the god Apollo and would only let their kids marry kids from families as wacked about descending from gods as they were. So they got more and more inbred, and weirder and weirder. Finally, one son goes nuts and starts killing people."

"Wow," Cyrus said. "I thought this was a funny story."

Diana shrugged. "The Avengel doesn't usually get involved until a story stops being funny. Anyhow, they'd named this kid Icarus, like in the myth. And he always freaked out in the dark. That's when he killed people, but he never remembered it when the sun came up. So he gets the fastest plane he can, and he starts flying west, chasing the sun like we are, only he actually keeps up and would even get ahead of it. He only touched down to refuel, and he just flew and flew. He burned through millions in fuel and replacement planes and a network of rogue ground crews, always changing where he touched down, and he just kept going. It took Rupe eighteen months before he caught him."

"Seriously?" Cyrus asked. "He flew with the sun for a year and half? He was never in the dark?"

"Nope," Diana said. "Not once. Icarus the Sun Chaser. Rupe said he was all the way nuts and practically blind when they caught him. He thought the guy would be angry or depressed, but he'd burned his eyes so bad, he always had this huge flaring afterimage. He thinks the sun follows him now."

"Where is he?" Cyrus asked.

"Back in Greece, in a hospital. Jeb said the guy was the saddest killer he'd ever seen. Tons of money, no mind, and the last survivor in his crazy family."

Even behind shades, Cyrus blinked and turned away from the bright horizon.

"Don't worry," Diana said. "It'll go down again. We're not flying that fast."

The sun did set again, but slowly. And the sky held on to its blue for hours, while down below, the ground was swallowed up by the darkest shadow Cyrus had ever seen.

Diana yawned and looked over at Cyrus's leg. An hour into the flight, Antigone had dragged him back into the cabin and their mother had bandaged it, warning him that they would have to dig the pellets out later. Just a little something to look forward to, Cyrus had thought. And Dan had rubbed his head like he was still a kid. Which he guessed he was.

Horace had been surly, refusing to even look at Cyrus. Antigone had hung the two paper globes from the ceiling to dry, where they looked like a pair of enormous, ridiculously droopy socks. Cyrus hadn't seen a drop of ink left on either of them.

Nolan and Niffy had been sleeping side by side. Dan had been sitting cross-legged on the floor, both eyes on Flint, who was hog-tied with Niffy's belt and curled up on the floor. All the vents were open and blasting cool air, but the little cabin had still smelled an awful lot like people.

When the sky had grown black and the time had

finally come to descend, Diana was asleep. Her arms were open in her lap, her head was tipped just a little back, and her shades had slipped two freckles farther down her nose. Her lips were parted slightly. Cyrus twisted in his seat and looked back into the cabin. He couldn't see Nolan and Antigone, but the others were all asleep. Only Flint's shoulder was in view, but even he was still.

Cyrus turned back to his instruments, and the darkness on the ground below him. He could see a city web of pinprick lights in the distance, but not a big city, and they weren't flying that far anyway. He had the coordinates Rupert had given Diana, but nothing else. There were stars above him, but no moon. He hoped there would be lights wherever they were supposed to land, because coordinates were only going to help him so much.

He nosed the plane down a little too quickly, and Diana's head lolled forward, then tipped toward him. Cyrus leaned over and pushed it back up. No good. Her chin hit her chest.

Oh, well. He'd have to wake her up soon anyway. He wasn't about to just pick a spot in the darkness and try to land.

"We overshot." Diana's voice was quiet in his headphone. She yawned. "Get low out over the lake and come back around."

"Lake?" Cyrus asked.

"We're just over it. That town out there is at the far end."

Cyrus leaned forward and stared at the ground. Then he looked out of his side window. Nothing. All blackness.

Diana tapped a little screen down at knee-level between them. And there it was. Small 3-D mountain ranges made of green lines, clicking slowly forward. A flat space was growing between them, broadening and extending. Cyrus hadn't paid any attention to the screen before because he hadn't known what it was, and no one had told him to.

"Nothing's that flat but water," Diana said. "I normally hate these things. I'd rather fly with my eyes. But it's nice on a night this dark, and without a lit strip."

Cyrus nodded, as if he had often flown and landed at night, let alone without a lit runway to land on.

He brought the plane lower and lower, until they were just below a thousand feet, and halfway out over the invisible lake. Then he went into a slow right turn.

"Tighter," Diana said. "We're between mountains here."

Cyrus banked harder, pointing his right wing down at water he wished he could see. His altitude dropped, but Diana didn't seem worried.

When he straightened out, he was below five hundred feet and aiming his plane at . . . he had no idea.

"Do you want to take it in?" Cyrus asked.

Diana looked at him and smiled. "You're doing fine."

"Yeah, right until I smack us into a mountain." Cyrus exhaled. The cockpit was cool, but his forehead was suddenly damp.

"Lower your gears and come in slow." Diana made it sound so simple. "Then I'll tilt the rotors and set her down."

Cyrus climbed slightly, just for his own sake, leveled back off, and then slowed until he thought they were going to stall.

"Nice," Diana said. And then she took over.

Cyrus flopped back into his seat, wiped his forehead, and tried not to pant. He felt the plane scoop and slow even more as the engines rotated up. It felt like they were in a helicopter, in a plane that could twist and slide and shuffle through the air as slowly as he could walk.

And then Diana flipped three switches, and spotlights on the wings and nose of the plane bathed the lake surface in icy halogen. Cyrus could see smooth dark water shooting past beneath them.

"Seriously?" Cyrus said. "Those were there the whole time and you didn't say anything?"

"You didn't need them," Diana said. "They would have just distracted you." She flipped a joystick down out of the instruments and pointed at it. "Find us a parking spot."

Where Cyrus swiveled, the spotlights swiveled. And up ahead, wedged between the still black water and a jutting mountain clothed in firs, there was a small cluster of cockeyed cabins. Huge cedar trees loomed between them, draping shadows over roofs and chimneys with heavy limbs, shielding structures from the spotlights where they could. Off to the right of the camp, there was a mountain stream descending into the lake, and beside it a small meadow.

"Right there," said Cyrus, but Diana had already seen it.

As the plane rose to hop the trees and settle in the meadow, down below the front door of a little cabin opened, and an old man rolled out onto the tiny porch, seated in a wheelchair.

He had a long rifle in his lap.

## ✦ four ✦

# EMPIRE OF BONES

CYRUS WOKE FACEDOWN on a bare mattress that smelled like dog. He blinked his eyes into focus and managed to lift his head. There was a brown Australia-shaped stain just beneath his face. The entire southern half of the continent had been flooded with his drool.

The mattress hadn't looked nearly so disgusting last night. With a little darkness and a lot of exhaustion, any flat surface can look pretty good. Last night, Cyrus would have given the grimy cabin floor four stars, let alone the bottom of a bunk bed.

Cyrus pressed himself slowly up onto his elbows. His right calf was shrieking with every heartbeat, which was probably what had woken him. Or maybe it had been the woodpecker doing major construction right outside the cabin's open window.

Cyrus sniffed, wiped his damp chin, and eyed a little window across the room. The sun was up, but big trees hid most of the light. He was pretty sure that Antigone had been on the bunk above him, but he wasn't even sure why he thought that. He could remember the plane landing in the meadow and sinking in the mud almost to its belly, and the crooked cabins, and the old man in the wheelchair pointing a rifle at him.

*Llewellyn Douglas.* The old free-diving kook who'd trained bull sharks in Lake Michigan. He'd forced Cyrus to drink something black and nasty. Then Cyrus had staggered into the closest cabin and picked a bed.

"Tigs?"

Nothing. He rolled slowly onto his side and lowered his bare feet to the floor. His right calf screamed with the increased blood pressure, and muscle fibers began to twitch and quiver beneath his skin. His bandage was new, but a dozen little bloody dots had soaked through.

Cyrus carefully slid his finger beneath the gauze and pulled it away from his leg. The top two puckers had been stitched shut.

The cabin door banged open and Rupert Greeves stepped inside. Cyrus squinted up at him.

"How's it feel?" Rupert asked.

"Like a shark bite," Cyrus said. "When did you get here?"

"An hour ago," Rupert said. "We got Jeb to a safe hospital and then stayed with him through most of the night. It's almost noon now." Rupert leaned his back against the wall by the door. "You've had a lot of shark bites, then?"

"Oh, yeah. Tons. Somebody stitched it up last night."
He straightened his leg out slowly. "How's Jeb?" He wasn't
sure he wanted an answer.

"Sorted," Rupert said. "For now. It was bad. If not
for Arachne, he wouldn't even have made it to hospital."

Cyrus exhaled relief. "And my mom?"

"Tired. Resting now." Rupert rubbed his jaw and
smiled. "Three years asleep, two months awake with
nurses all around to keep things calm and easy, and then
yesterday . . . her first day back with you lot."

"You mean *us* lot," Cyrus said. He flexed his toes and
groaned. "I guess I shouldn't be feeling sorry for myself.
Jeb almost died getting my mom out of Ashtown. I got
shot for those stupid paper globes, and they were ruined
anyway. I think I should make Antigone do my laundry
for life or something. Where is she?"

"Up and useful, unlike you." Rupert crossed the
room and lifted Cyrus easily to his feet. Cyrus sucked in
his breath through his teeth and hopped on his left foot.
He leaned against the bunk bed and exhaled, trying to
keep his breathing slow and steady. Rupert watched him.

"Can we at least stay here awhile?" Cyrus asked. "Or
are we running off again?"

Rupert smiled slightly. "You should see the whole
place before you ask that."

"I'm serious," Cyrus said. "For two months we've
been running. When do we just park somewhere?"

Rupert raised his eyebrows. "Not long ago, Cyrus Smith was begging to come along wherever I went. Now he just wants to park? You want me to drop you someplace comfortable and go on with this alone?"

"Come on, Rupe." Cyrus shut his eyes. "You know that's not what I mean. I'm just tired, and I hurt."

"Cyrus Lawrence Smith." Rupert's voice was a low growl. "You have witnessed the rebirth of an old war, the rekindling of a fire that once consumed nations like parched grass. The blame may not be yours, but you held the spark that set the flame. It is young and growing. Maybe, *maybe* it may still be quenched, so long as the Almighty bathes us in courage and luck and we do not rest and we do not tire and we do not listen to our own pain."

Rupert's chest heaved. His dark eyes did not leave Cyrus's. "Phoenix sets out to remake men according to his own demented imagination, but that twisted creature needs time. And so he stirred up the transmortals against the Order. Now the beasts have been loosed and our eyes must be on them. The great transmortals need no time at all to begin their destroying. Radu Bey will be drawing servants to him—men and women will flock to him without even knowing what draws them, like metal shavings to a magnet."

Rupert locked his jaw and gripped the side of the bunk bed. Old wood popped and Cyrus exhaled slowly. He'd rarely seen Rupert angry, and even now he knew the big man was holding back. Clenched fists and muscle-striped arms were ready to hurl the whole bed against the wall. Rupert's ribs rose and fell, and he seemed ready to shake the little cabin with a roar, but when he spoke again, his voice was calm and cold.

"My anger is with my own Order, Cyrus. Not with you. The O of B exists for such times as this. It exists *only* for such times as this, and yet it is the first to offer up sacrifices to the old darkness. Even good men and women of the Order now duck their heads and hide, hoping to avoid this war, hoping like so many fools through the ages have hoped before them, that only a few of the weak will die and then this storm of devils will quiet itself. You and I and your sister have been cast out to the Dracul, like the children of centuries ago, sent to feed a dragon."

He sighed, shook the bed slightly, and dropped his head onto his extended arms.

Cyrus had no idea what to say. His calf must have been ashamed, because already the screaming pain in his leg had muted slightly. He lowered his right foot to the ground and forced weight onto it.

"So," Cyrus said, "the last couple months . . ."

"Have been nearly pointless," Rupert said. "We have quietly gained a few assets, but fewer allies. Beyond the Boones and the Livingstones, there are no families willing to openly defy the Order."

"And the Smiths," Cyrus said. "And the Greeveses."

Rupert laughed, looking at Cyrus. "I had hoped to build an army. But we are the army. We must somehow quell the old gods, and even if we do *and* we survive, Phoenix will not have wasted his time. He and his new gods will be waiting for us."

Cyrus leaned against the bed. "But what about, you know, normal people? Cops? Soldiers? If the transmortals start smashing a town or something, won't everyone try to stop them?"

Rupert nodded. "Some will try. And that will add to the tragedy. When the great transmortals rise, the leaders and the powerful among men and women are the first to drop to their knees. Some will submit out of cowardice, while others have always worshipped and fed on power. When they encounter power raw, power primal, they will do anything to taste it, to be near it, to be enthralled. Sacred groves, ziggurats, fiery crags and labyrinths and valleys of bones, wherever the great transmortals make their homes, there also they will be worshipped with the shed blood of men and women and children. Agamemnon sacrificed his own child to such power, in exchange for his greatness. Babylon. Cambyses the Persian. The Scythians and their Amazon brides. All of them made blood sacrifices, all of them paid for strength and power with the lives of others. Wild and savage like the Picts, or ordered like the Aztecs, the Romans, the Nazis—it doesn't matter. The dark ones demand bodies, they give power, and they drive those who serve them into deeper and deeper madness."

Rupert turned and looked directly, deeply, into Cyrus's eyes. Cyrus blinked, but he could not look away.

"Cyrus Smith," Rupert said, "you and I were raised in a world where good men feared only the darkness of other men—and that is enough—where children could laugh at nonsense dragons in nonsense books, where monsters and giants had long ago been chained and hidden away in the deep places, devouring no one, so thoroughly defeated that even wise men and women believed *magical* to mean the same thing as *imaginary*. But the dark truths that lie beneath the myths and legends and storybooks are now erupting. We and the world will see the beginning of such . . . *magical* times. And, please God and all His angels, may we see them end."

Cyrus shifted on his leg, watching Rupert's eyes lose their focus and wander somewhere distant. Then Cyrus coughed.

"I'm sorry," Rupert said. "I shouldn't make this your burden."

"Why?" Cyrus asked. "Because I had some pellets in my leg? Because I whined about it? I promise I'm done. Next time I'm shot, I won't even mention it."

Rupert smiled, but his eyes were still heavy.

"Seriously," Cyrus said. "I'll just think about human sacrifice and bite my lip. And I always want to know what's going on, no matter how bad it is. I started all this—"

"No," Rupert said. "Cyrus—"

"Fine. I was *part* of starting all this," Cyrus continued. "It's kinda my burden already, Rupe. William Skelton made it my burden when he tossed me his stupid key ring and the Dragon's Tooth with it." Cyrus reached up and felt the keys and the empty silver sheath hanging from Patricia's cool body. "So just tell me what we're doing next. Another two months of hopping around and meeting with scared people? Hunting Phoenix? Hunting the *Ordo Draconis*? Even if it's all math with numbers and cartography, I'm in."

Rupert laughed. "You don't even realize how much you're like your dad. Just go jump in the lake. Get clean and move around on that leg. I have to skewer that Flint character and then listen to the ramblings of a Mohawked Irishman." He grinned. "We'll talk more after. I promise, you'll hear all the news."

Rupert gripped Cyrus's shoulder and then smacked him lightly on the back of the head before he turned for the door. Cyrus watched his Keeper go, and an old spring banged the door shut behind him. Whatever news had come in, it wasn't good. Rupert could always be a storm cloud, but he didn't worry easily.

Cyrus exhaled and did what he'd promised. He bit his lip and thought about the stories Nolan had told about

Radu Bey and the Dracul family, stories Antigone had refused to listen to, stories about kids his age being carried into sacred groves and stretched over mossy stone altars, about forests of stakes sharpened to hold bodies, about whole buildings made of bodies. Then he tried not to limp as he walked to the door.

Cyrus limped less as he moved over pine needles and roots and bare earth beneath the huge cedar trees. He passed two quiet cabins and a leaning outhouse and then made his way slowly toward the lake. Old Llewellyn Douglas was down by the water, seated in his wheelchair on a tiny battered dock, with a big wool blanket and a rifle across his lap. He was wearing a green stocking cap with a pom-pom on top, and a red flannel shirt under a puffy down vest that had once been cream with bright stripes across the chest but now featured a number of large coffee stains.

One of the Boones's amphibious jets was floating just thirty yards offshore.

Cyrus shuffled out onto the dock, barefoot and shirtless, and stood beside the old man in the wheelchair, squinting into the sun. The air was warm and dry, like California, and he filled his lungs with it. Even if he hadn't been the one flying the plane last night, the taste of the air was all he needed to tell him that he was in the west. Above the dark lake and its fir-covered mountain walls, the sky was low and large. A migrating herd of cumulus clouds seemed to barely clear the jutting trees as they slid east, and the loud blue all around them was close enough to taste. Cyrus loved being among old trees, breathing their breath, rich with age, and giving his own breath back. This air was mixed with the taste of running water from the mountain stream rippling the lake not far from the dock, and damp earth, and even in the sun, it had the small sharp teeth of air that has flown high and grown thin, air that has seen the poles and tumbled through skies of snow.

"Boy," Llewellyn said, "you gonna stand there sniffing the wind, or you gonna help me in?"

"It's nice to see you again, Mr. Douglas," Cyrus said. "I never said goodbye when you left. You taught us a lot."

The old man's face was carved with deep creases but it still looked hard and taut—like wet and wrinkled leather left to dry in the sun.

Llewellyn snorted. "Lie, truth, lie, Smithling. You can do better. There isn't a thing nice about seeing me again, not here, not now, not for you, not for me. No, you didn't say goodbye, and no, I didn't cry about it. I didn't even tell you I was leaving. And as for teaching you . . . ha! I taught you nothin'. Told you some things, but teaching means learning, and I don't know how as you learned a doggone thing." The old man glared up at Cyrus. "Can you fill your sinuses with water and pressure-proof your brain for a deep dive? You been slowing down your heart?

No?" He shook his head, bobbing the pom-pom on his hat. "I didn't think so. I talked *at* you. I didn't teach."

Cyrus laughed. "Well, I'm not lying. It is nice to see you. I never would have made Journeyman without you. Do you really want to get in the water?"

"Why do you think I'm sitting here, boy?" Llewellyn growled. "That plane ruins the view."

Cyrus looked around. He wasn't worried about the old man swimming. He'd never seen anyone more like a fish in the water. But with his own bad leg, he might not be able to help the old man back out.

Llewellyn Douglas set his rifle down on the dock and tossed his blanket on top of it. He was wearing a pair of very short, very old mustard-colored swim trunks, and his bare white legs were mostly bone and sagging skin where there should have been muscles. Cyrus tried to suppress a grimace.

"I have my suit on," Llewellyn said. "But only because that young Rupert says I'm not to go without one. Some nonsense about scaring the fish." He tugged off his hat, and his thin white hair floated away from his head, charged with static. The vest and the shirt were next, and Cyrus was left staring at a pale belly the color of a cave fish and ribs that marched up to the man's collarbones like two ladders in a skin bag.

Llewellyn eyed Cyrus's arms and chest, then assessed his own and sputtered out a laugh. "Boy, you're as brown as a nut, and you've strapped on some brawn beneath that skin, too. You almost look the Journeyman." He held out his hands. "Now get me in the water before I freeze in this sun."

Llewellyn didn't need much help standing up, and Cyrus was sure he didn't weigh more than a squirrel. The old man was vertical only long enough to fall forward, slithering into a dive that gave off more of a slurp than a splash.

Cyrus held his breath, hopped on his good leg, and then dropped into the dark rippling water feetfirst.

*Cold.*

Cyrus didn't gulp; he didn't flail. Time threw away whole seconds. His lungs were stone. His heart stopped. The fibers in his muscles paused, suddenly asleep. His skin was heavy, numb with shock. He drifted, a corpse lost in icy water. And then, slowly at first, his body began to burn. Icy teeth chewed at every cell, and their bite was fire. His feet bumped the soft, silty bottom, and his legs pushed off with the slow speed of a sloth. Drifting back up, he managed one pulse with his arms, and his head broke the surface into the sun.

He didn't gasp. Blinking, he opened his mouth and air came out, but he couldn't expand his lungs to inhale again. Llewellyn's face bobbed in front of him.

"Glacier lake," the old man said, and he spat. "The stream right there is fresh snowmelt, down from the heights. Nothing like it to make you know you're alive, and to ask if that's how you'd like to stay." Llewellyn smiled. "Don't take too long making up your mind." He slid through the water to the dock and dragged himself out.

Cyrus managed to inhale and turn back toward the shore. He had an audience. Rupert and Antigone were watching. Antigone held a towel and a shirt. Behind them, he saw Diana and Arachne approaching. Diana was tan and freckled and chatting, but Arachne was cool and quiet, with skin like spider silk woven and polished into pearl. Off to the side, hulking in the shadows beneath a cedar tree, he saw the huge shape of Gilgamesh of Uruk, looking surly and scratching his hairy cheek with a massive six-fingered hand. Gil was wearing a pair of blue oil-stained, oversize mechanic's coveralls that were too short for his legs, too tight for his thighs, and apparently unable to be zipped up past his bulging woolly chest. Gil looked too heavy for this world, denser even than the trees beside him. Cyrus didn't like seeing the transmortal without chains. Buried for good would have been even better.

Clearly on guard beside Gil, Captain John Smith stood with his arms crossed over a glistening gold breastplate. He was smaller than Gil, but just as dense. Beside each other they looked like men made of stone in a world made of cloud. But the Captain seemed to be enjoying himself a great deal more. He was wearing baggy camouflage pants tucked into his high Elizabethan boots, and his sword was low on his hip. His thick, square-cut beard almost reached his chest, and his rough hair was pulled back into a short ponytail. His cheeks were creased by centuries of smiles and songs, and his pale sun-bleached eyes shone, even in the shade.

Cyrus sputtered. He coughed. He wasn't . . . quite . . . able . . . to swim.

"Cy?" Rupert asked. "You coping?"

The Captain laughed. "Have ye never seen a rat drowning? The lad's a flesh anchor yearning for the bottom." The Captain shot Gil a warning glance, and then strode forward and marched out onto the dock, stepping over Llewellyn Douglas without a glance.

Spitting and kicking in place, Cyrus watched the Captain draw his sword. The dragon-etched blade sliced air and light as the Captain flipped it, catching the steel perfectly in his bare hand. Crouching, smiling through a squint, he extended the hilt to Cyrus.

Cyrus couldn't speak, but he shook his head. He shut his eyes, took a breath, and sank. Underwater, he followed the steps he'd been taught, contracting his torso around full lungs, forcing blood to flow. He felt his heart quicken in his chest. And then he contracted his will. The cold couldn't stop him. It was nothing. The fiery needle teeth were in his mind. He was loose. He was liquid. He pointed his arms and slithered forward. Moments later, he stood on silty stones, walking awkwardly up onto the bank. His teeth suddenly clattered without asking permission first. His skin was made entirely of bumps.

"Wow," Antigone said, worried. "It's really that cold? I think I'll skip."

Cyrus, shaking, glared at Rupert Greeves, and his Keeper spread his guilt out with a smile.

"What?" Rupert asked. "The water sorted your leg pain, yeah? How about a little gratitude?"

Cyrus fought to settle his quivering chest and steady his breathing. Then he nodded at Gilgamesh, still watching from beneath his tree.

"Why?" Cyrus managed. "Why. Gil's. Loose."

"Get dry," Rupert said quietly. "We are all that we will be, and it's time for a plan. Gil's part of that. Arachne's here to make him behave, and the Captain's here in case he doesn't." He turned to Antigone. She was hugging the towel and shirt to herself and chewing her lip. "Will you show him where to go?"

Antigone nodded and moved toward her brother.

"Grand," Rupert said. "Don't be long." He turned, striding away through the cabins, and the group trickled after him, with the Captain at the end, pushing the nearly naked Llewellyn Douglas in his wheelchair, beneath his mounded clothes.

Llewellyn winked at Cyrus as he passed. "I might have done a little teaching," he said. "The water ain't killed you yet, boy. And she's had her chances. Yes, she has."

As they rolled away, Antigone handed her brother the towel and he buried his face in its scratchy thread, rubbing his skin warm.

"Cy," Antigone said. Her voice was serious, and Cyrus looked up into his sister's wide eyes. "I know your leg is hurt and you're completely frozen and I got Rupe to agree to let us into his powwow, but there's something more important that I have to show you. Something I haven't shown anyone."

"Okay . . . ," Cyrus said.

"Like, right now," Antigone said. She handed him the shirt she had been holding. It was old and green with a white tadpole on the chest bent into the shape of a lightning bolt. "Symbol of the Douglases, apparently," she said. "Put it on." Cyrus obeyed slowly, still slightly shaking. As soon as his head was through, she grabbed his hand and began to drag him away. Wincing, hobbling over tree roots, Cyrus pulled back. Antigone stopped and assessed him, tucking her hair behind her ears.

"Fine," she said. "We really don't have time." She turned around and braced herself. "Jump on."

"Tigs." Cyrus laughed. "You're a bug. I'll crush you. And my shorts are soaking wet."

"I'm an ant," Antigone said. "I could carry Rupe if I had to. And I don't care about wet. Just get on before I get mad. I'm serious, Cy. You and your stupid leg are too slow right now. Do it."

Cyrus put his hands on his sister's shoulders and hopped onto her back. She groaned, and he felt her buckle a little as she grabbed for a grip on his legs, but she stabilized quickly.

"Giddyup, Tigger," Cyrus said.

"Shut up, Rus-Rus, or I'll drop you on a rock." Antigone gasped, and then she raced away.

Antigone carried her brother past their cabin and then veered for the stream. As the trees thinned and the stream and the meadow and the tilt-rotor plane appeared, she turned upstream and uphill, and the ground became rocky.

Finally, chuffing like a dying train, Antigone staggered around a boulder and stopped in front of an old outhouse. She dropped Cyrus, and he leaned against the warm stone, waiting for an explanation.

"Okay," Antigone wheezed. She bent at the waist, coughed, and straightened. "Rupert told us not to use this outhouse. Animals down inside or something. Will attack if you try." She put her hands on her head, breathless. Her face was flushed and wet with sweat, but she wouldn't slow down. "Perfect, right? No one would come here. So I did. And they're fine, Cy. They're perfect. It's solved. And it's crazy. Seriously, all-the-way, I-can't-even-believe-it crazy."

"Wait," Cyrus said. "What are perfect? The animals? You fixed the outhouse?"

"No!" Antigone barked. "The globes! Skelton's paper globes that you dropped in the motel pool!"

"I didn't drop them," Cyrus said. "The wind—"

"Doesn't matter!" Antigone said, and she held up both hands. "With everyone around all the time, I brought them up here. We thought the water ruined them but they're fine. They're more than fine. They're solved. And now I know why everyone was so mad when Skelton made us his heirs. Horace wasn't lying. Skelton was rich, Cy. Way crazy go-to-the-moon-and-back rich. And he didn't just show up to the motel and make us his Acolytes all spur of the moment. He knew what he was doing. It was all a plan."

Panting, she put her hands on her hips and smiled. "Wanna see?"

She didn't wait for an answer. Instead, she tugged open the old outhouse door and stepped aside.

"Get in there."

Cyrus stepped onto a sighing plank floor, and Antigone followed, banging the door shut behind her. Enough light trickled in through the cracks that Cyrus could watch his sister hop up onto the wooden toilet bench with one dark ominous hole, then pull the two stiff and folded globes and a flashlight down from a dust-covered shelf.

Antigone held up the first globe, and it looked like a collapsed umbrella.

"Okay," she said. "So no one could ever decode all that ink writing. Not Nolan, not Rupert. Nobody. Some of it almost made sense; some they thought was maybe a weird Sanskrit. But everything they tried to translate ended up being nonsense."

Cyrus nodded. "Right. Get to the new stuff."

Antigone beamed. "It *was* nonsense, Cy. The ink on the paper globes was a distraction all along. The real stuff was written into the paper. It just needed you to dissolve all that ink off in the Archer's stupid pool!"

Cyrus squinted at the paper. "I don't see anything, Tigs."

Antigone flicked on the flashlight and held the folded globe up to her brother's face with the light right on it.

At first, Cyrus thought he was seeing white fibers in the yellowed paper, much lighter than the rest. He leaned closer. The fibers looped together much too neatly, and there was a lot more of it than he had first noticed. It was writing as tight and sharp and fine as any he had ever seen. But it wasn't English. He couldn't make out a single word.

"It's tiny," Cyrus said. "We need a magnifying glass.

And it's not English, Tigs. I don't know what you're seeing that I'm not."

"Oh, come on," Antigone said. "Is it that hard to figure out?"

She carefully expanded the paper, pulling it out into something like the original globe.

"It's English," she said, and she slid the glowing flashlight up inside the globe. Then she rotated the paper carefully until she had found what she was looking for. "But it's all backward." She glanced at her brother with half a smile. "Don't you remember what came with it?" she asked. "A candle for the inside. That was the clue. I put the flashlight inside it and . . ." She pointed the lit paper at the outhouse wall, suddenly spraying a murky cloud of light across it. Inside the cloud, pale cursive letters crawled across knotholes and planks.

"Wow," Cyrus said. "Wow."

"Correct," said Antigone. "I know."

Cyrus stepped forward and put his hand under his sister's, trying to steady the wobbling light.

" 'To Antigone Elizabeth and Cyrus Lawrence,' " he read aloud, " 'I leave you this, my . . .' What's that say?"

" 'My Empire of Bones,' " Antigone said. Her voice was low. "And there's a whole letter that comes after."

## ❧ five ❧

# DEAD MAN'S TALE

ANTIGONE HANDED CYRUS THE PAPER and the flashlight. When he pulled back from the wall a little too far, the words disappeared in a blur. When he leaned forward, they sharpened.

Antigone tapped the planks. "Slide the light down. Read the letter."

Cyrus tried to adjust the flashlight and the paper, but he was hopeless, spraying blurry lines sideways or losing his place. He gave it back to Antigone.

"You do it," he said. "You were the one who kept that screen and the old movie projector in your room."

Antigone was distracted, her eyes on the wall. "This . . . is . . . nothing like that, Cy." But she stepped up close to the wall, adjusted the flashlight, and old, dead William Skelton's words immediately came into focus four lines at a time. She read the whole thing aloud as she went, pausing only to smooth the paper or shift the light. Cyrus watched the tight cursive words slide by as he listened to his sister's voice.

To Antigone Elizabeth and Cyrus Lawrence,

I leave you this, my Empire of Bones. Keep it tight to yourselves. Secret. You hold the Dark Tooth, and no one—no one—must know that you possess it. If Ashtown grows unsafe, run and don't ever look back. The O of B has been dying since your father was a kid, but if you can keep the tooth hidden, the Order might still win its war with Phoenix. Or it won't, but at least you'll be breathing. Every little thing that I collected and hid in my outlaw years is charted in this map. All of it is yours—allies and artifacts, weapons and wealth, enough hidden paths and hidden doors to last you through lifetimes of running. The keys I gave you will open every door. Do not use the keys to steal, or they will turn against you. When more is needed than keys, consult my ink bones. I've made notes of which bones will help you. Look closely. Trust no one but the caretakers named here. They are all staunch outlaws, haters of Phoenix as well as doubters of the Order. Tell them nothing about what you carry. Horace will serve you faithfully. Rupert Greeves is honest, but a fool who still believes the Order will stand for the good when blood begins to spill. I have left another globe for him—every little bit I learned about the *holdings of that devil, Phoenix. He must be hunted now and put down before he grows.*

*Be good. Be brave. I wasn't.*

*Billy B*

Antigone sighed as she finished.

"That would have been nice to have sooner," said Cyrus. "We've already lost the tooth, and to the worst guy possible."

"I know," Antigone said. "And we would have had this right away if the Order hadn't shoved us down in the Polygon instead of letting us move right into Skelton's rooms." She shifted the paper, searching for something. "But it could still help. Look."

A projected image of a large boat wobbled on the wall. Skelton had labeled it:

### S.S. *FAT BETTY*
LIBRARY, ARMORY, FUEL
MS. LEMON CHAUNCEY, SAGE

14.713791, 160.587158 (AUG.–NOV.)

Cyrus stared at the numbers. Latitude and longitude. Cartography, darn it.

"Where is that?" Cyrus asked.

"South Pacific," Antigone said. She was already moving on.

"And Lemon Chauncey?" Cyrus asked.

"No idea who she is," Antigone said. "Apparently, a Sage on a boat. But check this one out."

The flashlight sprayed up a drawing of a house on a mountain. It was oversize and cartoony, like a detail on a medieval map, but labeled with tight little rows of writing. Cyrus didn't even try to process the noted latitude and longitude. He only saw *"150lbs Gold, Boat, Quiet,"* and then Antigone had moved on.

A cave mouth.

"This one is in Mexico," Antigone said.

## CHICOMOZTOC
### RELICS, PLANE (SMALL), WEAPONS (ORDER BANNED), JEEP, FUEL

#### LEOPOLD MONTOYA, SAGE (EXPELLED)

"That's nice," Cyrus said. "Everyone needs relics and banned weapons."

"We might," said Antigone. She slid up a picture of something like a lighthouse. "This one is weird. It's in Istanbul."

# LEANDROS

## 60LBS. GOLD, 500LBS. SILVER, DRACUL GIN, DEATH THREAD, CURSES, FORBIDDEN. LEFT CLAVICLE. CRYPTKEEPER NEEDED

### MONASTERBOICE, IRELAND. RIGHT CLAVICLE.

Antigone lowered the globe and faced her brother. Cyrus looked from the blank dim wall to the paper in his sister's hands, and up into her face. Her brows were high and her eyes wide. *Cryptkeeper? Monasterboice?* They were weird words, and he knew that he had just heard them somewhere. Yesterday. From Niffy, that crazy Irish monk with the Mohawk.

"Niffy said he's a Cryptkeeper," Cyrus said. "And that he was from Monasterboice. Wherever that is. And I don't understand the clavicle thing."

"I think we should tell Rupe," Antigone said.

The outhouse door swung open and Rupert leaned his arm above the low jamb.

"What should you tell me, Antigone Smith?" Rupert asked. "Maybe why you two are plotting like a pair of villains in this dodgy loo?" He examined the tight space with his lip curled. "I should lock the door and leave you for the skunks."

"Skunks?" Cyrus asked. He glanced down at the wooden toilet bench.

Antigone faced Rupert and squared her shoulders. "I wanted to show you, but I had to show Cyrus first."

Rupert's eyes settled on the globe still in Antigone's hand.

"You've sorted it?"

Antigone and Cyrus were silent.

Rupert straightened. "Of course. Secrets, secrets. Why else would you dart off? I'll pry it out of you later. I've left that tetchy little mob waiting while I found you." He backed away from the outhouse. "Come on, then, and no more disappearing. Oh, and Cy, don't make your sister pack you around." He grinned, turning down the slope. "Shameful, mate! Her tracks looked like a squiffy two-legged pony's."

Antigone laughed.

"Her idea!" Cyrus said. "Not mine." But Rupert wasn't waiting, and Antigone had already grabbed the extra globe and was hurrying after him.

With his head whirling, Cyrus hopped out into the light and hobbled down the hill, trying to keep up.

The camp was like an old village, swallowed by time and trees, with only the cabins near the lake seeing any sun. Cyrus passed a boathouse with a sagging roof and walls lined with stacks of canoes buried in needles and moss. Rupert and Antigone led him around an old obstacle course crushed beneath the carcass of a fallen tree so old and rotten that moist wood fell away at the merest touch.

Cyrus's bare feet were silent on the needle-carpeted path, and the movement felt good for the most part, loosening his incredibly tight calf. Beyond the obstacle course, there were more cabins—some completely collapsed in on themselves, and others hiding beneath fallen branches and tufted ferns. And beyond these, in a pool of sunlight, there was a two-story stone lodge nestled against the base of a rising mountainside beside a thin ribbon of falling water. Moss-covered boulders stood guard around it. The roof was peaked twice, side by side, and the valley between the peaks was full of the accumulated forest slough of decades—drifted cones and needles and wooden decay. Two tall adolescent cedars had sprung up in this rooftop valley, but the lodge beneath them was still straight and strong.

Broad stone stairs ran up to plank doors on the second story. Hanging above the door, a large version of the lightning bolt tadpole on Cyrus's shirt had been burned onto a thick crosscut of cedar.

Rupert strode up the stairs and pushed through the doors, but Antigone waited for her brother at the bottom. On one side of the stairs, a steep wheelchair ramp of boards had been thrown down, and a rope had been tied to a post at the top. Cyrus could only imagine trying to pull himself up. Going down would almost be worse.

"This whole place belongs to Llewellyn?" he asked his sister.

Antigone nodded. "Rupe says Llew used to be one of the top trainers, and not just from Ashtown. Power families all over the world hired him and sent their kids here. He built this whole place himself."

"What happened?" Cyrus asked.

Llewellyn Douglas rolled out of the doors and stopped on the top step. "A man named Edwin Laughlin happened. Phoenix." The old man growled. "He came out here with grand ideas of how my training could be improved. Without so much as a do-you-mind, he picked an Acolyte and got started with his sorcery. I almost killed the villain and he almost killed me. I'm not in this chair because I love wheels."

"And the kid?" Antigone asked.

"Went nuts," Llewellyn said. "Died a year later. Now get up here if you're gonna."

The inside of the lodge was dim and enormous. The ceilings were vaulted on massive peeled logs, and low wooden chairs and tables dotted the room around a large stairwell in the middle. The Captain sprawled in a chair across from Gil and Arachne. Horace was sitting at a table, scratching something out on an old pad of paper. Diana was playing cards with Gunner, who had his long suit-clad legs folded up awkwardly beneath the table. The transmortals were like anchors in the room, like exhibits in a museum with mere mortals flitting past. Light treated them differently somehow. Or they treated light differently. The shadows they cast seemed deeper, the patterns in their faces exaggerated by centuries of extra expression, their eyes always staring out from another time. Especially small Arachne. Her blue icy eyes always seemed to be leaking light collected lifetimes ago. Only Nolan, lean and pale and strong like a whip, was capable of blending in with mortals, of making himself seem light enough for this world. At least if he wasn't angry and if you avoided looking into his ancient eyes, layered by time like limestone, and polished by trouble. When Cyrus entered the lodge, Nolan was the last transmortal he noticed. His old roommate from the Polygon had a small smirk and he was leaning back in a chair with his partially closed eyes on Gil. Gil, his ancient rival, the hero he had robbed and who had cursed him with his peeling serpentine skin. Nolan yawned and looked away from Gil to watch the slightly pimply Dennis Gilly, who was off in a corner, wearing short shorts, high striped socks, a head bandage that tufted his brown hair straight up, and a damp lightning newt shirt. He was attempting to copy an abdominal workout from a dusty booklet.

Dennis looked up and waved at Cyrus. Cyrus nodded, but his attention shifted quickly.

One end of the room was dominated by a huge stone fireplace full of cold ash. A small bed sat beside it, tidily made, and clothes were stacked neatly on top of it. The other end opened into a large kitchen. Cyrus could hear Rupert's voice coming from somewhere, but he was more interested in the walls than in where Rupert might be.

Old photos striped the lodge in rows. Men and women in faded color smiled on mountaintops, dove from cliffs, swam underwater behind fat-bodied sharks. Cyrus paused in front of two photos that hung together. A tall black teenager and a tall white teenager stood on opposite ends of a canoe, holding a green flag with a white lightning bolt tadpole between them. In the background, Cyrus could see the camp, the tidy cabins, the stream, and the meadow where the tilt-rotor plane now sat. The boys were both shirtless and muscled like young Olympians, and they were far from serious. The photo had captured them mid-laughter, mid-war—tugging on the flag, rocking the canoe with their bare feet, struggling to balance.

Cyrus stared at the younger version of his father, at the taut lines in his arms, at the blur of his smile, a little too quick for the camera. Then he studied the young Rupert Greeves. Rupert looked more determined, more insistent, and a little more likely to topple. But what struck Cyrus the most was that this Rupert had no scars. The boys were undamaged, ready for life and laughter and adventure. Now one was dead, and the other carried enough scars for three lifetimes.

Antigone stepped up next to Cyrus. Together they studied the next photograph.

Rupert Greeves and their father, now years older, stood shoulder to shoulder. They looked lean and sickly; their clothes were in tatters and their beards were ratty and out of control. Behind them, green cliff walls climbed up and out of view. Out of focus in the background, there was a stone structure like a ziggurat. Rupert's face was serious and his eyes hard. He had one arm extended, and a huge dragonfly was perched on his wrist like a falcon. Beside him, Lawrence Smith was grinning. He was leaning away from Rupert slightly, toward a girl with deep-olive skin and wide dark eyes. She was wearing a white dress intricately embroidered with swooping red and blue swirls that looked half bird and half wind. Her jet hair was pulled tight and wound into a tower on the back of her head. She wasn't smiling, but the corners of her mouth were tugging up as if she was about to.

She looked almost exactly like Antigone.

"Crazy, right?"

Dan's voice made Cyrus jump. He turned to see his older brother standing with his mother leaning on his arm. Her eyes were on the picture, too, and there was nothing tentative about her smile now.

"Mom," Cyrus said. He glanced back at the picture. "You're so . . ."

"Young?" his mother asked. "Frightened? In love with the crazy blond boy beside me?"

"So beautiful," Antigone said.

"So Antigone," Cyrus said at the same time.

"Why, thank you, Rus-Rus." Antigone laughed. "You're such a sweetie."

"Don't make me smack you," Cyrus said. "I just meant that she looks exactly like you."

"I'll take it," Antigone said. She stepped back, kissed her mother, and looked back up at the picture. "She's gorgeous, and I definitely want that dress."

This time Dan laughed. "Tigs, I haven't seen you in a dress in years."

"Yeah, well, I didn't have *that* dress, did I?" Antigone crossed her arms. "I had two brothers, no money, and thrift-store jeans."

Katie Smith moved from Dan and took Cyrus by the hand. Her touch was still a surprise, something long forgotten made new. She smiled at her son, and then pointed back up at the photo. There was a teenage boy standing next to her in the frame, trying to slide out of the picture. He was young and wiry, shirtless, but wearing what looked like a woven skirt belted with a wide scarf. A thick black blade like a machete was tucked into the scarf belt. The hilt was gold and nested with smooth emeralds.

"Hanno," Katie said. "Your uncle, my brother. He was your age when your father came to us. To my eyes, his blood is in you."

Hanno's face was worried as he tried to escape the camera. The boy and Cyrus were not the same, but even Cyrus could see the similarities. The jaw, the wide cheekbones, the aggressive brows. Cyrus felt like an echo, like the bouncing sound of someone else's voice thrown from very far away.

"I like his skirt," Antigone said.

"I like his sword," said Cyrus.

Katie sighed. "Your father and Rupert gave it to him on behalf of the Order, though the Order knew nothing of the gift."

The sounds of a struggle erupted out of the stairwell. Shouts, kicks, and a crash. And then Niffy backed up the stairs, carrying Flint by the shoulders while the man thrashed. Flint was tied, and he had a cloth blindfold over his eyes, but he was writhing and twisting like a gator. Rupert followed Niffy up the stairs, sweating and gripping Flint's ankles tight under his right arm.

"Knock him out," Nolan said. "Be done with it."

"No," Rupert grunted. "He needs to speak."

Nolan shrugged and the crowd watched Niffy and Rupert carry Flint toward the stone hearth. They folded him down into a low chair and Niffy stood behind him with one thick hand on each of Flint's shoulders.

"Cowards!" Flint shouted. "Bloody useless sacks—"

Niffy pinched down on Flint's shoulders and the man trailed off into a scream, trying to twist and shrink in his chair.

Rupert stood in front of him and crossed his arms.

"Enough." Rupert nodded at Niffy and the monk relaxed his grip. Flint slumped over the arm of his chair, panting. Niffy straightened him back up.

"Flint Montrose," Rupert said, "you sit before the Avengel of the Order of Brendan, Ashtown Estate."

Flint groaned. "I know who you are, you nit."

"I and these assembled members of the O of B, along with several of our allies, are currently operating in the field."

"On the run, you mean?" Flint laughed. "Sneaking about with your little gang of outlaw infants? You lot couldn't hatch flies in a backyard dunny."

The temperature of Rupert's voice dropped ten degrees. "You will therefore be tried under the rules of Field Governance and Martial Circumstance."

"Whoa," Flint said, shaking his head, trying to work the blindfold loose with his cheeks and eyebrows. "You can't do that. There's rules."

"Yes, there are," Rupert said. "The charges are murder and attempted murder. O of B witnesses stand ready to testify. A sufficient executioner for one of your rank is present and willing to perform his duty."

"You mean you!" Flint shouted. "You're going to kill me!"

"I'll strike the blow!" the Captain bellowed, jumping to his feet. "And from the looks of the holy friar, he'd be well pleased to pry a pirate skullcap with his fingers."

"If execution is deemed necessary," Rupert said slowly, "I shall be the one to carry out the sentence, though the accused shall choose the mode."

Flint jerked in his chair and tried to stand, but Niffy sent him shrinking back down.

"I have the right to see!" Flint squealed. "Let me see my accusers!"

Niffy looked at Rupert. Rupert nodded. Then the monk tugged off the blindfold and tossed it into the fireplace behind him.

Flint already looked like a ghost. Moisture hung beneath his nose and in the corners of his wild eyes. He took in the room quickly, and Cyrus saw surprise flash across the man's face when he looked at the Captain and again when he saw Gil.

Cyrus understood. Gil should have been off in some sort of secret prison. Of course, maybe that was what this broken-down camp had become.

"Cyrus Smith," Rupert said, "did you see who shot Keeper Eric Romegas at the Archer Motel?"

Cyrus coughed. Every pair of eyes focused on him, none more intently than Flint's.

"He did," Cyrus said, pointing at the bound man. "And he shot at me."

"Eric defied the Brendan's own orders," Flint pleaded. "He turned on me. He almost killed me. But I never tried to kill you, lad. Never. I only meant to hobble you. We were supposed to bring you in."

"Diana Boone," Rupert said, "did you see who shot and wounded your brother, Keeper Jeb Boone?"

Diana exhaled slowly, and then nodded. "He did. Twice. Once when Jeb was running, and again when he was on the ground."

Rupert stared at Flint, who was squirming in his chair.

"Keeper Flint Montrose," Rupert said, "I am the Blood Avenger, bound by my duty to avenge my fallen brothers and sisters, bound to mete out earthly justice upon thieves, murderers, and beyond all else, traitors. Do you deny these charges?"

"You can't do this," Flint said, his voice cracking with panic. "You can't."

"John," Rupert said, "will you lend me your blade?"

Captain John Smith stepped forward, drawing his sword as he did. He extended the hilt to Rupert, and Cyrus stared at the bright braided steel, traced with the scales of a dragon.

"Lean him back into the fireplace," Llewellyn said. "I don't want blood on the floor."

Flint's face hardened; then he spat on the floor at Rupert's feet. "You wouldn't dare."

Niffy jerked Flint's head back and leaned the chair into the fireplace. The man's jaw clenched. The lump in his throat bobbed and danced.

Rupert Greeves stepped over Flint, extending the blade with one hand until the steel hovered just above his throat. Cyrus swallowed hard. He had felt that edge against his own neck before. He'd even used it to part the Captain's last steel chain. It was beyond sharp.

"Rupe?" Antigone tried to push forward, but Diana pulled her back. "Rupert!" she shouted. "You're not really going to?"

Rupert raised the sword.

"Brendan's orders," Flint said suddenly. "Smiths were to be brought to him! Anyone aiding them was to die. Brendan's orders."

The sword hung in the air, ready to fall.

"To what end?" Rupert asked. "Why should Bellamy Cook collect the Smiths instead of leaving them for Radu Bey? Why anger the transmortals now after all the groveling he's done?"

"Skelton," Flint said. "William Skelton. He hid things. He stole things. And he left them to those Smith brats."

"Gold?" Rupert asked. "Money? What things does

Bellamy want? What's in Skelton's estate that's worth enough for this Brendan to defy Radu Bey?"

Flint twisted, gargled a laugh, and then spat again, this time on the hearth.

"You don't know anything, do you, mate? Bellamy doesn't work for Radu Bey. He answers only to Phoenix. Radu and his primeval beasties can tear the world down, for all Bellamy cares. Phoenix means for them to. They'll do the heavy lifting. They'll till the nations under and set the world blazing to ashes. That is their usefulness."

"Are all villains fools?" Rupert asked, shaking his head. "What good is that to Bellamy? Phoenix is hidden. Bellamy and his version of the Order will be destroyed."

"Out of ashes . . . ," Flint said, and he grinned. When he continued, his voice was hushed. "Phoenix rises. A new race, a new species, and we will be named for our father. We must be unmade to be remade. If we serve him well, he will give us new lives and new flesh. Beside us, you'll be the apes. Even Radu and his dragons will tremble in fear."

The blade flicked down. Antigone yelped, and Flint jerked in his chair. But Rupert had only notched the man's ear.

"What things did Skelton hide that Phoenix needs?" Rupert asked.

"People," Flint sputtered. "Exiles. Relics. Weapons. The Dracul Gin."

"He lies," the Captain blurted. "I hid away the dragon gin with my own two hands. Lop the little hedgepig's neck and set his craven skull a-bowling."

Cyrus saw Niffy look up at the Captain's words. His grip on Flint didn't slacken, but his interested eyes stayed on the Captain.

Rupert studied Flint's floury face. "Pythia," Rupert said, "does the man lie?"

No one answered.

"Pythia?" Rupert asked. He glanced back at the silent crowd. Cyrus turned as well, scanning the corners. He hadn't known the little rope-haired oracle was at the camp. Of course, he hadn't known that Gil and the Captain would be here, either.

"When you say *Pythia*," Niffy asked, "you wouldn't be meaning *the* Pythia?"

Nolan laughed. Rupert didn't answer. He focused on the Captain.

"John Smith?" His voice was hard. "Where is she?"

The Captain shrugged. "She's just a wee lass. I don't keep her in chains."

"The roof," Gilgamesh said, and his voice rumbled like a big bass drum. Cyrus felt it in the floorboards. Gil nodded his massive head up at the beams. "She roosts above." The giant man's cow-size eyes rolled back down and met Cyrus's. Cyrus looked away quickly.

"No lie," Flint said desperately. "I swear, I'm telling

only truth, mate. Skelton sabotaged Phoenix for years, ghosting away every relic he could, every time the boss sent him after something. No one knew until he swiped the tooth for himself, and then he took off running."

Rupert lowered his sword and backed away. Niffy stood the chair back up, and Flint sagged with relief.

"Oh, Lord love you, brother. I'll do anything you ask."

"Arachne," Rupert said, "put him to sleep."

Small Arachne slipped forward, her spider bag over her shoulder, where it always was. When she passed Cyrus, her arm brushed his and his skin tightened with the cold like he'd just touched ten years of moonlight. When she reached Flint, she unslung the heavy bag from her shoulder. Flint stared at her, confused, eyes wide.

"How long?" Arachne asked. Her voice was cool and quiet.

"A year," Rupert said. "At the least."

Arachne nodded and set her heavy bag on Flint's lap. She whistled lightly between her teeth, and Cyrus bit his lip as a large charcoal spider with white speckles scrambled out of the bag and up Flint's chest. Smaller spiders followed, but the man didn't notice. His eyes were lost in Arachne's, lost somewhere distant and cold, arctic and blue.

"Your dreams needn't be horrors," Arachne said quietly, and she touched Flint's sweating cheek. "They needn't mirror your darkness. Look beyond yourself. Dream in the light."

Flint jerked as the spiders bit. Cyrus wanted to look away, but he couldn't. The man who had tried to kill him blinked slowly, his tongue crept out of his mouth, and then his head lolled to the side. He was unconscious.

"Justice," Llewellyn said loudly, "would have been the blade."

"Aye," said the Captain.

"You can't be serious," Antigone said. "Rupert's not a murderer. We can't just kill people."

Rupert turned and faced the crowd, his shoulders slumping. He held out the sword for the Captain, and his words were as weary as his eyes.

"I am a man of blood, Antigone Smith. It would not have been the first time I have executed a man in the field." He glanced from Llewellyn to the Captain. "But wisdom can walk beyond justice. Look at us. Many in the Order are fearful of choosing our side in this war, fearful that we are nothing but ragged scofflaws with no creed but defiance."

"Cowards," grunted the Captain. "Fen-suckled foot lickers."

"Maybe," Rupert said. "But while we are outlaws in fact, we will not be in spirit. If we begin the hunt for Phoenix, we will need help, and our little band is off-putting enough already."

Niffy began to laugh, his round face split wide. "Off-putting?" He tipped Flint's head back and forth. "Oh, I wouldn't say that. You're a right lovely lot—the spider queen herself doling out doses." He curtsied at Arachne, and then eyed Nolan. "And he'll be the snakeskin thief, if I know my lists, and in the same band as Gilgamesh of Uruk, the hero thug who cursed him?"

"I am not of this band," Gil said. He shifted slightly where he stood and the floor creaked beneath his shadow. "But I am at peace."

"Brilliant," said Niffy, and he ran a thick hand over the stripe of curly hair on his scalp. "Just tagging along, then, to observe and report back to your brother beasts?"

Gil sniffed, and his nostrils flared. "And who are you, monk? Why are you here?"

Niffy ignored him, continuing on with a grin.

"And of course who could forget the traitor Captain, father of the Smiths turned transmortal Dracul killer? Your O of B is even ashamed of his crest." Niffy crossed his thick arms. "Rupert Greeves, your little band is beyond off-putting. You could execute a dozen of Phoenix's men in this fireplace and worry no one at all. You've had one trial already, and as grand and dramatic and lovely as it was, it's time for another. This time you'll all be on the block." Niffy looked around the room. His cheeks fell and the last residue of his smile vanished.

"The beast of Uruk has asked my errand. Well, I am

Brother Boniface Brosnan, Cryptkeeper of Monasterboice, numbered among the Brothers of the Voyager, the
first and only true Order of Brendan. The Brothers sent
me to make a judgment and deliver a message."

"Ignoring your petty rivalry, what are you talking
about?" Rupert growled. "What message?"

Niffy sniffed and wiped his nose on the back of his
hand. "Well, that will depend on the judgment, won't it?
You have been seeking allies for your war. I am here. An
ambassador. Are you to be the allies or enemies of my
order?"

"Irishman," the Captain said, "ye'd be wise to watch
your words."

"Sit, Captain," Niffy said. "Please. Transmortals to
my left, mere humanity to my right. This won't take long.
Will someone fetch the Pythian oracle from the roof?"

Rupert stared at Niffy.

"I'm a man of the cloth," Niffy said, smiling. "And
a possible friend. You need some of those, yeah? So in-
dulge me."

## ❊ six ❊

# JUDGE, JURY, MESSENGER

Cyrus squirmed in his seat until Antigone elbowed him in the ribs. Then, just for her, he squirmed a little harder. The two of them were wedged into a short wooden couch with itchy wool cushions on the humanity side of the room. Of the mortals, only Rupert stood.

Cyrus glanced back at the door. His mother had been pretty shaken by the interrogation of Flint. Of course she had been. And Cyrus hadn't even noticed. Not until Dan had asked that they be excused from Niffy's little show and had practically carried her from the room. And now Antigone was angry because Rupert had told her to stay. She was even angrier because she hadn't noticed how upset her mother was in the first place. And now her elbows were taking it out on Cyrus.

*Ten normal humans*, Cyrus thought. It was hardly an army. It was hardly even an outlaw band. And that was including his mother and Llewellyn Douglas in his wheelchair. But the mortals weren't really where this gang packed its punch. He looked across the room at the transmortals.

Nolan was slumping in his chair with his knotted paper-colored arms crossed and his eyes almost shut. His blue veins were faint beneath the surface of his skin, like long-healed bruises. He was calm, but no one who had seen Nolan angry would ever forget how dangerous he could be. Those veins weren't always faint. Cyrus had seen them bulge and writhe.

Arachne was beside Nolan, sitting straight up in her chair with her hands folded politely over her saggy bag of spiders like an etiquette instructor. Her icy eyes were focused on Niffy, where he stood on the hearth, and her obsidian hair was pulled back so tight that it looked like black glass. Cyrus wondered if her spiders had done it for her. Probably. Arachne was small and quiet, and he'd never seen her move quickly, not even when she'd faced Phoenix. Wherever there were spiders, she was danger-ous. And spiders were everywhere.

Gilgamesh overwhelmed a little wooden chair, and it squealed in pain every time he breathed. His legs stuck out like felled trees, and his six-fingered hands were splayed out on his knees. His serpentine lips were sneer-ing in his beard, and his cow eyes always seemed to be on Cyrus. He could explode like a humpbacked rodeo bull, and the small ice-eyed spider girl beside him might have been the only thing keeping him from tearing Cyrus's head off. Of course, Cyrus had saved Gil from Phoenix in a burning cigar factory on the Mississippi. Maybe that was enough to erase Gil's hate.

Cyrus met the huge man's eyes. They were still and dark and unblinking. Anger was trapped inside them, like a prisoner behind glass. Cyrus looked away quickly.

Gil was a problem.

The Captain stepped into the lodge, carrying Pythia on his back. The small girl with the wide eyes and the dark skin peered over the Captain's shoulder. Her thick ropes of hair were coiled around his arms, holding her in place. The other transmortals seemed almost normal by comparison. Her hair moved and gripped like the tentacles of an octopus, and life—ancient and mossy—almost dripped from her eyes. But unlike the other transmortals, her bright eyes looked young, and her focus seemed sharp enough to bend the world and time around it. She was mute, communicating in thoughts and dreams to seers like Dan, or in mysterious words written in fire on leaves so that they couldn't be kept and treasured.

From the Captain's back, Pythia cupped a dry leaf in her hands and blew it at Niffy. A fiery word sparked on the leaf as it fluttered through the air and settled on the hearth beside the monk's feet. Without a glance, he kicked it back into the fireplace.

The Captain lowered Pythia to a chair, but she slipped down onto the floor, wrapping her hair around herself and beginning to rock in place. Her eyes were locked on Cyrus, and he could see her lips moving in a string of endless whispers. He could guess what she was saying—the same thing Dan had been dreaming about for months, starting right before they had found their father's body and stopped Phoenix in the cigar factory where he had been using the tooth to redesign and resurrect a crop of New Men, where Phoenix had even managed to resurrect himself into the body of his nephew, Oliver.

Dan only ever came away from the dream with a string of words about the one called Desolation, and abominations, and the darkness of his shadow, and even the dragons being afraid.

It was about Radu Bey. Or Phoenix. One or the other, and as far as Cyrus could tell, it didn't really matter which. They were both terrifying enough without a crazy oracle or Dan's nightmare visions to spread the good news.

Nolan, Arachne, Gil, John Smith, and Pythia. Five transmortals. None if you figured that Gil was going to turn on the group eventually and the other transmortals would all be kept busy trying to control him.

How many transmortals did Radu Bey have? Rupert had been unwilling to guess, but Antigone had gotten a number out of him eventually. Over two hundred and climbing. Maybe two dozen of the great ones, at least as powerful as Gil. Two or three as powerful as Radu Bey himself. And how many New Men did Phoenix have? As many as he had had the time to make. And how tough were they? Nobody knew. Yet.

Cyrus looked up at Rupert Greeves, feet spread, strong arms crossed, narrowed eyes focused on a grinning Irish monk with a Mohawk. He knew that of all the obstacles they faced, Rupert's greatest fear—greatest *fears*—still lay beneath Ashtown, in the deepest vaults, behind hidden doors, beyond ancient seals. *The Burials.*

That number had been easy for Antigone to get out of Rupert. He had insisted that they memorize it. One hundred and forty-four Powers had been Buried before the first modern treaties and the settling of the New World. All had some form of flesh, even if stolen, but many were in no way truly human. The oldest and worst were gods and goddesses of war. Necromancers. Fallen stars. Leviathan. Panic. And worse. Seventy-two more had been Buried in the five centuries since the treaties, and they were mostly modern transmortals—once human, but no longer.

"Right," Niffy said. "Lovely little gathering. I'd been told you had Ponce along as well."

"We did," Rupert said, and he glanced at Arachne. "Now we don't."

"He's safe," Arachne said. "In hiding. This fight wasn't for him."

"Ah." Niffy glanced at Rupert as he said it. "Tight

ship you run, eh? What's it matter if the occasional hare slips the noose."

"I'm sorry," Nolan said. "You think we're prey? Last I checked, we're volunteers, all except Gil the vassal."

Gil snorted, shifting his glare from Cyrus to Nolan.

Rupert groaned and waved at Niffy. "Could we move along, then? Get on to the crucial bits. I'm only allowing this as a courtesy to your order."

Niffy grinned. "Right. Well, these are the crucial bits as far as my Brothers are concerned, and the very bits that Monasterboice requires me to press. Five centuries ago, we broke from the O of B when they chose to enter into treaties with the transmortals. We refused to make peace with darkness, and we would not lay down our strongest weapons even if all the transmortals had agreed to have their powers bound. The O of B has made do without us. But now that the treaties have been dissolved . . ." Niffy shrugged. "Ashtown's oldest weapons may be used again. Help us acquire them and put them to use, and we are your allies to the end, until the last dogs have been put down and the last pints have been hoisted and our voices are raw from the singing."

"Dogs?" Nolan asked, his brows rising. "Do we have a dog problem?"

Niffy stared at him. "Our call in this earthly sphere is to triumph over evil, not to arrange a cease-fire. Some enemies cannot be made into friends. Or pets."

"And we're evil?" Nolan's eyes hardened. Cyrus saw a vein quiver on the ancient boy's temple.

"You?" Niffy said. "No more than any mortal down the blood river from the first Adam. But for us, the struggle against our inner darkness ends at a headstone and full stop. For you, seeds of evil grow to weeds no matter how often you pluck them from the garden. One with eyes to see can spot it in you even now, Nolan, once called Nikales. Rage. Despair. Boredom. The asp sting of bitterness. You fight against it for lifetimes. You fall and you rise and you fall again, but your inner war can never leave off, it can never stay won. Mortals weren't made for it. We were made to run the race and hit the finish. Transmortals face pain with no end but the world's end. And most can't take it. They grow weary. They go mad. The flesh never dies, but the soul rots away inside."

Nolan was perfectly still. Cyrus waited for him to explode, but the monk's words seemed to have frozen him. After a moment, Nolan's jaw relaxed and he sank back into his seat. Niffy adjusted his rope belt and stepped forward, staring at the undying boy, older than empires. When he spoke again, Cyrus was surprised at how soft and sad the monk's voice had become.

"You've held up better than I ever could," Niffy said. "But you wear your guilt like a gaping wound. Evil haunts you, little brother."

Niffy turned back to the hearth while Nolan stared

at the floor. Gil smirked. The room was silent, and outside, tall trees popped and sighed in a breeze.

"The point," Niffy said, "is this. Those treaties locked away the O of B's most dire weapons. Blades and charms and chains and seals useful for the confinement and destruction of Powers of spirit and flesh. Why loose the devils and leave willing devil catchers unarmed?"

"There was a reason for laying those weapons down," Rupert said. "Some of those things were corrupting—the Dragon's Tooth not least among them."

Niffy ignored Rupert. "The monks still within the O of B, your so-called Brendanites, have requested our . . . *assistance* . . . in cleansing the Order from her cellars to her spires. They desire a purge, and no small one at that. They want Bellamy Cook, the traitor Brendan, tried, hundreds of memberships vacated, assets seized, and strict monastic orders instituted throughout the whole of the O of B." He grinned. "It has some appeal."

"But?" Rupert asked.

"But before we gave our answer, I was sent to find you, to see if there was yet hope for our mother Order." Niffy scrunched his face, and then grew serious. "Hear the questions of Monasterboice and my brothers. Will you take up the arms forgotten? Will you sign no treaty with the last Dracul and his *Ordo Draconis*? Will you hunt the dog Phoenix until his death or yours?"

"Brother Boniface Brosnan," Rupert said, and his

voice was edged. "I will take up no weapon that would darken my own soul. But while God and my fathers guide me, I will hurl every stone, swing every ax, slash with every blade, fire every gun, and loose every arrow and dart that I believe to be clean, holy, and fit for slaughter. I will sign no peace with Radu Bey or his *Ordo*, though I would rejoice to gift him with fresh chains. As for Phoenix, I hunt him even in my dreams."

Niffy's lips were tight, his brows low.

"And Gilgamesh of Uruk," he said. "Why is he among you unless you have already made peace with one of Radu's beasts? And here also is John Smith, a traitor to his own Avengel vows, who knowingly took up transmortality. Why have they not both been put down?"

Gilgamesh stood, nostrils flaring. "Monk," he growled. "You rope-belted Celts are no more than flies to one such as I am. I cannot count how many of your blood and cowl I have crushed and brushed aside when they came hunting for a hero. Your Druid magic does nothing more than tickle the hairs on my arms while my fingers crush your Irish skulls."

John Smith inhaled slowly and every hair in his thick beard seemed to crackle with static. The gold on his breastplate shone suddenly red, like copper. He reached up and put his hand on Gil's shoulder, and his voice was a low growl.

"Ho, now, beastie. The monk may be fool-born, but

he's not all misses. I deserve no better, nor does one as blood gorged as ye. Though this one and his crew couldn't do nay about it."

Niffy ignored them both and looked at Rupert.

"If Gilgamesh of Uruk is condemned, it will be enough. My brothers will put him away, and Monasterboice will aid you against Phoenix and the dragons. If not . . ."

Rupert inflated his cheeks and looked up at the ceiling. "Then you aid those tomfool Brendanites in opening the weapon vaults of Ashtown and attempting to purge the O of B."

Gil picked up his chair with one huge hand and raised it like a club.

"Gilgamesh." Arachne sounded like a disappointed kindergarten teacher reminding a boy in the back row not to pick his nose. She was tiny next to Gil, and she looked up at him from her seat with raised brows and wide eyes, still as the moon turning a tide, waiting for him to make his decision.

The giant set down his chair. And then he sat.

The room was silent. On the floor, Pythia resumed rocking in place. She looked at Gil and her eyes sparkled. Gathering up her hair to cover her face, she began to giggle. A leaf floated through the air toward Gil, and two burning letters said simply, HA.

Gil closed his fist around the leaf and shook the ash onto the floor.

"Make your choice, Avengel," Niffy said.

Rupert sighed and looked at Gil. "God knows he deserves it, but I gave my word. Until Gil breaks his, I will not break mine."

Niffy nodded. "Then you have already chosen the fool's path, laying out new treaties to bind yourself and give him time to betray you. Cheers, mate. Best wishes and all that, and I'm away for Ashtown."

"I'm afraid I can't let you leave," Rupert said. "Not knowing what I know."

"You've no choice," said Niffy, smiling. "I'll not stay on a dog's lead, and my brothers are waiting for me outside."

"What?" Rupert glanced at the lodge windows. "You led them here?"

"You led them here," Niffy said. "But I'll lead them away." He winked at Cyrus and Antigone. "Been lovely meeting the cheeky young Smiths. Pleasure and all that. Enjoyed the brawl and frolic." He backed toward the door and nodded at the Captain. "And you, guv. Bit of a hero of mine since I was a lad. Admire you still despite the circs."

The Captain drew his sword. "The Avengel bade you stand."

"Niffy," Rupert said, and he unsnapped the leather flap on his holster. "Please."

Niffy laughed. "And I bid the Avengel not to start a brawl he's no chance of finishing."

The lodge doors opened and four lean monks with hard, creased faces stepped inside. They were all unarmed, and Niffy was as thick as any two of them. The oldest-looking was also the shortest, with a ring of white hair on his speckled scalp and a pair of needle eyes peering out from a nest of wrinkles.

He stepped forward and reached up to his neck. Cyrus gaped as a small golden snake became visible in the man's hand. Patricia suddenly went frigid cold and cinched tight around Cyrus's neck, cutting off his breath.

Gripping the little snake by the tail, the old man lashed it forward like a whip. The gold serpent grew in size as it swung and a heavy writhing body slammed into the plank floor. It reared, hissing, ready to strike, with a head the size of a football, fangs dripping, and egg-size emerald eyes glistening against its gold scales. The monk still held the tip of the snake's tail. Surveying the room and the stunned crowd, the old man spat on the floor.

Choking, Cyrus forced two fingers beneath Patricia and behind the key ring at his neck, just managing to loosen her enough to take a breath.

The monks began to retreat.

"Wait!" Cyrus gasped. "Niffy! If I ever need, you know, a Cryptkeeper, how do I find you?"

Niffy blinked, surprised. "If you're in a true need, we're like to know already."

The old monk bullied Niffy out the door, and then backed through himself, trailing the massive snake behind him.

As the hissing head disappeared, Patricia finally relaxed.

Rupert and the Captain raced to the door. Gunner drew a long revolver and stood to follow them. Cyrus realized that Antigone was squeezing his arm almost as hard as Patricia had been squeezing his neck.

Nolan began to laugh. "Wow," he said. "Gil, I hope you feel loved. No allies for this little band while we have you."

Llewellyn rolled his wheelchair toward the door. "I'm not leaving, Rupert Greeves!"

Rupert disappeared outside.

Llewellyn only shouted louder. "I'm not! You all can scram-flutter to your next roost like spooked pigeons now that you've been found, but I'm going no place!"

Antigone let go of Cyrus, put her face in her hands, and moaned. "We're moving again, aren't we?"

Cyrus looked at Nolan. Nolan nodded. "A long retreat becomes a long defeat."

Rupert Greeves raged back into the room. Cyrus stood up, watching his Keeper, waiting. Rupert held his hands over his head, and then turned, raising a fist to punch the wall, He dropped it to his side instead, clenching and unclenching his fingers. He swore loudly, hooked a chair with his toe, and flicked it up into his hands.

"Rupert . . . ," Arachne said coolly.

"That one's always been wobbly," Llewellyn said.

Rupert Greeves turned, yelling, and the chair spun through the air into the fireplace. Ash and splinters exploded out over the hearth. A cloud of gray rolled slowly over the floor.

Breathing hard, hands on his hips, Rupert faced the group.

"Well," he said, "they're gone, and I don't know how. With enemies all around, they'll tear Ashtown down from the inside. Phoenix and Radu can pick through the ruins. And they know where we are, which means those fool Brendanites will know, and Bellamy will have eyes on them, which means he will know, and that's just as good as giving Phoenix an engraved invitation." He turned in a slow circle and then looked at Llewellyn. "I could eat."

The room was silent.

Llewellyn cleared his throat. "I have a whole summer larder of smoked meat. Fish, deer, elk, bird. Cheeses, too."

"Clever you," Rupert said. "Beer?"

Llewellyn grinned.

"Do we need a new plan?" Antigone asked. "Or do we just keep recruiting and . . . running?"

"I have a new plan," Rupert said. "I have a dozen new plans and more brewing. What I don't have is a full stomach."

Cyrus ate on the lodge roof, seated on the accumulated mulch of needles and cones and branches compressed by time and weather. Antigone sat on his left. Dan on his right. Five minutes earlier, Dennis Gilly, still in his short shorts and tall socks, had wandered out of the lodge door below them with a loaded paper plate in his hands. He had looked around for a grub buddy, but the Smiths had chewed silently and unnoticed above him. He'd gone back inside.

"How's Mom?" Antigone asked. She was picking at a small pile of oily smoked salmon.

"Tired," Dan said. He rolled his big right shoulder like it hurt. Then he stretched his muscled arm across his chest. "Sad. Asleep, I hope. It's strange, I was so scrawny and small and blond when we last saw her. I'm completely different now, and I notice every single change when she looks at me. It's like I've switched bodies."

Cyrus understood, even though his body had merely

grown. Dan's body had been overhauled from toes to nose—his hair had darkened, his eyes changed along with what they sometimes saw, and his underfed surfer physique was long gone. He looked more like a professional fighter now. His heart still tried to explode whenever he had serious visions, but Arachne's flesh-weaving touch had helped with that. It hurt him, but it hadn't been able to kill him.

Antigone set her plate beside her. "Why is Mom sad?"

"Why wouldn't she be?" Dan asked. "Think about it. For her, it's like Dad died two months ago. She was trying to swim after him and she passes out. We were a family when she fell asleep. Homework. Sports. Fishing. That stupid little garden she made us weed. Then she wakes up and the last thing she remembers is swimming. Dad's really gone, I'm completely different, Cyrus is grown up, and Antigone had no mother to dress her or teach her girl stuff, and on top of that we're all caught up in Dad's old world and people are trying to kill us."

"I did okay," Antigone said.

"Sure," said Dan. "But that's not the point. Mom lost more than we did, and she lost it all at once, right when she woke up. Her body is weak and her mind, well, she spent the last three years dreaming. All she remembers are some weird things about being in a bird. She gets distracted. She has trouble focusing. And when she does focus, she remembers everything and she cries."

Cyrus looked up at the swaying trees. They were almost too tall for their trunks, bending and rocking as they strained and stretched to reach the sun. It made him dizzy. But these days, everything made him dizzy.

"Will she get better?" Cyrus asked.

"Rupe thinks so," Dan said. "But not if we keep running like this." He tucked his final bite into his cheek and folded his greasy plate in half.

Antigone sighed and looked down between her knees at the forest floor below.

"Do you think we could get away?" she asked. "I mean just us. And Mom. Could we just change our name to Wankenschnitzel or something and move to, I don't know, Des Moines? Go back to school. Have friends."

"We have friends," Cyrus said.

Antigone laughed. "We have Diana, Jeb, and Dennis and a bunch of unstable people who don't die."

"And a short lawyer and his tall driver," Dan said. "Don't forget them."

"We have Rupert," Cyrus said. "And Rupert doesn't have much more than us." He Frisbeed his paper plate off the roof and watched it flutter into the trees. "No matter where we go, we are who we are. Skelton left us what he left us. I've done what I've done and started what I've started. People who don't die won't forget that. Those poor Wankenschnitzels wouldn't last very long with Radu Bey and Dr. Phoenix looking for them. Skelton knew a lot more than we do, and he only survived on the run for two years."

"You just don't want to go back to school," Antigone said.

Cyrus smiled and shrugged. Then he climbed to his feet.

Antigone nodded at his plate, caught in a spray of ferns twenty yards away. "You gonna pick that up?" she asked.

"Nope," said Cyrus. "But you can. Thanks for asking. I'm gonna go sit with Mom."

"Cy," Dan said. "Hold on just a sec."

Cyrus looked at his remodeled brother—at the muscles on Dan's too-square jaw, at the rope-size veins on his bull neck, at the deep brown eyes that had once been blue, the eyes that saw things. Those eyes were worried.

"More dreams?" Cyrus asked. "I've heard it, Dan. I know."

"Cyrus," Dan said. "This is different. I saw real things . . . like I did when I dreamed about Dad's body in Phoenix's cigar factory. That dream led us to him. You can't blow this one off."

"I'm not," Cyrus said. "But if I don't understand it, it doesn't matter anyway."

"My heart tried to stop," Dan said. "Twice. It hurt like . . . well, it hurt. Then my eyes stopped seeing everything around me and I fell down. Pythia was with me in there, in the vision."

Cyrus knuckled his eyes, groaned frustration, and turned away. Antigone, still seated, grabbed his ankle.

"Wait, Cy," she said. "Listen to him."

"Why?" Cyrus asked. "It's been the same thing almost every night. I almost have it memorized. Let me guess: 'Seventy weeks will soon be passed. One comes on the wing of abominations, and there shall be no end to war. He shall be called the Desolation and bad, bad, bad, worse, worse, worse.' Phoenix is scary. Radu Bey is scary. I know, Dan. I'm scared enough already without you reciting that to me all the time."

"But the dream has never been about Phoenix," Dan said. "And it's not about Radu Bey. Pythia helped me. I saw . . ."

Cyrus tugged his leg out of Antigone's grip and stared at his brother.

"Who?" he asked. "Super villain number three?"

Dan's dark eyes locked onto his brother's.

"You, Cyrus. It's about you."

## ❧ seven ❧

# THE DEVOTED

MERCY TRIED NOT TO PAY ANY ATTENTION to her warped reflection as she flowed through the people rivers and around the great glass towers of Midtown Manhattan. But only because her reflection looked pitiful. She was too small for the heavy mailbag on her shoulder, too short and too thin for her blue-gray shorts and her official uniform shirt. The shoes had seemed comfortable at first, but now every step on the uneven concrete sent needles up into her feet.

Her uncle had said this would be hard when he'd hired her. He'd said she wouldn't last the week. And yes, he had been willing to bet. If she did last, he would owe her a week of restaurant dinners. If she quit, she would owe him a week of cooking with her grandmother's recipes. Butter. Lard. And no more fat-free sour cream.

Mercy Rios, eighteen (and a half), temporary letter carrier. *Mailman. Mailgirl.* She puffed a strand of loose hair out of her face and stole a glance at her reflection in a pane of black bank glass. *Broken little beast of burden in borrowed clothes.*

Pausing before she reached the next street and putting one foot up onto a bench, Mercy adjusted the bag strap. It was her third day, and there was no longer any unbruised patch of shoulder willing to carry the weight. Not on either shoulder. But the pain wasn't what bothered her. She knew pain well. And physical pain could be pushed away and eventually forgotten. In the gym, she had been a fearless little gymnast, crashing on the balance beam and scrambling back up through the blood and tears, flying off the bars, tumbling onto her head. There had been pain every day, but she had never held herself back. She had never attempted only what she knew she could do. It was the unknown, the dangerous darkness of the harder, higher thing, that she had always chased.

In her last meet, two years ago, she had defied her coach. Her team's victory had already been assured when she'd chalked her hands and walked to the uneven bars. Her coach had crouched down, and with his nicotine breath and yellow smile, he'd told her which of the more difficult elements to drop. He'd told her to play it safe. And Mercy had nodded. She'd smiled.

She'd meant to. But once her blood was flowing, once she was flying and swinging faster and harder and higher than any girl was meant to, something else took over. She didn't drop her double back flip. She tripled it.

Mercy knew what it was like to hear a bone snap, to see and feel it jutting out of her thigh. That pain was long gone. But the pain of her coach's anger, the pain of being thrown away, of being pushed out and told not to come back . . . that was the kind of pain that could last a lifetime.

Hitching her bag, Mercy straightened up and stared down the sidewalk toward the next intersection. People parted around her, leaving her behind.

This next street, this next part of her route, was why she wanted to quit. It was why other carriers had already quit or pulled rank to be reassigned or had simply disappeared. It was why her uncle had been willing to give her a chance.

Mercy Rios never quit. Not even when she wanted to scream and sob and run away.

The small temporary letter carrier marched forward. Her eyes were on the corner, where the street's mouth waited. In the crosswalk, the rushing crowd seemed to accelerate, hurrying to get past. She knew they could feel it. Probably the same way she did. As she approached, the light turned red. The pedestrians should have stopped. They should have piled up on the curb and waited for cross traffic. But they kept rushing forward. There was no cross traffic. Not one car leaving, and not one of the hundreds of cabs and town cars and buses turning in.

Mercy approached the corner, holding her breath. As she did, the cross street became harder and harder to see. It wasn't invisible, it was just . . . pushing her eyes away, forcing her to look elsewhere, at pedestrians and cabs and bicycles. She felt like she was trying to push the wrong sides of two magnets together. The more she tried to focus her eyes—and her mind—on the street, the more they slipped away. It made her feel dizzy and a little motion sick. But she had spent years spinning on balance beams and flipping off vaults. She could handle a little dizziness. This time she was not going to hurry past.

Mercy stepped into the intersection and stopped. She was suddenly cold, and she began to sweat. In the crosswalk ahead of her, one man had stopped. He was in a suit and holding a briefcase. He was young. Pale. Sweating. But he was also crying. While Mercy watched, he walked slowly forward. With her eyes on him, she was finally looking into the mysterious street. She was walking into it, and as she did, the resistance disappeared. The magnet had turned. Now she was being pulled.

It was only one block of emptiness. Cars and people flowed past on both ends. Trash had accumulated uncollected at the curbs. Tourist shops and restaurants were silently entombed behind graffiti-speckled metal doors. A few cars had been abandoned in the road, and others were parked in front of expired parking meters. None of them had tickets.

A silent congregation of people surrounded a brown tower at the center of the block. The man with the briefcase was walking toward them. Men in sharp suits sat on the sidewalk with their backs against the building. Women in skirts had kicked off their heels and lay curled up on the concrete.

Mercy's pain grew as she walked, but not her physical pain. That had vanished since she'd rounded the corner. Her shoulder no longer ached. Her feet no longer felt needles in her shoes. The pain Mercy felt now was old, hidden away for years. She felt the throbbing shame of being thrown off her team, thrown out of her girlhood dream. It beat inside her fresh and raw until something older and deeper boiled up. Her father. The man who had so eagerly signed her away. She was suddenly eight again, out of her bed, peering into the filthy, cramped living room of the old Brooklyn apartment, watching her uncle gently explaining to her father why it would be better if he took custody of his niece. Her father had seen her. Unshaven, unshowered, sprawling on the couch with a bottle in his hand, he had turned his bleary red eyes on her.

"Take her," he'd said. "She's nothing special."

Mercy stopped in the street and her small body shook. Why was this happening? Why was she crying? The eight-year-old Mercy hadn't cried. She'd been eager to leave. That was the day the sun had begun to shine in her life. Cold sweat found her eyes and her stomach turned over, uneasy and sick. She could see her father's eyes. She could hear his voice. She shook her head and wiped away her sweat and tears. She didn't know what was wrong with this street, but it was a trick. She wasn't sad about her father. Not anymore. There was a small package in her bag, and she was going to deliver it.

The man with the briefcase was on his knees now, outside the revolving glass doors of the brown tower.

"Yes," the man said. "Please. Please."

The people around him weren't listening. Their eyes were open but empty, dazed. And they wore small frozen smiles, like dolls.

The man fell and rolled onto his back. Tears ran from his eyes as he stared at the sky. And then he smiled.

"Thank you," he said. "Thank you."

Mercy swallowed back a gag, and she stepped around the man. She reached into her bag and pulled out the package. It was wrapped in stiff brown paper and labeled with letters so black and smoky around the edges, they looked like they'd been burned on.

The street address was correct. But the recipient was strange.

To the Peace upon the Earth
40th floor

Where there would normally be a return address, there was only a city. *Phoenix.*

Mercy moved through the dazed crowd on the ground and stepped into the revolving door. Inside the marble lobby, she could see more bodies. People were crammed in tighter than hot dogs in a package. They sat back to back. They sprawled on top of each other. Skaters, bankers, models, moms, hard hats and cop hats and oil-stained coveralls and kids with school uniforms. Every race. Every age. She couldn't see the floor between the bodies. And they were all still.

*Child, you hurt.*

Mercy jumped. The voice had been deep and soothing. She stood in the door and looked around. And it had been inside her head.

*I see pain that even you cannot.*

An image erupted in Mercy's mind. Her mother. She'd only ever seen her in pictures. Now she was on a filthy floor. She was pregnant. Shaking. Foam dribbled from her mouth. Her father was there, talking stupidly, grabbing her mother, telling her not to play. An ambulance. Men and women in uniforms. Bright lights in a room. Blood. A baby. Little Mercy Rios. And her mother motionless.

Mercy was back in the glass revolving door, and her body was quivering.

*You cannot remember,* the voice said, *but you still feel. Child, there is a hole in your heart. A hole in your soul.*

"I'm fine," Mercy said, and she shut her eyes. She should quit. Right now. Turn and run.

*Mercy Rios,* the voice said. *I am the healer of souls. I am the Peace upon the Earth. Shall I heal you?*

Mercy doubled over and gagged. Her body was shivering and her veins itched with cold. She wanted heat inside them. She needed them filled. "No," she said. "Don't."

*Bring me what is mine.*

The words were hard, and when spoken, the bodies in the lobby rippled. Men and women suddenly rolled to the sides, leaving a narrow path from the door to silver elevator doors on the far side.

Mercy took a step back, but hands shoved her forward. She yelled and turned, but the people outside were on their feet. A dozen hands grabbed the revolving door, and they pushed.

Fighting, shoving, Mercy still slid around and stopped at the entrance to the narrow road through the human sea.

She stood, terrified, looking over the tangled mass of limp bodies. The room was silent but for one thing. The people were all breathing slowly and in sync, like a single organism. Chests expanded, and the sea around Mercy rose. They exhaled, and the sea sank.

On the other side of the lobby, a woman's arm rose from the floor, and she pushed the elevator button.

The sea rose.

*Ding.* The elevator doors slid open.

The sea sank.

Mercy looked behind her. The revolving door was jammed with dazed, smiling people. A side door was blocked as well. But the windows were glass. Glass could break.

*Bring me what is mine.*

The elevator doors tried to close, but the woman's arm flopped between them. The doors chewed on the arm and reopened.

Mercy had nothing to break her way out through a glass window. And everything in the lobby was surrounded. A flowerpot. A chair.

*Child, I can also grow angry. . . .*

"Let me out," Mercy said. "I'll leave your package here."

*Bring it to me.*

"Listen," Mercy said. "I don't care if you're in my head, or if I'm crazy, or what's going on. But if you don't let me go, I'm opening your package right now."

And then a young cop sat up in the sea. He wasn't looking at her, but the gun in his hand was, and his arm was as steady as the steel of the barrel.

*Bring it to me.*

The breathing sea of bodies quickened. And then the bodies rippled. Hands reached for her ankles and Mercy yelped, jumping over them, stomping on fingers. And she made the dash, sprinting through the narrow path for the elevator doors.

Mercy slammed into the elevator and kicked away the woman's arm that held the doors open.

As the doors closed, the cop with the gun fell back onto his side. The loud communal breathing had already slowed to the steady rhythm of a single sleeper.

The button labeled 40 was already lit. The elevator was rising. Mercy hit the 3. She could jump back off. There would be a fire escape. She could get out.

The doors opened on the third floor and Mercy jumped back. More bodies. The doors closed and she hit the 6. She began to rise again.

*Mercy. You cannot run from pain. You must be healed.*

Waves of memory rocked Mercy. Every awful thing that anyone had ever said to her, every unkindness ever done to her, every dirty look and insult and rudeness, every laugh from every boy, every slight from every girl, and every groan from every teacher. Crowds and crowds of men and women and children sprinkled through eighteen years of life now assembled in Mercy's mind in a chorus of disdain.

The doors opened. Even if the floor hadn't been lined with bodies, Mercy wouldn't have been able to move. As the doors closed again, she sank to the floor, gagging, choking.

*It can stop. I can heal you.*

"Of course you can," Mercy sputtered. "You're the one doing it."

The voices in her mind grew louder until the insults roared like breaking waves. The faces, the sneers, the spitting lips grew closer, and Mercy was suddenly washed in the sickening reek of foul breath. The air in the elevator was unbreathable.

"No," Mercy gasped. "No. It wasn't like that." Curling up on the floor, she squeezed her eyes tight. Through all the roar, through all the stink, she pictured her uncle.

Ramon Rios, short and broad, with a smile bigger than any room, teaching his niece to cook. Taking her to school, helping with her homework, smiling when she struggled, and telling her that beauty wasn't everything and brains would be useful, too. Presents and sacrifices, the extra jobs to pay for gymnastics, dinners out on her birthday, and trips to the shore.

The sickness inside her shrank away. The stink in the elevator retreated.

The elevator doors opened to the sound of breathing.

Mercy was looking through a tunnel made of people. The bodies on the lower stories had been a tangled mass. These bodies were all facedown and stacked like bricks. A wall of men on Mercy's left were stacked higher than the elevator. The man-wall leaned in, arching above the elevator doors. A wall of stacked women on the right leaned in, completing the arch above Mercy's head. Limp arms hung down from the ceiling of the human tunnel like fleshy stalactites. With every slow, synchronized breath, the tunnel expanded. With every long, collective exhalation, the tunnel contracted, and hot sour air wafted down around Mercy.

She crawled slowly out of the elevator. The doors slid shut behind her.

*Bring it to me.*

Mercy rose to her feet, clutching her bag, wiping her wet cheeks. The walls breathed around her. There was only one way she could go.

One step. Two. She couldn't help but scan the walls. Most of these people were well dressed—suits, skirts, nice watches, manicured nails. Blond and brown and red plumes of carefully styled hair dangled from the ceiling on the women's side. The tunnel curved slowly to the left, and Mercy followed it.

Here, there were cops. At first just a few, and then more. A dozen in uniform. Half a dozen in suits with badges on their belts. Detectives? Of course, all these people had families. They had friends. When the block had first gone bad and the first people went missing, the police would have come. They would have felt what she felt. The older they were, the more pain there would be to bubble up inside. Had all these people said yes to the voice? Even the cops?

*They know peace.*

Mercy sniffed. "Get out of my head."

*Bring me what is mine.*

The curve in the tunnel stopped, and Mercy stopped with it. Hot breath surrounded her. Ahead of her, the tunnel rose to a gaping hole in the roof. Men and women lay facedown across the floor, stacked like a flight of stairs, their backs waiting for Mercy's feet.

A breeze slipped down from the roof, and the hair on the ceiling rustled. Dangling arms swayed. Mercy began to climb.

Under each careful step she felt the slip of cloth, of skin over bone. She felt the rise and fall of the breathing beneath her, and she clutched the little package tight under her right arm.

Slowly, she rose into the sun, into the air, into the towering cityscape of New York. But her eyes were not on the buildings.

A huge man leaned back in a chair made of stacked people. He wore only a belted skirt of white linen, and his long, bare legs stretched out in front of him. Broken chains hung from his ankles and wrists. His rich skin glistened in the sun, and his short hair was black and curly. His jaw was strong, his hollow cheeks were smooth, and his eyes were all darkness. In the center of his bare, hairless chest, there was a deep-red dragon twined into a circle. At first, Mercy thought it was a tattoo, but it bulged beneath the man's olive skin like a blister full of blood. And while Mercy stared at it, she saw it ripple.

*Welcome.*

"Welcome," the man said, and the two voices were not the same. His accented voice was musical and alive, like wind through trees, like a distant parade, like the promise of the sea. The voice in her head had been cold and slight and edged.

Mercy tore her eyes from the man and looked around the rooftop. Three priests in black were on their knees, purple stoles over their shoulders, vials of water and crosses in their shaking hands as they whispered quietly.

"All are welcome," the man said. "Even those who labor to bind me. Their prayers weaken only them, and in the end, they too shall be given peace."

Behind the priests, there were other men. Mercy could see a rabbi lying on his face, still clutching a large animal horn.

"Who are you?" Mercy asked.

The man smiled like an animal baring its teeth. "I am the son of the moon and the sea. I am the Peace upon the Earth."

Mercy held out the package, her hand shaking. She couldn't make herself step forward.

"For you," she said. "From someone in Arizona. Can I go now?"

*Bring it to me.*

Hard and cold. Mercy blinked. The man still smiled. He spread out his arms and leaned farther back. Crude iron chains dragged beneath his wrists. The blister dragon quivered and darkened.

Mercy inched forward. "You . . . were in jail?"

The huge man laughed. He rattled his chains. "We were," he said. "Long. But here, in the sun, in this new Babylon of towers and lights, there has been much pain to be healed. We are now strong."

*Bring it to me.*

The voice had grown impatient. It bit into Mercy's mind like ice.

"Hear and obey," the man said. "I can drink your soul where you stand."

Mercy bit her lip. She looked at the slowly breathing couch of people beneath the man, at the sweating priests and the dazed rabbi. How many thousands were in this building already? How many more would come after her? Would she be a body in a wall when the next person passed?

Mercy Rios shook her head. She squared her shoulders and straightened.

"No," she said. "You're some kind of devil. Kill me if you want, but I'm not giving you anything." Turning, she flung the package like a Frisbee. It fluttered out into the air and over the edge. But one of the men from the couch—an armrest—exploded after it even as it left her hand.

The man leapt off the building. With his gray suit

coat flapping, he snatched the package out of the air, curled around it, and disappeared. Seconds passed and Mercy tried not to hear the sick sound that floated up from the street.

Mercy swallowed hard.

A woman spoke behind her.

"You've fed enough, Radu. Quiet the dragon gin."

Mercy spun. The kneeling priests still whispered, never breaking concentration. A woman like no woman Mercy had ever seen rose from the human stairs. She was taller than any man Mercy knew, and her red hair was pulled back into a braid that fell to her waist. She wore cracked leather the color of parched earth, studded with sea glass and smooth stones, and tight enough to be a second skin. Her freckled and scarred arms were bare to the shoulders, but large fish scales had been outlined onto every inch of them in deep-blue ink. The same scales crawled up her long neck, stopping just beneath her jaw. A deep scar underlined each stark cheekbone, too symmetrical to be accidental, and her eyes were the color of an angry sea.

"Girl," she said. "I am Anann the Morrigan. Breath and bone, you belong to me."

Behind Mercy, Radu Bey began to laugh.

# eight

# BOMBING RUN

CYRUS ROLLED OVER ON HIS BUNK. He knew it was no longer late. By now, it had begun to be early. Moonlight flickered and flashed on the floor beneath the cabin's little window, sliced and diced by tall swaying trees. Antigone's breathing was slow and steady on the bunk above him. Dennis was snoring on the bunk across the room.

For Cyrus, sleep was impossible. His leg wasn't bothering him. The throbbing had downgraded from shark bite to dog bite, and then down again to bike wreck. His mind couldn't stop chewing on Dan's words. Or maybe Dan's words were chewing his mind.

He was the Desolation? He would come on the wings of abominations? Suddenly, he cared about every word. The seventy weeks would soon be passed? Come again? Seventy weeks since when? He rolled over on his bunk, facing the wall. And then he rolled back. The keys hanging from the little snake around his neck jingled as he tossed. Reaching up, he fingered them, two of Skelton's gifts. He could remember the old man tossing them to him. He could remember the cold tingle he had felt when they were in his hands. But he could barely remember being that boy in the motel who knew nothing of real danger, who knew nothing about real Dangers. The tooth had been on the key ring then. There was no tingle to the key ring now.

Cyrus sighed, watching the moon paint spatter on the old plank floor.

He and Antigone had given Rupert both paper globes to study, not that there had been much choice. One had been meant for him, after all, and hiding the other one would have been impossible after Rupert caught them with it in the outhouse. Hopefully, the notations would make more sense to him.

Cyrus cautiously reached down to feel the little puckered pellet wounds in his calf. Maybe the pain was keeping him awake. No. Not the pain. The sharpness was gone, replaced by a familiar soreness that could have been caused by any number of things. He was awake because of what was going on inside his skull.

While the sun had fallen, Cyrus and his sister had sat with their mother, letting her squeeze their hands tight while she told stories of their father. Antigone had asked her for the old stories, the ones they had never been told, but their mother's eyes had wandered and grown heavy.

Cyrus kicked over onto his back and the bed rocked beneath him. Soon the sun would rise and they would fly. They would run and find some new place to hide, while Niffy and his monks were heading off to help the Brendanites wipe Ashtown clean. If they had their way, they would reset the O of B all the way back to the Middle Ages, when every member was a monk. But if the members fought back, then what? Kill them? It didn't make any sense to Cyrus. Why start a fight with your own side when there were real enemies all around?

They wanted Ashtown's darkest weapons.

Cyrus thought about the patrik the monk had held, how it had grown in his hand. Patricia had been afraid— terrified enough to almost choke him. Could she do that? Grow in his hand on command?

Cyrus slid Patricia off his throat. Her tail popped out of her mouth, and she appeared in his hands with a blink of silver to match the moon. The keys and the empty silver sheath that had once held the Dragon's Tooth dropped onto his chest, and he forced the little Celtic snake straight. She twined her neck around his thumb and he studied the sparking green of her emerald eyes.

"You didn't like that snake today, did you?" Cyrus whispered. Patricia tried to bite her tail, but Cyrus pulled it away. She tried again and was thwarted again. Resigning herself to visibility, she slid down his wrist, rubbing her cool back against him like a preening cat.

"What now, P?" Cyrus asked. "Where are we going to run next?"

The snake didn't answer. She reached Cyrus's elbow and stretched for his stomach. He smiled. She was heading back up to his neck.

"Do I look like the Desolation to you?" Cyrus asked, and his smile faded with the thought.

The screen door to the little cabin squealed open. A Rupert Greeves–shaped shadow stepped into the room.

"Rupe?" Cyrus asked.

Rupert nodded. "Come with me."

Outside, the trees swayed like upright sleepers beneath the silver moon. Shadows darted and swooped and dragged around Cyrus as he followed Rupert along a narrow dirt path. Patricia still glowed on his wrist, but now Cyrus had his forefinger in her mouth to keep her from gulping her tail.

"The leg fine?" Rupert asked, glancing back. "You're hobbling less."

"Yeah," Cyrus said. "Normal pain. More like a groan than a scream."

"Brilliant," Rupert said. "What comes after groan? A mutter?"

Cyrus didn't answer. Rupert had led him to the boathouse. They passed the burial mound of canoes, and rounded the building to an old wooden barn door on rails. It had been thrown open, and a single lantern sat on a workbench inside.

Llewellyn Douglas, complete with puffy vest and

green pom-pom hat, looked up from his wheelchair. Kayaks hung from the ceiling, and long rowing sculls were upside down in a stack of racks that filled the entire left side of the building.

The workbench in front of Llewellyn was covered with gear.

"I have what I have, Rupe," the old man said. "Nothing's too moth-bit, but it's all antique now."

Rupert picked up a pair of black leggings and threw them at Cyrus. They were featherlight, and the weave was oily and slick in his hands. A matching long-sleeved shirt followed. Black waxed canvas shorts and a waxed canvas shirt were heaped on top.

Cyrus caught them all and watched Rupert pick up larger versions of the same.

"What are we doing?" Cyrus asked.

"You don't like it when I vanish, yeah?" Rupert smiled, but there was no laughter in his eyes. "Tonight you vanish with me."

"Seriously?" Cyrus asked. "Where? How long? What about my mom? Dan? Tigs? Do they know?"

"If they did, it wouldn't be vanishing, would it? Get suited," Rupert said. "Diana and the Captain have their orders. They get your family out. If things go well, we'll meet up with them by lunch."

"And if things don't go well?" Cyrus asked.

"Then you will never see them again," Rupert said.

"And that, mate, is the truth every time you set foot outside your door, every time you sleep, every time you blink."

Rupert stripped off his shirt and began to pull on the tight black featherlight skin Llewellyn had given him. He nodded at the pile in Cyrus's hands and raised his brows, waiting.

Ten minutes later, Cyrus walked down to the lake beside his big Keeper. Patricia was hidden back around his neck. Waxy pocketed shorts had been belted around his waist, and the bottom of each leg had been cinched in tight just above his knees. The sleeves of his shirt had also been tied below his shoulders. The featherlight skin completely covered his arms and legs and felt like nothing more than cold air. He wore no shoes, but Llewellyn had given him socks of the same strange black cloth, dotted on the bottom with tiny rubber beads. Matching gloves, too, gripped with the same rubber dots.

Rupert led Cyrus out onto the dock. The moonlight split around the dock and stretched away to the far side of the lake. Cyrus adjusted his thick belt as he walked. He had a small spotlight, a tight coil of rope, a small nonlethal electrical pulse gun, and a long black-bladed knife at the small of his back. In Cyrus's last year at Ashtown, Nolan had spent hours training him with a knife of the same length, but this blade had felt heavier in his hand.

With knives, and against Nolan, Cyrus had always been awful.

Rupert reached the end of the dock, adjusted his belt, and checked the pouch of his shorts, where he had stored half of the lump of Quick Water. Satisfied, the big man dove, leaving dark rings in the moon-silver water. Ten yards away, he surfaced quietly and began to swim toward the floating jet borrowed from the Boones.

Cyrus stared at the water and inflated his cheeks. Ripples stared back up at him, waiting with daggers of cold. Rupert wasn't waiting. Heart pounding, jaw clenched, Cyrus dove.

He slid into the water like an eel. Cold bit the skin on his face, but it could only gum-chew the rest of him. The borrowed clothes worked. Cyrus surfaced, and he could breathe without gasping. His joints weren't locking up. Ahead of him, the plane's cabin door was already open. Rupert was reeling in an anchor.

Antigone jerked awake and looked around the cabin. She'd been dreaming about planes. But it wasn't all dreams. Jet engines were roaring.

"Cy?" She hopped off her bunk, winced at the sting of her bare feet on the floor, and slapped at her brother's bed. Blankets.

Outside, Antigone tiptoe-jogged toward the lake. Two

shapes and a wheelchair were side by side in the moonlight, watching the plane as it crawled away across the water.

Diana. The Captain. Llewellyn.

"Hey," Antigone said, and Diana looked back. Even in the moonlight, Antigone could see the sadness and worry on Diana's face. Her arms were crossed tight.

"Where's Cy?" Antigone asked.

Diana nodded at the jet. She began to bite a nail, noticed, and jerked her hand back down. "He's with Rupe," she said. "They're going to Ashtown."

Antigone opened her mouth and then shut it. She shook her head. Cy was . . . *no*. He couldn't be. He hadn't said anything. Why? Ashtown? Was there anywhere less safe for Cyrus right now? She should be worried. She should be mad. She was both. But there was something deeper, too. She was . . . *hurt*.

Antigone dropped into a crouch and hugged her knees. The plane was accelerating. A small hint of warmth brushed against her face. A breeze kissed her with the scent of fuel and flame.

"I don't understand," Antigone said. "Why didn't he wake me up?"

The plane was only two blinking wingtips now, rising in the air, banking left, climbing above the black shadow of a mountain. Antigone felt like someone was standing on her stomach. Tears were a real danger. She pressed her mouth against her arm. Diana sat on the ground beside her.

"Cyrus didn't know what was going on," Diana said. "But Rupert needs someone with him. Jeb isn't exactly available, and he wouldn't take me."

"Why not?" Antigone asked. "You've done a ton more than Cyrus."

"He had to leave another pilot behind," Diana said. "We're leaving early."

The Captain cleared his throat loudly. "The lad was nay wisdom's choice."

"Shut your hole, pirate," Llewellyn said. "The boy's as ready as he can be. And you were no choice at all, Captain, not if Rupe wanted one who'd obey an order."

The Captain sniffed and turned to face the man in the wheelchair. Placing one hand on his sword hilt, he bowed dramatically. "Insults unprovoked become not a man of gentleness. If not for thine age and thine lameness—"

Llewellyn snorted. "Oh, go put on your lace collar and cry in your hankie. Rupert told you and that Nolan not to let the big six-fingered oaf out of your sight, and yet here you are." Llewellyn wheeled his chair backward, and then turned it around, bouncing his way back toward the cabins. "Let the lonely girls cry and go do your job!"

"He's right, John," Diana said. "It's bad enough having Gil around with Rupert gone."

The Captain bowed stiffly, fluffed his woolly beard, and then strolled away in silence.

"Llew and the Cap were stuck here for a while before we came," Diana said. "Pretty sick of each other."

Antigone nodded, but she didn't care about that. She wanted to kick her brother.

Diana didn't need to be told. "Rupe was in a hurry. If Cy had said goodbye, how much time would Rupert have wasted telling you that you couldn't come?" Antigone didn't answer. "You would still be sitting right where you are now, but you'd be even madder."

Antigone exhaled slowly. She knew it was true, but it didn't make being left behind any more fun. And Ashtown? There was still plenty for her to worry about.

"Llewellyn was wrong," Antigone said suddenly. "About taking orders. If Rupe wanted someone who would obey, Cyrus was the last person in the world he should have taken. Dennis Gilly would have been better, even with his concussion."

Diana smiled. "Cy's not as stubborn as you think."

Antigone looked at the girl next to her. She cocked her head and blinked.

"What?" Diana asked. "What's the look for?"

"Cyrus? Cyrus Lawrence Smith? Not stubborn?" Antigone raised her eyebrows. "I mean, you've been around him, yes?"

Diana laughed. "Okay, so he's stubborn. But not *that* stubborn. Not when he really respects someone."

Antigone was stunned.

Diana groaned, embarrassed. "People don't scare him into doing things," she said. "And they can't just boss him into doing things." She waited for agreement, but Antigone wasn't saying anything. Diana swallowed, then continued. "Not unless he respects them, unless he wants them as a boss. That's what I meant. You know, he listens to Nolan about fighting but not languages. He listens to Rupe about pretty much anything. Me with flying. Dennis with sailing. You with . . . with . . ."

"With nothing," Antigone said. "I practically have to bite his ankles to make him do something."

Diana laughed. "Yeah, well, what would you think of a guy who did whatever his sister told him to do?"

Antigone stared at Diana's moonlit profile. "You like him," she said. It was hard to keep the accusation out of her voice.

Diana squirmed. "That's not what I was talking about."

"Well, you do," Antigone said. "I mean, you've always been super friendly. And helpful. But you're so much older than he is. I never thought . . ."

"Antigone," Diana said, and her voice had gone cold. "I'm not talking about this with you. It's stupid and pointless. I'm not talking about this with anyone. Not even myself. I'm not even going to think about it." She sniffed. "And I'm not that much older."

"You've totally thought about it. You're thinking about it right now."

"If you don't like centipedes, don't flip rocks," Diana said. "Don't take your temperature if you don't want to be sick." She paused, scrunching up her face. "If we're all still alive in four or five years, ask me to think about it then. Or don't. I don't care."

Antigone still stared at the older girl, waiting for her to at least return a glance. But Diana kept her eyes on the moon and the water.

"Do you worry about him?" Antigone asked.

Diana didn't answer, but she didn't need to. Antigone looked around. Diana had been standing on the shore in the middle of the night watching the plane fly away. It was gone, but she was still rooted to the same spot. Of course she was worried.

"More than Jeb?" Antigone asked.

Diana sighed. "Different," she said.

Once he had set the flight plan, Rupert wasn't interested in talking. While Cyrus blinked and stared at the instruments, Rupert had unzipped a waterproof bag, tugged out an old notebook and pencil, and begun flipping pages. He read, he scribbled, he sketched.

Cyrus had questions. He had tried to talk.

"Where are we going?"

The fourth time he asked, Rupert had finally licked the tip of his pencil and grunted.

"Ashtown."

"Why?"

Rupert had looked up for that one. "To make a vice a virtue."

Cyrus had asked about Phoenix and Radu Bey and the O of B and Flint. Only Flint had made Rupert look back up from his pages. His eyes had sparkled. Then he smiled and said nothing.

On Cyrus's fifth attempt to get Rupert to predict the behavior of Phoenix or the transmortals, he had mumbled his answer down into his notebook, his accent thickened by his distractedness.

"Give it a go, bruv. See if you can sort it. Good exercise. You've heard and seen enough. Look to the motives and what you know about character. Predict. Tell me when we touch down."

Nothing else had stirred the big man from his studies and his scratching and his whispered thoughts. Cyrus spent the next two hours staring at the panels in front of him, at the black sky, and then at the faintest hint of a glow in the east. And he thought.

Radu Bey and the *Ordo Draconis* wanted to reassert themselves as untouchably superior to mankind. The O of B was a reminder of centuries of their humiliation. So were the Smiths. They didn't care about structures or institutions or governments. They wouldn't want to govern any more than wolves want to govern sheep—that would mean worrying about roads and sewers and building codes. They would want to . . . Cyrus groped around for a word he had heard Nolan use—*transcend.* Prey. Be served. The transmortals were proud. Pride meant grudges. And living forever meant that grudges could be nursed for centuries into something more rank and sour than any petty mortal resentment.

Cyrus had seen bullies. He'd embarrassed bullies. He knew what came after. A bigger gang. Bigger weapons. Smaller kids surrounded.

*Lick dirt.* Or worse.

Radu Bey and his treaty-free transmortals wouldn't be hiding. They'd be looking for a chance to dominate, to thump their chests and remind the world of their nastiness, to make powerful people helpless, to make humans grovel. As for the O of B, they had only freed the transmortals to avoid a fight. But that would just make it worse. Needing to be freed at all? That would sting their pride. And there were still the Burials. . . .

Radu Bey wouldn't be happy until Ashtown had been crushed and pounded into dust, until every member was dead or on their knees, until the Burials were open. It was only a question of when he felt strong enough, of when his gang was big enough, of when he could find the Order alone and weak in an alley.

So . . . anytime, then.

But Phoenix was a different animal, making different animals. He would be hiding, designing, breeding. He would wait until the O of B was rubble. That was why he had killed transmortals and stirred them up against the Order. He might even wait until the nations of men were on their knees, licking dirt. Then he and his New Men would emerge. He would be the lion tamer, the one who held the tooth, the one to save mankind from the old destroying gods. Phoenix the Savior.

Phoenix would want to rule. He wanted to rule everything down to the cellular designs and shapes and senses of his people. Radu was power. Phoenix was control. Wherever he was, he would be preparing to tame the transmortals, to collar tornadoes, to make the beasts his own.

What did the O of B want? Not Bellamy Cook, the stooge Brendan working for Phoenix, but the regular people? They wanted the same thing all regular people did. They wanted it all to go away. They wanted the storm to pass without touching them. But when it did touch them, when it touched the ones they loved, when they were finally ready to stand and fight, it would be too late.

Cyrus could still remember the pit he'd felt in his stomach years ago in California, riding home in the first week of school. From the bus, he'd seen a small kid surrounded by bigger boys. And then they'd driven away.

He hadn't eaten that night. He hadn't done his homework. His father had taken him down to the cliff and they'd thrown rocks in the sea. What he had seen exploded out of him in a broken story. The boy, the bullies, he didn't even know them. Why did he care so much? Why did it make him feel sick?

They had talked. Cyrus couldn't remember everything, he'd only been in the third grade, but he remembered two things his father had said. "When everyone waits for someone else to do something, evil will always triumph. One bully defeats ten people when he uses fear. Ten bullies terrify one hundred people. Believe it or not, ten can frighten ten thousand."

Cyrus had asked him what he was supposed to do when the bullies were bigger than he was, when there were more of them. His father had smiled.

"It doesn't matter how big the bully is. What matters is if you're bigger than the one being bullied."

Cyrus's mom had walked to the cliff behind them, carrying two bowls of ice cream. She'd heard the last part and looked worried.

The next day, Cyrus had gone home with tissues wadded up his nose and a purple lip the size of a leopard slug.

Antigone had seen the whole thing and was appalled. At dinner, he'd let her tell the story.

Cyrus had eaten well.

It was the same thing now, just bigger and a lot more dangerous. Knowing what Radu would do didn't mean that they could stop him. It just meant they had to try. And they had to be ready to die.

"Cy!" Rupert slapped his shoulder. "Dozing off, mate? Lucky we're not in a car."

Cyrus blinked and shook his head. "No. I'm awake. Just thinking. Like you told me to."

Rupert grinned. "Well, I'm sure you have it sorted, then. You can tell me our next move shortly. Right now I need you to get to the tail door. There's a harness and a headset. Clip in and put it on."

Cyrus scrambled out of the cockpit, happy to stretch his legs and leave his thoughts alone. He pushed back between the empty seats and then let himself through a small door into the tail storage.

Flint was tied up on the floor.

Cyrus stumbled over him and grabbed at the walls, barely keeping his feet.

Flint's mouth was open and he was snoring. He was in a harness with a parachute on his back. A nylon strap ran up from Flint's pull cord and was clipped onto a rail on the ceiling. There was a note pinned to his chest.

*Dearest Bellamy,*

*He told us everything. Brace yourself. Cheers.*

*Rupert Greaves (Blood Avenger)*

Cyrus looked around, then spotted a headset on the wall and slipped it on.

"Cy?" Rupert's voice crackled.

"What the heck, Rupe?" Cyrus asked. "What are we doing?"

"Time we wagged our mouths a bit," Rupert said. "Remind Phoenix that we're in this fight, too."

"And that means dropping Flint out of a plane?"

"That and more. You clipped in?"

Cyrus grabbed a long harness that was anchored to a bolt in the wall. He stepped into it and clipped it tight around his waist.

"Okay," Cyrus said. "Now what?"

"Get your arms around Flint and don't let go till I tell you. Hop on it. Not much time, bruv."

Hydraulics whirred in the walls around Cyrus. The tail of the plane began to open. Cyrus dropped into a crouch and grabbed Flint's harness. Wind roared into the cabin, knocking Cyrus to his knees.

"Hang on tight!" Rupert's voice crackled in his ears. The tail door continued to drop open. The wind became freezing-cold suction. Flint began to slide across the floor. Cyrus flopped onto the man's chest, face to face with the snoring thug, and hooked his arms completely through the front of his chute harness.

This was no normal jump. Rupert was flying low, and he was flying at max speed, doing his best to wake up the entire state of Wisconsin. The tail dropped below floor-level, and the suction was like a tornado. Cyrus rode Flint toward the night air like a boy on a sled. His harness caught and held, and the suction lifted the two bodies up off the floor, off their feet, and banged them against the wall.

Gritting his teeth, Cyrus held on. Flint's straps were digging into his arms as streetlights and gas stations flicked by beneath them like the dotted yellow line on a highway, and the plane dropped even lower.

Even with the chute, Flint was going to have a rough fall. The man's head was bent straight back, his mouth was open, and his hair was whipping around his face.

Cyrus's headset began to slip.

The plane was over farms now. Then trees.

"Now!" Rupert said.

Cyrus let go and Flint shot out and up into the night like a toy eaten by a vacuum.

And there was Ashtown—stone walls and the great courtyard and the fountain and spotlit statues along the roofs and the airstrip and the zoo buildings and the harbor and the old stone structure where Cyrus and Antigone had lived—and it was all instantly tiny in the distance. Even tinier, swinging in the air above the courtyard, there was a red parachute and a blinking emergency light.

Still flapping against the wall, Cyrus stared at the strange place that had become his home, one more place that he now missed. His headset was gone, rattling in front of him just out of reach.

The tail began to close. Cyrus sank slowly to the floor.

Five minutes later, miles away, the jet rocked to a stop on the moonlit water of a small hidden bay tucked against the side of Lake Michigan. The engines whined their way down toward quiet. Waves slapped against the shore beneath rows of shaggy trees.

Rupert threw open the cabin door and looked at his watch. The glow in the east was growing.

Cyrus was exhausted. He dropped into a seat beside the door and shut his eyes. "What now?" he asked. Something thudded into his lap, and he looked down. Goggles and a snorkel. "We're swimming? Rupe, we're miles from Ashtown."

"Seven miles," Rupert said. "But we're not exactly swimming." He pulled a small metallic sphere out of his pocket and twisted it. Two halves popped apart about a centimeter and began ticking loudly. Rupert plopped it into the water. A moment later, the surface of the lake quivered with an underwater explosion and Cyrus's seat shook beneath him.

Shock waves.

"Oh, gosh," Cyrus said. "You're calling the shark."

## ✤ nine ✤

# PATHS OF SHADOW

RUPERT PULLED HIS MASK AND SNORKEL DOWN onto his forehead and leaned his arms above the plane's wide-open door. Cyrus eyed the dark water beyond him.

"Llew said it wouldn't take her long." Rupert glanced back at Cyrus.

Cyrus stood up. "You do know that there is more than one shark, don't you? Lilly is the trained one, but the last time we rode her, another great big one showed up that Llewellyn didn't even know."

Rupert looked back at the water, rippled with wind. "Well, I guess we need Lilly to show up first, then, yeah?" He slid to the side and let Cyrus step into the door beside him. "I'd get your rope ready."

"Why do I need a rope?" Cyrus asked.

"To tie on to a fin?" Rupert asked. "You're the one who has done this before, not me. I assumed it would be easier than hanging on for seven miles."

Cyrus rubbed his head and sucked in a worried breath through his teeth. He hadn't seen Lilly the Bull in a long time. And if he had, he would have jumped right back out of the water like every other sane person on the planet. Someone with a snarling, snapping dog on a leash will swear that their dog is actually a fluffy ball of fun. Llewellyn Douglas was sure that Lilly the enormous toothy bull shark was a tender little sweetheart. And apparently, Rupert had believed him.

"We're really doing this?" Cyrus asked.

"If she shows," said Rupert.

"And then we're sneaking into Ashtown. Won't they be expecting us now?"

"We are," said Rupert. "And no, they won't. They'll be expecting us to be long gone. A thief doesn't often ring the doorbell."

A black shape carved through distant water. Cyrus's stomach tightened. A bigger shape followed, and his stomach did flips.

"Rupe," Cyrus said.

"I see them," Rupert said. "Two. Which one is Lilly?"

"How am I supposed to know that?" Cyrus asked. "Jump in and see which one eats you."

"You're going in first," Rupert said. "Llew says she trusts you."

"Seriously? No way!" Cyrus began to laugh. "Trusts? He made me grab on to her one time for like a minute!"

Rupert assessed the glowing eastern horizon. The sky was bluing fast, prepping for the sun. He looked back at

Cyrus. "This is happening, Cy. And this is happening now. What's our best approach? You take the lead."

Cyrus inhaled slowly and leaned all the way out of the door. The two dorsals were swirling slowly around the plane, dipping, disappearing, and resurfacing to carve the lake in smooth figure eights.

"Okay," Cyrus said. "We need to get out onto the wing."

Cyrus pulled his snorkel mask over his head and let it hang around his neck while he watched the sharks. One was always coming when the other was going, and the last thing he wanted to do was jump out in front of either one of them.

And then the two sharks turned away together, rounding the nose of the plane.

"Now!" Cyrus said, and he dove out of the door. The water felt warm and oily. He dolphin-kicked himself forward, knowing the sharks would have felt his splash, would have already turned, would be gliding toward him. He surfaced, lunged up, and grabbed at the wing four feet above him. His bare hands would have slipped on the metal, but the rubber beads on his black gloves held like glue. He pulled his chin up over the wing, managed to hook his right leg over the edge, and with arms shaking, rolled up onto the top.

Two dorsals slid by beneath him.

Panting, Cyrus looked back at the door. Rupert had

stayed behind to shut it, and he now bobbed quietly in the water beside the plane. He watched the sharks pass, and then with one relaxed stroke, he slid through the water, grabbed the wing, and tugged himself up out of the lake and all the way into a sitting position on the wing with his feet dangling.

Cyrus didn't think Rupert could have looked any more relaxed, or his effort any more casual. The plane leaned a little and rocked with Rupert on the wing.

"I'm here," Rupert said, and he wiped water down his face. "Now what?"

Cyrus moved behind him, closer to the body of the plane. He knew only one way to tell which shark was Lilly. On that strange day, months and months ago, Llewellyn had used signals, commands. Lilly had obeyed.

"Scoot farther out, Rupe," Cyrus said. "Leave a big gap between us."

Rupert pulled up his legs and moved farther out on the wing. Cyrus got down on his knees and watched the water.

The two dorsals crisscrossed out beyond the nose of the plane. Cyrus raised his fist out over the water. One of the sharks veered toward him. Cyrus thumped his fist down onto the wing and the dorsal accelerated.

The lake erupted, spewing a geyser of water while the enormous snub-nosed, wide-mouthed, black bulk of Lilly the Bull surged up like a rocket. The spray doused

Cyrus's face, and then the thick-bodied shark landed on the wing. Steel and rivets screamed. The plane slapped its wingtip into the water and rolled onto its side. Rupert tumbled and slid down into the seething lake. Cyrus fell into Lilly, slamming his face and chest against her twitching side. She was as heavy and hard as stone wrapped in wet sandpaper.

The plane continued to roll, but slowly.

"Cyrus!" Rupert shouted. "What were you thinking?" He jerked himself up the wing and rose to his rubber-beaded feet. Lilly's bulk shifted, squealing as she slid inches down the wing.

Cyrus pushed himself off the shark. "Tie on to the pectoral fin!" He unlooped the rope from his belt and wrapped it around the base of Lilly's slowly flapping fin. Then he cinched it to his belt. Lilly's gills ruffled. Her baseball-size eye rolled. Rupert was tying on to the other side.

"She can't breathe," Cyrus said. "You ready?" He pulled up his mask and tucked the snorkel into his mouth.

"Ready!" Rupert shouted.

Cyrus slid forward, leaning past the shark's wild eye. Making his fist, he tapped the shark on the nose just like he'd seen Llewellyn do.

Lilly gaped her mouth, baring tooth armies. Her body quaked. She belched, and then vomited gallons of partially digested fish off the back of the wing and into the lake. Cyrus gagged at the smell. He'd used the wrong signal.

He thumped his fist on the wing, hoping that would work. Lilly didn't move. Reaching down right beside her eye, he thumped the wing again.

The shark jerked and writhed forward. Cyrus clung to her fin. He heard Rupert swear, and then the huge living bulk hit the water, dragging them both in with her. She dove. Cyrus heard the plane rocking and the metal shrieking above him. Lilly turned and Cyrus saw the wingtips slapping the water like a massive distressed teeter-totter. The other shark passed them, circling beneath the plane. Lilly left him behind, cruising out into the lake.

Grabbing at Lilly's pectoral fin, Cyrus pulled himself up as far as his rope anchor would let him. He could just see Rupert hugging tight to Lilly's other side.

Cyrus's Keeper looked up and smiled around his snorkel.

Seven miles to Ashtown. He hoped Llewellyn had taught Rupert how to steer. Cyrus ducked his head and let the force of the current press him tight against the shark's body. Soon he would need to breathe. He wondered if Lilly cared.

The spires and rooftop statues of Ashtown's great hall were on fire with daylight when Lilly surfaced for the twenty-first time on her lake cruise. Cyrus spat out his snorkel and shoved up his mask. They were fifty yards outside the stone harbor wall. Up the green slope and across the little airstrip and above the line of underground hangars, the towering kitchen windows were bright from within. An army of cooks was going to war in the predawn, preparing to feed the men and women who had all sworn to defend the world against the darkness and its secrets. They might not be keeping their vows, but at least they were going to breakfast well. Cyrus could see the smoke rising from the kitchen chimneys, and the smell of bread and bacon fat reached him across the water.

Or maybe it didn't. Maybe the sight of the kitchen windows was all his mind needed to recall the sizzling acres of bacon once tended by Big Ben Sterling, the always-laughing and occasionally evil no-legged cook. And the mounds of hot biscuits his flour-faced minions had heaped into baskets. And the bowls of soft butter they had stirred into thistle honey. And the smiles they had given to Cyrus as he had eaten himself into exhaustion.

The shark slowed, gliding into the harbor like she was waiting for them to make a decision. Rupert snorted and spat. "It's enough to break my heart, being out here and looking at that kitchen."

Cyrus laughed. "So it's not just me? I was thinking about Sterling's biscuits."

Rupert sighed. "You had to mention those. They've never been quite the same since we lost that old crook." He looked at Cyrus. "Eat a dozen in memory. We have to dive again. We don't need a dragonfly dropping by with a camera."

Cyrus licked lake off his lips. He nodded and pulled his mask back down. "Where to?"

"Beneath the zoo," Rupert said. "Not the Crypto wing," he added quickly. "The barns."

Rupert tapped Lilly's head, and Cyrus grabbed a gulp of air, tucking his snorkel back between his lips.

The big shark dove.

Deep water. Cold water. Lightless water. With one arm over Lilly's back, Cyrus kept himself glued to the swaying sandpaper body. He could feel Rupert's arm thrown over his own, pressing down, pushing left, tugging right, guiding the animal beside an underwater cliff and finally into a tunnel. Cyrus pressed his forehead into Lilly's side, hoping there would be no rocks, no jagged walls.

Lilly surfaced. Cyrus blew his snorkel empty, filled his lungs, and they were diving again. Another tunnel. Thirty seconds and they had resurfaced to the echoing roar of running water. Lilly was still working hard, but Cyrus wasn't sure they were moving. His feet skidded around on something hard and slick. The bottom? Could it be that shallow?

"Stay with her!" Rupert shouted.

What did that mean? What else would he do? What was Rupert doing?

"Rupe?" Cyrus asked. "Rupert!"

Electricity crackled. Large naked lightbulbs fluttered and then burned, hanging from an arched brown brick ceiling. The black water wasn't deep, but it was racing down a steep incline and seething up on itself below Cyrus, where the tunnel narrowed. Rupert was standing on a narrow brick walkway, his hand inside an open electrical box.

"Cut loose and send her off," Rupert said. "We're on our own from here."

Cyrus drew the long knife from the small of his back and slid the blade through the wet rope looped through his belt. While Lilly lashed her thick tail, swimming in place, Cyrus climbed up over her back toward Rupert. His Keeper crouched and held out his hand. Cyrus sheathed his knife and then jumped.

The downhill current swept out Cyrus's legs, but Rupert's hand clamped around his forearm, and the big man used the momentum of the water to swing Cyrus up onto the little walkway. Lilly twisted and slapped her tail against the side of the tunnel, flinging a wall of water over Cyrus. Crawling up to his knees, he spat and blinked and watched the big shark slide down into the froth and disappear.

"Llew was right," Rupert said. "She's a love." He pulled Cyrus onto his feet. "You sound? We've got a jog ahead."

Water beaded on Cyrus's sleeves and gloves and on the waxy black surface of his shirt and leggings. He shook it off and rubbed his hands through his hair.

"I'm ready," he said. "I've been in this tunnel before, haven't I?"

"You have," Rupert said. He turned and walked up the little walkway toward a crooked and broken narrow flight of brick stairs. "You and sister came through this tunnel when you first arrived in Ashtown, dragging poor, bloody Horace between you. But you got out further upstream, before this drop-off."

Rupert raced up the uneven brick steps two and three at a time. Cyrus paused at the bottom. The bricks were slick with moisture. Green slime coated the mortar. He took one tentative hop and then another, expecting to slide. His black booties didn't budge, and he let himself stride. Rupert disappeared over the top of the stairs without a glance back. Cyrus raced up after him.

At the top, a small black tunnel mouth waited for Cyrus, and he didn't hesitate. The brick ceiling was low but arched, and the walls grazed Cyrus's arms as he climbed. He stretched out his hands, letting his palms bounce along the sides in front of him. There was no light at all, but the stairs grew more even as he moved away from the water, and Cyrus kept a steady pace, matching strides with each breath.

"Cartography!" Rupert's voice poured down the narrow stairwell. "Draw everything in your head as we go, tracing from the outside in, counting your strides! Draw it in reverse, all over again with every new turn or junction."

Cyrus kept climbing. What? So he would start where? He pictured the harbor, the smell of biscuits, the shark dive. That was hopeless. So he started at the downhill river tunnel, the short walkway, the stairs up, and then the turn into the tunnel stairs. How on earth was he supposed to count and remember his strides?

His hands suddenly slid out into air. The stairs stopped and Cyrus's final stride slammed awkwardly down onto smooth stone. Cyrus turned in place, fighting the loudness of his breath, the thrumming of his heart, trying to hear any trace of Rupert. Down the tunnel behind him, he could hear the water running. Ahead of him . . . nothing.

"Start again." Cyrus jolted. Rupert's voice was right in his ear. Cyrus could smell the smoked fish on his breath from yesterday. He backed away.

"What do you mean?" Cyrus asked.

"I mean, start counting strides," Rupert said. "And keep track of the sequence in reverse order. Begin training your mind."

Cyrus said nothing. His chest still heaved.

"I have been in this place only one time," Rupert said in the darkness. "Years ago, when my own Keeper was the Avengel. From here, fifty-three strides down will take me to the river tunnel. With high current, almost fifty seconds' held breath will carry me out into the lake. Fifteen more seconds to surface. A quarter-mile swim to the harbor wall. He made me memorize every route in Ashtown—every route he knew."

"Because he was mean?" Cyrus asked.

Rupert laughed. "It's useful now, Cyrus Smith. And once your mind grows accustomed to the game, any new place and every new maze is memorized easily."

" 'The game,' " Cyrus said. "Right. You're not a normal person, Rupe."

"Nor are you," Rupert said. "Follow me and count. I'll quiz you along the way, but stay close."

Cyrus tracked the sound of Rupert's jogging. And he counted. At the end of every stretch, Rupert made him repeat a string of numbers and directions that would lead them back the way they had come.

Forty-nine, slight left, ten stairs down, right turn, thirty-three, full left.

They stepped out into another river tunnel, but the

sound of the water was more like a trickle. Cyrus wished he could look around. His eyes felt like they were bulging out of his head, they'd been in total darkness for so long. And every step he took, something inside him was expecting to fall. He stayed close to Rupert's footsteps and heard the sound of wooden planks squealing.

"Add the landmark," Rupert said. "Count it back."

Cyrus followed Rupert across the invisible bridge, counting his steps, praying that the squeaking wouldn't turn to cracking. At the other side, Cyrus rattled off the directions.

"Bridge, fourteen, forty-nine, slight left, ten stairs down, right turn, thirty-three, full left."

"Good," Rupert said. "Now we climb."

Cyrus walked into a wall.

"Over here," Rupert said. "Count, but we're not rushing these. Stay close to the rail. Wood doesn't always last."

Tread twenty-six of twenty-nine was missing, but Rupert made him note which one it would be when counting down. Tread four. At the top, they wound through a large room full of thick brick-and-plaster pillars and the smell of animals. Hay scuffed around Cyrus's feet.

Cyrus memorized and repeated the route, a little surprised that he still could. But the numbers weren't as random as he had thought they would be. Each one meant a different space, and each space, even in complete darkness, had felt a little different. But he still hoped

Rupert wasn't going to make him draw it all out when they got back from . . . wherever they were going next.

Light. Rupert pushed open a doorway, and Cyrus blinked at the brightness of what was actually a dim orange flicker. Rupert led Cyrus through the door and between rough plank walls hidden behind bales of hay. The light was coming down through open wooden traps in the ceiling. Cyrus stared up past two floors at the beamed ceiling of a massive barn. The smell of cow surrounded him.

"Keep count in your head," Rupert whispered. "Silence from here in."

Cows made their cow noises. Hooves stamped on boards above Cyrus's head. Stink rained down. Men in the barn were mumbling Latin. One moved by an open trap in the ceiling and Cyrus saw that he was robed and hooded. The Brendanites. He wasn't at all fond of them, not since his first week at Ashtown. But he'd never complained about their cheeses. Or their ice cream. Or even the yogurt. Nolan had promised Cyrus that one day he would also come to appreciate the monks' beer. According to the pale transmortal, the Brendanites were some of the only people to actually serve a purpose at Ashtown. That purpose was dairy. And brew.

For the first time, Cyrus had lost count. He bit down on his lip and took a guess, feeling like he was off by ten steps. In either direction. He recited the rest to himself.

Rupert peeked through a door and nodded at Cyrus to follow. They were leaving the barn's basement and entering a wide plastered brick hallway lined with oil lamps.

Cyrus began to count his steps. The hallway dropped, but only down three steps. It dropped again, but this time four. Cyrus didn't bother counting them.

Voices. The walls were now dotted with small alcoves loaded with candles and glaciers of molten wax in front of glistening tile mosaics of men with fingers longer than sloth claws and cheeks gaunt enough to belong to a Jolly Roger.

The passage rounded a slow corner and ended in a large wooden door with wrought-iron hinges. Cyrus whispered his steps aloud. Rupert took him by the shoulder and directed him into an alcove that held a miniature door instead of a mosaic. Behind the door, stairs. Tiny, extremely worn stairs, and a ceiling so low that Cyrus put his hands on the stone steps in front of him and practically had to crawl. Rupert's broad shoulders scraped slowly against both sides behind Cyrus.

As they rose, so did the voices.

Cyrus's head and shoulders emerged onto a tiny balcony, behind a stone railing. He wormed forward, but not all the way up out of the stairs. He was in a large, circular underground chapel. The domed ceiling was covered with bright mosaics depicting the slaughter of various bright-red monsters by monks with black swords. Twelve sculpted pillars ran up from the floor, through the tiny ring balcony that belted the room. The pillars were all people in robes—men and women—but every inch of them had been covered with inscriptions.

The floor of the chapel itself appeared to be a mosaic of the world, done in white and black and gold and jungle-bird blue. But it was hard for Cyrus to tell, because the floor was also covered with monks, clustered into murmuring groups, with their hoods on.

At the far end of the floor, there was a gold altar beneath a gold cross. Sitting alone on the floor beside the altar, with his thick white legs splayed out and his hood thrown back revealing his short Mohawk, Niffy was eating a biscuit.

A bell rang, and Niffy hopped to his feet, brushing crumbs off his robe. The monks quietly formed up in lines, and Niffy slid to the end of the front row, flipping his hood over his head.

Rupert tapped on Cyrus's back. Cyrus crawled along the cool stone floor behind the rail, grateful for his dark clothes. Rupert slid up beside him, squeezing between Cyrus and the wall.

The bell rang again and the monks on the floor began to sing. The words were Latin and the voices flowed in slow unison, even the echoes keeping perfect time.

"Niffy is down there," Cyrus whispered.

Rupert nodded. "We're in time."

"For what?" Cyrus asked.

The bell rang a third time and the voices stopped suddenly. The last echoes rippled around the domed ceiling and died. Behind the altar, the wall with the golden cross opened and three hooded monks in black walked out, shoulder to shoulder. All three held drawn black-bladed swords with gold hilts. Cyrus had seen a picture of a sword just like them back in Llewellyn's camp. His mother's native brother had been wearing it in his belt.

The monks laid the blades across the altar, bowed, and backed away, chanting as they did.

"Only one is real," Rupert whispered.

Cyrus looked at him, confused.

"The blades," Rupert said. "The other two are replicas."

Cyrus wasn't sure what that meant or why it mattered, so long as the edges were sharp. Two more men walked out from behind the altar. One man was old and large, hobbling from side to side, breathing hard. His hood was off and his bald head shone with sweat above his red face. Cyrus didn't know his name. He had only ever heard him called the Abbot, though his rank in the O of B was technically Sage.

The other man was the lean, wrinkled Irishman who had collected Niffy from the camp. His hood was also off and his scruffy white ring of hair made his spotted scalp look like an oversize leathery egg. His golden patrik slid slowly around his right arm, stretching from his shoulder to his wrist, visible to the room and glowing.

Cyrus felt Patricia tightening around his neck, and he quickly hooked his fingers beneath her.

"Easy," he whispered. He slid her off his neck and let her recoil around his left wrist. "Easy. He's down there. He can't see us."

The Abbot raised his hands to the room and wheezed in Latin. Cyrus's mind tried to keep up. He knew the usual holy words, but then . . .

*Uh . . . blessings . . . and something something brightness belonging to, no, originating in, or maybe descending down from sailors? From a sailor dream?*

"He welcomes the Irish," Rupert whispered. "The Brothers of the Voyager, their coming is 'as blessed as the rising light of the sun to men trapped in nightmare.' "

The Abbot continued. Cyrus knew most of the words, but they were coming too fast for him.

" 'The day has come, my sons and brothers,' " Rupert whispered. " 'The day long awaited and long feared, the day of abomination.' " He looked at Cyrus and rolled his eyes. "Brilliant."

The monk with the golden patrik stepped forward and took over. His Latin was quicker, his pronunciations archaic, and his accent made it sound almost like a song. Cyrus understood maybe one word in five. Rupert was listening intently, no longer translating.

Cyrus tapped his Keeper on the shoulder.

Rupert glanced back. "The old words," he whispered. "He's quoting the original covenant between the monks and the O of B." The force of the monk's voice rose. The old man's words were angry and slow.

"Now all the ways the O of B has broken that covenant," Rupert whispered. He shrugged. "And he's not wrong." The monk threw his arms into the air and began to shout, gold light from his snake haloing his wild hair. "'Enemies rise,'" Rupert translated in a low monotone. "'Dragons and flesh-mixing devils once again take root among men while the Order sleeps in its own rot and filth. Let fires burn away the dross. Let the storm winds rid us of the chaff. Let the Order once more raise holy hands; let us wear the robes and wield the tools of Reapers. Cleanse Ashtown of her impurity, empty her halls of vain unbelievers, open the terrible armories of the forgotten wars, rouse the Brothers Below, let every man feel the cold Breath of Brendan and tremble before our Justice and Wrath.'"

The monk dropped his arms and the room was silent.

"Wow," Cyrus mouthed.

"If this goes badly," Rupert whispered, rising to his knees, "you know the way out. Don't linger. Get to the plane."

Rupert ruffled Cyrus's damp hair, and then he stood.

"What are you doing?" Cyrus whispered. "Rupe!"

Rupert hopped up over Cyrus onto the stone railing, and he crossed his big black-sleeved arms. Cyrus bit his lip and pressed himself down against the floor.

The Abbot had once again waddled forward. His red face had paled while the monk with the patrik had spoken.

"Don't get too courageous, there, Irish!" Rupert's voice filled the domed room. "Or this lot might have to fight someone."

With that, Rupert turned and dropped, catching his hands on the rail. He winked at Cyrus and dropped again, down into the crowd of gasping monks below.

## ❊ ten ❊

# TWO BELLS

THE MONKS PARTED AS RUPERT WALKED toward the altar, his sleeved feet silent on the bright map tiles beneath. The old monk with the patrik tightened his lips and smiled. The fat Abbot wiped his forehead.

"Mr. Greeves," the Abbot said. "How did you . . . Why?" His Latin was gone.

Rupert laughed. "I am the Avengel, Abbot. I know every door into every one of your little chapels. I know your calendars and rituals and liturgies. I know your covenants with the O of B, and I know what recourse lies before you if, as dear Father Patrick of Monasterboice just informed us so eloquently, those covenants have indeed been broken."

"You have no standing in this gathering," the old Irish monk growled. Niffy, thick and hooded, inched toward Rupert.

"But I *am* standing in this gathering," Rupert said. He stopped in front of the altar. "And despite the lawless efforts of this Order's current Brendan, I have managed to retain my office and rank within the rule of law." He bowed to the Abbot. "But if the Abbot chooses to side with Bellamy 'Blasphemy' Cook, if he believes the office of Avengel was truly abolished and that our current Brendan is not, in fact, a lackey of Phoenix, then I will beg your pardon and make my exit." He faced the Abbot and bowed his head, waiting. After a moment of silence, he glanced up. "Abbot, I await your judgment."

Cyrus smiled. Rupert was enjoying himself. Niffy took another silent step forward. Cyrus opened his mouth to yell, and then clamped it shut. Not yet.

The Abbot stammered. Rupert kept his eyes on him but cleared his throat loudly.

"Brother Niffy," Rupert said. "If you touch me here, it will be no puppy scuffle."

Niffy froze where he stood. Cyrus saw him look up at the old monk Rupert had called Father Patrick. Patrick nodded slightly, and Niffy backed away.

"Right!" Rupert turned and faced the crowd. "As the Abbot has no objections, I ask that you, my cowled brothers, hear my proposal before you elect to burn Ashtown into a ruin. Bellamy Cook was duly appointed by the Sages of this Order." The monks began to grumble, but Rupert raised his gloved hands for silence. "Aye, he was elected when the O of B was under duress. He was elected with threats hanging in the air. And he serves at the pleasure of Phoenix, not the members of the Order."

"Liar!" a voice shouted. "He's a stooge for the bloody flesh-mixers and transmortal devils!"

The crowd murmured approval.

"So I thought as well," Rupert said. "But since I left Ashtown behind me, I have discovered otherwise. Radu Bey and Gilgamesh saw that they would benefit from his appointment. But Bellamy was not their puppet. It was Phoenix who ordered the treaties voided and the old bonds severed. Phoenix wants to freeze the O of B in fear while he builds. He wants Radu and the others to tear us down, and then he will tame the beasts with new collars. He will bind the wild ones to himself. And he can do it. Two months ago, I saw transmortals challenge Phoenix and fall before him, paralyzed by darts with poison spelled from the Dragon's Tooth, from the Reaper's Blade. They fear him already, and if he is given the time to prepare, he may even break them. If not, he falls, but only after we are already buried in the rubble of this place."

"We need the old weapons!" Father Patrick shouted. "Rouse the Brothers Below and see what Phoenix's darts, or even the tooth itself, can do to their stone flesh." He stepped to the altar and swept up one of the black-bladed swords. "These will sing with the Reaper's kiss as well, Avengel! Why is Radu Bey's head still on his shoulders?"

The monks cheered. Fists rose.

Rupert let his chin hit his chest. He stood still, silent, waiting for the storm to pass.

"The treaties bound this Order, too," Father Patrick said. "She once had tools of pain and madness to make even the Draculs weep. And she put them away! Forbade her own strengths! But the old curses on the dark tools are lifted now, Avengel. Mortals can once again wield them without fear. It is a day long awaited by the brothers of Monasterboice, by the Cryptkeepers, abandoned for centuries to labor long without the great arms sealed in Ashtown."

Rupert's head still hung.

Father Patrick paced behind Rupert with his glowing snake on his arm. The room quieted slowly. Finally, Rupert spoke, but to the floor, without looking up.

"Seventy-two," he said. "In 1859, the Brothers Below were roused by a fool of a Hungarian monk studying in this very cloister. Seventy-two people were killed in less than half an hour. The monk was the first struck down."

"I've read the account," Father Patrick said. "The number was inflated, to discourage the use of the Brothers."

The Abbot sputtered and suddenly found his voice. "I assure you, Patrick, our records are meticulous and serve only the truth."

"One hundred and forty-four," Rupert said. He finally looked up. "The Brothers' previous spree. In 1617, they obliterated a nearby Indian encampment. But what would a wise man expect from Brother Justice and Brother Wrath? We are all impure. We all need mercy, and the Brothers are heartless, soulless stone."

"They have been used wisely," Patrick said. "It can be done."

"Possibly," Rupert said. "But like all of Ashtown's dangerous residents, there is good reason why they were Buried in our deepest cells. Any man who seeks to free them seeks guilt—for his own death and the deaths of many others." He turned, gave Father Patrick a slow assessing look, glanced at the sweating Abbot, and then once again faced the crowd. This time he spread his feet and gripped his arms behind his back.

"Here is my proposal," Rupert said. "I will arm you. The old Sages wove many curses around many tools to prevent us from using them. Those curses may now be gone, but true evil cannot be lifted from a tool in the same way. I will choose which weapons will remain untouched. There will be no complaints about my choices. And even those weapons that I consider righteous are not to be used against a transmortal who begs mercy and willingly surrenders."

Grumbles rose from the crowd. Father Patrick laughed. The Abbot wiped his forehead.

"Without a trial," Rupert continued. "Unlike the Brothers Below, we have some wisdom to discern when mercy is the stronger weapon than wrath. We will remain an Order of laws, or we have already been destroyed." Rupert looked around.

"That's it, then?" Father Patrick asked. "You'll play at picksies in the deep vaults and then hand the weapons over? I know a promise with strings on when I hear it. Drop the other shoe."

"There are two stipulations and one difficulty," Rupert said. "I will hand the weapons over only if all seven Cryptkeepers renew their alliance to the O of B. The Brothers of the Voyager must resubmit their governance to the Brendan. Centuries ago, your founders left because of treaties that are no more. Your current ranks would be honored on reentry, and thus, six of your seven would immediately hold our rank of Sage. One would be Keeper. The last I tallied, five votes are all that is needed to remove Bellamy Cook as Brendan. Do that, and Ashtown, these assembled brothers, and the Cryptkeepers will be armed, a corrupt Brendan ousted, the O of B preserved, and the rule of law observed."

Father Patrick scowled. "And I suppose we are to name you in Bellamy's place, then?"

Rupert shook his head. "I am Avengel. Alan Livingstone would make a better Brendan than I. Or perhaps Robert Boone." Rupert smiled. "He would govern to your liking."

The old Irish monk was fidgeting with the snake on

his arm. "It is a lot to ask of us. But you've named the stipulations. What is the difficulty?"

"The weapons you seek are not all here," Rupert said. "Some were destroyed when the treaties were formed. Others were sealed behind the Brothers Below or used in the Burials, and must not be disturbed. As for the rest, over the centuries, many power-thirsty thieves have wormed through the vaults of Ashtown. Weapons have been taken, destroyed, or lost when curses fell on those who tried to use them."

Father Patrick laughed. "This seems a great deal more than a mere difficulty. You'll arm us, but there are no arms?"

"There is a map," Rupert said. "Left to me by an outlaw spy who lived and labored under Phoenix's nose. Many of the old weapons were collected and hidden. I will tend to their gathering."

"You and the young Smiths, you mean," Father Patrick said. "The map was William Skelton's making? The man called Billy Bones?"

Rupert didn't answer. Cyrus pressed his face all the way against the cool stone rail, watching the crowd of monks shift uncomfortably. Finally, Father Patrick nodded. Five of the monks, including Niffy, stepped out of the crowd and moved toward Father Patrick. Six of the Cryptkeepers.

Cyrus couldn't believe it. It couldn't work, could it?

Just like that, the Irishmen would rejoin the O of B as Sages and Bellamy could be removed? Rupert was smiling, but not because he had been joking. He was happy. Cyrus's mind began to race. Hope surged up inside him, and it felt strange, like being suddenly well fed after weeks of hunger. He hadn't realized just how hopeless he had become. But with Bellamy gone, everything would change. The Order would stop hunting his family. They could stop running and move back to Ashtown. They could train again. Rupert could unite the O of B to stand against Phoenix and the transmortals both.

"We have stipulations of our own," Father Patrick said. "About your transmortal 'allies,' so-called, and they cannot be negotiated."

A large cold hand suddenly slid over Cyrus's mouth. Another clamped tight around his throat, closing off his windpipe. Cyrus jerked and writhed onto his back. The arms were as solid as timber, long and bare to the shoulders. The skin was tinged green and traced with bone tattoos. One of Phoenix's men—one of the Reborn. Cyrus punched. He kicked and slapped and clawed cold skin, gasping in silence, watching small gills flutter on the sides of his attacker's throat. The world was suddenly slow, and Cyrus noticed everything. The man's wide eyes were lunar gray and scribbled with zigzagging black veins instead of pupils. And he wasn't even looking at Cyrus. He was looking down at the chapel floor, his steel grip barely even an exertion for him. More shapes flowed up the narrow stairs behind the tattooed man and slid around the ringed balcony like shadows.

Cyrus could hear Father Patrick speaking, but it didn't matter. Nothing mattered but getting breath into his lungs and blood to his brain. The world was growing blurry. The fingers on Cyrus's left hand couldn't quite close on the man's throat, but they could almost reach the fluttering gills. Almost. Cyrus writhed, trying to get his right hand to the knife handle that was digging into his back. He . . . couldn't . . . quite. He couldn't even bite the hand over his mouth. He couldn't uncrush his throat.

Pain. Panic. But pain was a message he could choose to ignore. Panic was the wrong reaction. He had been trained to suppress both.

Cyrus's feet scrambled, scraping on stone, bracing him against the wall. And then he grabbed the cold arms and jerked his throat and face up even harder against the hands. The world went purple with pain. His eyes felt like they were going to explode. He only needed . . . an inch.

Cyrus pulled himself harder into the pain. The purple went black and his body was suddenly warm. He threw his left arm up and clawed blindly for the man's neck. His fingers found the gills. He hooked them down inside, and he tore.

The man barely grunted. He grabbed Cyrus's left wrist, and his fingers closed around Patricia. Cyrus saw a silver flash and felt the snake strike from his arm. He gulped one breath down his crushed throat, and his right hand found his knife. Still blind, Cyrus stabbed and felt the blade bite deep.

The man's sharp bark of pain and anger rattled through the room. Fists hit Cyrus's face, but the blows were weak. Cyrus stabbed again, and the man slumped onto the stone floor beside him.

"Rupe!" Cyrus tried to shout, but his voice was a sandpaper whisper. He rolled onto his knees, coughing, and grabbed at the stone rail. As his vision cleared, he saw the monks below looking up and around at the dark balcony with wide eyes. Father Patrick was uncoiling his golden snake. Rupert held his knife in one hand and one of the black-bladed swords in the other. He looked up, and when he saw Cyrus, relief filled his eyes.

A single black sphere bounced down into the chapel, trailing smoke. The monks all turned. Rupert yelled, leaping away toward the altar.

*Boom.*

The blast stayed low. White fire, waist high, swept across the bright tiles, toppling monks, torching robes, and then breaking around pillars and washing up the outer walls. The balcony quivered. Smoke rose up, and rubble rained down. Moving like cats, the black shapes of Phoenix's Reborn leapt the rails and dropped among the writhing fiery monks.

Cyrus pulled his knife free and managed to stand. His windpipe felt as small as a straw. Patricia was bigger than normal and trying to coil back around his arm. He grabbed her tail.

"Stay big," he rasped, and he stepped onto the rail and jumped, swinging Patricia as he fell, aiming for a black shape in the smoke below.

Cyrus punched his feet into the back of a gilled man just before he finished off a burning monk. Then he slammed down onto the hot tiles. The last of his breath was knocked out of him, and his head snapped back against the floor.

He held on to Patricia's tail, and he could feel her striking, writhing across him. But the smoke was burning his eyes. So he shut them.

Bells were ringing. Big bells. Alarm bells. Cyrus opened his eyes and found that he was staring up through thin smoke at a red painted dragon on a ceiling. Patricia was long and visible, coiled up Cyrus's right arm and glowing silver in the smoke. Her green eyes were sharp and furious. Her tongue was lashing at the air, blood stained the underside of her jaw, and her body was taut. She was ready for more. Cyrus coughed, sat up, and coughed some more. Something was very wrong with his throat. And his head. And his eyes and nose were streaming.

A gilled man, one of the Reborn, lay dead beside him, slumped over the smoking body of a monk. Cyrus shifted onto his knees. More dead monks. Lots of dead monks. All of them smoking. He saw Father Patrick in a pool of blood. His snake was gone. He saw the Abbot, sprawled on his back without his legs. Cyrus gagged, but his throat was too tight to throw up.

There were gilled men, too, but not many. Four? Five? And one more on the balcony. No Rupert. No Niffy.

Bells. Ringing. They would be in the spires above the Galleria. They were telling Ashtown that something was wrong, telling everyone to hurry, to hide, to be ready, telling men with guns to race to find the site of an attack . . . *here*.

Cyrus spun in a quick circle. He had to leave. Now. Where was Rupert?

"If this goes badly," Rupert had said, "you know the way out."

Cyrus hurried to the big main door. It was ajar but only by inches. Cyrus pulled it open and peered out into the long hall with the alcoves. It was empty, but there was blood all over the floor. He could see the narrow entrance to the balcony stairs.

Ignoring his head and gasping for air like a drowning man, Cyrus forced himself to jog.

"Don't linger," he could hear Rupert saying. "Get to the plane."

Cyrus tried to straighten his course. He was drifting toward the walls as he ran. He almost slipped on blood when he reached the first stairs. There was a monk's body at the top. And another beyond his.

The hall bent, and Cyrus practically tripped over three of the gilled Reborn. They were all dead and their wounds were deep, clean hacks. Cyrus looked away and focused on his route. From here, he had to get below the barns. He knew the way. He could count his steps back.

Fear rattled inside him. He wasn't going to be able to count back anything. Not now.

"I can," Cyrus said aloud, but his voice was only a groan. He would get it right. He would. He had to.

Cyrus crashed through a door and into the paths beneath the barn floor. His head was clearing, and his breath was coming a little more easily. Above him, milk was dripping down through a wooden grate. Cyrus could see a monk's limp hand and the bucket he had dropped. Turning back the way Rupert had brought him, Cyrus staggered into darkness, trying to piece together the string of directions. Dodging pillars through the broad dark room that smelled of hay, he began to chant the directions aloud. Patricia was still glowing on his arm, but she was shrinking quickly now. Soon she would eat her tail and disappear.

Cyrus reached a door and banged it open, knowing what lay on the other side.

"Twenty-nine stairs down, tread four missing, bridge, fourteen, forty-nine, slight left, ten stairs down, right turn, thirty-three, full left."

Cyrus trundled down the stairs, hopping the missing tread. At the bottom, he jogged toward the dim shape of the bridge.

Patricia disappeared and darkness swallowed them both. Cyrus didn't care. He had run in; he could run out. He counted down his steps and left the bridge behind him, entering a tunnel. Dragging his fingertips on the wall, he counted down his steps again and then veered blindly left into an unseen tunnel mouth. Turning sideways, he counted ten blind steps down and then turned right. He pushed himself faster but tried to match the strides he'd used coming in, counting down from thirty-three. He was getting there. He would reach the river tunnel. What had Rupert said? Fifty seconds out through the tunnel into the lake? From there, a quarter-mile swim to the harbor. If Lilly didn't drop by, Cyrus would steal a boat and head for the plane.

Cyrus slowed, put his arms out, and felt for his full left turn.

Tiny bells jingled in the darkness behind him, and Cyrus froze, holding his breath. Metal legs squealed.

"Cyrus Smith, lad o' legend," a familiar voice said. "Go no further. Their nets are ready and waiting for a fresh catch of you."

A match struck in the darkness and Cyrus turned, staring at the grinning firelit face of a big black-bearded man. A small golden bell hung from each ear. Big Ben Sterling eased himself forward on his two thin metal legs, both of them bending and bouncing beneath his bulk.

"Look at you," Sterling said, still smiling. "Lad no more. You've grown to a right towering man."

"Stay back," Cyrus rasped. "I *will* kill you."

Sterling puffed out his match. In the darkness, Cyrus slid away.

"Is that any way to talk to old Ben?"

Cyrus didn't answer.

"I understand you might have a grudge or two gnawing on your insides, and I don't blame you, boy. But I'm just a simple cook who found himself in a difficulty. Don't forget, old Ben may have done some wrong, but he did save your life."

Cyrus snorted. He unwound Patricia from his wrist and popped his thumb in her mouth. He held up his glowing silver fist. Sterling's eyes widened in admiration.

"You saved my life?" Cyrus spat the words and then coughed, trying to widen his throat. "I was tied to a chair in your cellar. You poisoned this whole place for Phoenix. People died! You killed them!"

Ben's face grew sorrowful. "I regret that. I do. But I also set out the antidote to that poison and gave you a wink, now didn't I? I don't regret that, and I don't regret leaving your little Quick Water behind to help your sister find you." He shook his head. "I hoped no one would die, Cyrus Smith. I did indeed. But if I hadn't ruined that lovely sauce with poison, Phoenix would have killed people I loved. I tried to have it safe every which way and I failed. I did. I'm sorrowful about it, and here I stand to show it."

Sterling stepped forward, and this time Cyrus didn't back away. The silver light glinted on the man's eyes, his teeth, and the little bells in his ears. His black beard shifted light like oil.

"Cyrus Smith," Sterling said, "I'm showing my sorrow by clattering through these dank spider tunnels to find you. Those bloody green Reborn found your plane after you air-delivered Flint. They've had watchers lurking around Ashtown for weeks, but a whole platoon since Rupe managed to thieve your mother from under Bellamy's nose. The green beasties might answer to Bellamy, but it's just as likely to be the other way round. They're all filth regardless." Sterling's lip curled, and he sniffed disgust. His ear bells jingled. "I'd hoped Greeves would be with you, but as he's not, he's either dead already or playing fox to those green gilled man-hounds. If you want out of Ashtown, you'll follow the old cook with no legs."

Cyrus licked his lips. The cook's smile widened.

"There's some who might not trust old Ben," Sterling said. "But you can, Cyrus Smith. You can trust me with your life. If I wanted harm done to you, it would have been done long ago when that scareder, younger you was tied up in my cellar and my poisoned sauce was dropping bodies all around Ashtown."

"How do you know about the plane?" Cyrus asked. "How did you know to find me down here?"

"A cook rises early," Sterling said. "I saw your plane. I saw Flint drop. I saw you blaze away across the lake." He smiled. "And I know Rupert Greeves. I know him well. He wouldn't set a clatter at the front door unless he was coming in the back."

"But the tunnels," Cyrus said. "How did you know we'd come in here?"

"How many unguarded doors into Ashtown do you think there are?" Sterling asked. "Not many. The Avengel would know them, and so does an old smuggler turned cook. I was creeping in and out of Ashtown when I was just a wee two-legged Acolyte, *importing* things that may not have been strictly permitted on the Estate. There are other routes, but you were coming from the water and Rupert Greeves wasn't likely to risk the Crypto zoo."

"Phoenix's men," Cyrus said. "The Reborn. How did they get in?"

Sterling's eyes narrowed, and his smile disappeared. "They're not that bold yet. They keep to the outskirts. Bellamy Cook and his regular old-fashioned human thugs are the worst you'll find inside the walls. Those gillies will be waiting at your plane, as sure as sunshine, they will." Sterling winked. "But Big Ben is here to warn you."

Cyrus's mouth hung open. Sterling really didn't know what had just happened? Hot anger surged up into Cyrus's aching head. He tried to shout, and his voice rasped like it was passing through a saw in his throat.

"Where do you think I was?" Cyrus yelled. "What do you think just happened? The alarm bells were ringing! Phoenix's Reborn just firebombed a Brendanite chapel and murdered almost everybody. The Abbot is dead! Most of the monks are dead. Father Patrick the Crypt-keeper was there, but now he's dead, too."

Sterling's eyes narrowed in disbelief. "The gillies? Inside? Not Bellamy's thugs? You're sure?"

Cyrus chewed back his anger, and his words came out hard, like stones. "Gills. Eyes like lizards. Bone tattoos. One had me by the throat. Yeah. I'm sure."

Sterling hissed through his teeth; then he looked up and down the narrow stone passage, his bells jingling against his beard as his head turned.

"Rupert?" Sterling asked.

"I don't know," Cyrus said. "But his body wasn't there." Cyrus moved to the tunnel mouth that led to the stairs, that he knew would take him down to the river. "I have to go. Rupe told me to get to the plane."

Sterling shook his head. "The harbor is swarming. I told you they found your plane. An ambush will be waiting. But if the Reborn are inside, you need to be outside these walls, lad, and that quicker than quick."

"I'm sorry," Cyrus said. "I really can't believe anything you say. For all I know, you brought the 'gillies' in yourself. Why are you even here?"

Sterling grinned. "Why, Cyrus Smith, I thought you would have heard. I'm the cook."

Cyrus stared as the big man shifted his bulk on the two bent metal rods he used as legs. He was the cook? Again? Even after the poison? It didn't make any sense. But at the same time, Cyrus's mind drifted to the world's most perfect biscuits. His stomach growled loudly.

Sterling laughed. "I'll take that as the greatest compliment a lad can give."

Cyrus moved into the tunnel mouth, feeling for the top of the stairs behind him with his toe. He couldn't believe Sterling. He had to do what Rupert had told him to do. Rupert could be waiting for him right now. And if there was an ambush waiting instead, well, maybe Lilly the Bull would help out.

"Don't follow me," Cyrus said. "I don't want to kill you."

"You're too kind," Sterling said.

Cyrus turned and took one step down the dark stairwell. Below him, he heard shouting. Men cursed. Wet feet slapped on stone.

Sterling's hand landed on Cyrus's shoulder.

"Douse the snake light and follow me," Sterling whispered. "*Now.* I don't want them killing you."

## ❊eleven❊

# PLUMM

PLUMM, NEBRASKA, had been nothing but a railroad town. Some folks had worked on the farms that surrounded Plumm on every side, tilling and planting and cutting. Some folks had worked in town, trimming hair, scrambling eggs, making soap, plucking chickens, butchering beef, selling things like radios and milk shakes and couches to each other out of little brick storefronts with big windows and sideways signs that hung over the dusty sidewalks and had all been painted by the same old man who also welded the handrails for everyone's front steps. A few more people worked in government, telling everyone else where they couldn't park their cars or graze their horses, and what music was allowed at the one school dance that happened each year, and how long after dark people could stay in the tiny Founder's Park with the cracked statue of bald old Edward Plumm.

But most folks had worked in the rail yards and in the warehouses beside the rail yards. Big trains had rumbled through Plumm, trains heading all the way up to

Chicago, trains miles and miles long, loaded with cattle and corn. When those trains left Plumm, they were loaded with even more corn, spouted down from the big gray silos at the edge of town, and with pallets and pallets of Holy Soaps, made in iron vats with real animal fat and secret ingredients guaranteed to increase holiness after ten uses, and scented with things like lavender and honey and vanilla.

When Plumm was at its biggest, 251 people called the town home, and ten tons of Holy Soaps were loaded onto the trains every year. A woman named Sissy Plumm lived alone in a big brick house on top of the only hill. She owned Holy Soaps, designed fresh Holy Soaps, and invented new sins that Holy Soaps could cure. She never married and never had children, but one day a train brought her the pieces of a radio tower, and a pipe organ, and old silver microphones, and all put together, those were better than children. She started broadcasting the *Holy Soap Soothing Lunchtime Purity Hour Radio Show* from her living room, and everyone in Plumm, Nebraska, had to listen, and the mayor walked around at noon making sure that they did.

But the trains stopped coming. Bigger silos were built in bigger towns, and they were filled with more corn. And people stopped listening and stopped cutting each other's hair and selling each other milk shakes and making Sissy Plumm's Holy Soaps. And no one cared what music was going to be played at the school dance or where their horses could graze and how late they could stay in the Founder's Park. Because no one stayed in Plumm at all. Almost no one.

Sissy Plumm stayed in her big brick house, and she played her organ and she disobeyed her own rules, but then she washed her hands with some of the thousands of pounds of Holy Soap that would never get loaded onto trains, and every day at noon she sang her songs and taught her lessons about the dangers of sneezes and walking too quickly on Sundays. Every day she shared her wisdom on the *Holy Soap Soothing Lunchtime Purity Hour Radio Show*.

Until one day, she didn't.

The morning sun crept through tattered lacy curtains and found an old bed with four wooden posts carved with birds and flowers and rabbits, and on the bed, the sun found a boy with light skin and black hair. Oliver Laughlin was on his back and his eyes were open. But Oliver was new. He no longer looked out of his old eyes. He no longer thought with his old mind. A broken bamboo cane was in his hands, and the silver knob on the end was open, revealing a large tooth so dark it looked like a triangular hole in the sunlight, like a tiny door into some other reality, distant and cold. Phoenix pressed the tooth against his young new lips, savoring the cool electricity it sent into him. His new existence was more complicated than he would have liked, but there was such excitement in youth, such freshness in every nerve ending. How his grandnephew could have been such a pasty, mopey boy, he couldn't imagine. The lad had senses almost as sharp as some that Phoenix had designed himself, and that was even before Phoenix's extensive renovations after moving in. Oliver's mind had speed, too. Nothing like the speed of thought Phoenix had managed in his last body while wearing the Odyssean Cloak, but still, it had been a stronger starting point than he had expected.

Phoenix had overhauled his pale grandnephew in a shallow pool, in an abandoned factory, pouring force into wires and needles, violently reweaving every joint and bone and muscle and organ, sharpening and grinding the mind, heightening senses well beyond human levels, beyond most bestial levels. Except for smell. Smells were intrusive. He didn't want them, and he didn't need them. He had people to smell for him.

And then, when Oliver had lain in that pool, still and cold and broken, when his heart had stopped and his mind was void and his soul had fled, Phoenix had left behind his old ashen body, and he had entered his nephew.

There had only been one oversight: allergies. Phoenix had never before known the itching, sneezing torture of hay fever, and so he hadn't thought to search his grandnephew for that particular flaw. And so far, fixing the allergic glitch while living inside the Oliver body had been beyond him. After two months spent surrounded by fields, he hated hay fever almost more than he hated the Smiths.

Phoenix rocked off of the bed and his young feet found the floor. He faced an antique dressing mirror with speckled flaws in the glass. A tall shirtless boy with pale skin and symmetrical veins on his arms stared back at him. It was strange, this Oliver self of his, being a boy. Having two arms again and a mind that tried to move in straight lines. He brushed back his thick black hair and stared into the dark owlish eyes he had molded for himself, eyes that could see bright color in the faintest moonlight. There was an extra membrane hidden beneath the lids, tucked away for when he needed it, a lens for use in water. He blinked it now and smiled at the ticklish sensation on his eyeballs. He had set Oliver's gills low on the neck, just above his shoulders, in case he might ever need to hide them beneath a collar. He had decided against the photosynthetic skin for himself. The added energy gleaned from light was interesting, but not so enticing that he wanted to live his life tinted green.

Phoenix contracted his chest and torso, his abs and shoulders and arms. His lean body knotted up and vibrated like a plucked string. His veins rippled like whips beneath his skin. Grinding his teeth, he forced the tightness even further, into pain, into agony. He felt the scream jump up inside his throat and he smiled it back down, relaxing. The young muscles were only just beginning to reach the potential Phoenix had planned for them. The old Phoenix had shed his white coat and become monstrous to achieve strength, but this young Phoenix, fast and slight and fresh, already had the strength of an ape in his grip.

And of course, he'd narrowed Oliver's nose a bit. He'd never liked that brat's nose.

Phoenix flipped the broken cane and caught it, smiling. It was good being young. It was something he could happily be forever. And he would have done just that, infusing Oliver with the transmortality of Gilgamesh or even that red pig Enkidu before taking the boy's body for his own. But the Smiths had just managed to muck things up before he had been able to. No matter. Transmortality could wait. He couldn't be killed while he held the tooth anyway. He would let his Oliver body grow another inch or two before he captured an appropriately strong transmortal and stole his life from him. But the Smiths' meddling must be stopped now. Their role in Phoenix's story needed a dark and painful close.

First, they had taken the tooth from Skelton, along with everything else Skelton had hidden from Phoenix in those final years. They'd killed Maxi and burned the arm off the Old Phoenix when Ashtown was as good as his. They'd taken back their father's body just two months ago. They'd helped destroy the Odyssean Cloak. They'd prevented Oliver's transmortality. They'd taken his oracle, and they'd torched his cigar factory. He'd liked that factory. He'd expected to do a great deal of work there. Instead . . .

Phoenix turned away from the mirror and jerked back the lacy curtains. He was looking down over the tiny, crumbling town of Plumm, Nebraska.

Phoenix tapped the black tooth on the glass. Then he dragged it, watching glass powder rain from the sharp groove he was carving. The Smiths were meddlesome, and for that, he was grateful. They sparked a little extra desire deep inside him. It kept things *personal.*

Let the transmortals tear cities down. Let Bellamy Cook kick every brick of Ashtown into the lake. Let Radu Bey gut the Avengel and feast on the Sages if he liked. Phoenix had promised himself the Smiths, and promises to himself were the only kind of promise he ever kept.

The Smiths were out there. Somewhere. Following Skelton's steps. Collecting tools and weapons and charms that the old thief had hidden from him.

Phoenix had no plans to kill them. No. The Smiths deserved to experience many, many slow transformations before death could even be discussed.

Oliver Laughlin's lips tightened in sudden amusement.

At some point, he would design a spouse for himself. He would use a girl as clay and mold her into the mother of a truly new race. Why not the Smith girl? The boy could be carved and hacked and modified into something barely breathing and barely human. But the girl, why not make her more than perfect? She could be his Eve.

The door to the bedroom opened and a tall redhead in jeans and a white tank top stepped inside. He was one of the Reborn, greenish beneath freckles. His gills were high, just beneath his ears, and the bone tattoos on his arms were striped with precise symmetrical veins. His blinking blue eyes had the odd horizontal pupils of a goat.

"I thought I should wake you, Father."

"A statement," Phoenix drawled, "that implies I was asleep."

"I'm sorry. You have been sleeping more. . . ."

"I've been growing. Boys of the age of the one I now inhabit tend to have growth spurts. Boys whom I have modified as extensively as this one can expect to have even more. Am I asleep now?"

"Father—"

"I am not asleep." Phoenix turned. He was at least eight inches shorter than the man, but the redhead retreated a step.

"Word from Ashtown," the man said. "That's all. I thought you'd like to know."

"Indeed," Phoenix said. He tucked the bamboo cane into his belt, slipped on a shirt, and began working on the buttons. "That's very thoughtful of you. And what might that word from Ashtown be, or are you saving it for later?"

"Six Cryptkeepers were with the monks like Bellamy said they would be. But not just them. Rupert Greeves was there. And the Smith boy. They smelled him."

Phoenix raised Oliver's eyebrows and waited. "And?"

"And six of ours went down."

"Six? Who cares about six? I can make six more of you between breakfast and brunch."

"My brothers killed five of the Cryptkeepers and all the monks they saw. Greeves made it out, but they're tracking him."

"I'm sure they are," said Phoenix.

"They have his plane, but he never went back to it."

Phoenix nodded. Then he walked out the door and down a hall and into a living room with black-and-white portraits on the walls beside framed cross-stitched lists of rules, and filthy furniture, and a moldy rug, and boxes of soap stacked in towers. The redhead followed him along the dust-free path on the hardwood floor where Phoenix always walked, past silver microphones hanging from the ceiling, and a pipe organ, and the skeletal remains of a woman in a high-necked satin dress slumped onto the keys, buried in a shallow grave of dust.

At the wide oak front door, Phoenix stepped into sandals and walked out of the big brick house and onto the only hill in Plumm, Nebraska. The brightness of the morning sun forced his eyes shut, to give his oversize pupils a chance to adjust. Then Phoenix moved down the steps and onto the broken sidewalk, which ran beside a street that was more weeds than pavement. He enjoyed taking crisp, swift steps and not having a limp, but longer legs would be nice. He looked forward to it.

"Father," the redhead said behind him. "One more thing. When they got to the chapel, Greeves was talking to the monks about Skelton's map."

Phoenix wheeled around, suddenly a snarling old man caged inside a boy. Decades of fury poured out of his new eyes, and his lip curled as he spoke. "One more thing? That is *the* thing, fool, that and the Smith boy. If your brothers return without a Smith or that map, I will gut them each myself." He jerked the bamboo cane out of his belt and thumped the silver knob against the redhead's chest. "How many of my sons are still there?"

"Seven."

Phoenix clicked the knob open and pressed the tooth against the tall man's neck, just beneath the gill. He wanted to slash. To kill. To end this fool like every other fool who dared frustrate him.

"Then go join them," he said. He reached out with his mind, trying to grope his way inside this oaf he had created, to make him feel fear, to make him shake with terror and awe, to motivate complete obedience.

The redhead blinked in confusion and began to sweat. "Father, I'm . . . dizzy."

Phoenix lowered the tooth. He glared at his Oliver hand. He sneered at his Oliver mind. He was the Phoenix. He was the New Man. But this flesh was not yet what it needed to be. It channeled less power than his broken-down old carcass had. He needed time to train his Oliver self, to cut spirit doors inside his new skull so he could once again flood out into the skulls of others. Oliver could not be a mere flesh costume, a boy possessed. Phoenix knew he must truly be Oliver, and every cell of Oliver must be his.

He had time. Plenty of it. Radu Bey and the transmortals were only getting started. But if Greeves had Skelton's map, was that how they had found the cigar factory? Skelton had known that place. He had known many places.

"William Skelton," Phoenix said.

The redhead blinked.

"Was he ever here? In Plumm?"

"I don't think so, Father."

Phoenix made his Oliver head nod. "Good. Are the women ready? And the vats?"

"Both ready. The potion is bottled and the vats were cleaned last night." The redhead looked nervous. His blue goat-pupiled eyes were unsteady. Tremendous peripheral vision in those sideways eyes, Phoenix knew, but truly grotesque on a man. He turned away. The Holy Soap warehouse was waiting for him.

"My name is Dr. Oliver Phoenix," he said aloud. He closed the knob over the tooth and pressed it against his lips. "Oliver. My name is Oliver. I am Dr. Oliver Phoenix."

He sniffed as he walked, stepping around the tall dry forests of weeds that owned the sidewalk cracks.

"Dr. Oliver," he said. His nose itched, and he rubbed it with the heel of his hand. His eyes began to stream. "Oliver Phoenix. I am Oliver Phoe—"

A sneeze erupted out of him. He snorted and spat and widened his eyes while he walked. This could be fixed. He would find a way. Three more sneezes took him to the bottom of the low hill. Main Street was a rustling pastureland of weeds. Shattered storefronts gaped darkness. The Founder's Park had been swallowed by scrub brush.

Oliver Laughlin, lean, gilled, and furious, whose portrait hung in the Galleria of Ashtown, sneezed his way across the street.

Two large coyotes watched the strange one from their barbershop cave. He smelled like the other mans that now wandered their town, but rot and death clouded around this young one with the snout fits. He smelled like traps, like poisons in meats, like one whose eyes would soon bleed and whose snarlings would drip foam.

He smelled like mate-killer, young-eater; he smelled like madness and rage.

Lips curling, hackles rising, the animals growled loathing and backed deeper into shadow.

The plane jostled through another pocket of turbulence, and the wheel shook in Antigone's hands. Again. Her copilot headset rattled down onto her cheeks. Again. She pushed it back up. Again. Then she looked at Diana Boone. Tan, freckled Diana in her aviators and ponytail and khaki safari shirt with the sleeves buttoned up and the neck open, showing a long scar just above her collarbone. Diana who liked Cyrus.

"I don't like this," Antigone said. She was sick of her chair and the fizzly air-conditioning; sick of her headset and the noise it couldn't keep out; exhausted from too little sleep and too little food and too much worry. She didn't want to be flying the plane. It added even more stress to the layers of things she had to fret about. And it made her tense. Her shoulders were knotted tight.

"You don't have to like it," Diana said again. She glanced over from the pilot's seat and then rechecked the instruments. The tilt-rotor plane hadn't pulled itself out of the mud by the lake easily. For a while, it had looked like it might not pull itself out at all. But Diana had gotten in the air eventually, though they were still behind Rupert's mandated schedule. Four and a half hours in the air—three of them Antigone's—and another hour until their fuel-up at some nowhere airstrip in Mexico.

"Do you like this?" Antigone asked.

Diana looked at her. "What if I do?"

"You don't," Antigone said.

Diana shrugged. "I like this more than I like ignoring orders from the Avengel of the O of B. I like this more than I like the idea of explaining my disregard of orders to that Avengel when he eventually shows up mad."

Antigone twisted in the copilot's seat, looking back into the cabin. Dan was reading some old book he'd found at the camp. Katie Smith was leaning on his shoulder, her eyes open but blinking slowly. She gave Antigone a smile. Pythia ignored her empty chair and sat on the floor in a nest of her own hair. Nolan and Horace were both asleep. The rest were still at Llewellyn's camp. The division between those who had stayed behind and those on the plane had been part of Rupert's instructions. Dennis Gilly, Gunner, and Llew were the only mortals still at the lake with the Captain, Arachne, and Gil.

Antigone turned back around.

"I don't know why we brought the hair along. If we wanted protection, we should have at least brought the Captain. And Arachne is basically our doctor and we left her with all the people who will never need one."

Diana smiled. "The split makes sense if you think about it. You would never want to leave Nolan and Gil together. Dan is the only one who even talks to Pythia, so why leave her behind? The Captain and Arachne both have a chance at controlling Gil if things go bad, so they should stay with him. And if Bellamy or Phoenix or both take a shot at the camp, I think it's in pretty good hands. Would you want to drop in on that gang?" Diana laughed. "Gilgamesh, John Smith, Arachne and her ten billion forest spiders, and Gunner, too. Did you see all those rifles in the weaponry shed?"

The plane bounced hard and Antigone's heart skipped. Her headset slipped down. She sputtered her lips and pushed it back up.

"You don't like leaving, either," Antigone muttered.

"Of course not," Diana said. "Because I'm selfish. Because right now Cyrus and Rupert are in the fight, or at least circling the enemy. Because I haven't talked to Jeb and I don't know how he's doing. Because I'm anxious and curious, and because my job is to sit still for hours and make sure you fly straight and don't crash."

Antigone looked down at the globe Skelton had left them, folded neatly and tucked into a leather pouch below the instruments. Rupert had given it back but took his with him. After refueling in Mexico, she would be pointing the plane south and very, very west, all the way to a ship on the globe marked:

# S.S. *FAT BETTY*

## LIBRARY, ARMORY, FUEL

### MS. LEMON CHAUNCEY, SAGE

"Have you ever heard of Lemon Chauncey?" Antigone asked.

"I have," Diana said. "But nothing good." She turned her aviators at Antigone and smiled. "What would you expect from a friend of old Billy Bones? She was tried twice at Ashtown and got off both times. When they wanted to charge her a third time, she filed a trek and skipped out of there. Basically the same thing Rupert did before Bellamy could raise a tribunal."

"Charged for what?" Antigone asked.

"I only know the dining hall stories," Diana said. "From other kids. Not exactly reliable. They said she murdered three Acolytes she was training. Some other kid said she was charged with sorcery—curses, charms, dark stuff. You'll have to ask her." She laughed. "I'm sure she remembers."

Antigone adjusted her headset, thinking. "That map might be outdated," she said.

Diana nodded.

"Skelton died more than a year ago."

"Yep," Diana said. "And he even made the map before that." She smirked.

"And we're trying to find a ship. Ships move. What

if this Lemon lady decided she wanted to go somewhere new? What if Skelton didn't know what he was talking about?"

"Well," said Diana, "then we will fly for a very long time and look at a whole lotta ocean, and then we will run out of fuel and fall into it." One side of her mouth twitched up. "Don't worry, it's not a bad way to go. Popular, even. Been used a lot in the O of B since people started strapping wings on."

"Well, thanks for that," Antigone said. "Good to know. But if we're going to die, I'd rather keep the cause of death unique. Think you could you arrange that?"

"You mean like being eaten by a dragon? Tigs, you could have done that months ago. Opportunity missed. I think right now it's falling out of the sky or nothing."

Antigone looked out her window at the herd of clouds marching around the world. It was like being back in Radu Bey's strange open room on the pillar, looking out at sky that wasn't really there. She exhaled slowly, remembering how close she had come to death that day. She could still smell his hot dragon breath. Her ribs remembered the crushing strength of his tail. If Arachne hadn't woven her the Angel Skin, Antigone would have died right there. For weeks after, she hadn't wanted to take off that shimmering spider silk. Now she kept it in her pocket, folded into a tiny square as light as a pack of tissues. Two spiders lived in its center, always ready to march down her bare spine, binding her into her charmed pearly skin. They were friendly, but the thought still made Antigone shiver.

"Tigs?" Diana asked. "Are you okay? I'm sorry, I shouldn't have said that about dragons. You don't need to keep that memory fresh."

Antigone shook her head. "No, it's fine. I think I'll skip the dragon option. Maybe a meteorite. Lightning. A tornado."

Diana held out her hand, palm up. She waited, eyes hidden behind her glasses, strong jaw set. Antigone took the older girl's hand.

Diana squeezed. "Old age," she said. "Let's die of old age. In times like this, with what lies ahead, old age is as unique as it gets. Maybe even impossible, but we should definitely give it a shot."

Antigone felt her throat begin to tighten, but she smiled, and she meant it.

"Deal," she said. "And that goes for everyone."

Cyrus leaned against a shelf loaded with battered copper pots, and metal sheets ringed with the baked footprints of ten thousand cookies, and saucepans big enough for him to sit in. These were the rejects, the spares, the back-ups for special days when Ashtown was overflowing with members from continental Estates and family holdings around the world. The last time they had been used was most likely when Bellamy Cook had been named Brendan, when Ashtown had been so full the Acolytes had been forced out of their rooms and into a tent city in the courtyard. Cyrus wondered how many people were still around and how many had retreated to homes in faraway places to wait things out.

The storage room was at least fifty feet long, but narrow and dim. The walls were gray stone, the floor was cement, the ceiling was cement. Four large bulbs spread light that was more moon than sun and added to the quiet underground coolness of the place. Cyrus and all the pots were on one side. The other side was packed tight with towers of plates and bowls, wooden boxes stenciled with pictures of forks and spoons and knives, and then more boxes, bigger boxes, overflowing with foam and labeled with stenciled letters: CRYSTAL, SILVER, CHINA. There were dozens of them, and some were the size of hay bales.

Cyrus looked toward the door at the end of the room, where Sterling had disappeared. Then he looked down at his hands and feet, sleeved in black, and he looked back at the shelf, with the door hidden behind it, where they had entered. He had memorized his step counts and turns along the way, exactly how Rupert had shown him. He could duck back in and disappear before Sterling came back. He could get into the lake and swim for the harbor and steal a boat and try to find the plane. But he knew he was too late. Men had been in the tunnels, hunting for him. Of course, he could steal another plane. He could even call it borrowing. But if he did, where would he go? There was no way he could fly back to the camp. And it wasn't like there was a telephone number he could call for help if he just flew somewhere random and then hid.

He flexed his gloved hands and listened to his knuckles pop. Why was he trusting Sterling? He wasn't. Not really. Would he really be surprised if Sterling stepped back into this room with Bellamy Cook himself, if all the cook really wanted was to pack Cyrus up and ship him to Phoenix?

Cyrus knew that he needed his own plan, and he needed it soon.

Down the room, the shelf in front of the hidden door suddenly rocked and wobbled. Pots clattered together.

Cyrus backed away. He watched the shelf slide out into the room as the door behind it opened wider. His breath had stopped. His heart pounded on his eardrums. Run? Hide?

Dropping into a crouch, Cyrus pulled his knife and slid quickly toward the wobbling shelf. Tucking his shoulder, he rolled past it and froze, pressing himself tight against a large wooden crate.

The shelf stopped wobbling. Cyrus was stone. A single pot clicked against another as it rocked itself still.

Cyrus leaned forward, just past the crate, peering between pots at the narrow slice of darkness where the door had been pushed open.

"I smell you, boy," a man whispered. Hidden beyond the door, he inhaled long and slow. "Your taste hangs sour in the air like your brother's and mother's." He sniffed again. "But there's something more rotten, something more like . . . your dead father."

The door exploded open, flinging the shelf of pots across the room into towers of plates, knocking Cyrus back off his feet. In the rain of copper and china, a large shape stepped into the room, his head just below the lights. He was darker than Cyrus, but the bone tattoos were still easily visible. His hair was long and straight, his brow was heavy, and the bridge of his nose was wide, lined with folds, and tinted blue.

Cyrus crab-crawled back through rolling pots and shards of porcelain, and then scrambled to his feet.

The man drew two long, thin knives from his belt, then dropped into a low crouch, like an ape sitting on his heels. He grinned, baring the huge fangs of a baboon.

"Dear Cyrus Smith," he growled. "Please come play. From, your friend Oliver."

# twelve

# GARLICKER

CYRUS ADJUSTED HIS GRIP on the knife and shifted into the simple fighting stance Nolan had taught him. He kept his left hand loose and low; his fingers wanted to twitch, but he kept them still—*never show fear*—knees bent, weight lightly shifting from toe to toe like a boxer, body leaning slightly forward—*always show attack*. The man with the baboon nose and teeth stepped forward and flipped both of his long knives, catching the handles in big fists, blades pointed down. His black hair swung forward against his cheeks.

"Father wants you alive," the ape-man said, inching forward. "But that doesn't mean I can't kill you first. He can raise the dead."

Cyrus knew the strikes would come as punches—jabs and hooks that would land sharp steel instead of knuckles. And the man's arms were extremely long. Cyrus's breath quickened. He stared straight into the man's dark eyes—*worry him, be unexpected*.

"What was your name?" Cyrus asked. "Before Phoenix turned you into a monkey?"

*There are no real knife fights among mortals,* Nolan had said. *Only knife murders. The only true defense is a kill. . . .*

The man paused, straightening slightly, showing his fangs.

Cyrus managed half a smile. "Bobby? Wayne? Curtis, maybe? I'm sure you're quick and you can climb," he said. "And I know you have some nice little goldfish gills. But did Phoenix tell you about the monkey face before you signed up?" Cyrus did a bad imitation of Phoenix's southern drawl. "'I tell you what, Curtis, how about I make you look like the ugliest ape on the planet?'" Cyrus watched the man tense. "And you said what? 'Yes, please, I want a baboon face'? Did he give you the butt, too?"

The strike came even faster than Cyrus had expected.

A left fist, trailing vicious steel, flashed at his face. Cyrus ducked forward, between the man's long arms. Knuckles grazed his forehead, the knife nicked his scalp, and he knew the right fist was already coming. Cyrus jerked toward the blow instead of away, and the man's heavy wrist slammed into his temple. The blade missed its mark.

Slipping with the force of the blow, Cyrus stabbed and felt his blade find gut. He twisted and tore, hearing the man snarl in pain, but he knew it was only deep enough to irritate.

Cyrus dropped straight to the floor. Steel whispered in his ear. He landed and tried to roll away, but he was too slow and he knew it.

A foot pinned Cyrus's knife hand to the floor. Strong fingers gripped his short hair and jerked his head back, exposing his throat.

*The end*, as Nolan always said.

"Romeo," the man said. "My name is Romeo."

"Bummer," said Cyrus.

The room hissed with light. A white fireball swirled between the shelves and shattered around Romeo's shoulders and head, flinging him off of Cyrus and into the pots.

Romeo lay on a bed of saucepans that were glowing orange with heat. Cyrus coughed and rose to his knees. He could hear fat sizzling, and the smell in the room was vile.

Sterling raised a fat-barreled gun to his shoulder and smiled. He was wearing a white apron and a hairnet over his beard. "For all their gills and ugliness, they're still not fireproof." He nodded at the door and his gold bells rang. "Come on, then. Your carriage awaits. There are more of 'em sniffin' around."

Sterling turned and swayed toward the door on his metal legs. He pulled it open and peered out.

Glancing back at the cooked body, Cyrus wiped his

knife on his leg, sheathed it, and hopped through shattered plates and scattered pots to where the poisoner cook was waiting.

Two large trolleys with canvas sides waited in a dim hall outside. One was empty and one was filled to the brim with dried garlic cloves. Sterling tapped the empty one with his gun.

"Hop in and get down. These boys might as well be hound dogs with the noses they've got. We don't need you trailing foot scents."

Cyrus climbed over the side and curled up at the bottom. The trolley smelled like apples. Sterling dropped the gun with its fat barrel and little gas chamber in on top of Cyrus. It was heavy. And hot. A moment later, Sterling tipped the garlic trolley up over Cyrus like the bed of a dump truck. Garlic cloves rained down.

Cyrus saw Ben Sterling's smiling face, and then he couldn't see anything but cloves and darkness. He had been completely buried.

The apple smell was gone.

Sterling began to whistle. The trolley wobbled and rolled. Wheel squeaks mixed with the small sound of Sterling's ringing bells.

Cyrus felt the trolley tilt as Sterling pushed him up a ramp. He heard the rattle of an old elevator cage door. A moment later, a motor hummed, gears and cables whined, and Cyrus felt himself rising.

Cyrus squirmed. He didn't trust Sterling. Not at all. So why was he buried in a garlic bin, completely blind to where Sterling was taking him? Yes, Sterling had torched Baboon Boy, but if there was a price on Cyrus's head, that might not mean anything. To the pirate cook, it was probably only a question of who would pay him more, the transmortals or Phoenix?

"Hey," Cyrus said. He tried to sit up. "Where are we going?"

A heavy hand plunged into the garlic and held Cyrus's head down.

"Hush, lad," Sterling said. "Don't speak, don't move."

The elevator jerked to a stop. Cyrus heard the doors rattle open, and suddenly, he was surrounded by familiar noises—knives chopping, oven doors banging, pots clanking, yelps and shouts and laughs and songs. Sterling was pushing him into the great kitchens of Ashtown.

Even through the garlic the smells reached him, and his stomach rolled over on a bed of nails. How long had it been since he'd eaten? As he counted back the hours, the hunger inside him grew with the injustice of it all. And the hunger made him realize how tired he was. And the weariness made his calf prick up for some aching attention—yes, there had been pellets in his leg. And his head ached from slamming onto the chapel floor, and all of it together made Cyrus try to focus on how much trouble he was in, relying on Big Ben Sterling, of all people, to keep him safe in Ashtown. Maybe he'd hit his head too hard, or maybe the adrenaline from the chapel and the tunnels and almost being killed by Romeo had pushed him too far to worry about himself. His worry was real; the fear inside him was loud, but it was aimed elsewhere.

What had happened to Rupert? Was he alive? Was he in the lake? Had he been taken? Was he on his way to face Phoenix already? Or was his body sprawled in blood in some hallway Cyrus hadn't taken? What would happen without Rupert?

Cyrus wormed his face over to the canvas side of the trolley. He could see lights and shapes as they passed. He traced the cloth with his fingertips and found a tiny frayed square. He picked at the loose threads with his fingernails until he had a little peephole just big enough for one garlicky eye.

Sterling talked as they walked, calling out orders as he marched the garlic trolley past the fire island of lit burners and sizzling pans being shaken by fresh-faced underlings who had been sent to the kitchens to work off back dues or were simply failed Acolytes who had been kept on as staff. They were usually members of dying or depleted O of B families who knew no life outside of the Estates. You progressed through the O of B and lived on its upper decks as a member, or you slipped belowdecks and remained forever a servant.

Cyrus had asked Dennis Gilly why he had stayed in

Ashtown as a porter when he could have gone out into the wider world and become any number of things. Dennis hadn't even understood the question. He didn't know what kind of things people became, or why they would want to. He served the O of B. Oh, and leaving meant his kids would never be eligible for membership. Not that their father, pulling in staff wages opening doors in a bowler hat, would have been able to afford to pay their Order dues anyway.

Sterling turned the trolley and pulled it backward through a swinging door. The kitchen sounds muted as the door thumped on its hinges. Cyrus peered through his peephole and saw that they were in the dining hall.

Not many people. Less than half of what Cyrus would expect from a breakfast crowd. Empty tables. Scattered chairs. Low voices. Plates with no owners.

"Ben!" someone whispered. "Where are the monks? The alarms . . . awful rumors . . . that liar Bellamy says it was a drill."

"Show some respect," a woman scolded. "He is your Brendan."

"The Abbot and his monks are all dead," Sterling said quietly. "Attacked and murdered in one of their own chapels this very morning."

Cyrus was shocked. He'd expected a laugh and a lie. The trolley wheeled on. What was Sterling doing?

Cyrus could hear the news rolling through the room like a growing wind. He heard whispers hissing, chairs scraping, silver banging down onto plates.

"Who?" a man shouted. "Ben, who would dare?"

More voices rose.

"The transmortals, that's who!" a man bellowed. "The *Ordo* Bleeding *Draconis*!"

"No! No!" a woman shouted. "It's that bloodthirsty Rupert Greeves!"

Cyrus jerked in anger. He almost climbed out of the garlic right there. He wanted to see that woman's face; he wanted to know who would believe such a thing.

"Phoenix!" The voice was younger, a girl's voice.

"Hush, child," an old man said. "Our Bellamy has an understanding with that animal."

"Probably Bellamy himself," someone nearby muttered. "The monks were no friends of his."

"He would never," a woman said.

"Members!" Sterling said, and the trolley suddenly stopped. Silence settled on the room slowly, quieting every clatter. "I'm only a simple cook. I can't say who did this or why."

"Rupert Greeves!" The voice was female and sharp. "He dropped Flint with a note in the courtyard, and then the monks are attacked? You want us to believe differently?"

"But," Sterling continued, "I did clap eyes on the body of one of the attackers. The monks put up some defense."

Cyrus swallowed, waiting. The room was still.

"It was a man," Sterling said. "A big man. And he had himself a pair of gills."

The word *Phoenix* raced around the room in whispers.

"I knew it would happen!" the sharp woman shouted. "Rupert always was a man of blood; now he's joined with Phoenix."

Cyrus jerked his knees and then his feet underneath him. He pushed himself up and stood, overflowing garlic all around him.

Sterling sighed.

"Who said that?" Cyrus shouted. Hundreds of eyes locked onto him. No one moved. Cyrus sputtered and spat out the paper from a garlic clove. He scanned the room. The friendly and familiar faces he remembered were all gone. Rupert had told him most of the best people in the Order had left Ashtown and were hunkered down on private estates. This was a crowd with no fondness for Smiths, a crowd more concerned with their own wealth and status and survival than with any ancient mission or duty that might exist for the O of B.

Cyrus was breathing hard, his jaw cramping with anger. Sterling's heavy fire gun dangled from Cyrus's right hand. He searched eyes and saw fear in every one of them. One woman thirty feet away stood behind her chair. She had red hair, pinched cheeks, and a pointed chin. Cyrus stared at her, and he watched her wither.

"I was with Rupert," Cyrus said. "He was meeting with the monks. The Irish Cryptkeepers were rejoining the O of B. But then Phoenix's Reborn attacked."

Standing in garlic up to his knees, Cyrus looked away from the woman, scanning the crowd for opponents, daring anyone to challenge him.

"No one hates Phoenix more than Rupert Greeves," he said. "No one is more willing to die for any one of you cowards than Rupert Greeves. If you had any courage, you would throw Bellamy Cook out and stand with Rupert. You would help him hunt down and end Phoenix."

"Who gave him the tooth?" the sharp woman asked. "Who was that, then?"

Cyrus turned back to her. He threw one leg over the side of the trolley to step out.

The woman now held a long revolver. "Traitor," she said.

The trolley tipped. Cyrus slipped. As he fell, the echoes of the gunshot mixed with screams. He landed on his back in a rolling river of garlic. His right hand tightened as his breath left him, and he felt the heavy gun kick in his hand.

A white fireball swirled straight up toward the ceiling, exploding through the beams and chandeliers like a firework.

People were running. Chairs were tumbling. Women were screaming. White flame fluttered down through the room like snow. Gasping, Cyrus looked up as Sterling leaned in over him, golden ear bells grazing his bristly cheeks.

"Change of plans, lad," Sterling hissed. A metal leg thumped into Cyrus's skull.

Antigone jerked awake. Diana was punching her in the shoulder.

"Let's go, Tigs!" Diana shouted over the sound of the engines. "I need your eyes!"

Antigone blinked, sat up, tucked her black hair behind her ears—it felt oily on her fingers; she needed to wash it soon—and looked around. After Mexico, she had crashed hard. While the old, flat-nosed tanker truck had pumped fuel into the plane, everyone had stretched their legs on the small gravel airstrip with the sun-bleached wind sock fluttering above a tiny trailer that sat tipping slightly on uneven ground. A thick, smiling woman had lugged a pot outside and served up mounds of rice and beans on paper plates. Antigone had wolfed two platefuls and the woman had patted her cheek happily, as pleased with Antigone's dark skin and dark hair as she was with her appetite.

Cold, dripping glass bottles of Coke had been pulled from a rattling ice swamp inside an old metal cooler, and Antigone had downed two of those as well, even though they were sweeter than any soda she had ever tasted—strong sweet, like molasses.

The woman had kissed her goodbye, and had prattled long strings of Spanish love and admiration at Katie Smith once she'd realized that Antigone was her daughter. Katie Smith had smiled and thanked her, but in rough Spanish. Her own mother tongue was similar in rhythm but much different.

With too little sleep and a very full belly, Antigone had been blinking slowly before the plane finished climbing after takeoff. She'd been asleep before they were above the ocean.

Antigone crossed her arms and shut her eyes again. It felt nice.

"Tigs!"

This time Diana punched her hard. When Antigone opened her eyes again, the older girl tapped her own headset and pointed. Antigone's headset had fallen down around her neck. She stretched, yawned, and put it on.

"I've decided I don't like flying," Antigone said, hearing her own voice crackle in her ears.

"Oh, really?" Diana smirked. "Just now you decided that? Do you not remember all of our little training sessions when you would practically start bawling when I made you take the stick?"

"I didn't *bawl*," Antigone said. "I didn't even cry. I was just really uncomfortable with the whole idea of falling out of the sky."

Diana banked the plane, and Antigone looked out her window and down at the pale ocean and an island shaped like a fingernail-thin crescent moon, its two points bent until they were almost touching. A long, rectangular boat was anchored between them.

"I should fill out a trainer review for you on this flight." Diana laughed. "You've been a real gem of a copilot, snoring over there. Your brother did the same thing when we flew to Llew's. But now you've got to help me out. This is the place, but we have to decide where to set this bird down."

"Some random island," Antigone said. "With some freaky outlawed Sage woman who was on a map of Skelton's. Just land anywhere. This'll be great."

"In a little less than an hour, we will just land anywhere, thank you," Diana said. "We'll be floating without fuel."

The plane turned long and hard and slow, dropping as it banked. Antigone glanced at Diana, and the older girl smiled back. She was pushing the plane into a stall.

They weren't flying anymore; they were falling. Antigone grabbed her armrests. The plane drifted slowly nose-down and accelerated. Diana laughed as they picked up speed.

"Just getting their attention," she said. "We don't want to surprise anyone." She flipped a switch and shifted into a radio call. "This is Billy Bones to Fat Betty, hang on to your hats down there. Over."

The plane leveled out low enough over the ocean that the island stuck up in profile against the sky. Black lava rock rose in cliffs edged with pockets of white sand. Palm trees clustered like frond fountains. Long, curling waves rolled in over an outer reef. The island's crescent harbor clearly held deep water because the ship in the center was a fat-bellied freighter, its deck almost as high as the cliffs.

Diana roared over the island and down the length of the ship. The deck was green and dotted with trees. Dark shapes—not human—loped across it.

Then the island was behind them and Diana banked the plane again.

"We have to land in the water," Antigone said. "The deck is big, but it's covered with grass and trees."

Diana shook her head. "This is Billy Bones to Fat Betty, approaching to land on your bow. Instruct if needed."

"Fat Betty to Billy Bones." The woman's voice was a surprise in Antigone's ear. "Mind the trees and come out with empty hands high or I'll cook you for supper. Over."

"Roger that," Diana said. "Over."

She flipped the switch back off and looked at Antigone. "Nice. Lemon Chauncey, cannibal."

This time Diana slowed and tilted her rotors up on her approach. Antigone pressed her forehead against the window and watched the ship beneath them. On the stern, there was a large greenhouse with sparkling glass and fan blades spinning in the roof. The ship's bridge was three stories high and crowned with bent and battered antennae, a railed steel deck, and a glassed-in cabin. The whole bridge was equal parts white paint and rust, but in front of it, the long bow looked like a botanical garden. There were hedges and paths and trees and grassy lawns dotted with what looked like grazing curly-horned sheep diligently ignoring the plane above them. And there were larger shapes, too, clinging to the shadows, very much paying attention to the plane.

Diana twisted the plane in the air, facing the rust-and-white bridge, and set it down slowly on a flat, grassy platform at the very tip of the bow. Then she killed the engines. Antigone stared at the sheep, at the shapes hiding in the trees, and then up at the bridge. She could see someone looking at them from behind a window. The person turned away and disappeared.

As the propellers whirled their way toward silent, Diana tugged off her headset.

"Well," she said, "this isn't going to get any more normal with waiting."

Antigone nodded and then twisted in her seat, looking back into the cabin. Horace was on his feet, stretching. He checked his pocket watch, tugged down his vest, and began to polish his spectacles. Dan was stretching his thick arms straight up and his legs out in front of him. Pythia was motionless by his feet and completely hidden in her nest of hair. Nolan was already opening the outer door. Katie Smith ruffled her short chopped hair, widened her eyes at her daughter, and groaned.

"I do not like to fly," she said. "I am made for the ground."

Antigone smiled. "Me too, Mom. It didn't have to be that rough, though. Diana was showing off."

Diana slid past her into the cabin. Nolan threw the door open and kicked down an unfolding metal flight of stairs. Warm sea air filled the plane.

"Okay," Diana said. "We're supposed to get out with our hands up and clearly empty. Everyone listening? Nolan? Hands empty and high." She turned around. "Antigone, I think you should go first. You were Skelton's Acolyte and are more of an outlaw than the rest of us. If this Lemon lady is touchy, blame Skelton. He gave you the map." Diana pressed back into Nolan, clearing a path for Antigone to the open door. Nolan yawned, then crossed his pale arms.

Antigone stood, jerky on her joints, and moved back into the cabin. Diana dug a piece of paper plate out of her pocket and handed it over.

"From Rupert," she said. "This is the stuff he wants us to focus on. But don't mention him. Go as long as possible without saying his name."

Antigone looked at the short list of unexplained topics.

Radu's Dragon

Brendan's Breath

Tooth Tools (Weapons)

CryptKeepers (Brother Boniface Brosnan)

She shoved it into her pocket.

"Go ahead," Diana said. "And keep your hands up."

"Dan?" Katie Smith said. "Shouldn't you go first? Should you be with her?"

Antigone smiled at her mother. If Cyrus had been going first, Antigone would have been saying the same thing. But Cyrus was far away. It was her turn to do the worrisome thing.

"She's good, Mom," Dan said. "We'll be right behind her."

Stepping out of the plane, Antigone was looking over the rusty rail of the ship at the crescent island of cliffs and palm trees. She could hear distant waves crashing and the harsh laziness of complaining gulls. The trees along the cliffs swirled slowly in the wind, dry-mopping the sky. With her hands up, she hopped off the wobbly plane stairs and onto the grass-covered platform. She turned.

The ship was intensely gardened. Long, level lawns were densely framed with fruit trees in front of the tall white-and-rust bridge. She saw oranges and bananas, grapefruit and what she assumed were mangoes. Short, woolly sheep grazed in the open, but her eyes had already settled on three huge shapes creeping out of the shadows beneath the trees. They leaned forward on their fists, and as they entered the sunlight, she saw that they were covered with deep orange fur, a livelier version of the ship's rust. Huge hairless faces as round as they were flat were pointed at her. Nostrils flared. Thick lips curled. Orangutans. Sixty or seventy feet away. Big ones. Bigger than gorillas. She wondered how quickly they could close that distance.

Antigone lowered her hands.

"Guys," she said. "I'm not sure—"

A rifle cracked and turf kicked up at Antigone's feet.

"Hands high!" The metallic voice blasted over the deck from a loudspeaker. Antigone threw her hands back up in the air. The orangutans were still moving slowly forward, heads cocking, nostrils sniffing.

"Okay!" Antigone shouted. "I'm sorry! The monkeys startled me!"

"Apes," the loudspeaker barked. "Not monkeys. State your name and your business. And speak up!"

"Antigone Smith!" She looked up at the windows in the bridge. "I'm here to talk to Lemon Chauncey. William Skelton was my Keeper. He sent me."

The ship was silent. Antigone's eyes settled on the orange ape in the center. He moved around a nibbling sheep and the animal barely even took notice.

"Skelton's been dead a year," the speaker said. "Why should I believe you?"

"He left a message," Antigone said. "A map. It took us a while to figure it out."

The loudspeaker laughed. "Intelligent, are you? Well, I expected you here a year ago. Don't feel too bad; Billy Bones overworked everything by half. I told him the Empire of Bones thing would be too much for ignorant moderns, but he couldn't see past your last name. 'They're Smiths, Lemon,' he said. 'Smiths will crack it quick.' It was almost too simple, he thought, but I knew you would be a pair of fools."

The apes were getting closer to the platform. And their eyes were never off of Antigone.

"Well, Billy," the speaker said, "who was right and who is dead? Should have stayed here with us. The *Fat Betty* has more than enough."

"Um," Antigone said. "Can I put my hands down yet? Please. The apes are getting awfully close."

"The apes!" The loudspeaker cackled. "You're worried about them? They're just big cozy carpets, though they do stink in the rain. Jerome! Cadders! Jane!" The three apes sat down instantly, slouching over like beanbags. The biggest one snorted and began to pick its nose.

Antigone sighed relief and lowered her hands. The rifle cracked again, and this time the grass kicked up between her feet.

Antigone shrieked and hopped away. "What are you doing? Are you nuts? I asked if I could put them down!"

"And I didn't answer." The speaker chuckled. "Keep 'em up until every one of you is out of the plane and showing me empty palms."

Antigone backed away from the plane, hands high, and nodded at Diana crouching inside the cabin.

Diana exited, followed by Nolan, Horace, Katie, and Dan. Katie walked to Antigone and gripped her daughter's elevated hand. Dan hopped back into the plane to get Pythia. A second later, he was back outside.

"I'm sorry!" he yelled. "She's not going to do it. I'll have to carry her." Without waiting for an answer, he dove back into the plane and emerged a moment later with his own hands held high and Pythia clinging to his back, her arms around his neck and her ropes of hair wound around his chest and shoulders.

The silence was awkward. Antigone squinted up at the bridge, then cleared her throat to make introductions.

"This is my mother, Katie Smith," she said.

"You mean Cataan, daughter of Cataan, of the Cataan people," the loudspeaker barked. "Taken from her jungle city and the halls of her mothers by Lawrence Smith and Rupert Greeves. I know who she is."

"Well, you're the first," Antigone said. "Beside her is Diana Boone." Diana smiled and waved slightly.

"And you bring Nikales, the transmortal thief. I know that pitiful pale face."

At the word *thief*, Nolan hardened his eyes and lowered his hands.

"Hands," Antigone said. "Nolan . . ."

"She knows bullets won't stop me," Nolan growled.

The loudspeaker barked on. "And Skelton's short fool of a lawyer, John Horace Lawney the Seventh. He would be better tossed over the rail. But the real prize is at the end. You, the dark big lad, you can't be Cyrus. What animal do you carry?"

With his hands up, Daniel rotated so Pythia's face was toward the bridge.

"I'm Daniel Smith!" he shouted. "I'm sorry, she's a little shy. . . ."

A single burning leaf fluttered up on the breeze toward the bridge. The orange apes watched it drop into ash.

The loudspeaker erupted with shrill feedback, and Antigone slapped her hands over her ears.

"Pythia?" the voice squealed. "*The* Pythia? However did—Hands down, hands down!" Something thumped loudly against the microphone. "Come in! Come in! Bring her in now!"

Antigone lowered her hands slowly. The huge apes hadn't budged from around the platform.

"Still want Antigone to go first?" Nolan asked Diana. He stepped forward and dropped three feet off the platform while the massive orangutans watched. He curled his upper lip and showed them his teeth. The apes inched backward. Then a whistle chirped from the loudspeaker and all three orange carpets turned and began moving slowly away toward the trees.

Nolan smiled up at the bridge, his old worn eyes shining in the sun. "Look who spooked the monkeys. Come on, then, let's go have words with Madame Crazy and be done with this."

Led by Nolan, the pack of seven wound their way through the gardens, past the diligently grazing sheep with the curly horns, and down a steel path between the trees. A wide metal door into the bridge was propped open. Stairs ran up, and stairs ran down. Nolan began to climb.

"Down." The voice popped out of a small round speaker in the wall just above their heads. Antigone, still holding her mother's hand, squeezed in surprise.

"Ow," Katie said, squeezing back. Her eyes were wide and worried. She ran her free hand over her short black hair. "Tigger, I don't like this. Why are we here? Why would Rupert send us to this place?"

*Tigger.* Cyrus would have gotten a slap for using the name, but as far as Antigone was concerned, her mother could call her Steve and she wouldn't care.

"We'll see," Antigone said. Nolan and Dan were already leading the way down the steel stairs, and Diana was right behind them.

Horace looked at Katie, then Antigone. He polished his half-moon glasses on the hem of his vest as he descended the wide stairs beside them. "I have to admit to the same worry myself," he said. "Lemon Chauncey was a notoriously unstable and completely paranoid Sage prosecuted for witchcraft and unlicensed research into several extremely disturbing subjects. Skelton trusted her only because of her intense paranoia and her loathing of all living people."

"Why did she trust Skelton?" Antigone asked.

Horace sighed. "You're in it. He got her safely out of Ashtown and asked her to look after this boat. As for the greenery, Skelton required that I purchase whatever she wanted to make herself comfortable on board for the long term. The full contents of several exotic nurseries were delivered to her in a Japanese port. I never expected to see what she had done with it all."

Antigone stopped, and her mother stopped beside her. Horace continued two more steps and then paused, looking back up.

"So this boat . . . ," she said.

"Is yours," Horace said. "Congratulations. You own a freighter turned floating greenhouse. And you and your brother are now landlords to one of the craziest women I had hoped to never see again."

"Tigs!" Dan's voice floated up the stairwell. "You're wanted."

One steel flight of stairs down, a metal hatch was open in the wall.

Dan—still carrying Pythia—and Nolan stood on either side while Diana leaned through, looking around.

"Out!" a speaker barked. "Send in the Smith girl and the oracle. The rest of you skunks continue down the stairs. There's food and drink one deck down."

"Bad idea," Diana said. "Tigs, I wouldn't. Look in there."

The steel room was a maze of loaded shelves. Grill-covered lights were mounted on the low ceiling just inches above the crowded upper shelves. From where Antigone was standing, she could see little armies of jars filled with . . . what? Jam? Maybe. But some looked more like the jars that had held organs in formaldehyde in her science classrooms at her old school. Beyond them, she could see books and bones and bugs pinned to boards and racks of knives and rolled-up rugs.

"What else am I supposed to do?" Antigone said.

"Go back to the plane?" Dan suggested.

Nolan yawned. "I'll go in and find her," he said quietly. "She can shoot me as much as she likes. I tie her to a chair, then the rest of you join us for a chat."

"I'll go in with you," Dan said.

"Sure," said Nolan. "Just as soon as you're bullet-proof."

Pythia dropped to the floor. A leaf fluttered up out of her hands and floated away down the next flight of stairs. FOOD flickered on it in fiery letters.

The little oracle straightened up beneath her mass of hair and stepped through the open hatch and into the maze.

Antigone hopped in after her. "I'll be fine. I'm her landlady."

# thirteen

# TENANTRESS

THE SHELVES WERE OVERCROWDED in the same way that a brick wall is overcrowded with bricks. The shelving itself was virtually irrelevant, like a stencil used for the construction of solid walls. At some point, Antigone thought, they had to have bent under the weight of it, but now the weight of it was actually holding the shelves up. It was hard to comprehend this much . . . stuff . . . being so intensely neat and organized.

At first, what Antigone had thought of as the jam section had turned out to be the jar section. Strawberry jam was packed in tight next to jars of seeds, jars of tiny screws, jars holding animal—she hoped—eyeballs, jars holding yellow Lego bricks, and jars holding shells, ash, and colored sand. But regardless of the contents, every jar was the exact same size, with the same company name on the glass, turned at the exact same angle. Then came the slightly larger jars. Then the coffee cans. Then a whole section just of books with blue spines, organized in ascending height. Then red books. Then green books. It didn't matter if they were children's titles that Antigone recognized or bizarre titles clearly taken from some O of B collection, they were all sorted by color and size.

Pythia didn't seem to mind, or even notice. She moved slowly but steadily, trailing her hair behind her as she rounded corners or made hard turns. She knew where she was going.

They passed a solid wall of rolled-up newspapers, next to a section of densely packed fish bones, stacked like tiny logs, beside shelves of peach pits.

And then came the skulls.

Huge flat-faced orangutan skulls in ascending size. Below them, skulls that looked far too human and began much too small.

Antigone hopped up closer to Pythia, her mouth suddenly dry. The oracle strolled between them without a glance, but her hair seemed to notice, to tense and slightly tighten.

"Stop."

Two metal chairs sat in the aisle. Antigone stopped and looked around until she spotted the nearest speaker in the low ceiling. Pythia did not stop. She walked between the chairs and took a right turn around a shelf loaded with stacks of loose paper, sorted in towers by matching width.

"Stop!"

Pythia still didn't stop. Antigone hesitated and then ran after her.

"No! No! NO!" the speakers screamed. But it wasn't just the speakers now. The human voice was not far away. Pythia was accelerating, rounding another corner, and then a quick switchback turn; she was shooting the maze without hesitation, like one who knew and had always known.

The speakers squealed. Something crashed to the ground, and Antigone followed Pythia through a small gap in a shelf loaded with little swaths of fur artificial enough to go on teddy bears at a carnival.

They stood together in a small square room, walled in completely with shelves. A little mattress was on the floor, tidily made up with a pillow and one sheet. Black-and-white security monitors were stacked in a square at the foot of the bed, and an old-fashioned microphone was perched on top. A perfectly symmetrical arrangement of orange blossoms sat in a tiny vase on the floor beside the bed. In the corner, where a wall of coffee mugs met a bank of file cabinets, beside a tipped-over chair and a dropped long-scoped rifle, a woman was curled up in a ball, shaking. Her hair was blond going on silver, she was wearing old but clean coveralls, and her face was hidden in her arms.

"Don't look at me," she said. "Please. Go away."

Pythia dropped a fiery leaf onto the floor in front of the woman's face.

NO

The woman flinched. She sat up and scooted toward her bed. But only for a second. Then she dove back and frantically swept at the ash on the floor, dumping it into her pocket as she did. Finally satisfied, she set her chair back up and dropped into a crouch behind it, peering over the top with muddy green eyes nested in creased, sun-darkened skin.

"What do you want?" she asked, eyes darting to Antigone. "Why are you here? Why now? Where is your brother? Why do you have the oracle? How did you find her? Will she answer my questions?"

"Ms. Chauncey," Antigone said, "Skelton told us to trust you. And we need your help. Everyone says you know a lot."

"Questions," the woman said. "Mine for yours. One for one. We take turns, and you stop looking at me, you little Cataan devil with your Cataan devil eyes. Your eyes are cold midnight. I don't like eyes. Turn your back."

Antigone began to turn, but Pythia grabbed her and shook her heavy head. Pythia sat down, crossing her legs. Her hair swept backward, away from her face and her body. It wound around and around itself, forming a single thick braid down the center of her back. Antigone's mouth opened in surprise. Pythia always hid herself. She was always in the shadowy shelter of her hair, and Antigone thought of her as slightly more wild than woman. But with her hair back, she wasn't a woman at all. She was a girl—young and pretty with smooth brown skin, wearing a simple brown dress with no sleeves that could have been made from a potato sack. But her eyes were what grabbed Antigone. Without the shadow of her hair, they were wide and bright and warm, like . . . like burning leaves. Antigone had seen them like that before, but not often.

Pythia was showing herself to Lemon, and waiting for Lemon to return the favor. After a moment, Antigone lowered herself to the floor beside the oracle and crossed her legs.

"Fine," Antigone said, digging the slip of paper from her pocket. "One for one. But we look at you as much as we want. And my eyes aren't cold. I'm not an Eskimo. My mom was from the jungle. Now, you ask first."

Lemon Chauncey sniffed and shifted her weight, rocking back and forth in her crouch behind the chair.

"What happened to Billy?" she asked. "Is he dead?"

Antigone sighed. Then she nodded. "He came to a motel where I lived with my brothers. Some of Phoenix's men tracked him down. They killed him and burned our motel down. I was with him when he died."

Antigone saw tears in the woman's eyes. They glanced at Pythia, waiting.

TRUTH

The leaf and its burning word floated over the chair and Lemon Chauncey snatched it out of the air, letting it turn to ash in her palm and then dumping it into her pocket.

Antigone glanced down at her list. She might as well start at the top. *Radu's Dragon.* She exhaled, trying not to grow tense. Feeling nervous was just silly. He wasn't here. He was far away. He couldn't touch her.

"Tell me about the dragon in Radu Bey's chest." Her voice was steady, and she was glad. "The one he turns into."

Lemon grabbed the back of the chair, and she rose slowly. She pushed her silver-blond hair back behind her ears with rough-skinned hands, revealing a thin nose that turned up at the end and wide smooth cheeks speckled slightly with age. Creases clustered around her eyes. She was striking—pretty, even—but lost.

"Radu," she whispered. "The last Dracul. He and his dragon are gone. Bound. Buried. The Captain, your Captain, the noble traitor Smith, he ended the dragon gin."

Antigone scrunched her face. She didn't want to get off track with the big bad news that Radu Bey was probably running amok in New York City that very minute.

"Just tell me about his dragon," Antigone said. She felt her throat tightening and she couldn't stop it. She could see the chains he had used as whips, and the writhing dragon under the skin of his chest—the dragon that had taken over his body. It had almost eaten her just months ago, and now it was loose. They were going to have to beat it somehow. Maybe this woman had a jar of magic bullets next to the paper clips. Something. Anything. There had to be a way. Or . . . or she didn't want to think about the other option. She cleared her throat.

"Everything you know, please," Antigone said. "Is there any way to kill it?"

Lemon's eyes locked on Antigone's, but she seemed unaware that she was being seen, unaware of everything.

"Everything I know of Radu begins with a scroll," Lemon said, "written by the great Bar Yochai, who claimed to have been visited by the shade of Enoch himself."

"I don't know who those people are," Antigone said. "If you could—"

But Lemon cut her off.

"Listen, daughter of Cataan, heiress of Skelton. Radu Dracul, son of Vlad the Second, brother to Vlad the Third, was a powerful blood sorcerer and necromancer, one who feared no darkness. He was sent to the courts of the sultan, and among the royal magicians, he heard whispers of the old powers bound by Solomon and long hidden away by Hebrew wise men and Persian magi. With his bloodthirst, Radu became Bey of the sultan's armies, and he conquered many lands, always searching the synagogues while his men pillaged cities. He did much evil among the rabbis but loosened no tongues. With the armies of the curved sword behind him, he spilled rivers of blood and threw down walls until he found what he sought, sealed in the caves of an island on an Ethiopian lake, hidden with relics of the lost temple, guarded by African knights, claiming long descent from Levi. Radu cut them down but took only one relic—the scroll of Bar Yochai, the tale of the dragon gin, sealed by Solomon and cast into the sea, sought only by fools and dark ones."

Lemon was silent, staring straight ahead. Lost in memory and story, she moved around her chair and sat, with her rough gardener's hands restless on her knees.

"I am a Sage. I read and I do not forget. I found the accounts written by Vlad the Fourth, nephew of the great Radu Bey. He numbered the gin that had been recovered from the sea. He told Bar Yochai's tale, how he had stolen the gin jars and lamps and stones from kings and emperors and warlocks, and where he had hidden them. He told how the Draculs quested alone for them, how they were found, and the name of the beast Radu claimed for himself. He told of the blood magic Radu performed, and the union made between man and dragon gin." Lemon looked straight into Antigone's eyes. "Radu's dragon is called Azazel. He feeds on pain. His wings and his flesh were taken and destroyed by Solomon. Azazel needs a body. Radu is that body. Radu needs power and undying life. Azazel is that life and, when fed, provides power beyond any man. The two became one. You have asked and I have answered. Now tell me how the oracle comes to be with you."

Antigone glanced over at Pythia, wrapped in her hair. The dark-skinned girl's eyes were shut and her mouth was slightly open. She looked like she was sleeping.

"Phoenix found her," Antigone said. "He wanted her to explain how he could use the Dragon's Tooth to raise the dead. We rescued her two months ago and we've been taking care of her ever since. My brother—Dan, not Cyrus—sees things. He dreams, and then he talks to Pythia about what they mean. He can hear her. The rest of us can't really. Not usually."

"She is the seventy-seventh girl to be made oracle," Lemon said. "If Phoenix found her, it is only because he stole the journals I tried to burn before my trial in Ash-town. Her birth name is Pascha."

Pythia's eyes opened, not in surprise but with a smile. Lemon continued.

"When the seventy-sixth oracle died, Pascha was taken from a Byzantine convent and placed in Apollo's cave, where there is a stone seat at the end of a carved hallway full of arches. There, time folds and is not; there, all can be seen, and mortal minds bend and break. I sat in that seat for two breaths, and those breaths took half a year. And since then, my mind forgets nothing even when I want to. There are cracks in me, deep cracks in my mind and soul, and when Skelton found me, I was ready to fly apart. Pascha, the seventy-seventh oracle, sat in time's throne for centuries."

Pythia smiled. Slowly, she spoke, her voice dry and cracking. "Pascha sat," she said. "For breaths."

"Right," Antigone said. "Okay. I think it's my turn, and I'm still at the top of my list. I need to know more about Azazel, this dragon. How do we kill him?"

"Kill him?" Lemon asked. "Kill? He cannot be killed. But why? Radu Bey is bound and Buried, and his body is Azazel's cage."

Antigone puffed her cheeks and then exhaled out the side of her mouth. "I wish," she said. "I really, really do."

"I don't understand," Lemon said. She looked at Pythia. Her voice was edged and breathy. "Radu is bound."

LOOSED floated in the air, and Lemon stared at it, stunned.

"No," she said, shaking her head. "No, no, no. You don't understand what will happen. What is *already happening*. How long has it been?"

"Two months," Antigone said. "About."

Lemon jumped to her feet. She whistled through the gap in her teeth and both hands went up to her blond silver hair. "That's why you've come now. Where is he?"

"New York."

Lemon scrambled past Antigone, hopped over Pythia,

and disappeared into her maze, shouting back over the shelves as she went.

"Pain. Azazel wants pain! It makes him strong, and his strength becomes Radu Bey's. He gathers broken people first—killers, victims, it doesn't matter—and feeds on their deep hurt while they drift into a sort of nirvana and eventually die."

A crash came from somewhere behind Antigone. She heard Lemon's quick footsteps. A book slapped onto the floor. More running and a drawer opened. Finally, Lemon hopped back into the little room and dropped into her chair, out of breath. She handed Antigone an old leather notebook stamped with the black medieval ship that was the symbol of the O of B's Ashtown Estate.

Antigone opened it. It was full of sepia-brown photos and sharp, leaning cursive. The photos were of what looked like an archaeological dig. Men and women in safari helmets stood in trenches with shovels and brooms. Human skeletons were embedded in the trench walls like bricks—all facedown and densely stacked.

"Persia," Lemon said. "That book is from the 1850s. O of B Explorers found three different compounds apparently constructed entirely of people—big compounds, tens of thousands of people. Idiots that they were, they identified them as temples in some sort of death cult. They didn't know their history."

Lemon snatched the notebook away, dropped it onto

the floor with a thump, and handed Antigone a South American newspaper. The cover showed black-and-white photos of what looked like a ruined mountain temple, half eaten by jungle. The walls and arches and roofs were all bone.

"This one was a temple," Lemon said. "But only after the fact. Priests mortared the bones together and rebuilt with the scattered bones. The Chilean government found it and shut down the rituals in the 1960s." She tugged away the newspaper and handed over a stack of large glossy photos. "I took these," she said. "Thirty years ago. The first half were taken in an underground compound beneath modern Istanbul. You can only get in through the sewers. Long ago, it was the secret harem of Radu Bey. The bodies are all women. Some are now encased in limestone."

Antigone flipped through the photos, staring down long, arched tunnels of bones. Stairs of bones. Columns of bones holding high ceilings of bones. It was hard to understand, to process how many lives had been spent, how much pain there must have been.

"More than one hundred thousand women down there," Lemon said. "Just there. The rest of the photos I took in Romania. A hidden mountain valley, the last stronghold of the Draculs. That is where Captain John Smith took the heads of the Vlads. Humans subconsciously avoid it. Even the wolves will not go near it. For three days, I camped there, listening to the voices, to the whispered pain left unconsumed, and I watched the blue wisps of souls burn cold at midnight."

Antigone dropped the photos and shut her eyes. She felt like she was going to throw up. Cold sweat beaded on her forehead and she forced herself to breathe slowly.

Radu and his dragon had been beaten before. There had to be a way.

Antigone opened her eyes and was suddenly oppressed by the shelves. She stood up.

"I have to go," she said. "We'll finish this later. I need air."

"Already?" Lemon asked. "Did Phoenix loose Radu? Are they in alliance?"

Antigone shook her head. She thought about Cyrus, about the Captain's final chain in his underwater tomb. Cyrus had cut through it with the Dracul sword, not knowing that he was also loosing the last chain that bound Radu Bey and the power of Azazel.

"Come downstairs," Antigone said. "With the others. I need to ask you more."

Lemon shook her head. "No more. I won't come. The cracks inside me . . . Pythia can help mend them. She knows."

"You will come," said Antigone. "I own this ship."

Cyrus woke up on his left side, with his arms tied behind his back. He was on the floor in a small room, with very little light. There was a wooden chair tucked into a desk with an upper cabinet busy with at least a dozen tiny drawers. A small saggy-backed leather sofa lurked against the wall, and pictures of the sea were hanging on cracked plaster.

The door. Wooden. Shut. Old brass knob. Big keyhole. Light streamed under it and onto the itchy wool rug where Cyrus was lying. Low voices crept through the wood from the other side.

Cyrus rocked onto his face. Spitting dust and tiny gravel and woolly hairs, he leaned hard onto his cheek and managed to walk his knees up underneath himself. Pushing off the floor with his face, he rocked up slowly and fell back down, twisting to cushion the blow with his already whining shoulder.

He wriggled closer to the sofa and tried again. This time he barely got his face up onto the sour-smelling leather. From there, he swayed to vertical—knees first and then feet.

Blood drained from his head and he wobbled briefly. His skull was filing complaints with his brain, cataloging injuries, but none of that mattered. He was probably concussed after his jump from the chapel balcony and the crack he took on the floor. And then Sterling with that kick. Metal legs weren't fair for kicking.

Why had he listened to Sterling? Why hadn't he knifed him or at least kicked *him* in the head?

Cyrus thought about his ride in the garlic. Where had they been going before he had jumped out? Nope. That didn't matter. What mattered was where he was right now, and how he was going to stop being there as soon as possible.

Yep. He was concussed. Images of his old school fluttered into his head. He'd had a teacher once who had been concussed. Cyrus had spilled hydrochloric acid on the tile floor just a little bit on purpose. They'd cleaned it up, but afterward, the tile had been eaten so smooth it was slicker than ice.

Mr. Finney. With glasses and allergies and a mustache he was always stroking. Mr. Finney had stepped. Mr. Finney had slipped. Mr. Finney had smacked his head on the chalkboard tray.

Cyrus laughed out loud and sat down on the leather couch. Knots dug into his wrists behind his back.

*Shhh.* Cyrus eyed the door. The voices kept on voicing. No footsteps. He wasn't in trouble about Mr. Finney. No one was coming. But he was still tied up. He needed his keys.

"Patricia?" he whispered. "Keys, please." He shook his head quickly, jangling the key ring around his neck. "Unlock my knots."

Wait. Knots. The keys would be better for the door, not the knots. And only if the door was locked.

Grunting, Cyrus stood back up, blinked, moseyed to the door, and turned around. He gripped the door with fat tingly fingertips. He was willing to bet that his fingers were purple right now. They had been purple before. He'd seen them.

The knob wriggled slightly, but not far. He'd been right. Keys were needed. But something for his knots first.

Crossing to the desk, he bent over the chair and pinched his lips around the first little brass drawer pull that he could reach. He wobbled it open. It held an old map, folded up tight, sitting beneath a tiny ball of water no bigger than a robin's egg. Weird. Next drawer. It held a pipe and a pouch of tobacco, and a little metal tool that looked like a knife but wasn't. Drawer number three.

Knife! Bone handle. Folding blade. And also matches. Lots of little boxes full of wooden sticks with little red heads ready to explode.

Cyrus stared at the knife. Something was wrong. He was still tied up.

Slowly, Cyrus realized that he should get his hands in front of his body. He needed his purple fingers to pick up the knife and unfold the blade.

Cyrus crouched, lowering his tied hands below his rear end. Pausing, balancing, he raised his right foot to step back between his arms. And he fell. Not quietly. The room shook with his impact. He wheezed and coughed and shut his eyes, begging his skull to shut up. Things were bad all over. Not just in his head.

Hands, he remembered. Front.

He was on his back. Wriggling his hands under his rear, he hunched forward, forcing them as low as possible, pushing until his wrists and shoulders screamed. He lifted his knees and pulled his feet in. They were on top of his hands. With a jerk, Cyrus's hands slid up his smooth black leggings and popped over his knees. They were in front now, and easy to study.

Yep. They were purple. A thin rope was digging deep into both wrists. Cyrus climbed back onto his feet. He grabbed the knife and unfolded the blade. It was old, but the steel had been scraped sharp enough so many times that the edge no longer held a smooth curve. Cyrus shoved the handle between his teeth and raised his wrists to the blade. It hurt his teeth, but the rope popped loose. He tugged it off, put it in the drawer with the map, and closed it. Then he took two matchboxes, put them in his pocket, and stared at his hands.

Blood was moving through them again. And they were burning. Nerves were on fire. Cyrus poked his fingers with the knife tip. It hurt.

Behind him, the door opened.

Cyrus jumped, blinking, as Sterling stepped into the tiny room, bells tinkling. Behind him, in another little room, there was a small television with a curved, bulging screen.

"Sorry about Mr. Finney," Cyrus said. "I didn't know."

Sterling's eyes narrowed. "Who?" he asked.

Cyrus raised the knife. "I think I should stab you. And kick you in the head."

Sterling smiled and sighed. "I wouldn't blame you, lad. But we've got bigger troubles and that won't help them. You made a splash I couldn't hide. I quieted that eel of a woman who shot at you, told her that Bellamy already knew I had you and that I was acting on his orders. Of course, with another little exodus rush going on thanks to the gillies, Bellamy had his mind elsewhere and his hands full. But if he didn't know you were in Ashtown before, he does now, and he and his questioner will be waiting for old Ben. This place won't hold you much longer."

Cyrus looked through the door at the television. He hadn't seen one in a very long time. He wished for cartoons, but it was showing a man with a red tie talking about people missing in New York City. Then a cop started talking, laughing, offering explanations.

Sterling stepped in the way. "Cyrus? Are you okay? How are you feeling?"

Honestly? Cyrus thought he might throw up. And he was a little dizzy. And his skull was sulking. But there was something else, too. Something wrong.

"I was tied up," Cyrus said. "On the floor. You aren't friendly."

"Listen to me, Cyrus," Sterling said quietly. He took another step forward. Cyrus pointed the knife at him and swallowed hard. "You're in some rooms of mine," Sterling continued. "Not my official rooms. These are different. Not normal. Secret rooms with secret ways." He winked. "You understand me, lad?" He cleared his throat and raised his voice, changing his tone suddenly. "We want to help you. We want to talk about Skelton and Rupert and your little band. Where should we go to talk? Where would Rupert hide?"

"Biscuits and lies," Cyrus said. "And barbecue sauce. Liar."

Sterling put a heavy hand on Cyrus's forehead, his face concerned.

"You're not well, lad," he said loudly. He crouched slightly, until he was eye to eye with Cyrus. His bitter breath scratched its way out through his black beard. "Trust old Ben," he whispered. "Right now I'm your only friend."

Two shapes stepped together into the doorway behind the cook. Dizzy, Cyrus clenched his teeth and jabbed the knife at the cook's big belly. Sterling caught his wrist, quickly stripped the knife away, flipped the blade shut, and tucked it into Cyrus's shirt pocket.

"What is the point of this?" The sharp woman from the dining hall. "He should be with Bellamy already."

Sterling lowered Cyrus onto the couch. Two rough fingertips closed Cyrus's eyelids, but they couldn't close his ears.

"I've told you already," Sterling said. "Take the boy to Bellamy now, and we lose any chips we have in this game. We learn what we can about Skelton's holdings and hidings, then hand him over. Not before."

"Bellamy will just bundle him off to Phoenix," a man said. "Phoenix will get anything he wants out of him."

"Exactly why we learn what we can first," said Sterling. He was walking away.

"We don't have much time," the woman said. "We should be peeling back his fingernails. You've kept him napping all day. Bellamy will want to know what we've been doing."

"And I'll be the one to answer him," Sterling said. "Not you. This is my game, and you two will back me or back out. Run to Bellamy now if you like. Wag your wee tongues." The door shut behind him. The voices continued, muffled.

Cyrus opened his eyes. Sweat ran down his temple and into his hair. Above him, the ceiling was spinning slowly. He rolled off the couch onto his knees. His stomach was in his throat.

Sterling had left him the knife. Sterling was keeping

him from Bellamy. He was playing his game both ways. Gagging, Cyrus crawled to the desk. He pulled open a large drawer near the floor, hoping for a gun.

Papers. He threw up all over them. His head cleared, but only a little. He stared down at the vile, swampy mixture and then shut the drawer quickly.

Secret rooms. Sterling had said so. Secret rooms, secret ways.

Cyrus tugged at the next drawer up. It was locked. Wiping cold sweat from his forehead onto the back of his arm, he slid silver Patricia off his neck and dropped her key ring into his still-gloved palm. Empty silver sheath. Little pearl gripped in a claw. Small smooth nub of petrified wood. And Skelton's Solomon Keys: one gold, one silver. The silver one changed in his hand as he slid it into the keyhole. He turned it and heard the lock click. He pulled the drawer open. As he did, the entire desk—and the wall attached to it—swung toward him on invisible whispering gears. Cyrus crawled backward out of its way.

The opening was taller than he was, revealing only a narrow vertical shaft. Cyrus inched toward it. Dark, damp stone walls stained black with soot ran straight up and straight down. How far, Cyrus couldn't tell. He pried Patricia off of his wrist, where she had latched back on to him, and held her out over the shaft, feeling her tighten with the cool moving air.

Silver light up and silver light down revealed no end to the shaft. But the walls were grimed with old soot, and that meant that somewhere down there, Cyrus could expect a fireplace. And somewhere up there—he twisted his head, blinking away sweat and queasiness—he could expect a rooftop.

Cyrus's stomach turned over again. He shut his eyes and leaned his head against the wall, breathing slowly. Skelton had also used an old chimney as part of his route into Ashtown, but he'd left a ladder inside. There was no ladder here, and even if there had been, Sterling wouldn't have done well on it with his thin metal legs.

Cyrus opened his eyes. Leaning into the cool opening, he reached up into the darkness as far as he could. He didn't want to go down. He wanted fresh autumn air, exhaled by forests and cooled by the lake.

His hand found a leather strap. No, a leather stirrup. It slipped off a hook and dropped down in front of him, bouncing at the end of a thin rope. He tugged at it. Nothing. He reached back up and felt around all the stone walls. A lever. A gear. A crank. A coiled spring. More rope on a spool.

Something rattled in the room behind him.

Cyrus backed away from the opening. He stepped around the open wall and looked at the desk. One little drawer was shaking. Silver light oozed from its cracks.

Cyrus pulled the drawer open. The tiny ball of water

quivered and shook and bounced inside, as bright as the moon. Quick Water. He picked it up and dropped it into his shirt pocket along with the knife.

Outside the door, voices grew louder. He could hear Sterling, and the cook sounded angry.

Cyrus jumped back to his stone chute. There wasn't time for more investigation. He grabbed the cable and fished his right foot firmly into the stirrup. Then he reached for the lever.

The door opened and a new man stepped into the room.

"Bellamy wants him now!" he said. "I'll see—"

The man froze.

"You later," Cyrus said, and he jerked the lever.

Gears clicked. The wall swung shut even as the man drew his gun and jumped forward. Cyrus expected to drop. Instead, he shot straight up, rattling against the walls, clipping his shoulders and elbows and toes against grimy stone.

Patricia glowed around his wrist, showing Cyrus his speed as they rocketed up and up and up. They slowed. They stopped. They swung in place. A large spool of cable hummed quietly above Cyrus's head.

Cyrus banged around and twisted, searching for an opening in the walls. His leg was shaking, and he was dizzy enough already without the spinning. He needed to be sick and lie down and shut his eyes.

Shouts echoed from beneath him. He saw light flooding the shaft at least sixty feet below him. Cyrus groaned. He shouldn't have looked down. He threw up again, dampening his toes. A gun fired and a ricocheting bullet whined past him. He heard spattering liquid and loud squealing disgust.

Patricia popped her tail into her mouth and turned off the light. With his free leg, Cyrus kicked at the walls. He swung and slammed his body against them.

Heavy stone groaned and slid. A door opened, but there was very little light behind it, a whisper and nothing more. Cyrus lunged into a cool room and slammed onto a wooden floor. Sitting up, he reached back into the shaft and grabbed the swinging leather stirrup. Then he dug out the bone-handled knife and flipped open the blade. The rope was tough. He hacked at it, sawed at it, and the blade ate away millimeters with every bite.

The big spool began to spin and the rope went slack. More than three-quarters of the way through, he tossed the stirrup back into the shaft and slammed the stone door. Whoever tried it next would be going down, not up.

He put the knife in his hip pocket, wiped the sweat off his face, and looked around. Dim shapes sharpened as he stared. The place looked like an abandoned museum. Which meant he was in one of the Explorer collections—a collection he had never seen before.

Cyrus stood slowly. The walls were high. The room

was long. Stone columns rose to black wrought-iron beams that looked like something from an old-fashioned train station. The beams held up a roof of paned glass. The glass was coated with dust, but Cyrus could see the night sky and the glow of the moon on a row of monstrous winged statues. He was about as high as anyone could get in Ashtown. As high as the Brendan's chambers, even. And it was night.

Sterling had knocked him out during breakfast. For the first time, Cyrus wondered if he hadn't just been concussed. Sterling could have slipped him anything when he was unconscious. He licked the insides of his cheeks, fishing for strange tastes. Nothing but stomach acid. He spat on the floor and began to move forward between the pillars, and the moon swung slowly into view above him as he walked.

Considering the other collections Cyrus had explored, this place felt relatively empty. There were chests—all locked. There were bookshelves—locked behind wire cage doors. There were three solid blocks of stone covered with long, winding Latin sentences scrawled in white chalk. There was a cat carcass dried into a flat furry Frisbee on the wooden floor. And owl pellets. And bat bones.

Dust kicked up around Cyrus's feet as he walked. No one had been in this place for a long time—and definitely no one official. Any normal member would have wanted the floor swept, or at least the dead animals picked up.

A maid or porter would have been summoned with a broom immediately. Cyrus began to wonder if there had been another secret way out of Sterling's room, because this place was on the way to nowhere. He looked back at the solid stone wall where he had arrived. There was no sign of a door.

Cyrus turned between two pillars and into an aisle of statues. Three steps in, he stopped. Something was very wrong with the stone shapes. He backed up and assessed them all. Their feet were in solid blocks, but the rest was all too realistic, too exactly human in proportion. Artists modify and stylize. These were exact copies, and they were copies of people in pain. Those nearest him were dressed like the Explorers he'd seen in the oldest photos—men and women of the nineteenth century. But they had gashes in their necks or arms hacked halfway off or legs slit wide open or bullet holes in their chests. Farther down the row, the clothing grew older. All the way at the end, the statues were in monks' robes, and he could see stone weapons—arrows, knives, swords, darts—sticking out of them.

Cyrus roused Patricia and crouched with her light to examine the base of the nearest statue—a man with a big mustache wearing long trousers and a vest with a watch chain. His sleeves were rolled up, his fingers were spread wide and tensed, and there were four holes in his chest.

A paper card had been attached to the stone block that encased his feet.

**John Henry Holiday, Explorer, given to forbidden stone sleep November 8, 1887, confiscated with others from the Cult of the Reaper, December 21, 1921**

Cyrus reached out slowly and touched the man's leg. The stone was warm, even through his glove. Jerking his hand away, he hopped up and backed quickly out of the aisle. He didn't want to read the other names. They would be warm, too. They would all be warm, waiting for someone with the power to wake them and keep them alive.

Heart pounding, head throbbing, Cyrus turned and jogged past wide aisles without even trying to identify what they held. Sterling knew where he was, so he probably knew other ways into this place. And if he did, the others might as well.

At the end of an aisle, he saw a door. Holding up Patricia, Cyrus turned and ran toward it, passing racks of bladed weapons and dolls stuffed with straw and short fat jars shaped like people. The door was large, wooden with iron hinges, and without a knob or ring or keyhole to be seen. But leaning against the wall beside it, there was a tall ladder leading up to planks that stretched between the vaulted iron trusses in the ceiling. The planks made a walkway to a jagged hole in the glass.

Cyrus let Patricia disappear around his wrist, and then he grabbed on to the ladder and scrambled up as quickly as his dizzy head allowed. He crawled across the bowing planks, ignoring every pop and sigh beneath him. He stood, eyed the iron frame where the glass had been broken out, and then jumped, catching the metal with the grip on his gloved hands. With one kick in the air, he pulled himself up and through, onto the steep glass roof, and into a breeze off the lake.

"Move, and I'll snap your bloody head off," an Irish voice said behind him.

Cyrus jerked in surprise and almost fell. Slapping his palms down onto the glass, he looked back over his shoulder.

Niffy stepped out from the shadow of a huge winged statue. His robe was shredded and his face was a mess of blood and burns. Half of his Mohawk was missing.

Cyrus rolled over onto his back and then sat up, showing the monk his empty hands.

"It's me," Cyrus said. "Where's Rupert?"

"Rupert?" Niffy snorted. "Rupert's dead, mate. The Abbot's dead. My brothers are dead. We're all dead. Now tell me why your pocket's glowing."

## ❧ fourteen ❧

# EXECUTION

DENNIS GILLY BUTTONED UP THE WOODEN TOGGLES on
the heavy wool sweater Llewellyn had given him, and he
crossed his arms to watch Arachne work. A cold wind
was blowing down over the mountains, swaying the trees
all through the camp and ruffling the lake. Dark clouds
were piling up on the horizon, erasing the twilight. The
splitting in Dennis's head had calmed, and his mental
confusion was settling back down to its normal levels.
The dizziness was completely gone, but he couldn't remember anything at all from the last week. He remembered
breakfast. And he remembered following Arachne in her
long slow circle through the woods around the camp. He
had listened to her quiet hum, and he had looked away
quickly every time her arctic eyes had turned their icy
light onto him. He had watched the spiders work.

Millions of them were still working, nesting the camp
inside walls of silk.

Arachne was kneeling beside a flat stone on the bank
above the water. Her spider bag was empty beside her.

Dennis looked up at the shivering lake, once again wishing he could be sailing. Even in a cold storm, he was happier riding the wind across the water than anywhere else. Sailing was the one thing he was really good at.

Gunner dragged a wooden chair down the bank and dropped it beside Dennis. The tall Texan was wearing a dark wool coat with its collar pulled up beneath his ears and a cap pulled down all the way to his blond hooded brows. He lowered himself into the chair and stretched his long legs out in front of him.

"So . . . ," Gunner drawled. "Are we worried yet?"

Dennis looked at him. "What do you mean?"

Gunner ignored Dennis. "Excuse me? Ma'am? Little Miss Muffet?"

Arachne glanced back at him. "I'll try again soon."

"Try what?" Dennis asked.

"Rupert and Cyrus should have been back, what, four hours ago at the latest?" Gunner drew a long silver revolver from inside his coat, along with a small oil rag and rod. He began to polish the barrel. "Now here we are, with nowhere to go and nothing to go there in."

Arachne's lips tightened. She looked up at the sky.

"The Captain and Gil are fixing to brawl back at the lodge," Gunner added. "Old Llew is playing referee. That strike you as wise?"

"Do you think you could stop them?" Arachne asked. "Time must pass. And they are both men who must always challenge and test themselves and others." She looked straight at Gunner, her voice hardening. "As are you. But you trust that metal in your hand and the slyness in your skull. You are testing me now. Am I afraid? Am I worried? Will I hurry away to stop the scuffling of two boys? For they *are* both boys—bearded, brawny, bombastic boys."

Gunner smiled. "I woulda thought boyhood ended somewhere in the first century of life."

"It never ends," Arachne said. "Not for you. Not for them."

Through the woods, Dennis heard a shout followed by an enormous crash.

"And they're off," Gunner said. "May the best boy win."

Arachne didn't answer. She opened her pale hands and set a small wobbling ball of silver water on the stone in front of her.

"Quick Water," Dennis said. "Is that Cyrus's?"

"One-third," Arachne answered. "Rupert carries part, and Antigone carries part. Thus far, I have glimpsed only cloth." She parted the water with her fingers and then parted it again. Spiders swarmed up out of the grass to stretch the quivering spheres into threads. While Dennis watched, they began to weave two separate watery sheets.

"What do you mean, dead?" Cyrus asked. "Where? Who killed him?"

Niffy walked on the iron frames between the panes of glass, and then stood on the peak of the glass roof. His blistered face was chopped with little shadows.

"Dead," Niffy said. "Struck down. Soul and flesh parted. Breath gone from the body, lifeblood drained. Dead. We fought our way out of the chapel, and then we hunted gilled men through the bowels of Ashtown. Three escaped us. We parted, he to find you, and I to seek living brothers. We were to meet here and strike together. He swore that he would be here, or he would be dead."

Cyrus shook his head.

Niffy stared at him. "It was an Avengel's oath, no common promise. Sworn over the bodies of the fallen."

"He's not dead," Cyrus said. "Not unless you saw it happen. Not unless you were there and he said, 'I'm dead,' and you felt his pulse stop. I won't believe it."

Niffy shrugged. "Then he has broken his oath and matters not. Better men than he fell today, and I will not let my anger cool to grief. We strike now, together. Or I strike alone."

Cyrus's shirt pocket shook again. He dug his hand in and pulled out the tiny ball of water. While he watched, it sparkled silver and flattened in his palm. Niffy turned, staring while it fluttered up into a small, sharp silver liquid version of Arachne's head.

"Cyrus." The small water voice was barely a whisper. "Where are you? Where's Rupert?"

"Ashtown." Cyrus lowered his own voice to a whisper without thinking. "I don't know where Rupe is. We lost the plane. Phoenix's Reborn attacked."

Niffy crouched behind Cyrus and leaned in over his shoulder.

"Always love a chat," Niffy said. "But we're off to the battlefield. Must run, love. The bloody murdering Brendan himself is waiting to die, so if you don't mind . . ." He slapped the water flat on Cyrus's palm and stood back up.

Cyrus jumped to his feet and faced the monk. "What do you think you're doing?"

"Avenging my brothers," Niffy said. "And your Keeper, like as not. You can ring your spider-witch back later. Right now I need a guide. Which rooftop road do we take?"

Cyrus turned toward the lake and the row of statues, which overlooked the grass slopes that ran down to the airfield and the water. The statues were distant enough to be only dark shadows against the background of the moonlit lake, but he'd been in the Brendan's rooms before. He knew those statues were just outside his walls of glass.

"That way?" Niffy asked. "Grand. Are you armed?"

"You can't just go murder the Brendan," Cyrus said.

"Why not?" Niffy spat. "His allies murdered my brothers and my father." His voice wavered. "As my heart beats, I am at war with him, his vile people, and any who do not stand against him. The whole O of B can go burn with him if it likes."

Churning air beat against Cyrus's face and a shape shot above him in the darkness. Niffy drew a black-bladed sword out of the neck of his robe and dropped into a crouch. Another shape shot past, and the two huge dragonflies wheeled together in front of the moon and darted back toward Cyrus and the monk.

A sharp whistle pulled them away just as Niffy began his swing. The dragonflies darted around and through the statues and away toward the shape of a man jogging stiffly along a roof peak, hopping on and over chimneys.

"Ha!" Cyrus said. His whole body loosened, and he exhaled relief. Worry that he had denied and ignored washed away. The shape was Rupert's—broad shoulders, narrow hips, thick neck, easy gait—and it was running toward them, dropping cautiously onto the glass roof.

"Niffy!" Rupert hissed as he approached. "Now or never, Irish. They know we're up here. We move now!"

"Rupe!" Cyrus jogged toward him. "Man, I'm glad you're alive."

Rupert froze. "Cyrus?" He looked straight up at the stars. "Good God above, I'm a lucky fool." Looking back down, he smacked Cyrus's head. "You had me more than worried. I can't ever have that conversation with your mum, do you understand me? Never. Nor with Antigone. Outlive me, lad. Please."

Cyrus smiled in the dark, but Rupert didn't look good. His right sleeve was burned away, and his arm looked gruesome all the way up to his bare shoulder. He'd strapped on a gun belt with one revolver, and the long handle of an Asian sword peeked up over his shoulder.

"We have to get out of here," Cyrus said. "And you have to do something with Niffy. He wants to murder the Brendan."

"Not murder," Rupert said. "Execute." He pointed at the monk waiting behind Cyrus. "We spoke about this."

Niffy nodded. "You're here now, mate. Let's get on with it."

"Wait . . . ," Cyrus said. "What?"

"The blood is mine to shed," Rupert said. "The life is mine to judge. Stay as close as you can and do as I say. If I say nothing, do nothing. Hang back. No questions."

Rupert moved quickly away between the statues and onto another rooftop. Niffy and Cyrus stayed with him, jogging along the peak. Rupert dropped between roof peaks into a wide valley densely packed with leaves. A tiny aircraft, the size and shape of a hang glider, was tied to a chimney. It had a single black cloth wing, anchored to sandbags at both tips, and a small aluminum frame below the center, holding one seat perched between what looked like a pair of small silver rockets.

Cyrus stopped beside a small chimney steam-spewing stink.

"I heard Sterling was back," Rupert said. "He always had his rat routes in and out of this place. But I never thought his routes had wings."

Cyrus followed Rupert past the little flier, scrambled up a low wall, and stopped beside his Keeper. Niffy jumped up beside him.

From where they stood, the roof sloped gently down all the way to the final edge, where the last row of statues posed in silence and glass skylights glowed yellow. Invisible in the distance, Cyrus could hear the dragonflies patrolling the rooftops for Rupert.

The three of them crouched low and moved with quick soft steps down to the first glowing skylights. Rupert held up his hand, and Niffy and Cyrus hung back.

Slowly, Rupert leaned out over the glass, looking down. A moment later, he moved to the next one. And the next. Finally, when he'd nearly reached the extreme corner of the building, he signaled for Cyrus and Niffy to come.

Beside his Keeper, Cyrus looked down into the corner of a room where he had once faced the old Brendan, brother to Phoenix. Oliver had been there, too. Oliver, who had wanted friendship but refused to give any in return. Oliver, who had gotten much worse than he deserved. The unhealed slash on Cyrus's forearm tingled slightly beneath its tight bandage. It rarely felt like anything anymore, and Arachne's small bandage was smoother and more perfect than his real skin. Cyrus pushed away the memory. He could be sad for Oliver later.

The same couch and chairs were in the Brendan's rooms, beside the windows. And Bellamy Cook was pacing behind them. He was gnawing at his fingernails while he moved, spitting out the shards, talking, demanding, shouting, waving his arms, and tossing questions at three men who stood almost completely out of view. Cyrus couldn't quite see, but he was willing to bet that all three men had gills on their necks. There were other men and women, too—the room was full.

Snatches of Bellamy's shouting made it through the glass and were carried away on the lake breeze.

*done everything . . . ratbag thinks he can do . . . now . . . lies . . . promised me . . . dingoes listening . . . dragons toss . . . ending you . . . all ending*

Bellamy flipped over the couch and tore into a string of Australian curses. The three men didn't move.

Rupert drew his revolver and handed it to Cyrus.

"You fly past and put a few in the windows," Rupert whispered. "Niffy, help him launch the flier. Then we drop through the ceiling for hand-to-hand."

Niffy nodded approval.

Cyrus shook his head. "Fly that little thing? Then what?"

Rupert dug a small string-cinched pouch out of his pocket. "Your Quick Water," he said. "Fly as far as you have fuel, then hunker down until Di and your sis can get back for you."

"Rupe," Cyrus said, taking the pouch. "I'm not leaving you here. No more splitting up."

Rupert grabbed the back of Cyrus's neck and leaned forward, staring into Cyrus's eyes.

"Here I stand," Rupert said quietly. "Here I fall. If my vows mean anything, they mean this. I cannot turn away from the blood spilled today."

He smacked Cyrus's aching head and pushed him away.

"Quickly," he said. "The roof won't be ours for long."

Cyrus backed up the slope with the heavy revolver hanging in his hand. Niffy jogged past him. This didn't make sense. Tonight, Rupert Greeves fought for Ashtown. Without allies. The Captain should be here. And Nolan. And Arachne and Diana and Dan and the Livingstones and the Boones and Gunner and Dennis. They weren't much, but they were something. They were loyal and tough and . . . they were friends. Polygoners.

Rupert looked back and waved Cyrus away. He and a

thick Irish monk—no friend at all—were going into their Alamo.

While he, Cyrus, flew away.

And suddenly, Cyrus understood. He understood all the frustration he'd seen in his Keeper in the last weeks, the struggle, the anger. Rupert Greeves, Blood Avenger of the Order of Brendan, Ashtown Estate, was a protector, a guard, a shepherd. Rupert Greeves was no general. Generals spend men. Generals expect sacrifice from those who stand with them. Shepherds do not lead their sheep into battle with wolves. They fight alone.

Rupert had never settled on a path because down every path, he saw the deaths of others, the deaths of those he had sworn to die protecting—the deaths of his sheep. Some of his people had died anyway, and now Rupert saw a path open in front of him—a path that led to only one death. The only life Rupert Greeves would gladly spend was his own. Only that path offered him peace of soul.

Cyrus felt his heart thumping, and the hot anger began in his legs, tingling where the wind touched him. Heat roared up into his chest and pounded in his aching head. Niffy hissed at him, waiting. Rupert's eyes were on Cyrus's, quiet and peaceful and patient. And Cyrus knew something else.

Rupert would never wait for Niffy. As soon as they

were out of sight, they would hear glass shatter behind them as Rupert went in alone.

Cyrus's eyes were hot. It couldn't be this way. They had to fight Phoenix and Radu Bey and they had to win. People would die. But people were surely dying now, wherever Phoenix was. People would be dying wherever Radu Bey might have gone, unchained.

He, Cyrus Smith, had to be what Rupert Greeves could never be—a general.

*He shall be called the Desolation. . . .*

The memory of Dan's words sent tight chills up Cyrus's neck.

*You, Cyrus. It's about you. . . .*

And it started now.

*when he casts his shadow . . .*

Rupert was no longer the general.

*. . . even the dragon shall shrink in fear.*

Rupert Greeves was just one warrior, a warrior Cyrus had to be willing to risk. And if he died . . . Hot, wet anger rolled down Cyrus's cheeks. He turned away and began to run.

Niffy dropped off the low wall, and Cyrus dropped down after him. The monk was already untying the sandbag anchors.

"Niffy." Cyrus grabbed the monk's robe. "Rupe is going in alone. Get back there now." He was surprised at how calm his own voice sounded.

The monk blinked surprise. Glass shattered.

"Go!" Cyrus said.

Niffy exploded back up the low wall and disappeared. Another life risked. Cyrus shoved the revolver into his belt and flipped open Sterling's bone-handled knife. The ropes that held down the flier were weatherworn and parted quickly. Sandbags slumped to the ground, and black wingtips bounced up.

He could hear shouting. Gunfire.

The ropes were all cut and he gave the little flier a shove. It was heavier than it looked, and hidden down between two roof peaks. There was no way he was pushing it up. But he couldn't imagine that Sterling would be able to, either.

Cyrus ducked under the black cloth wing and slid into the little wire cage, spread his legs around the controls, and dropped into the seat. He didn't bother with the over-the-shoulder buckle.

There were two small pedals for steering, but there was no tail or rudder anywhere on the little thing, so he had no idea how they would work. The two fat silver tubes below him on either side had to be engines. The stick between his knees was obviously the throttle, and it had a trigger and thumb button—both under hinged plastic covers. Were there guns on this thing? He didn't have time to care. He had to start it. Now. Groping around beneath his seat, he felt a tank—fuel—

and then he found a small box. It opened. Yes. A key and switch.

A dragonfly shot past him. And another. He looked back toward the statues where he had first climbed up, and he saw shapes moving—a line of men, spread out, sweeping the rooftops.

Cyrus turned the key and flipped the switch.

The two silver tubes beneath him woke up, first with a yawn, then with a tornado roar. Leaves whirled up behind him and the little flier shook and bounced.

Cyrus glanced back at the rooftop hunters. He saw guns flash and arms wave, but he couldn't hear the shots or the shouts.

He held his breath, clenched his teeth, and threw the throttle.

The flier jumped forward into the pitched roof, banged its nose, tipped back, and then launched up and off the peak.

Cyrus should have buckled in. He was in the air, the flier was dropping, nose down, and he was still floating up. Grabbing at the stick, he managed to level it out and slammed back down into his seat.

The lake breeze pushed him inland. He tried to bank back toward the water. His pedals changed the direction of the engine thrust beneath him. The stick between his legs either bent in or released the cloth wingtips. Used together, he turned so sharply that he simply stopped in the air, and then began to drop into a glide.

Cyrus liked this thing. A lot. He accelerated past the buildings and wheeled back around over the airstrip.

The little Quick Water shook in his shirt pocket. The bigger lump was wobbling against his hip.

"Not now, Arachne!" Cyrus yelled, and the quivering stopped. He brought the flier in level with the Brendan's glowing windows and slowed until he was practically hanging in the air.

The room was a shambles. Rupert and Niffy were both on their feet, pressing against at least twelve men armed with guns and long knives. Rupert used only a sword and it was a blur in his hand. He was moving faster than Cyrus had ever seen, a man exploding forward into the teeth of Death. Niffy stayed beside him as they moved over a carpet of bodies. Niffy spun the black-bladed sword in one hand, and his dead master's patrik flashed like golden fire in the other.

Thirty feet from the windows, Cyrus banked slightly and floated down the length of the Brendan's rooms. Bellamy Cook stood alone, behind the brawl, watching with a gun in hand. Cyrus tugged his own revolver out of his belt. He handled the stick with his left hand and aimed the big gun with his right. He cocked the hammer and tried to steady the long barrel as he drifted and bounced on the breeze. He fired.

Three times, the gun jumped in his hand. Three windows shattered, and Bellamy dropped into a crouch. Cyrus had missed badly. He throttled the flier up over the statues and banked away in a loop to come back around.

A dragonfly banked with him, and Cyrus looked down at the line of rooftop hunters. They had reached the statues at the edge of the building. A few were already dropping into the Brendan's rooms. Reinforcements. The others were raising guns toward Cyrus. He had to work faster.

As Cyrus dropped level with the roof, he slipped his finger under the trigger cover on the stick, hoping for something.

Twin white fireballs corkscrewed down into the stat-ues, splattering light and heat among the stone winged creatures that guarded Ashtown. The statues flashed with angelic fire, and shadows tumbled and rolled and fell into the darkness below. Cyrus nosed forward and then banked along the roofline, firing the whole way, close enough to feel the heat on his face and to nick an angel with his own wing.

Bright images seared onto his eyes—the angry faces of weather-stained stone warriors suddenly enlightened, and living men tossed by living flame.

Engines humming, wings bouncing, Cyrus accelerated away into cool darkness. Behind him, the roof smoked like a volcano. Below him, men now fired up from the ground. White fire that was not his own swirled up past his wings and died slowly in flocks of small suns high above him, brightening the night. Bullets puckered the cloth of his wings.

Ignoring the ground fire, Cyrus filled his lungs with lake-cooled autumn air and wheeled his little flier back around.

Rupert was fighting from his knees. Niffy was down, back up, and down again. The men they were facing now were hardly men at all. They were the Reborn.

Cyrus pointed his nose toward the first windows he had shot out and throttled forward. He sent two fireballs toward the Brendan's rooms and then switched from the trigger on the stick to the thumb button on top.

With a sound like air cannons, twin pipes beneath the flier's wings spat a pair of small spiraling football shapes through the windows and into the white billowing furnace. His flier was right behind them. Too close.

Boom.

Glass shrapnel hit Cyrus in a cloud of sound. Cloth wings tore. The roof above the Brendan's rooms bulged up and then collapsed. Two of the great angelic statues teetered and fell. Cyrus ducked, covering his eyes, kneeing the throttle forward.

He felt the first jerk of impact. He heard metal scream and glass shatter. He felt himself spinning and floating out of his plane, passing through heat.

Cyrus Smith skipped across the top of a long table, caught his leg in a chandelier, tore it from the ceiling, and then slammed into a wall.

Behind him, a huge stone wing and arm punched down through the ceiling, smashed the table, and disappeared into the floor, caving it in all around it. Cyrus slid down the sloping floor and thumped into the statue. He blinked, expecting unconsciousness. Expecting painlessness. Darkness. Sleep. But it didn't come. He could hear slow crackling fire, beams groaning beneath enormous weight, water spattering somewhere, and one man coughing.

"Rupe?" Cyrus sat up, grabbing his ribs. His right hand still clutched the revolver, his fingers locked as tight as the claws of a corpse. He managed to hook his gun hand over the top of a huge stone angel feather and fought his way to his feet.

"Rupe!"

The coughing stopped.

Cyrus climbed up onto the angel and crawled forward through the smoking, sparking rubble, pushing through dangling ceiling plaster.

"Rupe!" Cyrus shouted. "Answer me now!"

"I told you," Rupert said quietly. "Fly away."

Cyrus's eyes were streaming rivers down his cheeks, trying to flush away smoke and rubble and grit. "You said to fly as far as it would take me." Cyrus slid beneath a beam, and dust avalanched down onto the back of his neck. "Well, it took me this far."

He could see into the front room now. His little flier was a crumpled mess, the frame bent, the wings torn into tattered black flags. Wind from the lake blew in through blasted-out windows, stirring smoke and pushing low flames across carpets and couches and up the walls. On the few unbroken windows, the flames reflected, warped and flickering like surreal liquid. A shape too quick to be friendly darted across one of the reflections.

Cyrus froze, blinking, holding his breath. Slowly, he pulled back the hammer on the revolver. The reflection moved again.

A man stepped out from behind a slab of rubble that had once been ceiling but now rose from the floor like a wall. His hair was gone, and his bone tattoos were hidden beneath his charred skin. Blood oozed down his neck from a fluttering gill. He held a long knife.

Another man, shorter and broader but also one of Phoenix's Reborn, moved into view beside them. His face was a swollen, bloody mess. His jaw was broken and dangling open, but it didn't seem to bother him. None of Phoenix's sons were much affected by pain.

Cyrus heard Rupert groan. He rose slowly into view

from behind a toppled sofa, his sword raised. He was covered in dust, ghost-pale everywhere but where his wounds mixed the dust into bloody mud.

"Weapons down," Rupert said. "You are trespassers, enemies of the Order of Brendan, murderers of our brothers. Your lives are forfeit."

"You are the grandest nutter of them all, aren't you, mate?" The accented voice belonged to Bellamy Cook, Brendan of the O of B. The rough, lean Australian limped into view from behind a pile of ceiling and wall. Cyrus had last seen him up close when Bellamy had put his name forward in the great Galleria for the office of Brendan, when he had stared at Cyrus and made his position clear on all things related to Smiths. That night, the transmortals had rioted. The next day, Cyrus and Antigone had gone on the run. They hadn't stopped.

Bellamy's sharp eyes were hooded in his creased and grimy face. Gray stubble lined his jaw, and his mud hair, usually slicked straight back, now fell loose around his temples. His clothes were blackened, but Cyrus could see no wounds.

Rupert inhaled slowly and coughed dust. "Bellamy Cook, Keeper from the Barrier Estate, who stands in this Order for Brendan, I name you murderer, traitor, oath breaker, and disciple of darkness. Stand before the Sages to receive your judgment, or stand before me and die."

Bellamy laughed and then winced, grabbing at his

side. "Rupert Greeves, still playing at lords and ladies and dead saints and oaths. So serious, mate. What is darkness? Tell me. Do you even know?"

Rupert hobbled forward a step. "You brought in these flesh-mixed monsters to kill your own people."

"The Breed," Bellamy said. "That's what we call them. The Reborn. And shortly I shall proudly join them." He smiled. "To be honest, mate, I hurt. I know you do, too, but look at them—barbecued and battered and they'll still have your throat out in half a tick. And the eyes, the endurance, the speed, the strength. I look forward to it. Of course, you should know that I didn't bring them in to kill my people. I brought them in to kill those bloody Cryptkeepers. Couldn't have them creeping about, or worse, joining up and ousting me. Not that it matters now."

Both of the Reborn moved to flank Bellamy. The shorter, thicker man with the shattered jaw passed in front of what remained of Cyrus's flier. From beneath one crumpled wing, the golden patrik struck, snapping up and stretching long like a crackling electric wire. The stocky man snatched its head out of the air faster than Cyrus could even see. The snake wrapped around him and the two dropped to the floor.

For a moment, Bellamy watched the struggle; then he cocked his head and looked beneath the flier. He nodded at the tall man with the bleeding gill.

"Finish the fat monk."

Cyrus fired, and this time his hands were steady. The tall gillie crumpled, and the window behind him shattered—another gaping hole, open to the night.

Rupert scrambled forward, grabbed the flier, and lifted. Niffy exploded up, blade raised, and Bellamy limped quickly backward. The monk ended the thick, gilled man on the floor and the golden snake shrank quickly, coiling up around Niffy's arm in a bright spiral.

Cyrus turned his gun toward the Brendan of his Order.

Rupert marched after Bellamy, stepping over bodies. Cyrus stood up and followed, tripping and slipping as he did but keeping the gun on the chest of his target.

"'Not that it matters now'?" Rupert asked. "What does that mean? Why doesn't it matter now?"

"You can't kill me," Bellamy said. "You can't break your vows."

"To kill you," Rupert said, and his voice was ice, "is to keep my vows. You have declared war on your own people and mine. You conspired with their enemies. Blood runs in Ashtown and the knife is in your hand. If the Avengel of this Order cannot pluck your worthless life, then who can?"

"You're not Avengel," Bellamy said. He backed into a buckled wall beside an open window and stopped. "There are no more Avengels."

Rupert raised his sword to the man's chest. "I always knew you were a thief and a pirate, but I would not have called you a coward until now. Answer my question."

"Radu Bey is coming," Bellamy said. "Phoenix has not forgotten to watch the dragons. They are coming. They will open the Burials and topple the walls and till the earth and take every life they find. The O of B will be no more. Ashtown will be destroyed."

"On your knees," Rupert said. "Now."

Bellamy smiled grimly and shook his head. "You're done, mate. All of you. Radu bloody Bey is coming, and he has what he needs to unleash every last sleeping hell beneath this place. And once he's done his violence, Phoenix will make him kneel and fit him with a collar. He and his dragons will serve the Breed before this war ends and the world is remade." The Brendan's teeth were bright in his soot-stained face, and he leered at Cyrus. "Pity I won't be here to watch the brutes peel open a Smith and feed. Boy, you won't even be wearing skin when the sun rises."

Niffy stepped closer to Rupert. "Take the villain's head or I will."

"Where is Phoenix?" Rupert asked. "Were you going to meet him?"

"I am no traitor," Bellamy said calmly. He looked into Rupert's eyes. "And I am no coward. My work in this flesh is now done, and I have been faithful to my father, Phoenix." He pulled up his sleeve, displaying his bare forearm. Ghosts of removed bone tattoos were still visible on his sun-rough skin. "I shall be Reborn," he spat. "You will be offal on the floor of a dragon's cage."

Bellamy Cook lunged forward onto Rupert's sword. Gritting his teeth, snarling, he threw his arms around Rupert's head and drove him back toward the open window. For a moment, the two men teetered, and Rupert let go of the sword and punched his open hand into Bellamy's face, ducking out of the wild embrace and falling to his knees.

A sword hilt on his chest, a blade out his back, Bellamy Cook slipped away, grabbed at Rupert, grabbed at wind, and fell, swallowed by the night.

Low flames crackled, dying in the rubble. Wind swirled dust around Cyrus's feet. He blinked at the open window, at the airstrip, at the harbor, at the moonlit lake. Then he turned to Rupert. The big man crouched slowly and buried his face in his hands. He looked like he was going to be ill.

Niffy stepped up beside Rupert, and Cyrus saw tears on the brawling monk's face. The monk closed his eyes, and then he spoke, his voice lilting with Irish sadness.

"You who knit me in my mother's womb and plucked me into life, be not far from me. I am alone in grief's broad sea. My brothers are fallen, their laughter is stopped, their voices are silenced. The pride of Monaster is poured out like water, and my courage is no more than ash. Be not far from me. Dogs encircle me. Bulls surround me. Troubles melt my heart like wax. Evil has drained a draught of greatness, and I am left alone, to be pierced and broken."

Rupert rose. "Be not far from me," he answered. "Walk with me through the shadow of the grave. Tear this curtain of darkness. Make your face to shine upon our fallen, and give them peace."

The silence was long. The men were still. Cyrus listened to the wind and mixed it with his own slow breathing.

The Avengel had slain the Brendan.

The dragons were coming.

## ✤ fifteen ✤

# SCURRY

MERCY RIOS OPENED HER EYES. She was on her back. The ceiling above her was made of people. Women. All of them. Limp arms hung down with perfectly finished nails and glittering rings and delicate watches. Above the arms, the ceiling was a carpet of dangling hair.

Mercy remembered the rooftop and the man with the dragon chest and the chains. She remembered throwing the package she had come to deliver, and she remembered the tall woman with the fish-scale tattoos and the scarred cheeks touching her—and in that touch, she had felt seas crashing and cliffs crumbling and crows calling and men shouting and bones breaking and cold wind daggers on her face and the hot sticky warmth of blood pooling in her mouth. And then it had all vanished and she had vanished with it.

Now . . . this room of bodies. The place was hot and moist with breathing, sweet with perfume, sour with the stink of the living, edged with the reek of the dying.

A heavy black crow hopped onto Mercy's chest and

she jerked, trying to smack at it with both hands. But her arms were only made of smoke, and the smoke broke around the bird.

The crow's feathers barely rustled. It cocked a twitching yellow eye at her and gave her nose a quick peck.

Mercy ghosted up and through the bird. Sliding off a table-high platform and onto her feet, she looked down at her smoky arms and hands, and then faced the bird. She had to be dreaming.

Or she was dead.

The crow wasn't looking at her. At least not the smoky her that had jumped away.

The flesh-and-bone body of Mercedes Rios lay on a table of stacked gray-haired men, all facedown. She was still in her letter-carrier uniform, but the sleeves had been cut off of her shirt and her shorts had been cut much shorter; below the knee before, now they only came down to her midthigh.

Scales had been traced in sea-green ink onto her bare arms and legs, two small cuts had been made just below her cheekbones, and black feathers had been woven into her black hair. Crow feathers.

The crow pecked the body's cheek. Smoky Mercy felt it.

"Hey!" She billowed forward, waving her arms and stomping, trying to shoo the crow away.

The bird looked at her, and then went back to pecking.

"No!" Mercy screamed. "No, no, no, you stupid bird!"

She smoked up onto her own body and puffed a barrage of fists and knees and elbows all around the crow. Then she sat on the bird. At least, she sat all around it. Finally, the crow cawed and hopped backward. She sat on it again. It flapped and hopped back. Mercy sat on it all the way down to her body's feet. The crow dropped to the floor. Mercy stayed on her own legs, staring at what was between her feet.

The little package she had delivered had been neatly opened. Inside, there were four small compartments. In one, fine white powder had been partially mixed with what looked like blood. In the next compartment, there was a torn and creased paper with a sketch of a stone floor. On the floor, human bones had been arranged in a large circular design crisscrossed with strange symbols. An inner circle had been formed with skulls. In the third compartment, there was a tiny glass vial with no label and a small syringe. The syringe had been used. The fourth compartment was empty.

Beside the package, a small note was resting against the bare foot of her own body. It had been unfolded, but the edges had contracted part of the way back in. Mercy grabbed at the paper, but it barely moved with her touch. She crouched and craned, and finally just shoved her face into the letter so that one eye was inside the folds.

The handwriting was scratched out neatly in small, sharp cursive.

Honored Bey, Breaker of Chains and Men, Flesh Companion of the Great Serpent Azazel, Builder of Bone Cathedrals, Chief Among the Ordo Draconis, greetings.

Please accept these tokens of my goodwill toward you and of my ill will toward our mutual enemies, the dogs of Ashtown. For too long, they have resented the truly powerful, suppressing greatness wherever they found it. It is my sincerest wish that the Burials be opened and your people freed. There need be no enmity between us. I possess the tooth and the power thereof, but should you destroy the persecutors in Ashtown, I swear that I shall not use it against you or any member of the Ordo Draconis.

To this end, I include: I) Bone flour milled from blood relatives of the entombed victims in the Burial of Bald Catha. II) An ancient sketch of the bone rune shaped from seven (six men and one woman), on the very floor of the Burial in which Bald Catha is bound in sleep. III) A tooth potion as evidence of my own power. Test it only on one you do not need for a day or more. IV) Feathers *plucked from the sleeping head of Babd Catha herself.*

*You know the rite. You have gathered the strength. Wield it.*

*With respect and admiration,*

*Phoenix*

Smoke Mercy drifted back from the paper and the table of men on which her body slept. Six men. She was the one woman. And she had black feathers woven into her hair. Feathers plucked from the head of Babd Catha? Who was Babd Catha? Now the table of men seemed a lot less like a table and a lot more like an altar. She backed away, and for the first time, she looked down at the smooth tile floor beneath her smoky feet. A large design like a star had been faintly traced onto it with gritty blood—blood and bone flour.

She tried to kick it, to rub it off with her feet while the crow watched—hopping, cawing, cocking its black head.

Mercy Rios wanted to scream, but her insides were too soft with fear. She shook without a body to shake. She felt cold sweat without skin or pores. All around her, the women in the walls breathed.

And then one wall opened. Unconscious people rippled and parted. The tremendously tall woman who had called herself Anann the Morrigan stepped into the room—freckled and scarred, bare arms and bare neck all tattooed with scales. She still wore her cracked and worn leather studded with sea glass and stones, but her long red hair was loose and wild, and her feet were bare.

The huge man with the broken chains on his ankles and wrists stepped into the room after her, and the bloodred dragon blister twisted on his chest. Anann stepped to the body of Mercy. The crow fluttered up onto her shoulder.

Radu Bey turned dark eyes onto the Mercy of smoke, and he smiled.

"There is much life in this place. Her soul takes on a body of vapor."

Anann turned, looking into Mercy's eyes.

"Let me go," Mercy said. "Please."

Anann said nothing. She turned back to the Mercy on the altar and began delicately tracing every scale that had been drawn on the girl's arms. Smoke Mercy writhed, slapping at her own arms, feeling every touch.

"You were not meant to be awake," Radu said. "But so many souls, so much breathing, so much life draining into this air, daughter, you are the moisture of many lungs."

"It is time," Anann said quietly. "Babd Catha, my sister, has waited long." She leaned slowly forward, draping her red hair over Mercy's body. Smoke Mercy shivered in the corner with the ticklishness of the touch that blanketed her.

"Soon," Radu said. "The others are coming. She can wait a little longer." Dragging his chains, he stepped toward the smoky girl in the corner, huddling beneath the arms that dangled from the breathing walls.

"This isn't real," Mercy said. She wrapped her ghostly arms around her ghostly knees and began to rock in place. "It isn't. I'm asleep. I was hit by a car. Something. This isn't real. There aren't people like you. There aren't. No one is called Babd Catha."

Radu Bey extended a huge hand. "It is time you left this place."

Mercy reached for it, and as she did, flame sparked in the huge man's palm. Heat jumped through her. Her hand and arm swirled away in twisting steam. Her world, her pain, her worry—it all evaporated into nothing.

Antigone sat with her legs crossed on the roof of the bridge of the S.S. *Fat Betty*. Below her, the ship deck rustled in the evening wind. Off to her right, the island's palm trees shook their fronds at the moon, while to her left, as far as she could see, the moon was painting the world's straightest road across the sea.

Beside her, an enormous orangutan sat like a rug

mountain, peeling bananas. The huge animal smelled like—she groped for any possible comparison—like the flooded interior of a car left in the sun with the windows up. Like a carpet so tired of being peed on that it had eaten the cat. Like the girls' locker room at her old school had somehow been trapped inside a hay bale. Even in the warm tropical night air, he was sitting close enough that she could feel the heat coming off his body.

Cadders and Jane had been steering clear. This one was Jerome. Lemon had sworn that he was as friendly as a tired dog, and she hadn't been far wrong. But he was a tired dog that had decided to follow Antigone everywhere. His lower lip hung low as he hunched over a single banana, peeling it carefully with fingers the size of traffic cones. When he'd finished, he turned his huge, leathery moon face to Antigone and extended his backhoe-size arm, holding the naked banana directly in front of her mouth.

At first, Antigone had resisted—bananas were not her closest friends in the fruit world—but Jerome had persisted. *No, thank you* meant nothing to him. Finally, she'd nipped off a tiny bite with her teeth, and the happy ape had shoved the rest into his own mouth. Then he'd plucked another banana off the bunch at his side and had begun the process all over again.

Antigone had now eaten more banana in one night than in her previous five years. And while the orangutan worked, she stared out at the saltwater world around her, and up at southern constellations she had never seen, and she thought about everything Lemon had told her, everything she had shown her, and the volumes of terrified warnings that the nervous woman had issued with every other breath.

Antigone had spent the whole day grilling Lemon with Rupert's questions, poring over pictures and files, and listening to her grow hoarse. It had been awful stuff to hear, but she hoped it would be helpful to Rupe, helpful in preventing horrible new layers of awfulness from being added to the story of Radu Bey. So far, no magic bullets.

Of course, there was also the chance that she was only on this boat because it was warm and far away and safe. Thinking that made her angry. So she didn't.

A banana appeared in front of Antigone's face and she bit it. She still had Rupert's list in her pocket. She pulled out the creased paper and looked at her Keeper's handwriting in the moonlight.

*Radu's Dragon.* Azazel. Really, really bad news. But she'd known that already. She'd seen Radu's dragon form. She'd felt the crushing weight of its tail, and if not for the Angel Skin, it would have been the last thing she ever felt. According to Lemon, now that Radu was unchained, he and his Dracul would be collecting vast quantities of pain, huge numbers of devoted victims, and their slowly expiring lives would be the strength behind his sorcery, assembled into a temple of their still-living bodies. It was a gross thought—gross in the pictures with all the skeleton walls, even grosser when Antigone thought about those bodies with their flesh still on, still alive, still breathing, crushing each other slowly. In such a place, Radu would be virtually untouchable, and capable of old, old sorcery beyond even what Lemon could imagine. But according to Lemon, the right blade could cut Azazel from Radu's chest. Then Radu could die, but the dragon and the man would have to be faced separately.

*Brendan's Breath.* Lemon had laughed at the phrase. Antigone had assumed that it was talking about the current Brendan, Bellamy Cook, but it was something much older than that. An old legend about the original St. Brendan himself. An old lie, Lemon had called it. Sappy Victorian Sages had even talked about Brendan's Kiss. Allegedly, it was the kiss of life, a kiss that could awaken not the dead, but the unliving—stone, wood, steel, cloth. Other stories said that Brendan had sealed his last breaths into two stone jars, which had never been opened. Theoretically, that breath could be used for powerful blessings. But the truest and oldest story—at least according to Lemon—was darker. Brendan's breath wasn't life-giving at all. It was judgment. She'd told the story to Antigone after brewing tea, and she had clutched her little cup tightly as she spoke.

"The touch of life belonged to a repentant Druid, no one knows his name now, who considered it a curse and a burden and begged St. Brendan to give him the sleep of Burial. St. Brendan agreed, but first, he spoke all of the laws of righteousness into twin limestone jars, using the lost tongue of creation. Then he sealed them with Solomon's name for God, and asked the Druid with the touch of life to make the stone live, to make them giants, and to make the laws he had spoken their hearts, and judgment their only purpose. The Druid agreed, but he was more fearful of such judges than Brendan, and when he livened the jars and the stone began to quicken and grow, he gave them voices. The two grew into stone giants, brothers in shape and strength, and they looked on men and judged them all to be guilty and deserving death. But when they spoke their judgments, Brendan's breath—their laws, their hearts—left them, and they grew still. Statues of living stone, the Brothers were taken deep into the vaults, where they keep silent watch over the oldest hall of Burials, and only fools have dared disturb them."

Antigone had asked questions, but Lemon had refused to say more.

Jerome held out a banana and Antigone nipped off a bite. Next on her little list . . .

*Tooth Tools (Weapons).* Lemon had taken her to a small armory belowdecks, full of knives and swords and strange spears and muskets and musket balls and flintlock pistols and huge sawtooth traps hanging on chains next to clusters of strange lumpy bombs, all forged in black steel under some kind of influence from the tooth. Lemon had said the blades were nearly unbreakable, and while they couldn't kill a transmortal, they could inflict intense pain. The closer the tooth was when they were used, the more intense the pain. Skelton had laid them away for years against the day when the tooth should be recovered. And Lemon wanted them all gone. She refused to touch them, and while Antigone had walked the racks of black steel, Lemon had looked away.

Antigone had been excited. Weapons were obviously helpful. And then Nolan had picked up one musket, recoiled when the steel touched his skin, and thrown it onto the ground.

Antigone had seen the old anger erupt in his normally weary eyes, the blue veins seething beneath his paper skin. She could see it still. Antigone looked at Jerome, the orange ape. He had run out of bananas and was now carefully stacking empty peels.

Nolan had practically snarled at her.

Antigone had backed away, watching the ancient boy clench his fists and grind his teeth. Slowly, Nolan calmed, exhaling the storm inside him one steady breath at a time. His hands unclenched. Sweat slipped down his temple and onto his cheek.

"I'm sorry," he finally said. "Antigone . . . pass such cursed and Reaper-charmed steel through my blood and I will still be screaming in a year. It is charged with a pain and madness I can feel from here."

Antigone sighed. Rupert might want them to collect weapons, but that wasn't happening. Not with Nolan on the plane. And she was pretty sure she didn't want it to happen, either. Torture like that felt wrong. Until she thought about Radu Bey . . .

A sharp whistle floated up from the deck below. She looked down and saw Dan standing between the trees. Jerome grunted and leaned forward onto his knuckles, peering over the edge.

"Di's been talking to Arachne and Cyrus!" Dan shouted. "You need to get down here."

Cyrus was pacing in the small dusty room where Rupert had left him. There was one chair, one light, a small folding table dotted with oil cloths and a gun-cleaning kit, two walls covered with books, and two walls covered with loaded gun racks. The sagging bookshelves surrounded the locked door. More bookshelves had even been mounted directly onto the door. Rupert had called the place his lesser study.

The glowing Quick Water wobbled on the table.

Bells were ringing. And ringing. And ringing.

Cyrus heard shouts in the hall outside his door, and he froze.

"Cyrus." Arachne's voice was tiny and thin. "Cyrus! Stand still, or come closer. This is hard enough as it is."

"Cyrus?" The voice was Antigone's. "Cy? Are you—" His sister gurgled silent.

Cyrus stepped back to the table and dropped into a crouch, staring at the blob on the table. He had lumped Sterling's little drop in with the rest, but it was still a small sphere.

Arachne's pale, distorted face bobbed inside it. Warped and magnified spiders raced across it.

"Divide the orb, Cyrus." Arachne's voice was sharp and clear. "And press the halves flat against a wall. I will do the rest."

Cyrus split the clear jelly sphere and looked around. There wasn't much in the way of open wall space. He stepped over to a bookshelf and squelched both little balls flat against the leather spines of Rupert's books. Jelly oozed out between his fingers, but then slurped quickly back through. Letting go, he backed away.

Two silver splatters clung to Rupert's books. They swirled and sagged, dripped and climbed back up. Eventually, they flattened. Almost. The liquid was ridged with the spines of the books, but the books themselves faded away behind the water. On the right side, Cyrus was looking at a ripply Arachne, and Dennis was peering over her shoulder. They were in Llewellyn's lodge or somewhere like it. On the left side, he was looking at Antigone, Dan, and Diana. Nolan lurked in the background with his arms crossed. They were in what looked like a cafeteria with painted metal walls and caged flickering lights above them.

"There," Arachne said, and the liquid rippled. "This is easier."

"Cy?" Antigone said. "Can you hear me? What's that ringing? The water keeps rippling."

"Alarm bells," Cyrus said. "Bells of summoning. I don't know. It's crazy right now. Rupert shut me in here and now he's off being Rupert. I don't know how long I can talk, so let me get this all out. First, is Mom okay? Everybody good?"

Antigone nodded. Diana retreated and Cyrus's mother leaned into view, her dark eyes even bigger and brighter in the warped liquid, her raven hair even shorter. She smiled slightly and puckered Cyrus a quick kiss.

"Where are you, my son? Is it safe? Will you be safe? You should come here where it is warm. This air makes me stronger."

Cyrus blinked, surprised at how he felt, at how much he suddenly wanted to be with his mom. He had risked never seeing her again more than once today, and bigger risks were coming. Everyone was watching him. Dennis and Diana and Nolan and Dan. He coughed, unsure of what to say. He was badly out of Mom practice.

"Love you," he said quietly.

"And you," she said. "Be safe."

Cyrus nodded, and his mother retreated. He was sure she could still hear him, but saying what he needed to say was suddenly easier.

"Right." Cyrus coughed again and then filled his lungs for a quick rundown. He told them about the attack in the chapel, about Niffy and Rupert attacking the Brendan's rooms and Bellamy Cook dying and what he had said before he went out the window. "So Radu Bey is on his way, and he's planning to destroy Ashtown and open all the Burials. We still don't know where Phoenix is or if he's going to come and try to tame Radu Bey. I think he's coming, or else Bellamy wouldn't have said he was going to be Reborn. He was expecting Phoenix to get his body."

Cyrus paused. Dan didn't look surprised at all. Of course, for all Cyrus knew, everything he was saying was just confirming some dream of his brother's. Antigone's mouth was open. Diana was covering hers with her hand.

Nolan stepped forward. "When?" he asked. "How much time do we have?"

Cyrus shook his head. "Not enough. That's all I know. Rupert is gathering everyone still here who isn't running. He's telling them everything, and fingers crossed they don't kill him on the spot. But here's what we need." Cyrus turned to Arachne's silver face. Dennis was blinking in shock behind her, his mouth drooping. "Arachne, Gil has to fight for us. We need him—and the Captain—here as soon as possible." He looked back at the cafeteria. "Diana?" Diana Boone slipped forward. Dan leaned away to let her get closer. "Could you have your dad pick up Arachne and her crew and get them to Ashtown right away? He should come, too, with his biggest guns and every last one of his crotchety friends who don't want to see the Burials opened."

Diana nodded. "I'll try. It might not be easy."

Cyrus knew that already. And he knew what he was asking them to risk. None of this was from Rupert. This was all from him. Every spent life would be on his shoulders. Cyrus ignored the cold lead settling in his gut, swallowed hard, and pushed on.

"If your dad can't get to Llew's camp, you'll have to do it, Di, and right away. But it would be better if you all started collecting absolutely as many of Skelton's weapons as you can find and came straight here. Are there any there?"

"Yeah," Antigone said. "But, Cyrus . . ."

Nolan pushed forward. "Cyrus—"

"Good," Cyrus said. "Start now. Get here as soon as you can. Like, by sunrise, and pray that Bellamy was wrong and they're not planning to hit us tonight."

Someone began pounding on the door to Rupert's little room. Cyrus jumped to his feet.

"Di, get someone to Llew's. Tigs, weapons. And put your Angel Skin back on. Love you, Mom!" Cyrus swiped the liquid off the books and dropped the slopping ball into the little pouch Rupert had used to carry it.

"Cyrus!" Niffy bellowed through the locked door. "Needed! Now!"

Cyrus slid an iron bolt and pulled the door open.

"How'd it go?" Cyrus asked.

Niffy shook his head. "Not well. The goodies already trickled away under Bellamy. The baddies already had the word to run. A few bounced us in the hall, but Rupert tapped a pint of rage and they scattered. Most of the remainder are staff, and they seem to be looting and leaving, but Rupert hasn't given up yet. I need you to get me to the zoo. Crypto wing. Little lad called Jax. Rupert wants his giant turtle."

Antigone watched the two separate sheets of Quick Water slurp toward each other and wobble into one. Arachne's face was still waiting when the rippling stopped. Cyrus was gone.

Antigone said nothing. Dan groaned, dragging his hands down his face. Diana turned, looking for Lemon.

"Do you have a phone or something like one?" Diana asked.

Antigone didn't hear Lemon's answer. Her older brother leaned in tight, whispering through her hair. "We can't keep moving Mom like this," Dan said. "I'll go. You stay here with her."

Antigone thought about the tall, smooth-skinned man with the stone face and the hard eyes, with the chains on his wrists and ankles and the bloody dragon on his chest. She thought about the huge dragon he had become—the hot breath that had parted around her face, the stumps where wings should have been, the spiked tail he'd used to hurl balls of fire . . . the dragon's voice crawling through her head.

She would need to put back on her Angel Skin.

"I'll go," Antigone said. "Mom will feel safer with you. She'll *be* safer with you." She glanced at her brother. Dan's eyebrows were up. "I have a better chance of controlling Cyrus than you do," Antigone added. "And I know Ashtown."

Dan nodded. Antigone looked around. Katie Smith was watching her with worried eyes. Antigone tried to smile, but it felt like a lie. She let it fall off her face. Diana and Lemon were gone. Horace was sitting at Katie's table with his short legs crossed, scribbling in a small notebook with a pencil too small to keep a bowling score. Nolan leaned against the back wall with his arms crossed.

Antigone turned in her seat and met the boy's time-polished eyes.

"Nolan," she said, "I know you don't like it, but we need weapons that can scare a transmortal. That's the whole point. Not evil stuff, just . . . awful."

Nolan turned his head and slowly scratched the side of his neck. The tips of his fingers were red and pink. He'd been chewing his nails.

She went on. "If Radu tries to kill Cyrus, I don't care if I make him scream for a year."

"You don't understand," Nolan said quietly. "Some of these things . . . Fight devilry with devilry and it doesn't matter who wins. Devils triumph either way. You become what you defeat."

Antigone scrunched her lips. "So find us some angels, Nolan."

Nolan smiled sadly. "That is what *we* are meant to be, what the O of B has sometimes been."

Arachne's watery voice slipped out of the Quick Water, and Antigone jumped in surprise. She'd forgotten Arachne was still watching.

"Some tools corrupt the user. Others are redeemed in holy use. Assess the weapons fairly, Nolan."

The pale boy yawned slowly, stretched, nodded, and finally turned away.

Antigone looked back at Arachne's silver face.

"Now for the storm," Arachne said. "And an end."

## ❧ sixteen ❧

# REMNANT

THE LAWNS WERE DOTTED with bobbing flashlights and lamps. Shouting men and fretting women and a few children were lugging bags and packs and overflowing pillowcases toward the crowded grassy airstrip. Some passed it, heading toward the dark harbor.

One plane after another bounced down the airstrip and then climbed into the night as dozens more were wheeled out of the underground hangars or sat idling outside the doors.

"Zoo!" Niffy shouted. The thick monk slapped him between the shoulder blades. "Focus, lad!"

Cyrus jerked back into the moment and began moving again. Most of these people had always been distant to him, some even unfriendly, but there were a few faces that had been kind to him in the halls, faces that had grinned and laughed with Rupert Greeves. And they were running. Running like none of it—the O of B, the vows, the history, the darkness Ashtown quarantined—really mattered. Cyrus understood the families that had avoided Ashtown under Bellamy Cook, but this was different. This was an evacuation. This was surrender. The war was lost before the fighting had even started. To these fleeing people, the O of B was a club, not a calling. Asking them to stand and fight, to stand and possibly die to prevent the taking of Ashtown, would be like asking someone to die for a neighborhood baseball team. They just didn't care. Not when their lives were at risk.

The fear was contagious. Cyrus could feel it in the air, feel it prickling his skin as men shouted at each other, as taxiing planes cut each other off—tails smacking wings—to race down the grassy strip and veer away into the night. They were risking their lives so they wouldn't have to risk their lives.

He looked back and up at the mountains of stone of Ashtown. By the light of the moon and the low flicker of fires, he could see smoke still rising from the ruined rooms of the dead Brendan.

"These people," Cyrus said. "What was the point of everything if they won't stay now?"

"The point," Niffy said, "was to live comfortably in the way that they saw fit. The point now is to continue doing the same thing elsewhere and as soon as bloody possible."

"But if the Burials are opened, if all the transmortals are freed . . ." Cyrus trailed off. It was hard to imagine a world made in the image of Radu Bey. Or Phoenix.

The charred and bloody monk grew more serious as they walked. "In every herd, many stampede, while only a few turn to face the lions. Cowards live for the sake of living, but for heroes, life is a weapon, a thing to be spent, a gift to be given to the weak and the lost and the weary, even to the foolish and the cowardly."

Cyrus slowed to a stop. The stone and steel shape of the zoo loomed in the trees ahead, its glass roofs higher than the highest leaves. He looked back at the scattered and fleeing members of the O of B. Two young men scurried past, dragging four packs each.

"Aye, even them," the monk said. "When mothers lay down their lives for children, when brothers die for sisters and sisters for brothers, when fathers die for wives and children, when heroes die for strangers on the street, they do not pour out their blood because the one they save deserves such a sacrifice. Nah, lad. Love burns hotter than justice, and its roar is thunder. Beside love, even wrath whispers. Not one of us snatching breath with mortal lungs deserves such a gift, and yet every day such a gift is given." He thumped Cyrus in the shoulder with a heavy fist. "To love is to be selfless. To be selfless is to be fearless. To be fearless is to strip your enemies of their greatest weapon. Even if they break our bodies and drain our blood, we are unvanquished. Our goal was never to live; our goal is to love. It is the goal of all truly noble men and women. Give all that can be given. Give even your life itself." Niffy stretched one open hand out toward the crowded airstrip, the blinking lights, and the shouting. He splayed his burnt fingers like he was dispensing a blessing. "What do they deserve, lad? A flogging. The old bamboo rod in the hand of the late Abbot. Death. And yet Rupert Greeves would gladly die even for the least of these. For you. For your sister. For me. Do we deserve that gift?" He laughed and turned, looking straight into Cyrus's eyes from beneath his own sooty brows. "There is only one Rupert Greeves, Cyrus Smith, and many undeserving fools who need him. He walks the boneyard path, following in the steps of the one Mortal from whom even the Reaper fled in fear. That path runs beneath headstones, down through the lightless cold of lonely loss, through the dark valleys where death was borne down to the black soul river and the final battle line. Only love can set a man's feet on such a path. Only love can see him through, into rest and the hot light of the sun."

Cyrus blinked. Niffy smiled slowly, still staring. The blistered and soot-covered monk didn't look at all like someone ready with a homily on love. In the dark, he looked barely alive. Which, Cyrus figured, was his point. Niffy was very willing to die for others. That had been clear from the beginning.

"Right," Cyrus said. "Honestly, I don't care about those people at all right now. They can go wherever and do whatever. There are people I care about protecting. And there are things that I hate. I want them dead no matter what."

Niffy's smile disappeared. "Aye," he said.

Cyrus kept pace with the thick monk, his ankles slicing through tall, cool grass as they moved beneath the trees. People didn't often come this way.

"This morning in the chapel," Cyrus said, "your own Abbot, the one with the gold patrik . . ."

The monk cocked his blackened, mostly bald head. "What do you know about patriks?"

Cyrus smiled. "I know that you didn't take it from him, because they have to be given. If he'd died with it, that snake would go with him into the grave to live among his bones. I know that they aren't mortal creatures, and that they are named after St. Patrick. I didn't know that they could be controlled like that."

"How do you, lad, have opinions on their control?" Niffy asked. His voice was sharp. "I know only of the golden patrik—called the endless serpent—of the Brothers of the Voyager, and he is always held by the First Cryptkeeper of Monasterboice. And yes, the serpent passed from my master's hands into my own before his death, as he passed from his master's hands into his, and thus all the way back to the day of our beginning, when the serpent was first gifted to Brendan by Patrick himself."

"Well, I hope you know how to use him," Cyrus said.

"We're going to need as much help as we can get. I wish we could just throw Radu Bey in the Crypto wing."

"He is the greater monster," Niffy said. "Any beast would tremble before the dragon Azazel. We should be seeking the Brothers Below."

Cyrus stopped. They had reached the zoo. It climbed up from the darkness below the tree canopy and into the moonlight well above the highest branches. The uppermost level was entirely glass framed in black steel; below that, smooth stone plunged to the ground, decorated only with smooth pillars and tarnished copper waterspouts that ended in open-mouthed beasts well out of Cyrus's reach. Up close, it was like standing beside a small mountain sliced in half.

There was a large wood and iron door in the center, beneath a stone arch. Cyrus veered away from it, toward a tiny one-story building attached to a corner.

"The Brothers Below," Cyrus said quietly. "Are they in a Burial? How do we wake them up?"

"They are named Justice and Wrath, they are not people, and they are not in a Burial," said Niffy. "Under their judgment, any impurity is cause for death. If my master knew of a way to rule them, he took it with him into death."

Cyrus nodded. He'd heard Rupert say that much in the chapel that morning. The moon shadows were dense, and the path to the corner of the zoo was rough and uneven. Patricia was still around his wrist. Cyrus slid his hand around the key ring that she carried, then slid his fingertips beneath the cool scaled body, pulling her invisible tail slowly out of her mouth.

Patricia appeared in his hands. Cyrus looked up into Niffy's surprised face, lit with silver. In a flash of gold, the monk's snake appeared, quickly unwinding on his forearm, growing, extending, tongue flicking. Patricia writhed in Cyrus's hands, crushing his fingers as she fought to disappear.

Niffy's mouth hung open.

"Hey . . . ," Cyrus said, backing away.

The golden snake struck.

Cyrus jumped backward, tripped, fell onto his back in the long grass, and the hot, heavy golden body landed on top of him.

Niffy was shouting. Cyrus rolled, shoving his hands and Patricia beneath him, but the snake was too quick. Powerful coils slid around him, crushing Cyrus's arms to his sides. They lifted him, twisted him, and slammed him onto his back.

Cyrus's breath was gone. Bones were cracking in his hand where the now-invisible Patricia was still shrinking, squeezing, grinding the key ring into Cyrus's knuckles.

The golden snake forked Cyrus's face with its tongue. It butted its hot nose into his chest, worming down along Cyrus's arm toward his hands.

"Patrick!" Niffy was shouting. "No!"

The monk was pulling at the coils. He was grabbing at the head, but he only managed to lift Cyrus and the snake both off the ground before dropping them again.

The coils tightened and Cyrus's ribs screamed and popped.

Niffy found the tip of his snake's tail and grabbed it hard. Cyrus watched him pinch the gold point, and he felt the coils loosen. As the monk backed away, the snake began to shrink and unwind. The head rose, and Cyrus stared into its green glowing eyes. The forked tongue snapped out like a whip and dragged down Cyrus's face once more before Niffy tugged the animal all the way off him and into the grass.

Cyrus sat up, coughing. He raised Patricia and his pained fingers to his lips.

"It's okay," Cyrus whispered. "He's gone. It's okay."

Niffy was backing away through the grass, dragging the limp and shrinking snake like a golden garden hose. Finally, the patrik dangled from his hand, once again slender and small. It wound around Niffy's arm and disappeared. Breathing hard, the monk looked up at Cyrus. He wiped sweat onto the sleeve of his robe, then began to laugh.

"Funny to you?" Cyrus asked. "Your stupid snake almost killed me."

Niffy laughed harder. "You have a patrik! And she's a girlie! Do you know what this means?"

Cyrus stood up, tugging Patricia's tight body down off his hand and onto his wrist.

"Babies!" Niffy bellowed, raising his arms. "A brood of patriks!"

Cyrus shook his head. "Not going to happen. No way."

Niffy seemed confused. He dropped his arms. "How's that then? Why not?"

"I don't know if you were paying attention," Cyrus said. "But she doesn't like yours. Not even a little bit." Cyrus shivered and rubbed at his face where the snake had tasted him. "And I'm not going to make Patricia do anything she doesn't like."

"Patricia! Ooh, that's lovely." Niffy raised his own arm and whispered loudly to his sleeve. "Her name is Patricia!"

Cyrus smiled despite himself. "Come on," he said. Then he turned back to the zoo. Niffy whispered snatches of snaky poetry as he followed.

The little outbuilding attached to the corner of the zoo was unlocked. The lights didn't work, but the electricity was still on—two large refrigerators hummed in the darkness inside. Cyrus banged into large piles of stacked bags of grain, but he didn't dare light up Patricia again. In the end, he managed to find the door he was looking for, and he tested the steel handle.

Locked.

Cyrus banged on it.

"Jax!" he shouted. "James Axelrotter! Hey, Zoo Boy!"

Nothing. Finally, he glanced back at Niffy.

"Turn around," he ordered. "I need Patricia and I don't want your stupid snake seeing her again."

Niffy was probably grinning, but it was too dark in the building to tell. Cyrus heard the monk turn, whispering advice to his snake as he did.

Cyrus recovered the key ring as quickly as he could and examined the door with Patricia's silver light. She was tinier and fainter than he had ever seen her—barely longer than a big night crawler.

There were three locks. The silver Solomon Key opened two of them, and the gold opened the third. More silver and gold. He wondered what color Patricia's eggs would be. Or maybe she wouldn't even lay eggs. Maybe she would give birth to her young like a rattlesnake.

He pushed the door in slightly. The warm smell of zoo rolled through the dark crack to greet him.

"Jax!" Cyrus whispered as loudly as he could. There were a lot of things in there that he didn't want to wake up if they were actually sleeping.

Cyrus stuck his head all the way into the room. Moonlight filtered down through high, dirty skylights, softening so much it barely reached the ground. Cyrus could just make out the tall waterfall at the extreme end. From this far away, it actually sounded more like wind than water.

"Jax!"

"I'm not leaving!" The voice was faint, echoing off the walls and the ceiling.

"No one's asking you to!" Cyrus shouted back. "Jax, it's me! Rupert needs Leon!"

Something distant crashed. Cyrus instinctively pulled back his head. This part of the zoo was inhabited by at least half of his nightmares. And Jax.

"Are you inside?" Jax asked. "Don't be inside. I'm turning the lights on, Cy. Watch yourself."

Cyrus slid his keys back onto Patricia and let her vanish around his wrist. As long as stupid Patrick was around, she wasn't going on his neck.

A switch popped loudly, and small spotlights buzzed to life above old black cages that ran down the length of the nearest wall.

A bird shrieked. Something large and unseen and uncomfortably nearby snorted itself awake and then bellowed irritation.

But Cyrus's eyes were up, scanning the high steel rafters overgrown with canopies of hanging vines. He saw distant white wings flare in a roost, but no serpents dropped into flight. Nothing dove out of the roof or off the upper mezzanine of cages.

Niffy squeezed into the doorway beside Cyrus. The monk's odor was a dozen shades of rank, but he didn't smell any worse than the zoo—or Cyrus, after the day they'd had.

James Axelrotter moved into view. He was a small boy, wearing wrinkled clothes and sporting an overgrown head of bed-messed hair. And he was pedaling a bicycle welded into something that looked like a shark cage on wheels. A hammock was strung up inside the cage beside him, and a little canvas folding chair and a shelf were in one corner. Jax pedaled furiously, but the cage moved slowly as it drifted toward the door. Heavy bars were spaced well apart to handle any of the big beasts that might want to try for a Jax snack, but Cyrus could see a wire mesh woven between the bars that would more than deter flying vipers.

"Strange," Niffy said.

Cyrus laughed. *Strange* didn't begin to describe the only kid on the planet who got homesick when sleeping in a room that *wasn't* filled with certified monsters. Jax hadn't lasted more than a week on the run with the Smiths, away from the transmortal beasties in the Crypto wing of the zoo he'd grown up tending. He had been unable to sleep, and spent his days alternating between incredible grouchiness and designing the bicycle cage in a notebook. Once Cyrus had promised him that he could go back to Ashtown and still be a for-real Polygoner and friend of the Smiths, the kid was as good as gone. The Boones had managed to arrange a lift back for him.

The bicycle cage and its kid engine approached at about the speed of a granny in a walker. Jax stopped fifty feet away, breathing hard, resting his hands on his knees.

"Cage looks good," Cyrus said. "Nice work. Can you shift gears?"

Jax shook his head, struggling to speak. "Perhaps, when I'm older," he gasped. "But with my adolescent stature . . ."

Cyrus smiled. *Adolescent stature* was generous. Jax was small and, short of sorcery, always would be. But he was also crazy smart, and while he could be emotional, he was almost impossible to motivate with fear. On his home turf, he was a sharp and very verbose rock. Growing up with flying vipers did that for a kid.

"You look like you've been swallowed and regurgitated by something unpleasant," Jax said. "And burned," he added. "I'm sorry, I don't know your acquaintance."

"Brother Boniface Brosnan," Cyrus said. "He's a friend." He glanced at Niffy. "Sort of."

Niffy grinned and nodded. "Cheers, mate. Love a full tour of the facility and all that—some other time, yeah?—but I've been sent to fetch a giant ferocious turtle. Is this where I apply?"

Jax began to pedal again, but slowly. The cage inched forward.

"Leon is sleeping. What do you want with him?"

"Rupert wants him to play guard dog at the court-yard entry. Ashtown is awaiting an invasion and is short on defenders. Good help being impossible to find, Rupert desires an angry turtle."

"Leon isn't trained," Jax said. "He wouldn't know what to do."

"Let's not worry about that," Cyrus said. "Let's worry about doing what Rupert wants. Can you get Leon up to the courtyard?"

Jax nodded. "Yes, but only with a massive quantity of cheese. And after that much cheese, his stomach will be quite upset and he'll be incredibly irritable. More than he already is."

"Brilliant," Niffy said. "Irritation is ideal."

"Right," Cyrus said. "Great. Do we need to get cheese?"

Jax shook his head. "I have a stockpile of old nasty stuff. He likes it fuzzy and rotten."

At the far end of the room beneath the waterfall, Cyrus saw a car-size shadow move. Leon, the centuries-old snapping turtle, rose out of a pool and smacked onto the tile floor in a turtle-and-water avalanche.

Niffy swore.

"I know," said Cyrus.

"After the turtle, Rupert wants us in the Galleria," Niffy said quietly. He looked at Cyrus. "I'm telling you now in case I die."

Leon was bigger than some cars, his spiny shell was taller than Cyrus, his spiny tail could have sent a buffalo tumbling, and the beaked mouth in his massive, rotten-pumpkin-ugly head could bite a man in half. But the turtle was able to focus on only one thing at a time, and his favorite thing to focus on was cheese.

Cheese crumbs led him to the big wooden doors.

The zoo exploded in noisy chaos when the doors were opened and the night air rolled in. Striped bears leapt out of cages. Jaculus Vipers swirled in the rafters and slapped down onto the floor, hissing at the sight of freedom, but Leon merely moseyed. He dragged his bulk through the doorway with his asymmetrical nostrils snorting at the ground, searching for lumps of stinky cheese.

Niffy screamed, slapping the turtle. Cyrus shouted. And then Jax jumped out of his bicycle cage, smacked a lump of cheese directly in Leon's face, and then jerked it away before he lost his arm. He hurled the cheese outside.

Leon became a snorting volcano of shell and lashing spiny tail. He cleared the doors, and Jax barely managed to shut them before something large and snarling slammed into the other side.

The rest was relatively easy. Jax climbed up onto Leon's back, avoiding the shell spikes as the turtle heaved his weight from leg to leg. Then Jax began lobbing chunks of cheese out ahead of him. Cyrus hopped onto Leon's huge tail and ran up it, grabbing the scaly spines, and scrambled up to sit next to his small friend. Niffy followed the same way, but he refused to sit.

With the hard shell rocking beneath him like the deck of a reptilian ship, Cyrus couldn't help but smile—even with the planes still trailing away as the panicked residents of Ashtown fled. The smell of doom wasn't as strong as the smell of turtle.

By the time Leon had reached the great courtyard, he was wheezing and tired. He paused by the towering sculptures that rose out of the fountain in the center of the lawn and shoved his head into the pool, bubbling furiously.

The courtyard was empty. Cyrus stood up on the shell of the gurgling turtle, looking at the big stairs and pillars that led to the heart of Ashtown. The tall wooden door was open, and yellow light flowed out around the shape of Rupert Greeves, standing alone.

Two more small planes whined up into the night sky, one after the other, wingtips blinking. Ashtown was bleeding out.

"Okay, Leon," Cyrus said, tapping his foot lightly. "Let's go."

Leon looked up and geysered water out of his nostrils, and Jax lobbed a piece of cheese toward the big open door even as Rupert Greeves turned away.

When the exhausted turtle had finally climbed the stairs, Cyrus saw that Rupert had looped a heavy chain around the base of one of the pillars. The chain ended in a thick belt strap. Leon collapsed onto his belly and shut his eyes. Niffy hopped off and walked into the bright hallway. Cyrus helped Jax cinch the leather strap tight onto Leon's baggy back leg, as thick and coarse as an elephant's but with webbed feet and banana-long claws. Leaving Leon panting, they hopped over the turtle's tail and jogged into the glowing hall.

The Galleria was virtually empty. After an empty acre of wooden chairs, no more than fifty people were scattered through seats in the front. There were white-haired heads that belonged to Sages, hunched in clusters. There were staff members, terrified and young, scattered in bunches. Big Ben Sterling stood against a wall with his arms crossed. Young men and women—Journeymen and Explorers—sat upright in the front rows. All of them had their eyes forward, focused on Rupert Greeves.

Cyrus jogged down the center aisle between the chairs, flanked by Niffy and Jax. His Keeper looked up at him, his face burned and battered, his eyes quiet with sadness. Cyrus had expected defiance in Rupert Greeves. He had expected a battle roar and confident, quick steps and surety of purpose. Rupert was still wearing all black—cinched shorts and pocketed shirt, tight sleeves and leggings. His hands were on his hips, and he let his head sag forward between his broad shoulders.

Rupert Greeves looked heavy with death, like a man

at his mother's graveside, like a man beside a deathbed. The Order was dying.

Cyrus stopped. Jax slipped into a chair. Niffy sat down across the aisle.

Cyrus stood in the middle of the aisle, all in black himself, counterpoint to his Keeper.

Rupert rolled his head slowly, and then looked up at the vaulted roof. His voice was low.

"Father of our Lord, vouchsafe to bless this grave in which we are about to place the bodies of thy servants."

Cyrus looked around. He had heard those words before. Was this a funeral? There were no bodies. And then cold realization drained through him. There were bodies. About fifty of them, sitting in chairs.

Rupert looked at the sparse crowd. His voice was rough.

"The fallen Brendan," he said.

"Hail," one voice replied quietly.

The crowd was silent.

Rupert exhaled slowly. Then he squared his shoulders and set his jaw. Cyrus knew his Keeper well enough to know that Rupert had chosen his course.

"You," Rupert said, "few and faithful, Sages, Keepers, Explorers, Journeymen." He looked up at the back rows. "Staff. The Order, in her decay, does not deserve you. She does not merit your courage, your blood, your lives. She has betrayed you, and yet you are faithful. I, Rupert

Greeves, Blood Avenger, standing for this moment in the Order on behalf of our older brother, Brendan, thank you. You are my brothers and my sisters. You are my betters. I am ashamed that these halls I love cannot defend you. I am ashamed that you who are willing to remain to face our Order's ancient enemies and the terrors of her darkest years must see such disarray." Blinking, Rupert looked from face to face. "The dross has burned away. You are the gold, the true treasure of Ashtown. And now the gold goes beneath the hammer."

Cyrus heard a girl sob. He looked over to see little Hillary Drake, green eyes and curly hair, sniffing into her apron. She was the last of an old family, now unable even to meet the standards for Acolytes. She wasn't here out of courage. She had nowhere else to go.

Rupert cleared his throat and continued. "The assets of the Ashtown Estate belong to those who chose to remain, and they are to be used in the preservation of this Order. What you carry away in your hands may be the only seeds of Ashtown to survive these final days. You must choose wisely and quickly. Sages, gather volumes. Staff, assist them. Keepers, choose from the collections. Explorers, the Estate planes must be prepared to leave with your load of refugees and relics for the African Carthage Estate in four hours. Journeymen, we will not leave our dead unburied. Our Brothers of the cloth still lie in the chapel where they were murdered."

The small crowd was restless.

"We didn't stay just so we could leave," a thin boy in the front said. Cyrus didn't know him, but he agreed.

"You stayed," Rupert said, "to preserve and defend the Order of Brendan, and that is what you will do." He held out his hands, palms up. "Members, rise."

Everyone in the front rose. The staff, Niffy, and Jax remained seated. Rupert looked back at the nervous groundskeepers, porters, and housekeepers.

"Rise," Rupert said. "Courage is your only qualification. You are truer members than all who fled."

Even Hillary Drake stood.

"The Order entrusts her remains to you. Regrow her greatness if you can." He sighed, and for a moment, his formality fell away from him. "Whatever gold and silver is still in the vaults should be divided equally among you before you go. Work quickly, and as fairly as you can."

Small gasps and whispers did laps through the staff. Cyrus suddenly understood why Sterling had stayed. Or he thought he did. But the big cook's face was grim.

Rupert drew himself back up, raised his hands, and shifted his voice.

"Flesh and blood of Brendan, the storm grows," Rupert said. He was beginning the chant of departing. Cyrus had only seen it used a few times, and always at funerals. It had once been meant for earthly treks, but now most members just signed a book and slipped away without any ritual.

"Let us fill our sails," the crowd replied. The voices were scattered and uneasy.

"The storm grows!" Rupert shouted.

"Let us spread our wings!" the crowd said, and this time their voices were in time. Even Sterling had shouted out the reply. He was no longer leaning against the wall, and his big fists were clenched.

"The sea rages!" Rupert said.

"Let our ships till her waves!"

"Flesh and blood of Brendan," Rupert said, "let us give . . ."

"And not count the cost!" the crowd shouted, and Cyrus with them.

"Let us fight . . ."

"And not heed our wounds!"

"Let us toil . . . ," Rupert said, and Cyrus could see that his Keeper's eyes were wet.

"And seek no rest," Cyrus said. He forgot the crowd. He looked at Rupert, and Rupert looked at him.

"Let us labor," Rupert said.

"And seek no reward," said Cyrus.

"Until our dust is dust," said Rupert.

"And our ash is ash," said Cyrus.

The room was silent.

Rupert dropped his arms. "Yeshua defend us," he said. His voice was a whisper.

Beside Cyrus, Jax wiped his eyes. Cyrus didn't bother wiping his. He didn't care if his cheeks were wet. He knew what had just happened. A trek of travelers had been blessed.

And Rupert Greeves had presided over his own funeral.

The big man up front breathed evenly. Body no longer sagging, but relaxed and ready. Eyes no longer weary, but alight with victory.

"Cyrus Smith," Rupert said, "Journeyman of the Order of Brendan, Ashtown Estate, come forward."

Cyrus blinked. Then he wiped his cheeks quickly and walked forward, stopping even with the front row.

"Cyrus," Rupert said. "Will you take up my badge when I fall? Will you defend and avenge the blood of your brothers and sisters in this Order? Will you go with these people and be their Avengel? If so, kneel, and prepare—"

"Nope." Cyrus shook his head. "Absolutely not. No way."

Rupert's mouth hung open for one slow moment before he clamped it shut.

"I know what you're doing," Cyrus said. "And I'm not going anywhere."

Antigone waited in the moonlight beside the platform that held their airplane on the nose of the S.S. *Fat Betty*. The engines were roaring. Diana was wearing headphones and checking instruments by the glowing yellow light of the cockpit. Horace was waiting in the plane.

Antigone looked at the rustling palm trees on the crescent island. This would have been a nice place to stay. Maybe someday. Maybe never. She smelled orangutan and turned back to see Jerome knuckling his way toward her. The great ape dropped down beside her and turned his eyes toward the island to see what she saw. He looked as serious as a poet.

"It's been nice, Jerome," Antigone said. "Though I wish I was in a bed right now and not getting back on a plane."

Jerome was silent.

"You take care of my mom, all right?" Antigone tried to meet the ape's eyes. "If bad people come, throw them in the ocean."

From beneath the trees, Lemon emerged, walking beside Dan and Katie Smith. Nolan trailed behind with a long and obviously heavy duffel bag over his shoulders.

Antigone forced a yawn to loosen her tightening throat. She was not going to cry. Her mom would be safe. There was absolutely nothing to cry about.

Katie Smith, as slender and silver as an aspen tree in the moonlight, moved ahead of the others, straight for her daughter. Her eyes were lit like lesser moons, and the darkness in their centers pulled at Antigone like they were trying to drag her into another place and another time.

Katie's slender arms wound around her daughter. Lips found Antigone's cheek.

"My Tigger," Katie said. "Your father loved you more than life. And so do I."

Antigone cried.

Katie Smith pulled back, cupping her daughter's face in her hands. She smiled at Antigone, her eyes pouring out raw, unfiltered affection.

"I would rather that my daughter could sit and sing with me beside this warm sea, but in dark times, there are claims greater than a mother's. Be wisdom for your brother, but trust his boldness."

Antigone nodded. She had no words. Her mother kissed her on the forehead.

Dan stepped up beside his mother. His face was pale, and he looked sick to his core.

"Antigone . . ."

"I don't want to argue," Antigone said. "I have to go."

"Nothing in me wants to argue," Dan said. "Everything in me wants to lock you in a room and go myself."

"Well," Antigone said, "thanks for being reasonable."

Dan licked his lips. He was sweating and almost green.

"This isn't reasonable," he growled. "This is me trusting . . . trusting a girl who writes with fire on leaves. This is me trusting a ridiculous dream."

Katie Smith shook her head. "True dreamers do not trust the dream. They trust the one who sends it." She looked at Antigone. "Daniel is meant to stay. You are meant to go."

Nolan climbed up past Antigone. He was wearing gloves and sneering with slight disgust. His heavy bag clattered with the unseen weapons that he, and no one else, had chosen.

Daniel put his hand on the back of Antigone's head and pulled her into his chest. When he let go, her mother took her hands, kissed them each twice, then dropped them and backed away.

When the plane rose, when it banked away from the freighter with its gardens and its apes, when Antigone slid over the crescent island fringed with cliffs and trees and away from the shapes of her mother and brother and onto the road of silver moonlight over the sea, she felt like she had felt beside her father's grave beneath that ancient redwood tree. Something was stretching inside her. Something was tearing. Something was already torn.

It wasn't exactly the same. This time she felt like the one inside the grave while others stood beside it.

## ❄ seventeen ❄

# LIVE BAIT

OLIVER LAUGHLIN MASSAGED HIS EYEBROWS. Outside, the sun would be rising, but he didn't want to see it. Right now he needed things dim. His feet were up on a rusty handrail, and he was leaning back in a rickety bent-wood chair. Twenty feet below him, on the cracked concrete floor where large vats once burbled with Holy Soap, dozens of women were sleeping in neat rows.

Phoenix yawned, and then groaned. In his last body, the white Odyssean Cloak had magnified his mind and multiplied his cunning, but living in—no, *being*—Oliver was different. He had broken down barriers in the boy's skull before he'd bothered to move in. He had doubled and trebled the boy's capacity, pushing it well beyond mortal levels. But oddly, he hadn't needed to do any real redesigning or even rebuilding. It had all just been there . . . walled off, unused, and more powerful than he could have imagined until he'd been able to think his way around inside it for himself.

Man, Phoenix felt, had been meant for tremendous

things. More than ever, as he cautiously explored Oliver's new mind, Phoenix was certain that he was doing God's work. Or gods' work. Or more likely, the work of a god. He smiled.

It had been difficult at first—painful, even—to achieve his old levels. But his consciousness was flowing more easily through Oliver's brain now. And there were still corners unexplored, potentials that Phoenix had not begun to touch. Psychic potentials. Telepathic potentials. Destructive, creative, invasive, and matter-altering potentials. Exploring them was like opening present after present on Christmas Day and always seeing more beneath the tree.

Phoenix smiled again. He thought of things like presents now. Oliver, after all, was much closer to childhood than Edwin Laughlin had been.

Of course, in addition to the thrill of discovery, testing each new ability gave Phoenix a headache that was equally beyond mortal capacity. His forehead felt like a double-barreled volcano ready to blast screaming tangled nerves out of his eyebrows.

Yes, he could turn off the pain—he'd done it in some varieties of his men—but not without turning off all of it. There would be a more delicate switch in there somewhere. He'd figure it out. Or his skull would adapt. Eventually.

"Father."

Phoenix dropped his Oliver hands and looked up.

The angular red-haired man who loomed over him was one of the few of Phoenix's failed creations. The rest of the failed had been thrown into early action at Ashtown. Phoenix had not mourned their destruction, though he had not expected such high casualties.

This man—Hal, his name was—was physically perfect on every level. But he was a worrier. And worriers made every strength a weakness.

"Father," Hal said again. He scratched a freckled cheek. "We haven't heard anything new from Ashtown. Do you think the transmortals suspect something?"

"Of course they suspect something," Phoenix said. "But that won't stop them. There is more than enough bait in those Burials to draw them."

Hal cleared his throat. His gills fluttered. "I can't help but wonder if including the tooth potion in the package for Radu was a mistake. They may be too scared of you to take the bait."

Phoenix dropped his feet off the rail and thumped his chair down. He began to laugh, and then he grabbed his throbbing forehead.

"Scared? Radu Bey?" Phoenix stood. Hal took a quick step backward. "I have brandished a tiny weapon. I have threatened him meekly and shown that I am the one who feels fear."

"But, Father . . ." The redhead's gills flared, and his freckled green face flushed.

"He will sniff the bait," Phoenix said. "He will circle. And then he will strike with the wrath of the old gods, and we and all the world will know."

Phoenix stretched inside Oliver's new mind. His skull hatched Phoenix's influence out between his eyes.

Hal's arm bent jerkily at the elbow. He extended one wavering finger and then tucked it into his own nostril. He stood there, eyes wide with terror.

"Stop picking your nose, Hal," Oliver sneered.

Hal's finger twisted and wiggled, picking diligently. Hal began to sweat and shake. He fought to lower his hand, but the finger popped right back into his nose.

"Hal," Oliver said. "Your nose is bleeding."

And it was. Streaming down around the man's knuckles. Hal began to sob.

"Do not bring me such childish fears," Oliver said coolly. "Bring me no fear at all. I gave you strength; find courage, you pitiful, gutless . . . *human*."

Hal turned and ran, his bloody hand suddenly free.

Oliver closed his eyes. His head was crackling. It felt like it was levering slowly open, yawning in his forehead. And as it did, his pain muted slightly, like a long splinter was being dragged out him, like his mind had just grown a new limb.

He had just made a grown man pick his own nose. Phoenix let Oliver's mouth twitch into a smile.

Children could be so spiteful.

Cyrus stood on the belly of a huge stone statue, floating on its back in a quiet black sea. And that is how he knew it was a dream. Stone. Floating.

Cold wind tightened the skin on his face, but his body was warm. The stone statue beneath his feet wore carved mail and had outstretched sinewy arms. One hand gripped an ax and the other held the severed stone head of a bearded man. Cyrus walked up the statue's belly and chest and the stone bobbed like a log, slapping the arms down into the dark water and rocking back up again.

Cyrus looked down at the stone face as it emerged from the water. He had expected a man. A king. A Viking chieftain, maybe. But the statue had the face of a woman. Not even a woman—a girl. A pretty girl. Her eyes were shut and her brows were low with worry. Her stone mouth was slightly open, like the mouth of a sleeper straining to speak. Black water trickled out between her lips. She wore no helmet, and instead of hair, long stone feathers erupted from her scalp.

"Do you see her?" The voice was Dan's. Cyrus looked around. To his left, Dan was seated in a metal chair at a small metal table, both on the surface of the water. He was leaning forward, resting his head on his crossed arms. His eyes were shut, and a caged light hung in the air above him.

"Yeah," Cyrus said. "I see her. I'm standing on her."

"That's how the dream goes," Dan said. "She's floating, right?"

"Yeah," said Cyrus. He looked back down at the black water licking the stone. "Not friendly water."

"Death," Daniel said. He yawned, but his eyes were still shut. "The water is death."

"Creepy," said Cyrus. "And weird. I'm dreaming a floating statue and my brother napping at a table." He smiled. "But now that I know I'm dreaming, I think I'll fly away. Wanna come?"

"You're not dreaming," Dan said. "Well, you are. But it's not your dream. It's mine. I'm giving it to you. I thought you should see it."

Raindrops started puckering the black water around Cyrus. A few slapped the statue. A fat one hit Cyrus in the ear. Not the top of his ear. Somehow, it shot right into his ear hole. He squeegeed at it with his little finger.

"That part's all you," Dan said. "Not me."

"So if the rest is all you . . ."

"It is," Dan said.

Cyrus stared at his napping brother. "Okay," he said. "A couple things . . . First, it's kind of creepy having you in my dream. Cool, yes. But also creepy. Second, why this? You thought I should see it, so what's the point?"

"Pythia has been teaching me," Dan said. "She started by coming into my dreams, and she doesn't just write on leaves. She helped me figure out that all the abomination, desolation, seventy-weeks stuff was about you."

"We're not talking about that one," Cyrus snapped. "Don't show that to me."

"Not going to," Dan said. "But she taught me how to send dreams, and she's helping me to interpret. This one is easy. The water is death. And the statue is floating in it. But it shouldn't be floating. It's stone. It's meant to sink. It—*she*—should be deep in darkness, but she is rising."

"She," Cyrus said quietly. "Who is she?"

"She is called Babd Catha. She was a Celtic war goddess the last time people let her run around. She's a storm crow who gathers vicious human followers and demands, in Lemon's words, 'much unpleasantness' in her service. Child sacrifice. That kind of thing."

"Okay," Cyrus said. "And she's floating. Not staying in darkness. Check."

"She's in the Burials, Cyrus," Dan said. His voice was barely louder than the rain pattering on the table around him. "In one of the oldest and deepest vaults. If *she's* coming up, then she won't be the only one. Also, that's not her face. Babd has no face. She has only a feathered skull. Whoever that girl is will be her first victim, the required sacrifice when the storm crow wakes."

Cyrus didn't want to look back down at the face of the sleeping girl, at the stone features struggling to speak.

But he also couldn't help it. The girl's mouth bobbed underwater, choking on liquid darkness. Cyrus felt sick.

"I think I'd like to wake up now, thanks." He shut his eyes and turned his face up to the sky, hoping for cool rain. Another drop hit him in the ear hole.

"Last thing," Dan said. "And it's not good. Babd will rise up from the depths of darkness, but how do we keep her from leaving the water for good? If she receives a sacrifice, her awakening will be complete, but we don't know who that girl in the statue is or where she is, or who is meant to stop it. There has to be a key in the dream. Something. A promise. A clue. Or else it's just awful news with nothing we can do about it." He sighed. "Pythia says most dreams are like that, but this one can't be. I've seen what Babd will do and . . . and that sacrifice can't happen. It just can't. You can wake up now, Cyrus. I need to talk to Pythia."

Cyrus looked down at the massive floating stone statue beneath his feet. Dan wanted a clue. He rocked slightly and watched dark water ripple up into the statue's mouth.

Babd was *beneath his feet.*

"Dan," Cyrus said quietly. "Am I usually in the dream? And I'm standing on her?"

"Oh." Dan swallowed. "Cyrus. You're right. You're the last thing between her and total reawakening. You have to find the girl, Cyrus. If Babd receives a sacrifice . . ." Dan's eyes were still closed tight. "Cyrus. Look around. Look down. She would only be the first."

Cyrus scanned the water. All around him, stone fingers and stone faces were beginning to break the black rain-puckered surface. Hundreds of them.

"Cyrus," Dan said. "I've seen Antigone die. I've seen her live. I've seen Diana and Jeb and Rupert and Dennis. . . ."

"Stop it." Cyrus bit his lip. "Jeb's not even here." He stomped on Babd's stone shoulder.

"Cy? Have you thought at all about the words from the other dream?"

"I try not to, thanks," Cyrus said quietly.

"The seventy weeks will soon be passed," Dan said. Cyrus could have recited the rest, he'd heard his brother say it enough times. "One comes on the wing of abominations, and there shall be no end to war. He shall be called the Desolation, and when he casts his shadow, even the dragon shall shrink in fear."

Cyrus stared at the black water, at the slowly bobbing fingers.

"Seventy weeks . . . ," Dan muttered. "Seventy weeks of what? From when? Any ideas? We need the dragons scared now. . . ."

"Dan," Cyrus said. He faced his brother and opened

his mouth to fire irritation. Dan was sitting up now. His arms were crossed. His eyes were open.

Dan was blond. His eyes were blue. He had thinned down to the tan California boy that now lived only in fading pictures. Cyrus was looking at the brother he'd lost, the brother Phoenix had erased and rewritten.

Cyrus's irritation fell out of him; it was swallowed by the black water. He owed Dan better. He owed Dan everything.

"You can wake up now," Dan said. "Anytime."

Cyrus nodded.

"Hey . . . ," Cyrus said. "Thanks. And, I, uh . . ."

Dan gave him a wide, sun-bleached surfer grin of years ago. "I love you, too, man. Now look behind you. You're not alone, little bro."

Cyrus turned. Antigone stood on the statue right behind him. She wore her leather jacket belted, with a revolver on one hip and a long knife on the other. A slice of pearly Angel Skin shimmered in the open neck of her shirt, and her fingers were threaded into her glistening black hair as she wove it back into a tight braid. She smiled at Cyrus as she worked.

"Cowboy up, Tarzan. Let's go."

A raindrop hit Cyrus in the ear hole.

He opened his eyes.

Cyrus blinked. He was curled on his side beneath a heavy blanket with his knees pulled up against his chest. And he was on a rooftop, tucked against a small wall beneath a wet morning sky. A dissipating trail of black smoke wandered away from the Brendan's destroyed rooms on the far side of Ashtown.

Niffy nudged Cyrus with his toe.

"Well, you're a keen little watchman, aren't you, then?"

Cyrus sat up and dug for a raindrop in his ear.

Niffy smiled. He had bathed, and his visible portions were striped with bandages. His robe had even been washed. More likely, he had swiped a new one. His stripe of hair was now uneven on his gauze-dotted scalp, but it was clean.

"Rupert told me to let you sleep," Niffy said. "But enough is enough."

Cyrus's brain slowly shook off the image of black water and his blond brother. In the Galleria, when he had refused to run to Africa with the others as a sort of Avengel in waiting, he had expected Rupert to argue, to banish him from Ashtown, to grow angry. He hadn't. After the first flurry of activity, Rupert had sent Cyrus onto the roof to keep watch for incoming planes. But now it was day. Niffy wouldn't be standing here if Radu Bey was downstairs.

"What happened?" Cyrus said.

"What happened is that wily Rupert Greeves sent a bone-weary lad to keep watch over the safest place in all of Ashtown." Niffy winked. "He even sent you with a blanket. I think he hoped that the war would come and you would sleep through it, tucked up here on the rooftop, watching for planes behind your eyelids."

Cyrus felt his damp face growing hot. "No planes came. I would have heard."

Niffy's grin widened, his high round cheeks pinching his happy eyes into slits.

"You slept through the grave digging and the funeral bells, and the final wee air fleet as it flew away. Vesuvius couldn't have roused you."

Cyrus stood, wiping his rain-wet face. He ran his hands over his short hair, flinging an army of tiny drops up after his fingers.

"One plane dropped by," Niffy said. "Landed not thirty minutes ago, claiming to have been summoned by some right daft prat named Cyrus Smith. You know him?"

Cyrus sucked in a long breath. Rupert had wanted to die alone. He had spent the night shuttling people away. And Cyrus hadn't bothered to tell him that he had sent out a slightly different message.

"Is he mad?" Cyrus asked.

"Yes," Niffy said. "Aye. Indeed. Verily. And in more ways than one."

Niffy turned and Cyrus followed him around chimneys back toward the hatch door that the monk had left open. Cyrus glanced back at the black smoke curling up from the far corner of the world of Ashtown rooftops.

Rupert had wanted to be alone then, too.

Nervousness floated up behind Cyrus's sternum and settled in his throat. Yes, he had undermined Rupert.

Oh, well. On this point, Rupert needed undermining.

It was strange, walking an empty Ashtown. Hall after hall, stair after stair, Niffy and Cyrus moved in near silence. The floors were a mess of things cast off and left behind, too heavy to carry or too useless to pick up when dropped.

Members' quarters had been left open. Beds unmade. Trunks open and overflowing. Water dripping in unseen tubs.

Only fifty of the faithful had remained.

And then there were five.

Niffy led Cyrus through the main hallway, past the black ship of Brendan on its pedestal, past the empty dining hall, and into the kitchen.

Sterling worked one small block of the massive fire island of stoves that would normally be ablaze. Omelets sizzled. Bacon shook and cracked small whips of grease.

Rupert sat on a stool across from Sterling, his eyes shut, his head in his hands, his mouth open. He looked asleep.

Jax sat on a stool beside Rupert, glaring at Sterling.

A butcher-block table usually reserved for vegetable-dicing prep cooks was mounded with heavy charge guns that could stun a transmortal.

Rupert stirred. "Cyrus," he said. "Who else is coming?"

The big man sat up slowly and turned.

Cyrus didn't answer. Sterling winked and flicked a hot piece of bacon through the air at Cyrus's head. He caught it, shuffled its heat from hand to hand, and then tucked it between his teeth.

Rupert stood up, crossed to Cyrus, dropped a heavy hand on his shoulder, and steered him toward the swinging door into the dining hall. He pushed it open and held it, looking down at Cyrus's face as he did.

The Captain and Gilgamesh and Arachne sat at one table. Gil and the Captain were both wolfing massive piles of some special Sterling scramble. A dozen plates were already empty.

Arachne sat quietly with her bulging bag on her lap. She'd gained a lot of spiders in the woods, and she looked like she was waiting for something. She turned her frigid eyes to Cyrus and smiled slightly. It wasn't a happy smile.

Robert Boone, Jeb Boone, Gunner, and Dennis were eating loudly and talking at another table. The creases on Robert's face were as hard as canyons. His brows were low, and white scruff lined his unshaven jaw. Jeb had stitches down his shorn scalp and across his temple.

And he was wearing an eye patch. Diana's father and brother both looked as serious as death. Gunner looked lost in thought. Only Dennis was smiling, clearly glad to be in Ashtown.

Rupert let the door swing shut, then marched Cyrus back through the kitchen and into the long hallway lined with Explorer displays.

He pushed Cyrus away from him and crossed his arms.

Cyrus staggered at the force of the shove and turned to face his Keeper.

"What were you thinking, Cyrus?" Rupert asked. "Do you want your friends killed? Robert says his daughter and Antigone are on their way as well."

Cyrus swallowed. "Ashtown should be defended."

"And it will be," Rupert said.

"By you?" Cyrus asked. "Alone?"

Rupert inhaled slowly. "What do you think Radu Bey will do to John Smith?" he asked. "Do you think Arachne's spiders can face a dragon? Do you expect loyalty from Gilgamesh? Every mortal in this place will die, Cyrus. But any transmortal who stands with us . . . they can expect decades and decades of horror."

Rupert stepped forward, uncrossing his arms. "You and every other wakeful soul in this place will get on Robert's plane, and you will leave."

Cyrus shook his head. "You need help. Do you even

know where the Brothers Below are? You still have to find them, and there aren't even any Sages left to ask."

Rupert blinked.

"You were going to try to wake them up, right?" Cyrus asked. "In the chapel, you said you wouldn't because they would kill too many innocents. And you've done nothing but chase people away since then. You were going to wake them, because even if they killed you, they could stand against Radu Bey."

"It is an option," Rupert said. "If I find them. But only if I am alone."

"But aren't they evil? Don't they kill everyone and everything?"

"No man is pure in heart, mind, body, and soul. There are stains in all of us that the Brothers see, and because they see all things without grace or mercy, because they are Justice and Wrath . . ."

"They kill everyone," Cyrus said.

Rupert sighed. "They issue a just judgment. If I want justice for Radu Bey, I will bow before it for myself."

"Rupe." Cyrus shook his head. "You don't deserve to die."

"Before I was born, did I deserve to live?" Rupert asked. "I was made and life was given to me so that I could be standing right here, right now. So that I could be spent."

Cyrus bit his lip, thinking. He understood what Rupert was saying. But that didn't mean he had to accept it—not just yet.

Rupert leaned forward, eyes wide. Cyrus studied the floor.

"Our race is flawed, Cyrus. Mortality is meant for us. We will take our faults into the grave, and in the grave, we will leave them. Pity the transmortals, living forever with their stained souls. We can lay our burdens down; we can offer up our lives for the ones we love."

"Exactly," Cyrus said, looking up, meeting his Keeper's eyes. "*We.*"

A sharp whistle shot out of the kitchen.

"Rupe!" Niffy shouted. "Planes! One low and landing, and one coming in fast—"

Engines roared. Air shrieked. Glass shattered. The ground shook Cyrus off his feet as white fire billowed out of the kitchen, sucking the air dry.

Rupert was on his face. Cyrus rolled over and elbow-crawled to him. He grabbed for his Keeper's pulse, but Rupert knocked his hand away and pushed himself up, his back smoking slightly.

"Niffy!" Cyrus shouted, but he couldn't hear his own voice. The only noise now was a shrill shrieking in his head, the impossibly loud ringing of some internal fire alarm.

Rupert scrambled up and ran into the obliterated kitchen. Cyrus staggered after him.

The wall of windows had become a gaping hole. The wall between the kitchen and the dining hall had been split wide, and the smoking remains had been thrown across the smoking tables. Everywhere, things were burning.

Tucked in the shattered shadow of a half-gone fire island, Sterling lay across the bodies of Jax and Niffy. All three were moving slowly.

Rupert turned to the dining hall.

Cyrus could hear him shouting but his voice was muffled and distant.

The Captain erupted out of the rubble, his square beard gray with dust, his breastplate dented, and his camouflage pants smoking. Bellowing curses, shaking with rage, he drew his sword and stomped toward Rupert.

Gilgamesh rose slowly, uncurling himself from around the body of Arachne. She was untouched and her bag uncrushed, but Gil's broad back was a bloody swamp, studded with shrapnel.

"Robert!" Rupert waded into the destruction, heading toward the table where Robert, Jeb, Gunner, and Dennis had been sitting. A solid slab of wall lay across that part of the room.

Dennis emerged on his hands and knees from beneath it.

"We're fine, Mr. Greeves!" he said. "All fine!"

Rupert spun back around.

"Cellars!" he shouted. "Everyone into the cellars. Get belowground! We'll get pounded before we make our stand."

Just as they touched down on the little green airstrip, Antigone saw the jet scream over and the fireball swallow the kitchen. And the Brendan's rooms looked like they had already been destroyed.

"Not good!" Horace yelled behind her. The little lawyer was out of his seat and pressing his face against a window. "Not good! Not good! Not good!"

Nolan leaned forward between Diana and Antigone, looking up the slope at the smoke rising from Ashtown. The jet responsible was out of sight, but at the speed it had been moving, it could be back on top of them between two heartbeats.

"Let me out," Nolan said. "Then take off and disappear."

Antigone shook her head. "Diana can leave, but I'm coming with you."

Diana pointed to a plane at the end of the runway. "That's my dad's," she said. "I'm staying."

As the plane stopped, Antigone pulled off her

headset and Nolan threw open the cabin door. Still wearing gloves, he had the heavy black bag slung over his shoulder.

Nolan, Antigone, Diana, and Horace jumped out one after the other. The props were still turning as they ran up the hill.

Low on the horizon, Antigone saw the jet approaching again. Nolan dropped to one knee and unzipped the long black bag. He jerked a short, fat brass tube from the jumble of gear. It had a brass wheel on the side, a handle and trigger on the underside, and an oversize musket-style hammer on the top. Nolan flipped a tiny lever, and the tube suddenly telescoped out to at least six feet long. Nolan's hands were moving fast, digging back through the bag.

"Crank that wheel!" he yelled, and Antigone and Diana both jumped forward. Antigone had her hands on the wheel first, and she began to crank it clockwise as fast as she could. Three twists. Four, and it clicked.

Nolan dropped a dark canister down the wide end of the tube, grabbed the handle, and cocked the oversize hammer.

The snub-nosed, dual-nostriled jet roared in over Ashtown. Black spheres dropped from its belly as it came.

Nolan pointed the fat end of the tube straight up and pulled the trigger.

With a crack, the long telescope sprang back together, lifting Nolan off his feet and hurtling the canister up into the wet gray sky.

The jet's bombs were erupting in a chain as they slammed into walls and roofs and grassy earth.

Nolan's lonely canister slowed at its peak and crumbled into barely visible dots.

The jet roared beneath it.

The dots struck faster than Antigone could see. While bombs marched down the grassy slope toward the airstrip, hundreds of small explosions punched into the jet's wings and cockpit.

Bomb heat lifted Antigone off the ground and flung her back onto the airstrip in a cloud of earth. She landed and rolled. Spitting dirt and blinking, she looked back up at the sky from her belly.

Trailing smoke, the jet hit the lake at full speed. A pillar of flame and water marked its end.

She could hear Nolan laughing. He was on the ground only a dozen feet away.

"Two hundred pyro-newt eggs in a crank launch!" He looked at her, eyes gleaming in his dirty face. "Not a banned weapon, but an antique!"

"Is it done?" Antigone asked. "Is that it?"

The pale boy leapt up easily, the fat tube dangling from his hand. He looked happier than Antigone had ever seen him—full of a strength and energy that was, for once, not powered by rage.

"Done? Antigone Smith, it hasn't even started." Nolan shook his head. "That was just Radu knocking on the door."

## ✤ eighteen ✤

# THE QUICK AND THE DOOMED

CYRUS WAS STANDING ON A STATUE floating in black water. She was higher now. Inches higher. He wheeled around. There was Dan, eyes shut, head resting on his arms. There was Antigone, braiding her hair.

"Dan!" Cyrus yelled. "We're being bombed! I don't have time for this!"

"Have you found the girl?" Dan asked. His voice was tense. "You have to find her. There's not much time. Go! You shouldn't be here right now!"

Cyrus couldn't breathe. He had been on the cellar stairs when the last round of bombs dropped the world on him. Stone rubble was pressing down on his chest, and his mouth was full of blood. He wormed free of the pressure and began to hack out dust with his first weak breaths. At least he wasn't burned. He hated burns. He managed to twist onto his side and pulled himself in the direction he believed to be up. It was up. He could see fire. And gray daylight.

Cyrus crawled up the rubble slope into what had been the kitchen. Now it was a crater of smoking stone with walls that were mostly holes. He snorted and spat out blood made black with dust.

"Cyrus!"

He looked up. Antigone was climbing toward him over a hill of glass and stone where the kitchen windows had once been. She was wet from the rain, and she was dirty, but she was wearing her leather coat belted. Gun on one hip and long knife on the other. Angel Skin alive with light at her throat. Her hair pulled back into a tight braid. She was dressed exactly as she had been in the dream.

She was hurrying forward. She was pulling rubble off of him. She was checking him for broken bones. She was talking.

Cyrus wasn't listening.

"Hey," he said. "Antigone."

She paused, her eyes spilling worry.

"We have to get into the Burials. Like, now."

Radu Bey walked barefoot through his human hall, chains dragging behind him. Anann the Morrigan walked with him, stride for stride. Muffled by the walls of bodies but still audible, sirens whined in the world outside. The full force of the *Ordo Draconis* had assembled in his temple. They were silent. They were ready. But with so many transmortals in one place, the city blocks around them had slipped into chaos.

Outside, the police. Again. Emergency, emergency. Humans are weaklings. Azazel, the dragon inside him, could sense every breathing body the police dragged away from his temple. And before they could be taken too far away, Radu felt Azazel ripple and slither beneath the skin of his chest as the serpent used the power of the temple to snip their soul strings and send another servant into death.

This building had never been meant as a long-term home. Radu smiled. It was a launching point. An egg that would hatch into his new empire. And it had been his first real feed. Something quick and easy after centuries of chains.

Tonight, when every Burial of Ashtown had been emptied into his temple, he would lead his army of gods out into the crowded streets and show them the tall towers of light, and he would make them his. Together they would shatter the City of Man with chaos, ascend the great towers, and then turn their eyes to the world.

Tonight, he would claim his capital city.

Radu's first wave had reached Ashtown, and he could see fire when he shut his eyes. The second wave would be sweeping the rubble for survivors . . . and for any of Phoenix's Reborn with their tooth potions. The potions were a worry, but Phoenix would not have sent the sample to him unless he had wanted Radu to worry. It was potent, but it was a bluff. Phoenix couldn't possibly have produced enough of it to down two dozen transmortals for any length of time, let alone two hundred. It was a complicated ritual preparation that required at least one full phase of the moon to mature. Since Phoenix's factory had been destroyed, there hadn't been time for that many new batches. One batch, maybe, but he would have needed vats and vats boiling down the mixture for a month to get as much as he would need. The sheer strength of Radu's force was enough to overwhelm even one thousand of the Reborn if they were foolish enough to engage the gods with only a few tranquilizing dart guns.

"The road is long ready," Anann said. "Your army is waiting. My sister is waiting."

"Yes," Radu said. "And she can wait a little longer."

Anann grabbed his arm and the two stopped.

"You swore to me," she said. "She will be the first. She is waiting."

"As is Phoenix," Radu said. "We will tread cautiously when the path is prepared by an enemy, even one as weak as Phoenix."

He studied the hard, scarred face of Anann the Mor-

rigan. There was beauty in her bloodthirst, in her dedica-
tion. She was like the cliffs along the North Sea—jagged
of soul, pitiless, unmoving. He traced one of the blue ink
scales on her neck with a long bronze finger.

"We will wake your sister," he said. "We will bring
her here. The altar is ready. I myself will stand with you
as she receives her sacrifice, and Azazel shall honor her
power with a temple of ten thousand souls when this
city falls."

The charge guns had all been buried or burned. When
Cyrus and most of the mortals had been helped up out
of the rubble, Nolan began passing out weapons from his
bag. Some he handled casually and quickly, but others
received his full attention, and he was careful to touch
them only with his gloves.

Horace took a stone hatchet with a heavy black head.
Nolan handled it like a jeweled egg.

Gunner and Jeb both already had sidearms, but they
took long black knives that made Nolan's lip curl, and as
many small glass canisters of pyro-newt eggs as he would
give them. The eggs themselves were packed tight inside
glass and surrounded with clear fluid. They looked like
large charcoal olives, but Cyrus could see a dull orange
glow in the center of each one.

Cyrus watched Jeb, stitched up and grit covered, one eye patched and one eye squinting at the glowing eggs in his hand. Jeb was coming straight from the hospital back into battle.

Nolan, shivering, handed Jax a short black machete, and Diana a black trumpet-mouthed blunderbuss, along with a bag of powder and a heavy sack of tooth-charmed shot.

"Jeb," Cyrus said.

Jeb looked up at him.

"Thanks," Cyrus said. "For helping get my mom out of here. I haven't seen you since."

Jeb cracked a dusty grin. "Anytime. You'd do the same for me."

Diana was watching the two of them from beside her father. Cyrus glanced at her, at her father, and then back down at Nolan's bag.

Yes, he would. For Jeb's mom. Diana's mom.

Rupert was helping Sterling to his feet. Niffy was nowhere to be seen.

The Captain and Gilgamesh exploded up from another buried cellar. Arachne crawled out behind them.

The Captain roared, his face red and purple, his body shaking with anger. He stomped rubble off of his knee-high boots and then jerked his dragon sword out of its sheath.

"Where are the beasties?" he bellowed. "Where are the fools who desecrate these halls with flame and fire?"

While the Captain raged, Gilgamesh crossed to Nolan and held out his huge six-fingered hand. Nolan hesitated. Then he drew out a thick horn bow, unstrung. He handed it to Gil along with a quiver packed tight with thick black feathered shafts. The arrowheads were made of glistening obsidian.

"Don't touch the tips," Nolan said. "Or maybe you should. Touch them with your chest."

Gil smiled.

Sterling was wobbling on his metal feet.

Nolan carefully handed Rupert a long, gently curving black sword and a belt of six glass spheres. Cyrus had seen them used before. Break them and a crackling lightning ball would rip through a room. Rupert strapped them on above the double holster he already wore.

"Transmortals with me," Rupert said. "Robert, get the mortals down to the planes and out of here."

"Hold on!" Gunner blurted. "I didn't come to run."

"Rupe," Jeb said, "I stand with you."

Cyrus reached into Nolan's bag and grabbed one canister of pyro-newt eggs and a long fat-bladed knife. When he touched it, a cold electric whisper shot all the way up into his shoulder. He and that knife had both known the Dragon's Tooth. But he didn't have time to wonder or remember or wish about what had been. He grabbed Antigone's arm.

"Come with me," he whispered. "Right now." Then he turned and ran.

He heard Rupert groan. Glancing back, he saw Antigone on his heels. Diana watched him go, and Dennis danced in place, eager but too afraid to follow.

"John," Rupert said. "Go."

The Captain jumped after them.

Cyrus scrambled through the gash in the wall where a door had been and slid into the great hallway. Up ahead, he saw that Brendan's boat had toppled from its stand. Chandeliers and portions of the ceiling had dropped onto the tile floor. At the far end, the tall wooden door to the courtyard had been blown in, and its splintered remains leaned against a wall of crushed displays, still smoking, its jagged edges licked with flames.

Beyond it, an unseen Leon began to snort and roar.

Cyrus didn't know exactly where he was going, but he had to trust in Dan's dream, and he had to move fast. There was girl somewhere who was going to be sacrificed, and he was meant to find her. He was meant to send Babd Catha back down into the dark, along with the hundreds of others who would try to rise behind her if he failed. And that meant he had to go down himself. Way down. Through doors Nolan had never let him open. As deep as or deeper than he had ever been.

He knew where to start. Picking up speed, dodging rubble, he veered around the toppled boat and slammed against a locked door that he knew would lead him to a hallway with stairs down into hallways with stairs down into chambers with even more stairs down. This was the way to the Polygon. But there were forks to some of those stairwells as well. There were doors on those lower levels that led to whole subterranean wings of Burials.

From the main entrance, Leon belched rage and Cyrus paused, listening to the echo. He couldn't see past all the rubble, but he could hear shouting and the turtle's chain rattling and jerking. Antigone stopped beside him.

"Hold this," Cyrus said. He handed Antigone the pyro-newt eggs and tucked the knife into his belt. Then he slipped Patricia off his wrist, slid the keys off her tail into his hand, and raised the snake up to his neck.

The Captain grabbed Cyrus's shoulder.

"Come on then, lad," he said. "Back to the flock with you."

Cyrus looked up into the grizzled face and sea-sharpened eyes of his ancestor.

"They're here," Cyrus whispered. "They're coming."

A tall shape ran up to the distant shattered door and leapt onto the side of the toppled boat. He wore leather on his arms, a long chain-mail shirt with loose flaps that hung between his knees, and a gleaming silver onion-shaped helmet with a single gold spike on the crown. He had a thin black beard that looked like lichen drooping off a tree branch, but his face was too solid for a mortal's, and his eyes seemed to eat the light. Perched on the boat, he raised a sword in each hand, pointing them stiffly at the little group.

The Captain backed into the middle of the hallway with his sword arm.

"Tamerlane," the Captain said.

"Dog," said the man on the boat. Another shape jumped up beside him—a man's shape, but his face was hidden behind a mail mask. Three stones dangled from cords in his right hand, and he held a spear with a long, forking blade in his left.

"Crescens," the Captain said. "Will I find every maggot in the rot of this carcass?"

A blond woman walked slowly around the boat, and the air seemed to ripple away from her like heat on a highway. She raised a long, slender, jewel-encrusted musket to her shoulder. Leon the turtle was still bellowing. More were coming.

"Rupe!" Antigone shouted, and she threw the jar of pyro-newt eggs.

The glass shattered at the foot of the boat. The eggs bounced out and rolled across the floor. The transmortals watched them, unworried, like bored children. For one moment, nothing. And then each egg flickered to life and sought a target, darting for the closest warm body.

With concussions like gunshots, eggs punched into all three transmortals at once. Red fire slammed them into walls and sent them tumbling. One egg slammed into the Captain's breastplate, throwing him backward. The red flash kicked Cyrus and Antigone up against the door, but they kept their feet.

Cyrus fed his gold key into the locked door, pushed through it into cool darkness, and dragged his sister inside. Slamming it behind them, he locked it as quickly as he could.

"Rise if ye dare!" the Captain was shouting. "I'll reap your devil guts for chum!"

More gunshots. Or eggs. And shouting.

"Cy, what are we doing? Where are we going?" Antigone was breathless. Cyrus couldn't blame her. His heart was pounding and his lungs were fluttering. Just three transmortals. And there would be dozens. Hundreds? The reality of it was sinking in. Rupert wasn't a pessimist. He might have actually seen the only way through this. Even if he and Antigone stopped the sacrifice and kept things from getting worse, Radu and all his transmortals would still be waiting for them after. And probably Phoenix. Along with his Reborn.

Justice and Wrath and Rupert might have stood a better chance.

Patricia slid easily off of Cyrus's neck and wound her glow around his hand. He slipped his finger through the key ring and pulled his sister down the hallway.

"We have to get down," Cyrus said. "Into the Burials. There's one we have to find. Dan had a dream. We can't stop all of them. But there's one . . . we have to." He tried not to picture all the stone fingers rising out of the water in the dream. He tried not to think about leaving his friends under attack. Doom seemed heavy in the air around him, slowing his blood, slowing his limbs. "And a pair of huge statues," he added. "It would be good if we found them. Just in case this goes as bad as Rupe thinks it will."

They reached the first stairs and Cyrus turned, raising Patricia, studying his sister's terrified face in the silver glow.

"I'm sorry I told you to come," he said. "I . . . this might be it, Tigs."

Antigone shook her head. "No. It's not. No way. Cowboy up, Tarzan. Let's go."

Cyrus actually laughed. He felt lighter just hearing her use the line from the dream. Antigone forced him down onto the stairs.

The first part of the descent was familiar. They ran down halls crammed with storage and furniture mounded beneath sheets. They watched for the ominous-looking doors—the oldest doors, the doors of foreboding that they had always been told not to open. Those would lead them down.

The first door they tried led to a massive amount of antique and very clearly forgotten janitorial supplies. The second door led to spiral stairs that only ran up. The third door led to a completely empty room, with a stone floor layered in dust and rattraps in the corners.

They ducked back out and moved on.

"So," Antigone asked, "what else can you tell me about this Burial we're supposed to find?"

"It's bad," Cyrus said. He was distracted and breathing hard. He slowed down in the hallway. Something was nagging at him. "Nasty woman war goddess human sacrifice girl going to die to bring her back." He didn't even hear himself. He'd been in two Burials before. One had been the Captain's drowned vault. The other had been Rasputin's, and he'd been sneaking around with his Solomon Keys for the first time when he'd found it. That was one of the most recent Burials, so it had been higher up, but it had still been hidden—the floor of an empty room had fallen away into stairs.

Boom.

The sound was distant enough, but the stone floor vibrated slightly under Cyrus's feet. That had been huge. His friends were up there. Diana was up . . . No. He couldn't think about that right now. He couldn't be Rupert. Individuals might die. They all might die. But they couldn't lose this fight.

Antigone was looking around at the walls. She was thinking about the people they'd left behind.

"The Burials don't have doors," Cyrus said suddenly. "I mean, they do. But not normal wood-and-hinges doors."

Antigone faced him. "Cy, do you—"

"The empty room," Cyrus said. And he ran back the way they had come.

Inside the empty room, Cyrus began scraping at the dusty floor with his feet. Rasputin's Burial had been opened with a single keyhole set in a stone. The Captain's had been a keyhole in an epitaph.

Antigone worked beside him. A dust cloud billowed up around their knees. Soon they wouldn't be able to see at all.

Antigone moved along the walls. She paused in a corner.

"Cy?"

Cyrus jumped over beside her. Antigone dragged her foot across a tiny silver chain with seven links inlaid in a single stone. In the middle of the last one, there was a keyhole.

Cyrus dropped to his knees, slid his silver key into the hole, and turned.

The room echoed with the sound of grinding stone. The floor sank away into a flight of stairs.

Ancient air crawled up through the dust to meet the Smiths.

"Okay," Cyrus said. "Stay with the keys until I call you. It will shut again if I pull them out."

Cyrus raised Patricia above his head and stared at the dark spiral descent at his feet. He didn't have time to be afraid. He didn't have time to worry. He drew the fat-bladed knife he'd taken from Nolan's bag and pointed the dark naked steel in front of him. His hand buzzed with cold power, a charmed memory of the Reaper's Blade itself.

From here, it was all new—very old—territory. He dropped onto the stairs, counting every quick step with a tongue-tip whisper inside his teeth. From here, he had to track his direction like Rupert had shown him.

The stairs were longer than he had expected. The dropping floor had simply bridged him down to solid permanent stairs that bent and curled and twisted instead of keeping a consistent spiral. His legs tightened and grew heavy. His whispered count slurred into one prolonged but punchy hiss.

The air was suddenly cooler on his face and in his lungs. It thickened so much, he felt like he was splashing through it.

And his feet hit the bottom. He stopped, breathing

hard. Heavy dust, undisturbed for centuries, swirled away from him.

There was no choice of paths. A single arched corridor stretched away from the stairs, disappearing in nothingness beyond Patricia's glow.

He waited. He listened. Something hidden dripped. Something invisible scratched. The corridor was creepy enough to send any sane person right back up the stairs. But Cyrus had lived in the Polygon, bathing in icy drips, sleeping just out of reach of thousands of scratching feet. And he was here in search of one of the sleeping never-dead because his brother had shown him dreams.

"Eighty-four, up," he whispered. He extended Patricia left and right. No doorways, no keyholes.

"Tigs!" He threw his voice back over his shoulder. A second later, grinding stone echoed above him. The floor vibrated beneath his feet.

"Wow, that was close!" Antigone's voice rattled down around him and the grinding banged to a stop. He could hear her incredibly slow footsteps, like she was stopping to tie her shoes on each step.

"Cyrus? Cy? Could you turn Patricia on, please? It's so dark, I feel dizzy."

Cyrus raced back up the steps, three at a time, burning his legs and his lungs all over again by the time he reached his sister.

Antigone handed him the keys as he caught his breath.

A dozen steps above her, the stairs simply stopped. The floor had closed. The ceiling was solid above them and well out of reach.

"Great." Cyrus dropped the keys into his pocket. "One light, one set of keys, we stay together now. And we have to hurry."

At the bottom, Cyrus didn't stop to let Antigone take in the corridor. He settled into a jog, whispering his step count as he did, sweeping Patricia back and forth, trying to watch the walls.

The corridor began to slope down, and at the same time, it bent slowly to the right.

"Cy!"

Cyrus stopped before his forty-second step. A large single slab of stone was built into the left-hand side. It was peaked and slightly smaller than a door, though bigger than the epitaph stone that had sealed the Captain's underwater chamber.

Cyrus extended his snake hand toward it, and Antigone ran her hands over the stone's uneven surface. A tiny trickle of water from the ceiling had marred the stone over centuries, striping it with bulging mineral deposits that looked like vertical sinews. Right in the center, there was a small inscription and a single silver chain-link inset around a keyhole.

"It's in Latin," Antigone said.

"This is why I brought you," said Cyrus. "What does

it say? The nasty female we're looking for is called Babd Cathy."

"Pietru Cax-something," Antigone said. "The name isn't Latin. It's Greekish, and it's definitely not Babd or female." She looked back at her brother. "It's like an epitaph, but it's mostly hidden now. Do we open it to check?"

Cyrus shook his head. "No time. Come on."

He picked up his count at forty-three, but the next stone was only ten steps farther on. And it belonged to someone named Ambrosius. Antigone skimmed the epitaph.

"Something about being a father of witches," she said. They moved on, but only ten more steps.

"Horsa," Antigone said. "Never heard of him. Or her, I guess. Might be a feminine ending." The inscription was badly obstructed. "Invader, blood drinker, brother to someone, so definitely a guy."

Ten more quick steps around the curve and Cyrus slowed before he even saw the stone.

Slab number four. Another silver link around a keyhole. There had been seven links in the floor of the entry room, and Cyrus was starting to think he knew why.

This slab was already different. The stone was gray, but veined with green smokelike swirls. And when Cyrus wasn't looking directly at it, the green veins seemed to be moving. The wet mineral deposits from the ceiling parted around this stone, leaving it clean. There wasn't even any dust.

The inscription was in the sharp chopped lines of Sanskrit or something like it.

Antigone touched the stone and jerked her hand back. The surface had depressed under her fingers like mud. While Cyrus watched, his sister's finger dents disappeared. The Sanskrit disappeared. With a low, wet sucking sound, another inscription formed.

In English.

Smoky green veins writhed through it. The silver link sprouted silver branches and tiny silver leaves.

# QUICK

Self-submitted to this cold peace, here sleeps he of
the ancient young,
burdened with the touch of life.

"Okay . . . ," Cyrus said. He turned to move on.

"The touch of life," Antigone said. "I've heard of him. He wanted to be Buried, but Brendan had him make two living statues first."

Cyrus looked at his sister. He looked back at the stone that should have been stone but was acting like clay—if clay could rewrite things, and if it could swirl colors like water.

"The Brothers Below?" Cyrus asked. "Those living statues? This guy made them?"

"That's what Lemon said," Antigone answered. "A Druid with the touch of life."

Cyrus wanted to forget Babd. If this guy had made the Brothers, then maybe he could change the Brothers. He might be able to tell Cyrus where to find them. He could definitely tell him how to wake them, and how to keep them from killing absolutely everything. Maybe.

Cyrus tallied his step count in his head. This was not what he was supposed to be looking for . . . not if he believed Dan. And he did. He had to. But the maker of the Brothers?

He needed to stay on task. Cyrus nodded at Antigone, sheathed his knife, and jogged on, dragging his fingers down the wall as he went, no longer counting his steps.

The next three slabs in the curving corridor turned up an Italian name, a French name, and more Latin. But no Babds and no Cathas. Not even a Cathy.

And no other stairs. No other doors or corridors. Nothing.

Cyrus kicked the dead end. He kicked it until his foot screamed, and then he kicked it one more time. Breathing hard, he turned around, put his hands on his knees, and leaned against the wall. The cool stone pulled the heat from his back but not from his frustration. Somewhere up above him, people who died were fighting people who didn't. They needed him to get this done and get up there. He had to be faster. He had to find the Burial of a feather-haired war goddess with a skeleton face and stop a human sacrifice so that the real versions of every statue in Dan's black dream water wouldn't rise up around them and destroy the real world. And now he couldn't even stay focused on that.

QUICK. With the touch of life . . .

He breathed slowly, trying to clear his head. Dream Dan had told him that Antigone would die if he didn't find Babd Catha and prevent her from rising. In which case, he should be sprinting back up those long stairs already, trying to find a way out of this place, and a way into the next dank suite of Burials.

Cyrus wiped his forehead on the back of his wrist.

"Cy?" Antigone asked. "What are we doing?"

Cyrus slid down into a crouch. He had to make a decision now.

"Quick," he said. "We find out about this touch of life."

Oliver Laughlin yawned and stretched his Reborn but still adolescent body. He crossed his feet at the ankles and folded his hands around the Dragon's Tooth, letting them rest on his stomach. The plane was absurdly loud and absurdly cold, but collecting as many aircraft as he had over the last few weeks had required the remainder of his wealth and a great deal of theft. Pickiness would have been foolish. And he could, after all, silence the noise inside his skull; he could push warmth through his body. The flip-down stretcher he had claimed for himself was uncomfortable enough that it must have been intended for use by the dead. But that could be altered within his mind as well. Complaining nerves were tamed and his mind focused on the broader game at hand.

Phoenix was striking for the throat.

Radu was testing the trap. He had firebombed Ashtown and sent in a team of at least nine transmortals. Somehow, Rupert Greeves was on-site, but he wouldn't be for long.

Radu Bey would enter Ashtown. The Burials would be opened, and Phoenix and two hundred of his sons would be in place, ready to constrict.

The old powers would be offered a choice.

Mortality: true, complete, and final death.

Immortality: but only in blood-bound allegiance to Phoenix.

Phoenix knew that some would fight. But his Reborn would be firing darts full of tooth potion already tested and proven in that skirmish in the cigar factory. If the darts could stun Gilgamesh, a sufficient number could temporarily drop any of the transmortals. Phoenix had even sent Radu a little sample along with the ritual tokens to help him enter Ashtown—a threat to accompany his gift.

In the end, Phoenix expected to execute many with the tooth that tipped his cane—perhaps even rebestowing transmortality on a few of his most-trusted Reborn sons. But surely most of the dragons would kneel. They were lovers of power, unused to fear. They would feel terror and awe, and they would be bound to him.

And then he would govern the storm.

Oliver yawned and felt the pleasure of young lungs inside a taut chest, undecayed by age. The human authorities were scurrying. A plane had crashed in the lake. The smoke rising up from Ashtown would be visible for miles. Some fools were sure to investigate.

Oliver closed his eyes and smiled at the thought of what those people would be walking into.

The living stone was warm beneath Cyrus's palm. It felt like mud, but it was dry, and as dense and heavy as stone. Because it *was* stone. If he punched it, his knuckles would break. But when he pressed on it lightly, it depressed beneath his fingers. If he had time to experiment, he could probably stab his knife right through the slab, one slow centimeter at a time.

"Cy, are you sure about this?" Antigone chewed her lower lip while she watched.

"Of course not," Cyrus said. "I'm unsure about everything right now."

The silver Solomon Key rippled and morphed into a long, jagged leaf as he slid it into the hole and turned.

The slab bent inward slowly in the center, and then swung open.

The room inside was on fire with sunlight. Cyrus staggered back across the hall, blinking. Antigone threw an arm up over her eyes.

Warm air swirled out into the corridor. The floor of the chamber was covered with vines and grass and bright flowers that looked like they were made of pottery or porcelain, but all of it was moving, bending slightly in a breeze. The chamber was deep, the vaulted ceiling high, and the far wall held the white fiery orb of a false sun. It was setting, inching down toward the floor. Every pillar had sprouted branches, and they were heavy with fruit and blossoms. Huge clusters of grapes hung down from the ceiling.

Cyrus stepped inside, and the grass bent around his feet, light enough to be real.

In the center of the room, water burbled out of the stone floor and flowed in a small circular river. Inside that circle, the grass was thick and emerald bright, bent and tangled in a ring like a nest.

In that nest, a small boy was sleeping. He was on his side with his knees pulled up to his chest. He wore pale rawhide trousers but was shirtless. His skin was the color of caramel and was thickly spattered with dark chocolate freckles. He had no hair.

"Um, excuse me?" Cyrus inched forward. "Hello?"

The boy's eyes opened. They were even greener than Patricia's. As green as two glowing leaves held up in front of the sun.

He sat up, looking from Cyrus to Antigone in the open doorway. He blinked, and then stretched, bending slowly backward until his body was shaped like a horseshoe. In a flash, he snapped back upright. Apart from the baldness, he didn't look more than eight years old.

Cyrus cleared his throat. "I'm Cyrus, and this is my sister, Antigone. We need your help."

The boy's bright eyes narrowed. After a moment, he leapt to his feet. As he did, his legs changed, and a goat's body sprouted below his waist. He landed on four prancing hooves, now a young goat centaur. He turned in a circle, while Cyrus and Antigone gaped at the boy's freckled torso on the spotted goat's body. Finally, he faced them, a rear hoof still scraping at the grass. When he spoke, his voice was a wide whisper that seemed to be coming from everywhere at once but was still barely louder than the little stream that encircled him.

"I plucked Cyrus the mighty Persian from his

goatherd home," he said. "You are not he, but perhaps his distant echo. I wept for Antigone as she hung in the cave, her tomb. You have not her darkness."

"Different people," Cyrus said. "Not us. But we really do need your help. We have to stop the sacrifice of some girl we don't even know, though I did see her face in a dream. And I think we're going to need the Brothers Below or something just as strong. Is there any way we can find them and wake them up without dying?"

The boy cocked his head. "I do not know them."

"Justice and Wrath," Cyrus said.

"Law hearts," said Antigone. "You made them for Brendan in exchange for this Burial."

The goat boy shut his eyes, breathing slowly. He shook his head.

"Listen," Cyrus said, moving forward. "The transmortals are coming. Radu Bey is coming. He's going to wake up some crazy war goddess without a face, and if she gets this sacrifice, then she'll be too strong to stop and all the people I love are going to die, and these Burials will be opened, and the world is going to get absolutely hammered with pretty much every single member of the awful villain hall of fame all at once."

"My sleep is older than these words. I do not know them." The boy's eyes stayed closed. His sun was sinking fast and the color of the room was shifting to red and orange. A small moon was rising on one wall.

"Immortals," said Antigone. "Radu Bey is a Dracul, a blood sorcerer and dragon gin. He shares his flesh with Azazel."

The boy flinched at the name, but his eyes stayed firmly closed.

"They're coming to wake Babd Catha," Cyrus said. "And everyone else will follow."

At that name, the boy's eyes snapped open. He stared straight into Cyrus's and down inside him. Cyrus coughed. He felt heat in his head, in his gut, in his chest. And in a flash, it was gone.

"It is now the truth," the boy whispered. "It must be made a lie. But you do not have the strength to face her. The Reaper has kissed the knife you now carry, but only the Reaper's true blade can harm the storm crow, mother of death and devils."

"Right," said Cyrus. "Well, I lost that one. So we should find her Burial and make sure she doesn't come out and no one kills this girl for her."

"Her place of sleep is sealed with living stone from my hands," the boy said. "There is no door, no keyhole, no hinge. The stone will swallow ax and pick and blast. A way cannot be opened from without." His bald, speckled brow furrowed, and he shut his eyes again. "And yet she rises. A dragon has been given charms to guide him. He spends the strength of a thousand souls to come to her. A thousand more to wake her and open the stone from within." His eyes opened, and their green was dimmed by sadness. "She will walk these halls. She, the oldest of evils but one, will see the sun."

"What about the sacrifice?" Cyrus asked. "The girl. Can we stop that? Where is she?"

"Many hundreds of miles distant," the boy said. "On an altar of men, in a chamber of bodies, in a temple of pain and slowly departing souls."

Cyrus groaned. So Dan's dream had simply been an announcement. It was done. Babd Catha was rising no matter what, and her human sacrifice was hundreds of miles away. All the stone shapes would rise up from the water, and he knew what that meant. Dan had seen death for all of them. That was all that was left—for Cyrus and for his sister and for his friends, for everyone he had called to join in the impossible defense of Ashtown. Some general.

Antigone shivered. She had actually seen pictures of Radu's old body buildings. There was a new one? And some girl was inside one on an altar made of people? It made her feel sick.

"Okay," Cyrus asked. "So how do we wake the Brothers Below?"

The boy's goat legs vanished and he was human again.

"The kiss of law," he said. "Breathe your law into them and stop their throats. They shall arise and slay."

"Us first," Cyrus said. "Right? I mean, if it has to be that way, it has to be that way. But I'd rather it not. And there are others, too."

The boy didn't blink. His eyes were still.

"Listen," said Cyrus. "Please, help us. We're not looking to purge silly people. If you made the Brothers for anything good at all, this is it. I have to stop Babd and Radu. There are people we love, and they are upstairs, fighting for us right now."

Antigone moved up beside Cyrus, her face on fire in the false sunset. She tucked a loose strand of hair behind her ears and met the boy's eyes.

"A boy called Quick," she said. "Is that really your name?"

"I have worn many names," the boy said. "I have taken many sacrifices. With a stolen spark of life I have grown much folly and seasoned much wine and spread much foolish love. Always, in every temple, in every rite, I was the fool, always I was Quick and Quickening." He looked from sister to brother and back. "A greater Fool came. A greater Folly. I was broken and found peace."

Cyrus looked at Antigone, impatient. She was smiling.

"We're not in this situation because we're wise," she said. "Please. Help us."

The boy nodded. "There is one deep rite to turn Justice, one only to shield men from Wrath."

Quick spread his arms and the grass flew out of his

circle. He stood on bare, slowly swirling stone, ringed with water.

"If you would belong to the Fool, slay me," he said. "Your black blade can bite." And in one second, his freckles vanished and his skin became perfect. In the next, he dropped to the ground, no longer a boy but a small sheep—short-haired and young.

*Slay me.*

"No," said Cyrus. "I can't do that."

Antigone drew her brother's knife and stepped across the water.

*Throat.*

"Tigs!" Cyrus jumped forward, but he was too slow. His sister bent quickly, grimaced, and jerked the blade up across the lamb's throat.

Black blood stained white wool and ran down over the stone and into the water. The little river ran red.

The lamb leapt back up into the shape of the boy, one side of his throat gaping. But he didn't seem to mind. The bloody boy traced three circles in the stone at his feet, and small living bowls sprouted up, pooling with his dark liquid life. The bowls didn't stop growing until they had closed all the way into spheres the size of small oranges.

He handed two to Antigone, and they were as heavy as solid stone in her hands.

"To stop their mouths," he whispered. He handed the third to Cyrus. "For those you love." The boy looked at them both. "Kneel in the water."

The round stone was hot in Cyrus's hand. Antigone dropped to her knees in the tiny stream, and Cyrus followed her down, more than a little confused. Sharp, frigid water climbed over his calves and numbed his knees.

Quick reached out with both hands and tore Cyrus's tight black sleeves off at the elbows. He threw them away. Shocked, Cyrus watched them unravel and sprout up into black grass where they landed.

With a snap of Quick's hands, Antigone's leather jacket was gone. He threw it aside, and Cyrus watched it roil on the ground like it was trying to stand up or take root or slide away. Antigone was wearing a short-sleeve olive safari shirt, buttoned only in the center. Beneath it, her pearly Angel Skin glowed. Winged images moved through the visible threads.

Quick smiled at the sight. Then he plunged his cupped hands into the cold water and slapped it up into Cyrus's surprised face. Cyrus spat, blinking and dripping even as Quick did the same to his sister.

"Lay down your life," he said, "and find that you have picked it up. Fear no raging beast."

Quick dragged his fingers through the black blood on the stone. Then he touched his fingertips to Cyrus's temples and painted a dark stripe down Cyrus's forearms onto the backs of his hands, and did the same to Antigone. He pointed to the stone ball in Cyrus's hand.

"Place those you love in a sealed room. Wipe that blood or your own blood around the door."

Antigone studied the backs of her hands. "What about when it wears off?"

Again Quick smiled, and his eyes flashed spring and summer. "It is the Fool's symbol, the mark of the lamb who ravaged ancient lions. The symbol fades, but what it symbolizes will live on, growing with every drumbeat of the sun. I am Quick; it is I who say this. Believe, and it is done."

Cyrus looked at his sister and then at his bare arms. Patricia had been striped with blood as well. "This will keep us safe?" he asked.

The boy called Quick ran his hands over his soft stone, and his blood began to sprout back up into long emerald grass, spreading through the whole ring as it did, swirling into a nest. His throat had healed, and his freckles were returning.

"Safe?" he asked. "I am older than this world. It will not make you safe; it will make you dangerous—light to the darkness, life to the dead, love to the loveless, folly to the wise. Wage your war. Wake the Brothers."

He curled himself back into his nest of grass.

"But where are they?" Cyrus asked. "How do we find them?"

"Follow your feet down when the floor falls," Quick said. "Run. Justice and Wrath wait below the rising water. If you seek, you find. Live for those you love. Until the end"—Quick yawned—"of sorrows."

Cyrus stood up in the little stream. He looked at the heavy stone ball in his hand, and then down at the sleeping boy, mottled with chocolate freckles. Antigone rose, dripping, beside him.

"May the Brothers burn the feathers of Babd Catha," Quick whispered, his eyes blinking slowly. "And grind her skull to meal. As for the wingless beast, the dragon you called Azazel, feed him no pain." He breathed in long and slow. "Tell only tales of laughter."

The sun on the back wall set completely. Only the light of a moon and Patricia lit the sleeping boy in the grass.

## ❧ nineteen ❧

# THE BROTHERS BELOW

RUPERT GREEVES KICKED the heavy oak door open and stepped into the room with Horace slung over his shoulder and bleeding down his back.

Jeb, Robert, Diana, and Gunner ducked through the door after him. Gunner had Nolan's big black weapon bag slung over his shoulder, and it looked a lot heavier now that he was carrying it. After a glance back into the hallway, Gunner shut the door and threw a heavy bolt.

The room was three floors above ground level and served as a council hall for Sages. The long, low ceiling was held up by dark carved beams, and a table of the same wood filled the room below it. The stone walls were painted but undecorated. There were three doors but no windows, which was why Rupert had chosen it.

He shrugged Horace's limp body onto the end of the dark table and stepped back, breathing hard. Robert and Diana jumped forward and quickly tore open the little lawyer's vest and shirt, searching for his wound.

Rupert saw the deep gash just below Horace's ribs, and he looked away, wiping the sweat off his face.

Gunner dropped his weapon bag and rounded the table, bolting the other two doors. Not that bolts would do much good against the hunters behind them.

Jeb was leaning against a wall with his eyes shut. The stitches in his scalp had blown halfway open and his ear and neck were painted red down the shoulder.

Rupert looked back at the other two Boones.

"Come on, Horace," Diana whispered. She was working on the lawyer with gauze while her father used a needle, fighting to stop the bleeding inside the small man.

Horace's breathing was short and sharp, never quite filling or emptying his lungs. Rupert had seen too many ends not to know what was coming. While the Boones worked, he stepped over to the table and grabbed the little lawyer's hand.

Horace turned his head toward the big Avengel, and he squeezed. He licked his lips and tried to catch enough breath to speak.

"Too many lies," he said, "to forgive. So many . . ."

Rupert shook his head. "Not now, Horace. Not now."

"Then . . . when?" the lawyer asked. "Forgiveness . . . I don't . . ."

Rupert leaned in. "Forgiveness is given, not earned. You have mine."

Horace shut his eyes. "Gunner," he whispered.

Rupert looked up at Horace's tall nephew, but Gunner shook his head and backed away, wiping his face with his sleeve. Robert Boone had given up. He backed away. Diana gnawed her lip, still pressing down on the wad of gauze.

"My accounts," Horace said. "Sewn in my vest. All Gunner's." Gasping, he grabbed at Rupert's arm. "The old words," he said. "Say the words."

Still gripping the lawyer's hand, Rupert placed his left hand on Horace's head, and he spoke in Latin. The words were firm and certain, and as he spoke, John Horace Lawney VII relaxed. His breathing eased. His bleeding stopped. And he was gone.

Rupert folded the lawyer's hands on his chest and backed away.

"Dennis?" he asked the room. "Jax?"

Robert and Diana looked around, noticing the boys' absence for the first time.

"Dennis was with us on the first flight," Jeb said. "I slipped and he helped me. Jax could be anywhere."

Rupert sighed. Niffy had insisted on standing with the transmortals. How long the monk would last, he didn't know.

"And Sterling?"

"Didn't even try," Gunner said. "He fell back when we started the push."

"How many were there?" Robert Boone growled.

His crease-lined eyes were still on Horace. "I expected more."

"Nine by my count," Rupert said. "Scouts only. The rest will be on their way." He reloaded both guns in his holsters, and then drew the short black-bladed sword in his belt.

"Keep the doors open while I'm gone. Eyes and ears at all three. No surprises, and do not get holed up in here. Lock the door and get out."

Robert Boone cracked knuckles on both of his rough hands. "Jeb here knows his way around this place better than I do. He'll take the lead."

Jeb looked even more exhausted at the suggestion, but he nodded. Rupert gave the body of Horace a final salute as he moved back to the door they had entered.

Diana followed him. "Rupe," she said, "I want to come."

She had the black-barreled blunderbuss strapped to her back, and it was loaded with her very last round of tooth-treated shot. At least three of the transmortals were hobbled by pain because of it, but the ammo shortage had moved her on to a short heavy shotgun. It might not hurt them as much, but it could still send them rolling.

Rupert looked at Robert.

"Bring him back whole and entire," Robert said to Diana. "But don't let him slow you down."

Diana almost smiled.

Cyrus and Antigone ran down the long corridor. Antigone had left her coat behind, given that it had sprouted leather twigs and leather leaves.

"Where do we start?" Antigone asked.

"We have to get out of this dead end and find some other way down," Cyrus said. "But 'the rising water'? Where is any water rising in this place?"

They were approaching the base of the long stair. Was there a spring Cyrus didn't know about? A fountain?

Crack.

Stone shivered and groaned. The floor of the corridor heaved and leaned to the left. Cyrus and Antigone tumbled, flew, slammed into the wall, and then slid to a stop. Stone shards rained down from the ceiling. Whatever had just happened, it was big.

Cyrus coughed, climbing to his knees. Patricia had popped her light off again, but Cyrus could feel the floor angling left.

Cold energy hissed through the stone beneath him. Faint blue-and-white shapes like flames wisped through the walls around him, unhindered by the rock, too fast for his eyes to catch and hold. And then they were gone.

"Tigs?" Cyrus asked. "Did that seem like the strength of a thousand souls to you?"

"Shhh," Antigone said. "Listen."

Voices. And not from inside the corridor. And not from above the corridor. Cyrus lowered himself back down, pressing his ear against cool stone.

Many voices, all of them mingling together like the sound of falling water. And then silence.

One voice, a great voice, a man's voice, rose from beneath the stone.

Antigone recognized it.

"Cy!" she whispered. Reaching out for her brother, she found only his foot, and it was sliding away. The floor was cracking. It was crumbling.

Together in the darkness, they fell.

Radu Bey stood in a tunnel of bodies on the uppermost level of the temple. One moment ago, the bodies had been breathing, but no more. He and Azazel had thrown the pulse of one thousand souls through the symbols on the floor, and then at the wall. Blue-and-white fire still danced around the hole that should have opened onto the air above the city streets. Instead, it opened into a perfectly spherical tomb. A large grisly shape was stretched out on a stone bed.

Azazel burned inside Radu Bey's chest. The dragon held a second flood of souls ready, gathered from the temple floor below. Anann the Morrigan stepped up beside Radu Bey. Behind them both, the armed *Ordo Draconis* waited.

Radu Bey gripped the chains that hung from his arms, and he raised them both in his hands. The dragon writhed in his chest, sizzling with fire. Radu lashed his chains forward into the tomb, and the second storm of souls exploded like thunder.

The temple of bodies shook. But the tomb's stone walls shattered and crumbled. They cracked and splashed into unseen water, and dust billowed out of darkness.

Radu Bey waited. As the dust settled, he listened to the whine of sirens. He listened to his now-silent human walls. He was truly a blood sorcerer, possessor of dragon gin, savior of gods.

Black water was flooding Babd's newly opened tomb. It flowed out of the ancient tunnel and around Radu's bare feet. He walked forward, dragging his chains against the current, and stepped through the gaping hole in his temple wall. He stepped into darkness, into the deepest belly of Ashtown.

Dan sat at his suspended metal table, looked at Cyrus, and said nothing. Cyrus bobbed, treading water in the black lake beside the huge statue that now floated high on the surface.

"I know," Cyrus spat. "I know." And he grabbed on to Babd and tried to pull himself up. But he kept slipping back down. He kept sinking.

In the darkness, Antigone found her feet. The water wasn't deep—waist-high in places—but it had been deep enough to break her fall, and it was deep enough to drown in.

There was light coming from somewhere close—through a jagged crack in the wall, glowing through the rubble dust that filled the air. More blue-and-white wisps darted around and through her, finally disappearing beyond stone and below water. Grisly, monstrous carvings lined what was left of the broken walls.

She turned around and saw Cyrus floating facedown in the water.

Antigone splashed forward, grabbed her brother, and flipped him onto his back.

A huge laugh echoed around them.

Radu Bey was coming.

Antigone got her arms under Cyrus's and looked for a place to hide. Giant shapes and shadows were moving past the lit crack. Voices. Loud, excited shouts. A woman began to chant.

They had to get out of there. Antigone veered toward

a deep shadow in the opposite wall, a tunnel mouth. Praying a string of pleases, she pulled her brother into it, wrapped her arms around his chest, and shut her eyes. He was breathing. But not for long if anyone found them.

The transmortals were not silent. The chanting was growing louder. Other voices were laughing. And then there was splashing. Large shapes were moving through the crack. They passed Antigone quickly—dark silhouettes of women as tall as Gil with swords drawn, thin men who seemed to leave ripples in the shadows, huge men with heads like buffalo, shapes that were bent and sharp like scythes, unarmed women that emitted an aura of dim light that bruised the air—yellows and reds and greens. More and more and more of them splashed past, until they were only distant voices falling down whatever shaft they had chosen to climb up.

"Cyrus," Antigone finally whispered. "We shouldn't be here. No one should."

Cyrus sighed a dreamer's frustration. Antigone slapped his face and he jerked awake, kicking and splashing in her arms.

"I'm sorry," Antigone said. "But I can't hold you up out of the water anymore and we have to work fast. A whole army of nightmares just marched by."

Cyrus flailed, smacked her by accident, and stood up.

"Where?" he asked. "Who?"

"Radu Bey is here somewhere. I heard him. A ton of others came out of that crack."

Cyrus looked back at the jagged crack in the wall. Then he messed with Patricia until the surface of the water was silver all around them. He held the snake high. Not too far behind them, in the tunnel Antigone had chosen to hide in, low wide stairs rose out of the water.

Cyrus waded toward them, and Antigone followed. At the top of the stairs, there was a stone door. More than thirty silver links were inlaid in its surface around a center keyhole.

"Oh, great," Cyrus said, but he was already digging for his keys.

Diana slid on her belly toward the stone stair rail. There was a diamond cutout in the stone that would let her look down into the main hallway. She glanced back, and Rupert nodded.

Diana set her shotgun on the step beside her, slid the barrel of her blunderbuss through the gap in the rail, and studied the floor below. She could see four transmortals flat on their faces with their arms bound. The Captain paced around them, muttering furiously. His face was a bloody mess, but his golden breastplate glowed like it was fresh off a bed of coals, and his dragon blade was drawn.

Beyond him, and beyond the smashed front doors, Diana could just see one of Leon's legs, and the heavy spattering of rain on the steps outside.

Diana scanned the rubble throughout the hallway but saw no sign of Gil or Nolan or Arachne. Nothing of Niffy or Sterling—though she hadn't expected him to be around—and no sign of Dennis or Jax.

In her peripheral vision, Diana saw something move in Brendan's black boat, where it lay tipped onto its side. She stared for a moment longer, and saw it move again.

Dennis Gilly. And Jax. Together, and not in a bad hiding place, though close to where the fight had been the hottest.

Of course, she was glad Dennis and Jax seemed to be fine. But they weren't really whom she had been thinking about. She had no idea what Cyrus and Antigone were attempting or where they had gone. She did know that she wanted to be with them. She'd hesitated. She'd waited. And then they'd been gone.

Niffy and Nolan entered the hallway. Niffy was limping badly, and Nolan was peeling skin off his bare arms as they walked, dropping the thin sheets behind him.

Where were the other five attackers? Where were Gil and Arachne? Where were Cyrus and Antigone?

"Do you hear that?" Rupert asked. He dropped into a squat behind her.

"Shouting?" Diana asked. She wasn't sure. It was definitely voices.

The Captain could clearly hear it. He tensed and turned in place.

Niffy and Nolan froze. Niffy dropped onto his belly and pressed his ear to the mosaic tile floor. A split second later, he jumped back to his feet. He grabbed Nolan, and they ran.

The floor erupted in fire. Diana jerked back as tile shrapnel whistled and chattered through the hallway. Larger stone blocks smashed into walls and skidded across the floors.

A huge bare-chested man with glistening olive skin and a bloodred dragon on his chest climbed out of the hole. He wore a bright white cloth bound with gold around his waist. Broken chains hung from his wrists and dragged from his ankles.

The Captain stood to face him.

"Smith!" Radu Bey roared, and he began to laugh. "This is joy in truth."

Diana blasted her last tooth-treated shot into the back of the huge man's head. His roar became a scream of pain, but he turned, snarling and undamaged, looking for her. Transmortals with thick arms and wild eyes were scrambling up out of the hole around him like ants out of a mound. The whole building shook with the thunder of their weight.

Niffy and Nolan had regrouped, both holding blades and lobbing jars of pyro-newt eggs, but not enough for the swarm that came to meet them. The hallway was filled with shouts and explosions. Diana dropped her blunderbuss and then emptied her shotgun, and still the Captain and Radu Bey eyed each other like they had forgotten all else. Niffy and Nolan retreated out of sight.

More transmortals were climbing out of the hole. They scanned the hallway and the walls for enemies, and Diana prayed that Dennis and Jax would keep still in the boat. Radu waved a few away. Others circled around him and pressed the Captain's flank.

Captain John Smith stood alone, his eyes brighter than his breastplate and his beard smoking. His smile, whitened by years of sun on the sea, flashed at the massive man with broken chains—the transmortal he had tricked and Buried so long ago.

"You are my brother, Smith," Radu snarled. "You and I are bonded in blood. But I gave you my true brothers' heads. What shall I do to you?"

"What shall ye do?" The Captain laughed. "Ye'll see that dragon scite cut from your flesh with your father's own blade. Then ye'll face a man as man, with no dragon puppetry to aid you." He sliced the air with his sword and raised the tip at his enemy. "Come, Radu. A fourth

Dracul head in the crest of Smith would make a better symmetry."

Radu Bey used only his chains, and they lashed and snapped forward faster than Diana could see.

The Captain whirled and ducked, shattering links on the edge of his blade. As he danced, the transmortals edged all the way around him, swords and spears and daggers raised.

"Rupe!" Diana said. She drew a revolver and put another round in Radu Bey. The blood sprayed from between his shoulder blades, but he barely seemed to notice. "Rupert! What do we do?"

Rupert Greeves put a hand on Diana's shoulder and began to pull her away. But she couldn't go. She fired and fired and fired on the circle of transmortals, but she was like a bee trying to defend a man from wolves.

Surrounded completely, the Captain's blade was still fast enough to keep the ring from closing. He laughed as he fought, and his smile was as grim as any reaper's. And then he began to sing. His accent and his effort slurred his words, but Diana recognized the song. Her own mother sang it in the kitchen, and her happiness in the singing always belied the sorrow of the words.

The Captain sang and he danced and he slashed the ring around him. He sang even when Radu's chain found his legs and lightning forked from the links and felled him. He sang as the transmortals tore the blade from his hand, grabbed his wrists, and stretched his shaking oak-strong arms out from his sides.

He was singing as they tore off his breastplate, and singing as Rupert pulled Diana back from the rail, away from what was about to happen.

"You are no immortal," Radu spat. "You are a beggar with a scrap of Odyssean Cloak hidden beneath your skin."

"Their mouths they opened wide on me," the Captain sang. "Upon me gape did they, like to a lion ravening and roaring for his prey. For dogs have compassed me about; they pierced my—"

The Captain's voice broke into a shout of pain, and then he sang on, louder still, filling the vaults with what sounded like triumph, like joy.

John Smith was ready to sail.

Diana shook as Rupert pulled her away. But she heard the beastly snarl as the scrap of Odyssean Cloak was taken from inside the Captain's chest. She heard a blade sing. The snarling stopped. Mocking laughter began.

"We have to get you out of here now," Rupert said. "All of you."

Diana didn't argue. She couldn't, even if she'd wanted to.

Oliver Laughlin paced the length of his descending plane, with his chute strapped to his lean adolescent shoulders. Radu Bey had taken longer to strike than Phoenix had expected, but the timing would work, so long as Phoenix wasn't there first. The transmortals would ravage the place for a while. They would open Burials. Hundreds would dance in the ashes of Ashtown. They would rejoice in the glory of their own strength. That was easy. They could be there for hours and Phoenix would still have time to gather his harvest. But if he was there too soon, a cautious Radu Bey might withdraw to strike another day.

But would there be another day like this one? A day when all the great ones would be in one containable, cageable place? Before they inevitably feuded and fought and scattered?

Phoenix raised the silver knob on his broken bamboo cane to his thin Oliver lips. He knew this breed of last-minute anxiousness was courtesy of youth, but he still felt it. He wanted this more deeply than he had once been able to want anything. And with wanting came fear.

He flipped open the silver knob and studied the black tooth, the sharp black triangle that swallowed light. He pressed the tooth itself to his lips and felt calming cold electricity flow through him. His plan would work. His intellect knew it. The trouble was with his young nerves.

Oliver walked toward the cockpit, even as he felt the plane banking into descent beneath him.

He could see Ashtown smoking ahead. He could feel a young man's adrenaline pumping through him.

"Father!" The two largest of his sons stood behind him, ready to help him jump. He walked back toward the cargo doors and positioned himself between them. Oliver smiled and bounced in place. Anxiety was becoming excitement.

"Aim for the fountain, Father!" one of the big men said. Once, he had been a Marine. "We don't want you initiating too close to hostile structures."

Phoenix smiled. He had molded a terrific crop of sons, the first seeds of his new world. Hal, the coward, excepted. But Hal was still in Plumm, watching over the collection of women chosen as wives for those sons who would survive this day.

A red light began to flash beside the cargo door. Let the countdown begin.

Cyrus and Antigone had descended back into water. The Brothers were in a chamber beneath rising water, but there had been no springs anywhere, and no fountains. The water was black and still, and the walls were wet. The chain of chambers behind the sealed door hadn't been easy to navigate. Ten stone markers in and Cyrus and Antigone had been forced into a hard right turn, and a room much larger than any they had seen belowground. It was almost the size of the dining hall, but with slightly lower ceilings and some kind of dais at the far end.

The water was thigh-deep. Antigone sighed, but Cyrus was staring straight ahead.

"Tigs," he said. "Look." He slid Patricia's tail out of her mouth and stood beside his sister in silence.

"Cy . . ."

"Let your eyes adjust."

There was a vertical seam on the far wall and it was glowing. That was how Cyrus had seen the dais at all. And that was how he could see the two huge shapes on either side.

Cyrus began to water-jog forward. He tripped, dove, stood again, and kept running, the heavy stone ball in his pocket banging against his leg with every step. Antigone dove more often, managing to stay just half a step behind him.

As Cyrus drew nearer, he slowed, sliding his finger back into Patricia's mouth and holding up her light.

Steps rose to a circular door with the glowing vertical seam. But the top of the steps was buried beneath a layer of bones carved from stone—stone bones, from monstrous beasts and monstrous men, strewn around the feet of the tall statues.

The Brothers and their clothes and all their weapons were shaped from the same stone. They wore the robes of monks with hoods up, hiding hard features in shadow. But solid stone or not, both heads seemed to have turned, to be looking down at Cyrus and Antigone.

"What do you think is behind the door?" Antigone asked. "And where's the rising water?"

"Right now, I don't care," Cyrus said. "I want these guys up top."

The Brother on the right gripped three spears in his left hand; a long sling dangled from his right. Instead of a stone, the sling held the skull of a king wearing a gold circlet crown. More skulls were pulled behind.

"You must be Justice," Cyrus said.

"Why?" Antigone asked.

Cyrus pointed at the Brother on the left. "Because he's Wrath."

The huge stone monk held only a long carved jawbone—like a giant crocodile's—in his right hand. The sleeve of his robe had been torn off at the right shoulder, and his stone arm was knotted in permanent tension.

Cyrus inflated his cheeks. These guys alive would be able to crush him like a cheese puff. They each had to weigh as much as a garbage truck.

But he had been marked. He could wake them. When they looked at him, they wouldn't see all the things he wished he had never done; they wouldn't see the cracks in his soul. They might not see a friend, but they wouldn't see an enemy, either.

He hoped.

Cyrus climbed up the steps and stood at the foot of Wrath. The statue was four feet taller than he was. The mouth was closed and the stone jaw tense, but there was a hole at the base of the man's throat right between his collarbones. It was about the size of a baseball.

Antigone stood beside Cyrus, handed him a stone ball, and cupped her hands to give him a boost. He used it to hop up and grab on to the stone giant's shoulders. They were warm, and the stone depressed beneath his fingers. He grimaced and shifted his grip, suddenly feeling very much like he was climbing all over something alive.

What was it Quick had said? "Breathe your law into them." What law? Thou shalt not kill? No stealing? Smoke the villains? "Live for those you love." That was just about the last thing Quick had said. Cyrus thought about why he wanted this beast of a man-shaped stone to wake, about why he was willing to die. Because of Diana. And Rupert and Jeb and Dennis and Jax and Nolan and the Captain and Arachne and even Niffy. He was angry because he loved.

"Um . . . Cy?" Antigone was beginning to shake.

Cyrus leaned forward until his lips were inside the hole at the statue's throat, and then he gave the statue a law for his heart.

"Live for those I love," he whispered.

Then he smacked the stone ball into Wrath's throat hole and watched as it melted and molded into the rest, until the giant monk had a completely human-looking neck. The statue's eyes lit up green with burning orange centers.

Cyrus jumped down and the eyes followed him. Antigone was backing away.

"Hurry!" Cyrus said, and he dragged his sister to the feet of Justice. She handed him the next ball and cupped her hands to boost him.

Cyrus scrambled up and spoke his law without hesitation. The second ball melded into the throat, and he jumped back down.

Two pairs of fiery autumnal eyes stared down at the siblings. Two massive statues shifted their weight, and the stairs beneath shivered with the force of it.

Wrath's fist clenched his jawbone, and living stone knuckles popped like tree trunks snapping. Justice rattled his three spears and then stretched his arms out from his sides. His chest expanded with a sound like wind in a canyon. The sling and crowned skull rocked beneath his arm.

Antigone slid her arm into Cyrus's and inched behind him.

Cyrus was braced to die, waiting for a blow to fall.

"Cy," Antigone whispered. "I think they're waiting for you."

Cyrus pointed straight up at the ceiling. "Go!" he said. "Defend what I—what *you*—love."

The Brothers looked at each other. Then Justice tore his feet free of the stone and leapt down off the stairs. The splash enveloped Cyrus and Antigone when he landed. The room shook. Loose stones rained down from the ceiling.

Justice reached for Antigone.

"No!" Cyrus yelled.

Wrath splashed into the water behind Cyrus. A stone hand closed around his thigh and he was lifted up. Dangling upside down, he saw Antigone hanging from Justice's hand beside him.

So this was it, then. The end. Killed by statues.

At the same instant, the Brothers dropped the siblings in the water. Then they turned, leapt up onto the stairs, and with two blows, smashed open the round door with the glowing seam.

Justice and then Wrath ducked through into light.

Two rows of lanterns hung from chains attached to the high ceiling. They were white balls of flame, each one suspended over a carved stone sarcophagus. A shallow river ran between the rows, and the Brothers strode through it.

Cyrus and Antigone sprinted behind, barely able to keep up. This was a tomb for mortals, not transmortals. One of the sarcophagi had been split open by a ceiling collapse, and normal grimy bones had spilled out. As the two rows ended, the Brothers reached a larger sarcophagus, carved like a boat. Water poured down over it in a delicate stream.

"Saint Brendan?" Cyrus said.

"You're just getting that?" Antigone said. "Yeah. I'd say so."

The stream dropped down the center of a stone-lined cylindrical shaft. A spiral stair coiled up around the sides toward a distant stone ceiling, but the Brothers were too big for the stairs. Instead, they began to climb the outside of the spiral like a ladder.

"Hey!" Cyrus shouted. "A little help? You're going to destroy those."

Justice leaned back and extended his bundle of spears toward Cyrus and Antigone, blades down.

"You asked," Antigone said. "May as well."

They each hooked their arms over the spears and Justice lifted Antigone up onto Wrath's overly large shoulders, and set Cyrus on his own.

Radu Bey dodged Leon's snapping head and stepped out into the pouring rain, the sword of his ancestors at his side, the blood of the Smith running off its edge in the water.

A dense ring of parachutes was settling on every side of Ashtown, like mushrooms from the sky.

It couldn't be Phoenix. He wasn't that foolish. And the O of B would never throw away this many men. The human military? That could be. He smiled at the thought. But he hadn't expected to swallow up the simple soldiers in fatigues for a few months yet.

Anann stepped out beside him.

"How long here?" she asked. "The resurrections are well begun. My sister thanks you, but she has slept long and desires sacrifice."

Radu Bey pointed his sword at the sky. "And this?"

At least twenty parachutes were touching down all around the courtyard.

Radu Bey filled his nostrils with the promise of battle and strode down the stairs in the rain, rattling chains as he went. He moved toward the nearest chute.

The man slipped out of his harness and rolled into a fighting stance, as lithe as a cat. As Radu Bey approached, he could see the gills on the man's neck, the power in his limbs, the strange symmetry of his features, and the wildness of his eyes. Here was mortal art worth making. He could enjoy the victory in felling such a creature.

Radu Bey raised his sword as the man raised a gun dangling a belt of darts.

Needles punched into Radu Bey's chest as the dart gun spat its tooth-brewed poison.

Radu Bey lashed the man's legs with a chain, and lightning cracked. When the mortal staggered, Radu's blade flashed and sent the man's head rolling. Then Radu Bey dropped to his knees.

"Poison!" he bellowed back to his men. And then he fell forward, giving himself to the dragon gin within.

Azazel, scales the color of dried blood, spun, flinging the body of the headless man across the courtyard with his spiked and smoking tail.

He stretched out his mind and found another stretching back.

*Phoenix!*

He had come in a boy's flesh, and to the dragon's ancient senses he felt as cold and unyielding as the Reaper's Blade he carried. And so very . . . *young.*

Diana let her reloaded shotgun dangle at her side. She stood at a window three stories up, looking down at the courtyard. Behind her, Jeb and her father and Rupert were shouting. The four of them were trapped in a room with only one door. Rupert had rallied them and they had tried to reach the airstrip, or even the water, but the transmortals were everywhere.

They had been attacked and then chased and then forced back and back into this room with no retreat.

Rupert and her father and her brother were struggling to hold the door, even as it splintered under the assault.

Horace was dead. The Captain was dead. Gunner was dead. When Diana had fallen, he had stood over her with one gun blazing, while the other hand wielded a long black knife.

The tall Texan had been picked up by a fiery woman and smashed against a wall while Robert Boone had managed to drag his daughter away.

It was hard to imagine Dennis and Jax and Niffy being alive in the swarm of unkillable hate that now prowled the halls of Ashtown. As the Boones and Rupert had fled, she had heard the rejoicing. The Burials were being smashed open.

Were the Smiths lying dead in some dark hall, or had they escaped? Were they hiding?

In the courtyard below, there was a dragon.

Behind her, Rupert's shouts were growing louder and more desperate, his threats more impossible. She filled herself with a long calming breath. It was time to die. She began to turn from the window.

And then, in the courtyard below, the central fountain exploded. Water swamped into the grass. The obelisk toppled. Statues lost limbs as they fell.

Two huge monks who looked like they were made of clay climbed up out of the hole. For a moment, they stood, assessing the field like two living monuments. And then they raised weapons. One picked up a man and seemed to weigh him. Then he dropped him into a sling and flung him completely out of the courtyard and into the trees. The other monk grabbed the dragon by the spiny tail and spun it around, ignoring the fiery blast that billowed around him. He leaned forward, studying the dragon's snarling face, and then he struck at it with a massive jawbone.

The monks were brutal and methodical, and as calm and unafraid as two men choosing fruit. Men were crushed. Transmortals were flung. The dragon took blow after blow and retreated, its claws and teeth and fire useless against the unflinching stone giants.

Beside the monks, ducking blows intended for others, dodging massive feet, Diana saw the Smiths.

Cyrus slipped in the mud and fell on his back, almost stabbing himself with the fat-bladed black knife. Steel was shattering, men were shouting, transmortals were cursing, a dragon was roaring, and the Brothers were loudest of all. Every blow shattered bone. Every step was an earthquake, pounding the grass into a swamp. The monks of living stone moved with the sudden force of explosions, and every motion of their joints groaned like giant sighing timber. The Reborn fled before them. The transmortals stood but were toppled like saplings facing an avalanche of boulders.

Rolling over, Cyrus looked for Antigone. She was crawling toward him through the mud. But behind her was Oliver Laughlin, looking startled and afraid between two large guards, standing with his back near the wall of the courtyard.

Cyrus blinked the rain away. Phoenix was here. Which explained the gilled men. But why? And Oliver looked both horrified and amazed by the Brothers.

Wrath picked up a transmortal and threw him down the hole beneath the fountain. Justice crushed two men with his cluster of spears and flung them toward the wall. The dragon embalmed Wrath in fire, but he merely picked up a statue from the fountain and hurled it at the dragon's head. Azazel leapt away, and the statue disappeared in an explosion of mud. The dragon sprang forward again, hacked wing stubs flailing, and lashed its tail around Wrath's head, throwing him to the ground. The earth shook. Swords and spears bit into the Brother's soft stone, but there they stayed, ripped from attackers' hands as the statue twisted and stood. Darts shattered on him and ricocheted away.

Yes, Cyrus could see that Phoenix was impressed. His Oliver face had the look of a boy admiring a new toy. And he had a wall at his back. He felt safe.

Cyrus scrambled to his feet and ran as hard as he could to get out of Oliver's peripheral vision.

He slid over a dead gilled man with his chest caved in by a crowned stone skull. Then he sprinted toward the courtyard wall, aiming for a spot less than forty yards from Oliver.

Twenty transmortals were drawing Justice away from Wrath, separating the Brothers. The dragon circled Wrath alone.

Breathing hard, Cyrus hit the courtyard wall and pressed his back against it. Oliver was clutching his broken cane, rubbing the silver knob at the top. If one of his two guards turned . . . but they didn't. Apparently, they had never seen a dragon fight a man of stone, either.

Glass shattered. Three stories up on the main building, Cyrus saw four bodies falling together. He saw Rupert's dark skin. He saw Diana's red hair. And his heart stopped.

They hit the ground hard, but they bounced and rolled like Cyrus had been taught. Then they were still. The bodies on the grass were well away from the Brothers. A few eager shapes began to move toward them.

Cyrus had no time for anything but rash. He might never get this close to the tooth again. Keeping his shoulder as tight to the wall as he could, he sprinted toward Phoenix from the side. He saw Oliver raise his silver knob to his lips.

Four seconds. Three. The guards still hadn't looked. One. Cyrus slipped in behind the first large guard, closed his hand on Phoenix's bamboo rod, and smashed his shoulder into the side of the boy's head.

He felt a shot of cold vibration thrill up his arm as he rolled free. And then a large gilled man stepped over him and emptied a gun into Cyrus's stomach.

The other man was firing now, too. Darts and bullets both. Heat punched through Cyrus's ribs. Darts dangled from him.

Cyrus couldn't breathe. But right now, holding the tooth, Cyrus also couldn't die. He pushed away the pain and rose, clutching the tooth to his chest and slashing at the guards with his black knife. He split one man's knee and kicked his gun away when he fell. The other was reloading. Cyrus threw his knife and watched him crumple.

Cyrus turned to face Oliver.

Cyrus's arm straightened, shaking, slowly extending the tooth to give it back.

"No," Cyrus said.

"Yes," said Oliver.

Cyrus turned and ran with Oliver behind him. He ran toward the Brothers, but as he did, he saw Rupert being dragged by his arms back toward Leon's steps.

A transmortal with a forked spear was prodding Diana. Cyrus forgot everything else. He forgot Oliver. He forgot the pain in his chest. He ran toward the ones he loved, and he heard swamping thunderous footsteps as two stone mountains ran with him.

"Crescens!" Cyrus shouted. It was the name the Captain had used.

The transmortal turned and raised his spear in surprise. His mail mask was up and he had a black pointed beard. He clearly wasn't worried about Cyrus, but there were stone giants right behind. As Crescens prepared to roll out of the Brothers' reach, Cyrus slashed at him with the short bamboo rod. He missed, slipped, and fell.

But Nolan didn't miss. A black blade sprouted out of the transmortal's chest, thrown from behind.

The man dropped his spear and sat down in the mud, his eyes wide with pain and surprise.

Nolan wrenched the long knife from the man's back with gloved hands, and he looked at Cyrus with rain parting around his eyes.

"You hold the tooth," he said, and he raised his own blade. "Beside it, true tooth-forged steel strikes with the Reaper's own bite."

Wrath's jawbone nearly took Nolan's head off, but he dropped to the ground just in time.

"No!" Cyrus shouted. "No!"

Justice bent to pick up Diana's body. Cyrus dove over her, spreading himself as wide as he could. He dug into his pocket for the stone ball Quick had given him to mark the ones he loved. Not knowing how to open it, he squeezed as hard as he could, and drops of Quick's blood fell onto Diana's cheek. She was breathing. Barely, but it was there, hot on Cyrus's hand. He quickly dabbed the blood onto her temples and then dragged stripes down her forearms. He climbed to Robert and Jeb and did the same for them. Jeb was coughing, but Robert was unnervingly still, and his breath was quiet.

"You see?" Cyrus looked up at Justice. The monk bent over the bodies. Then he turned back to the courtyard. It was scattered with gilled bodies and dart-drugged transmortals, stirring slowly. The dragon was gone. Oliver was nowhere to be seen.

Antigone was racing around the fountain hole, heading for Cyrus.

"Stay with her!" Cyrus shouted to Justice. "Keep her safe!"

Nolan was still dodging Wrath. Cyrus scrambled after them, and when Nolan doubled back, Cyrus was ready with blood on his fingertips.

Wrath picked Nolan up with the delicacy of a back-hoe, studied him, then dropped him in the mud and turned his orange and green eyes on Cyrus, waiting for a command.

They had to find Rupert. But he couldn't leave Diana.

"Tigs!" Cyrus shouted. "Guard them!"

Without waiting for an answer, Cyrus and Nolan ran toward the main door into Ashtown. Wrath followed, splitting stone stairs with each step. At the top, Leon had retreated into his shell and was still. Through the doors, Cyrus saw Radu Bey, back in his own form but bruised and bloody. He was grinning, watching four others nail Rupert Greeves up onto the door of the Galleria.

"Radu Bey!" Cyrus shouted, every cell in him ready to explode with anger. He was quivering with cold lightning, with a feeling he had never had before, not even when he'd first struck with the tooth as a weapon. Slowing his breaths seemed like slowing time itself. His heartbeats felt years apart. Radu Bey and his crowd turned as Cyrus bent and picked up a short spear with a broken shaft but a head and throat of blackened, tooth-forged steel.

"Good," Nolan whispered.

Cyrus inhaled and familiar words filled his mind, and for the first time, he knew their meaning. He felt Dan's voice inside him, and he wondered if his brother was having his old vision, but this time his vision was real, and it was happening now.

"The seventy weeks have passed," Cyrus said. "I lost the tooth and hold it again. I am the one come on the wings of your abominations. I am called the Desolation, and even the dragons will shrink from me in fear. Now leave my Keeper be and back away."

Radu Bey took one step back, but not on Cyrus's command. He was making room for another figure, walking through the crowd.

It had the tall body of a woman, wearing cracked leather armor studded with smooth stones. But her hands had talons like a bird's, and she gripped a single white bone. Her face was an empty-eyed skull thick with black crow feathers.

The skull hissed wind instead of speech, but the sound took shape.

"I bring the peace of carrion. I make the quiet of the lifeless. Babd Catha has come."

## ⚜ twenty ⚜

# SCATTERED

ANOTHER WOMAN STOOD BESIDE BABD CATHA, wearing the same leather but with a scarred face and red hair and bare arms tattooed with large fish scales. She carried an ax.

"I will end all of you," Cyrus said, and he believed it. "Is the girl still alive? I know you need a sacrifice. Where is she?"

The skull spoke again. "Where is my son, Quick, whose power wakes the stones?"

Wrath did not need to be told what to do. He had seen, and he had judged. He stepped around Cyrus and raised his stone jawbone.

And then Babd lifted her raptor hand and pointed a single talon. The stone giant froze. Wrath shook and shivered.

"No." Cyrus shook his head. He couldn't fail now. He had the Brothers. He had taken the tooth. But Rupert had been nailed to a door, and Diana was hurt outside, and who knew how many others had fallen.

Cyrus charged, shouting something in Latin that

Antigone would have corrected. He raised his spear, and then Nolan grabbed him and pushed him to the ground. The pale boy was on top of him, forcing his head down, covering it with his own body.

Babd hissed and Wrath shattered. Every shard of the Brother's huge bulk flew back toward Cyrus and Nolan in a storm of stone, spinning them away across the floor. Shrapnel ripped up tile, stripped walls, and tumbled the great shattered doors out into the courtyard.

Leon bellowed terror, but his chain was broken.

Nolan was limp on top of Cyrus. The transmortals were silent, but the skull was laughing like midnight wind.

Cyrus rolled out from under his friend. Nolan's back looked like he'd been sanded by an avalanche. His eyes were open but unfocused. Another friend fallen.

Cyrus turned and faced his enemies, dizzy, his ears ringing, shrapnel splinters dotting his arms.

He could see Babd. And Radu Bey.

He could see Rupert Greeves nailed to a door.

How many could he kill before they took the tooth from him? Before Babd shattered him like she'd just shattered Wrath?

It didn't matter.

Cyrus shoved the bamboo rod into his belt and picked up Nolan's sword with his left hand. Gripping the spear with his right, he charged.

On the other side of the crowd, he saw the flash of

the golden patrik and heard Niffy's shout. Babd turned and Cyrus threw.

The scaled woman slid in front of the spear, and the blade split her sternum. She smiled, raising her ax, and then seemed surprised as it fell from her hands and she sank to her knees.

Cyrus was ready to die. He was mortal. His life was meant to be spent. And it was meant to be spent now.

Niffy's Irish cries proclaimed the same. Ancient black blades whirled on both sides as lambs without fear ravaged lions, as undying devourers felt bones unknit and strength unmade and lives torn away.

Mortals need not fear death. It is as common as birth.

The lesser immortals fled. Only the great ones stood.

Babd deflected Cyrus's blow with a breath. His sword slid away from her and sparked on the floor as her talons plunged into his shoulder and a needle pierced his throat. Twisting, he brought the sword back up and took her claw off at the wrist. Radu's chains swept out Cyrus's legs and pulled him down. Babd bent over Cyrus, raising her bone and hissing a curse, but Niffy sliced at her back. She brushed aside his sword, but he leapt, locked his thick legs around her, and slammed her to the floor across Cyrus, and Cyrus was already swinging.

Babd Catha's feathered head rolled away from her body, and the storm crow crumpled, sizzling at the wound.

Cyrus rose slowly. Only Radu Bey remained beside

the hole in the floor where he and his army had emerged. Niffy and Cyrus circled the sorcerer, watching the blood dragon in his chest writhe in anger.

"Cut the beastie out," Niffy spat, "and we face a grimy mercenary prince and a coward."

Radu Bey lashed his chains, and lightning crackled between the final links.

"Today I took the head of a Smith," Radu said. "I am owed only two more to complete my own crest."

*You have pain.*

The dragon's voice was in Cyrus's head. He gripped his sword.

*So many have fallen. Give me your pain, your anger.*

"I have laughter," Cyrus said. He thought about his father and running with him on the cliffs beside the sea. He pictured his mother awake after three years of sleep and smiling with her short dark hair; Dan, who had kept him alive on waffles for two years; Antigone, who had laughed with him and bossed him through the darkest times; Diana, who had taught him how to fly; and Rupert, who had tried so hard to die alone. Hot tears rolled down Cyrus's face, and the fire of a loved life flowed through his limbs, wiping away weariness with a fierce fury. He looked back at Rupert, head hanging, body propped up against the door with thin blades through his arms, like an insect pinned.

*The great ones are free. The Burials are open. Do you not fear?*

"Would that be wise?" Cyrus asked. "Because I am not. And I have this Irish brother to plunge into death with me."

"Aye," Niffy growled, spinning his own black blade. "In and out again. As many dips as she takes."

"What can you do, dragon, to erase the life and the laughter I've already lived and already laughed?" Cyrus asked. "What can you do to frighten one as foolish as me?"

Radu Bey lashed a crackling chain at Cyrus's head, but he caught it winding around his blade.

"What can you do?" Cyrus asked again.

Radu dropped to his knees and spun, giving his flesh to the dragon. The huge spiny tail snapped forward, hurling churning orange fire and barreling Niffy headfirst into the wall.

Cyrus jumped forward, and the dragon turned, snapping huge jaws. Cyrus swung, and the black blade shattered Azazel's teeth and severed the forked tip of the dragon's huge tongue.

The dragon backed away and Cyrus pressed forward, sword raised.

The tail lashed, flinging fire as cover, and the dragon turned, slithering down into the jagged hole in the floor.

Cyrus dropped his sword and dove, grabbing on to the spikes of the smoking tail and dragging behind it down into the darkness.

Slowly, Rupert Greeves raised his head. His eyelids fluttered and the corner of his mouth twitched up.

"What," he asked the world, "can you do to erase my laughter?"

Cyrus slammed against a wall and splashed once more into deep water. He had his arms and legs around the tail now, and it twisted and thrashed as the creature raced through the water, down the long tunnel, toward light that poured in through a crack in a broken wall.

The creature smashed into the crack and through, scattering rubble. For one second, Cyrus glimpsed the inside of an empty, spherical tomb, and then the dragon leapt into a hall made of people. Cyrus blinked in horror, unsure if he was now dreaming as the tail dragged him across walls of people and through the dangling hair of hundreds of women. The dragon raced on until it reached a wide room lined with arches formed by sleeping people.

The long tail vanished in Cyrus's clenched arms as Radu Bey resumed his human shape. Cyrus thumped to the floor and tumbled. With chains dragging, Radu disappeared.

From the floor, Cyrus looked up at the wall of people, at the dangling hair and arms, and he shivered. Beside him, there was stack of old men, facedown. Cyrus sat up. Lying across their backs, there was a girl.

She had a straight cut on each cheek, black feathers in her hair, and fish scales painted onto her arms where the sleeves of her letter carrier's uniform had been torn off.

Cyrus recognized her face, even though he had only ever seen it carved in stone.

He jumped to his feet and felt her neck for a pulse. Her skin was cold and damp, but her heart was beating. Barely.

Out of all the people trapped in the walls and the ceiling and the altar, Cyrus chose her. He slid his arms beneath her shoulders and knees and picked her up. From somewhere in the labyrinth of bodies, Radu Bey roared, but the voice in Cyrus's head was sharper.

*Thief! She'll die if you take her.*

Cyrus turned in a circle. He could hear rattling chains. Radu Bey was returning. Cyrus quickly crossed the room to one of the human arches. He could see nothing through it but darkness, but he could hear the sound of falling water. It led somewhere.

*She dies now!*

Cyrus backed away until he could rest Mercy's legs on the altar, freeing up one arm. Then he tugged the bamboo cane and tooth up out of his belt and set it on her stomach. He grabbed her limp hand and closed it around the silver knob.

With the loss of the tooth, his body sagged. Pain dragged daggers through him. His vision blurred.

He scooped up Mercy's legs and staggered for the arch.

*Fool.*

"Yep," Cyrus said, and he stepped through.

Dan had been holding the dream patiently, watching for any kind of news. He sat at his metal table, and he stared at the empty black water around him.

Pythia sat beside him, but she didn't like to be seen. Not by Cyrus, at least.

Dan yawned, sleepy even in his sleep.

Pythia elbowed him and pointed. A low bank had appeared in the water, a bank made of bones. Mobs of stone statues rose to the surface around the little table. They floated toward the bank, then quickened, climbed out, and walked into fog.

"So many," Dan said.

Pythia put her finger to her lips, watching every shape closely. There had been no Babd Catha, and she sat back and crossed her arms happily.

"They're not all out yet," Dan said. He pointed at three shapes drifting toward them, low in the water, just below the surface.

Dan leaned forward over the table.

The shape was Rupert Greeves.

After him, a girl floated, her lips parted, pooling dark water. Her face was haloed in a swirl of red hair.

Diana Boone.

At first, the last shape looked like a cross. But then Dan could see that it was actually two shapes together. A girl—*the* girl—had her face just barely above the water. She was clutching the tooth to her chest. Completely submerged beneath her, carrying her, Dan saw the shape of Cyrus.

Dan turned away from his brother, unable to look at his battered and swollen face.

Alan Livingstone had known that they would likely be too late, flying in from Africa. But he hadn't been prepared for what *too late* might look like.

His twin boys, George and Silas, went silent at the first sign of smoke. But as they circled low, approaching to land, smoke was the least of what they noticed. Huge holes had been punched in Ashtown. The kitchen was gone. The Brendan's rooms were gone. The courtyard was cratered and dotted with bodies. The front doors were in splinters, and the pillars beside the main entrance had toppled down the stairs.

When they had landed and were walking solemnly up the slope toward what had once been the kitchens, they saw Big Ben Sterling talking to some sheriffs who had arrived by boat. He was doing an excellent job of keeping them out of the buildings.

Inside, they found a limping, wounded monk with a Mohawk collecting the O of B's dead and wounded with help from Arachne and Antigone Smith.

Alan Livingstone was a hard man, and his boys just as.

John Smith was a headless body. Robert Boone had leapt from a third-story window already mortally wounded. John Horace Lawney VII, and Gunner beside. Little James Axelrotter had been crushed by falling stone, but he was still breathing. Somehow.

All those were grief, but it was the barely breathing body of Rupert Greeves that broke Alan's heart.

Antigone Smith sat by the broken doors overlooking the destroyed courtyard of Ashtown. When Wrath had exploded, Justice had collapsed, melting into a boulder dotted with embedded blades.

Antigone felt the same. Cyrus was gone and she had turned to stone, unable to feel her own small wounds. Damaged Diana sat beside her, trapped in the shocked daze of loss.

Together they looked at the future, and it showed them nothing.

The sun set and the moon rose, and still they sat. Finally, Niffy joined them, with a glass of something the color of the autumn. He made them drink and he told them everything he had seen of Cyrus up until the end.

And Jeb came on crutches and sat with them, and he stared at the moon with dry eyes and thought about his father and said nothing. And Dennis Gilly sat with them and cried more than anyone. And Arachne sat with them and let her spiders drain out of her bag and flow down the cracked steps in search of food. And she was sad, though she tried not to show it, and they knew it was because Gilgamesh had broken his promises to her and to all of them, and had vanished in the first wave of the attack.

All the while, Antigone wandered through thoughts that she had never allowed herself to think. And she pushed them away like rotting fruit and focused on a new day, with a new sun and fresh smells and a young wind bringing back her brother, the brother who could never be taken from her, because he had already been written.

Beneath the bright moon, in one of those muddy places where land becomes liquid, not too far from where Antigone sat in the smell of smoke and the memory of harm, two tons of Leon eased himself into Lake Michigan and sank into cool forgetfulness.

He never wanted to see people again.

# EPILOGUE

CYRUS SMITH COULD HEAR A WATERFALL. And birds. And insects. And . . . monkeys? He slowly managed to force his eyelids open. He was staring straight up at a thick green jungle canopy.

A girl's face appeared above his own. She had deep brown eyes and cuts on her cheeks, but the black feathers were gone from her hair. She didn't need them. Her hair was already black enough.

"You're the sacrifice," Cyrus mumbled.

"No," she said. "I'm Mercy. I thought you were going to die. I gave you your stick back. I was going to bury you with it."

Cyrus shut his eyes again. Both of his hands were on his chest. He clenched his fist and felt his fingers close around the bamboo cane. He felt for the silver knob on top. The jolt of cold when he touched it told him that the tooth was still inside.

"Where are we?" Cyrus asked.

"When I woke up," Mercy said, "we were in this

weird temple made of bones up the mountain from here. I dragged you as far away from there as I could as soon as I could. You should drink something. We've been here two days and you've been sweating the whole time."

Cyrus was drifting off into a strange dream with black water. Maybe he could drink that.

"There is water pretty close," Mercy said. "You can hear it. But . . . hey!"

Mercy opened Cyrus's eyelids with her fingertips. "You won't believe this. It's patrolled by these giant dragonflies. And I mean *giant*."

Cyrus furrowed his eyebrows and his eyelids snapped back shut.

"Fine," Mercy said. "Pass out again. But tell me your name first."

Cyrus exhaled slowly. "I am called the Desolation."

Mercy said something, but he didn't hear. He was floating in black water, and his ears were below the surface. For some reason, it was easier to open his eyes here.

Dan was seated at a little metal table with his head in his hands, staring at the water.

When he saw Cyrus, he exploded out of his chair. His laugh sent ripples across the surface.

## ❧ GRATITUDE ❧

Paul S. for the push
Jim T. for the bittersweet
Mallory L. for the first launch
Lovely for the dreams
My attic-dwelling bunk-bed readers for the excitement
Every last one of y'all for joining the Smiths in Ashtown

## ❧ ABOUT THE AUTHOR ❧

N. D. WILSON is the bestselling author of the 100 Cupboards series and *Leepike Ridge*. Once, in the fourth grade, he split his buddy's arrow while shooting at a mattress from twenty yards. Now he writes at the top of a tall, skinny house, where he lives with a blue-eyed girl he stole from the ocean, their five young explorers, two tortoises, and one snake. For more information, please visit AshtownBurials.com.

THE SUGARCANE FIELDS HOLD SECRETS YOU
CAN'T EVEN IMAGINE. . . .

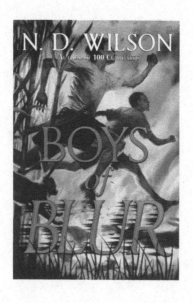

TURN THE PAGE TO DISCOVER
WHAT'S HIDDEN . . . IF YOU DARE!

# ONE
## MUCK

Out in the muck, where a sea of sugarcane stops and swamps begin, sitting beside a lake bigger than some countries, there is a town called Taper.

Taper has only one hill, a flat-topped mound just above the northern edge of town, ringed by cane. On that mound is an old white church with nothing but a stump where its steeple used to be before it was torn away by some long-forgotten hurricane. As for the church bell, it crashed through the floorboards and settled into the soft ground below. It's still down there, under the patched floor, ringing silence in the muck.

Most Sundays, the little church sees a few cars, and a minister under a wobbling ceiling fan preaching at old men and women who have heard it all before. But when this story starts, one of those men has moved right on beyond old and straight into dead. There's a whole herd of cars parked below that white church, and a whole herd of people standing around the rusty iron fence that cages in the graves.

The dead man's name was Willie Wisdom. And if he hadn't died, a boy named Charlie Reynolds might never have set foot on that mound in Taper, Florida, and this story would already have run dry of words.

Charlie Reynolds stood with his stepfather and his mother and his fidgeting little sister near the front of the crowd. From where he was standing, he could see loose black dirt mounded up on a tarp, ready to fill in a hole. He could see one end of the long box that held a man.

His neck itched. So he scratched it.

Charlie was not a boy who usually wore suits. And his neck wasn't the only place crawling with itches—just the worst of them. He had brown hair that went blond in the summer, a cluster of freckles on his nose that multiplied like weeds in the sun, and gold flecks in his hazel eyes in every kind of weather.

Normally, he wore old T-shirts and heavy shorts with deep pockets that were empty when he left the house in the morning and full when he returned at night. While he had a closet full of clothes and a dresser overflowing with shirts and pants that still smelled like store, he never touched them. He dressed from the laundry basket at the foot of his bed, and in the laundry basket he always found a T-shirt and a pair of shorts. On cold days, he added a raggedy hoodie that had belonged to his father.

Charlie hadn't worn a suit since his mother's wedding

five years ago. He'd only been seven then, and he'd hated it, but he'd understood. Without the suit he couldn't hold the rings, and his mother had really, really wanted him to hold the rings.

For a moment, Charlie tried to pay attention. He looked at the flush-faced minister beside the grave. A sweaty roll of neck was bulging above his ministerial collar. For some reason, the man was talking about gardening.

Charlie couldn't listen. Not with the Florida sun shining and the wind rattling through miles of sugarcane fields and itches dribbling down his neck and in between his shoulder blades.

Not while he was sinking.

Charlie took a step back and stared at where he'd been standing—two wet footprints dented the turf on the hilltop. His stepfather's feet weren't making dents, they were making craters. Charlie leaned on one foot and bounced, testing just how far he could sink into the turf.

A hand landed on his shoulder and Charlie looked up.

Charlie's stepfather, Prester Mack, knew how to wear a suit. Big square shoulders, brown skin a little slick in the sun, he looked down at Charlie and shook his head no more than a centimeter, then let go of Charlie's shoulder. Charlie knew his stepfather's football knees would be hurting, but Mack was tough, and the old man sealed in the box ready to go down into the hole had been the closest thing to a father Mack had ever had.

The minister was talking about bones now, a whole valley full of them. More than in the muck, he said. More than in a thousand fossil beds. His voice sounded like he was almost done.

Charlie inhaled slowly and the air tasted charred. He turned. A tower of smoke was roiling up from the fields.

Some people didn't care that old Coach Wiz had died. They had sugarcane to burn.

Three women sang.

Six big men stepped forward and lowered an old coach into the ground.

Willie Wisdom, foster father to twenty-seven, head football coach of the Taper Terrapins for thirty-two years. Rest in peace.

The crowd shifted and frayed around the edges. Men and women were hugging Mrs. Wiz where she sat by the grave in a white plastic chair. People were setting food on tables in the shade beside the church. A man was clattering glass Coke bottles into a little plastic swimming pool full of melting ice.

"You ever drink one from a bottle?" Charlie's mother asked. He looked up at her and shrugged.

"If you had, you'd remember."

Natalie Mack smiled at her son, but the smile didn't reach her eyes. Real smiles brought creases to the corners. Her look bounced away through the crowd before taking in the tower of smoke and then returning to Charlie.

"Mom?" Charlie asked.

His mother didn't answer. Standing barefoot in the grass, she dangled her high heels from one hand and Charlie's sister, three-year-old Molly Mack, from the other. Today and every day, his mother's hair was pulled back into a high doubled-over ponytail, but it seemed blonder than normal above her black dress.

As Charlie watched her eyes, he felt something tighten in his chest.

Charlie had been four when he'd learned how his mother's eyes looked when his father was on his way home. He'd been four the first time his mother hid him behind pillows on the top shelf of a closet. Five the first time he'd called the police. Five when he'd felt his first broken rib. Five when he'd learned to keep his face empty and five when his mother had loaded his backpack, taken his hand, and led him out the front door of their little house, past the rusted swing set, past his bike and his sandbox and an old worn football in the grass, and down the cracked sidewalk toward the bus station, never to return.

For a while after that, his mother's eyes had always looked the way they did when Charlie's father was on his way home, like he might be waiting around every corner, in every motel, in every restaurant, or walking behind them on every street.

Charlie had been six when his father had caught up with them, but by then, Mack had been there, too. Mack had changed everything.

"Mom?" Charlie asked. "What's wrong?"

Natalie sighed. Her eyes were on Mack, where he was laughing with three other old football men in the crowd. She shook her head. "Nothing." She smiled again, forcing eye creases this time. She cocked her hip and tugged Molly up onto it. "We'll be leaving soon, so make sure you eat something."

Charlie nodded. Molly looked at him, widening her brown eyes and making a big fake surprised face. Then she curled her lip into a snarl—her very best monster face.

Charlie gasped silently in fear. His sister laughed and threw her weight at the ground until her mother set her back down.

"I know you, Charlie," his mother said. "Wander if you like, just don't go far." Molly grabbed her mother's hand and began to drag her away. "And eat something!"

Charlie ignored the food tables. He slipped past church ladies in hats, men in suits, and clusters of boys slouching in red and white jackets. Each jacket had a football patch on one shoulder and a nickname on the back. Charlie saw ROCKET and SLIDE, J.TAG and WEAZEL. Free of the crowd, he moved through the taller grass, down the shallow side of the mound until only a narrow ditch in the black silt held him back from the cane fields.

The sugarcane looked like giant grass, bundles of green sticks taller than men tufted with long dry leaves like scythe blades. Separated by narrow, dark gaps, the rows marched away beneath the quiet blue sky. Not far from where Charlie stood, the sky's belly was rough with swamp trees. The fields and the trees both ended at the foot of a steep grass-covered dike—an earth wall taller than the white steepleless church and its mound combined.

A breeze slid around Charlie and on through the cane. The air was warm, but the field shivered like an old man with a chill.

Charlie looked at the sky, held up by nothing more

than the column of smoke he'd noticed during the service. The flats were wide open, but he still felt strangely enclosed. He felt like he was standing on the bottom of a deep hole, a hole so wide the sky came all the way down inside it.

He didn't mind.

Charlie was in the cane where his stepfather had been raised and played his first football. Over the dike and across the water, he knew he would find more cane and the town of Belle Glade, where his real dad had been raised and played *his* football.

Both of his fathers had roots in the muck. Maybe Charlie did, too.

"Hey," a boy said behind him. "I guess we're some kind of cousins."

Charlie turned, squinting against the sun. The boy was thin, black, and about Charlie's height. He was wearing a creased red tie with an untucked dress shirt, canvas sneakers, and jeans. His hair was short, his eyes were big, and his smile was wide.

"I'm a Mack," the boy said. "Your stepdad is my pop's coz. So you and me are, too."

"Not really," Charlie said. "That would make us, like . . . step–second cousins."

The boy shook his head. He took one step and jumped, gliding over the ditch and landing lightly in the cane field.

"Nope," he said. He stripped the leaves from one of the cane stalks and snapped about a foot from the top. He broke it in two over his knee. "Cousins is cousins." He tossed one of the pieces to Charlie. "Try it."

Charlie examined his cane. Where it was broken, the end was gritty and wet with what looked like sap. He nibbled at a green corner. It tasted like sugar. Tiny bits of cane grit crept across his tongue.

"It's sweet," he said.

"Sweet?" The boy grinned. "Naw! Not sugarcane." He laughed, gnawed at the end of his own hunk, and then pointed it at Charlie. "Call me Cotton. Everybody does. I already know you're Charlie. I even know that your pops was Bobby Reynolds from Belle Glade who went to jail, but just about everybody knows that. You go to school?"

Charlie nodded.

"I'm homeschooled. My mom's crazy for books. Stacks and stacks of books I'm supposed to read and that's about it. And I can't play football." He tapped his sugarcane against a wide smile. "But I will. Next year I'll play. You play football? You fast, Charlie Reynolds?"

"Fast enough," Charlie said. "But I've never played."

Cotton exhaled disbelief. "You've got Bobby Reynolds for a pop and Prester Mack for a step, and you don't play?"

"Not yet," Charlie said. He prodded the sticky end of his sugarcane with a fingertip.

"But you will?"

Charlie shrugged. "It's my dad's sport. Both my dads."

Cotton chomped on his stick, studying Charlie. Finally, he dropped it in the trough.

"You scared of snakes?" Cotton asked.

Charlie shook his head.

"Good. Come on, I'll show you something." Without waiting for an answer, Cotton began running along the edge of the field, rattling through the leafy fringe.

Charlie dropped his cane hunk and hopped the ditch. When he landed, the damp muck rose around his feet. The first steps were the hardest but none of them were easy, and Cotton kept going faster. Charlie fought to stay in his new cousin's wake, thumping his shoulder against cane and turning his face away from brittle, slashing leaves, tugging every step up from the sucking ground.

After forty yards, Cotton suddenly veered, disappearing into the wall of cane.

Charlie followed. Cotton had turned into a narrow

dirt road exactly one truck wide. The cane leaned in on both sides.

"Hey!" Charlie shouted. "Where we going?"

Cotton laughed and kept moving. His feet were lighter than Charlie's, barely touching the ground. Where Charlie planted and pushed, Cotton quick-stepped, floating into the air, gliding between the tire tracks and soaring over puddles. Charlie was quick enough, and he had never been clumsy, but trailing Cotton made him feel like a bulldog puffing after a greyhound.

Cotton turned again, and this time the road ran beside a ditch full of black water. Up ahead, something that looked like a busted old tire slid off the bank and splashed into the ditch.

Charlie wanted to stare at the water and get a better look at his first gator, but Cotton was still moving.

One more turn, and then trees. Cotton slowed and stopped. Charlie staggered up beside him, wiping his face on the sleeve of his suit coat. He was breathing hard, grass cuts stung his hands, and at least one blade had nicked his face. Cotton didn't seem to be breathing at all.

A narrow grass strip ran between the cane field and a deep canal. On the other side of the canal, thick swamp forest overwhelmed the bank. Ahead, a three-foot-high mound ran out of the swamp, bridged the canal, and disappeared into the cane. Swamp brush and scraggly trees crossed the canal on the mound's back and even grew out in the cane—a finger of wild stretching into tamed fields.

"This is it?" Charlie asked. "This is what you wanted to show me?"

Cotton's eyes were hooded. "The trees have been creeping," he said. "A lot longer than I've been alive. The mound has a stone core—tractors can't till it."

Cotton scrambled onto the mound. Charlie followed, grabbing slender trunks as he did. The ground was suddenly firm beneath his feet and with just that little bit of elevation he could see over the cane—the narrow mound ran through the field directly toward the little white church on its hill.

Cotton was moving again. Charlie turned and followed him along the top of the mound toward the swamp.

"Old shacks back in there," Cotton said, pointing toward the trees. "Shacks for cane workers—Haitians mostly. Now they just use tractors."

Cotton stopped over the middle of the canal, before they reached a wall of looming cypress trees slung with vines and bearded with moss. Charlie saw a snake on the far side slip down into the black water. The mound didn't just bridge the canal, it worked like a dam. On one side, a murky pool spread back into the trees, surrounding dozens of trunks. A tongue of water slid through a deep notch in the top of the mound and ran down into the canal on the other side. Cotton hopped the thin stream and crouched down.

At the boy's feet, embedded in the mound, was a chalky stone the size of a manhole cover but not quite circular. It was more egg-shaped. Cotton was scraping moss off the edges.

Charlie didn't care about the edges. Right in the middle of the stone, there was a dead snake, gray and speckled and twisted halfway onto its back. Beside it was a small dead rabbit.

"You killed them?" Charlie asked.

Cotton shook his head. "I didn't. I don't know who does. Sometimes I just think they come here by themselves when they're ready to die. Or someone collects them and leaves them here. There's always something, usually pretty small. Rats. Birds. Squirrels or skunks. Once they're here, nothing touches them. Nothing eats them." He looked at Charlie and lowered his voice. "When I found this stone, it was under moss and a whole pile of little bones."

He pointed into the trees at a short row of broken-down shacks. Only one still held up its own roof.

"I put all the bodies and bones in there," Cotton said. He looked at Charlie. "Wanna see?"

Charlie did want to see. And he didn't. The black water beside him and the looming trees and the chalk stone and the bones all felt very different from the cane fields with the white church on the hill beneath the blue sky and the sun.

"Well?" Cotton asked. Charlie nodded, staring at the collapsed and rotten shacks. And then something moved in the shadows.

Cotton picked up the snake by the tail and stood, grinning. "Wanna hold it?"

"Cotton," Charlie said, and he took a step back.

Cotton laughed and jiggled the snake. "Dead. See?"

A tall man stepped out from under the trees and into the light.

"Cotton!" Charlie grabbed his cousin and scrambled backward, smacking into a young tree.

Cotton dropped the snake and spun around. The man was walking toward them. He stepped onto the mound.

He was wearing a helmet.

He was holding a sword.